Alison Giles graduated from Leeds University in the early 1960s and later trained as a psycho-dynamic counsellor, working mainly with young people. Now, settled in Kent and with her family grown up, she has turned to writing. *Meadowland* is her first novel.

MEADOWLAND

Alison Giles

FOURTH ESTATE • *London*

First published in Great Britain in 1998 by
Fourth Estate Limited
6 Salem Road
London W2 4BU

Copyright © 1998 by Alison Giles

A catalogue record for this book is available from the British Library.

ISBN 1–85702–609–8

Typeset in Palatino by
Avon Dataset Ltd, Bidford on Avon B50 4JH

Printed and bound in Great Britain by
Clays Ltd, St Ives plc, Bungay, Suffolk

CHAPTER 1

I knew it was a mistake to go and see Flora; but nonetheless I went. Although it was the weekend, I dressed for the occasion in the tailored red suit with its fashionably short skirt which I normally reserved for the office. As a concession to my destination I settled on lowish heels.

The final miles of my journey, an hour and a half's drive west of London, led me away from the drone of the motorway and into a valley. The road, a thin yellow line on my map, coiled itself loosely round the river across a series of what had once been packhorse bridges, now strengthened but rarely widened. February sunlight glinted on fallowed fields and on pastures churned up around the feeding troughs into waterlogged mires.

As I drove, I glanced at the pile of books perched sedately on the passenger seat. The bundle, secured with doubled string, had the air of some little old woman – not quite tall enough to peer through the windscreen; too polite to complain of the lack of view; occupying herself instead with scrutinising the dashboard. I half expected remonstration at my speed.

I eased off the accelerator. The whole thing was ridiculous, of course. I could have posted them back; I should have posted them. But to do so would have been to refuse my father's last request.

He had waited until my mother left the ward to speak to the sister. Then, lacking the energy to lift his head from the starched pillow, he gestured me closer. 'I want you to do something for me,' he whispered. He described where to find the volumes. 'Return them to Flora. Yourself. Please!'

My mother had tripped back before I had time to reply. But as we said our farewells that evening, his eyes pleaded with me; reluctantly, resentfully even, I nodded. He died that night at about the time my mother and I, hastily summoned, fretted at a red light at the bottom of the hill.

Now three weeks later here I was, deep into unknown countryside, propelled by a collection of dog-eared books towards the home of a woman whose existence I had for over twelve years dutifully ignored.

Rounding a corner, I found my way blocked by a tractor silhouetted against its cartload of hay. I slammed on the brakes. My God, this really was the back of beyond. I pulled over against the hedge and winced as I heard the scrape of branches along the Astra's polished paintwork. To my right, the tractor teetered up on to the verge, avoiding tipping its trailer into the ditch by scarcely the width of a theatre ticket. The driver – round-faced under a tangle of curly hair – grinned down at me, mouthing his thanks. I nodded acknowledgement, forcing the corners of my mouth upwards against the downward thrust of lips clamped tight in irritation. The books – which had shot forward into the well – seemed to stare at me reproachfully.

Jerking at the gearstick, I revved the engine and the car leapt forward. The parcel shuddered, held its point of balance for a moment, then toppled sideways, leaving the page edges uppermost. They looked vulnerable, less powerful. That pleased me.

I relaxed a little, slowed to negotiate another narrow bend and began to ponder just what I would say to Flora when I came face to face with her. The road was beginning to climb now, up through an avenue of oaks and beeches merging on either side into gladed woodland. Through the trees to the west, a light airiness hung above the dip of the valley, the hills beyond curving the horizon. Despite all my misgivings, it was hard to resist the serenity.

Was it for such a sense of peace that my father had initially come; once in a while, and armed with fishing rods and a box of assorted flies? I remember – I must have been about ten at the time – his setting out the bright screws of fur and feather on the dining-room table and challenging me, with that great chortle of his, to recite their names. His favourite was his own design: the

'Golden Retriever', he called it. He swore he'd enticed more trout with that one fly than with any conventional nymph or dun.

In those days, he would return on a Sunday evening smelling of damp leaves and moss; bearing his pungent catch in an old wicker shopping basket scrounged from the cupboard under the stairs. Mother would squeal at him to 'leave those filthy wellingtons outside', and wrinkle her nose as he plonked his booty on the draining board.

'Come on, Carrie,' he would say to me. 'You wash and I'll fillet.' And so I would hold the slippery ovals under the cold tap and, with numb fingers, brush away the mud and grass; and watch as, wielding the brown-handled kitchen knife I was forbidden on pain of direst retribution to touch, he deftly cut away the fins and sliced along the belly of each scaly creature, stripping out the skeleton with practised ease.

Then my mother, having banished Father upstairs to 'make yourself presentable for goodness sake, dear', would arrange the speckled bodies in rows under the grill and whip up a delicate butter and herb sauce to pour over them.

The taste – once anticipated with so much relish – was now nothing but a soured memory.

To start with, I only noticed that Father was returning almost, and sometimes entirely, empty-handed from his increasingly frequent fishing weekends; and that my mother turned away, her expression curiously blank, when he apologised

4

awkwardly for the poor catch. Perhaps, I thought, she had looked forward to our trout suppers more than she had ever given reason to suppose.

Then one Friday evening, as he was about to set off and I went to shut the garage doors, I realised his rods were still leaning up against the wall at the back. I ran after him down the drive and, skipping sideways parallel with the moving car, banged on the window. 'You've forgotten your rods,' I puffed. I teased him triumphantly: 'You won't get much fishing done without them.'

His smile, as he pulled the car to a halt, was strange; faraway. 'Oh, of course!' He fetched the bundle of canes and stowed them in the boot. He seemed to hesitate before going back to collect the battered red tin box in which he stored the rest of his tackle.

'Happy now?' he said. He patted me on the head before sliding his long legs under the steering wheel and driving off.

I knew then that something wasn't right.

All my mother said, when she saw bewilderment written loud on my face, was, 'Her name is Flora.' We never spoke of her again.

There were times when I was crying out to do so, but somehow I knew that to ask for explanations would endanger some sort of balance that held my world precariously in place.

It wasn't that I didn't understand the meaning of Mother's cryptic announcement; by the time of that revelationary Friday, I was already into my teens – just. In the early days, I spent long hours wondering. I found myself hoping Flora didn't look like the bewigged and powdered Madame de Pompadour of my school history books; Nell Gwyn, I decided, presented a far more acceptable image of my father's mistress. On the other hand, Flora must surely be some sort of witch, pointed hat and all, to have lured my father into her lair. I should have liked to speculate with my friends, but the taboo that hung over the subject at home extended to an unspoken prohibition on it being mentioned outside. My fantasies remained secret ones and, undernourished, eventually withered. And, with them, my curiosity.

About Flora herself, that is. My father's betrayal and my mother's acceptance of it continued to puzzle my pubescent mind. It was not the stuff of which the romantic novels, into which I escaped to revive my faith in the happy-ever-after, were made. But eventually even those queries succumbed to the practical routine of Father's regular weekend absences.

For the benefit of the neighbours, he made a point of ostentatiously packing his fishing gear in the car each summer Friday, and on his return nodded comments over the fence about the state of the water. The close season was more problematic. But, each year, something was dreamed up. One winter, he was – Mother would explain as she nodded her way along the Avenue – 'helping a friend do up a country cottage'; the next, he was 'tutoring an OU course'. If the Mackenzies or our then neighbours, the Brandons or the Williamses, whispered cynicism among themselves, they were careful not to do so in my hearing.

For my part, I surmounted the difficulty by teasing my peers with the notion that his weekends were spent on top secret government assignments. 'You mean he's a spy,' gasped Penny Kingsley, reliably gullible. Pouring scorn on my giggling claims distracted the others from probing the reality.

At home each Friday evening, after Mother and I had cleared away our supper for two, she would pick up her embroidery and dictate a shopping list for the following morning. Curled up in Father's big Minty chair, I would, every now and again at Mother's behest, disentangle my legs from its depths and scurry out to the kitchen to check the stock of some item. (As I grew older, such sorties took on a more self-consciously languid air – but the ritual was maintained right up to the time I went away to university.)

Next day in town and before embarking on the supermarket marathon – traditionally reserved for Saturdays, for unspecified reasons which it never occurred to me to query – we often treated ourselves to coffee in the department store in East Street; and afterwards, wandering back down the escalators, inevitably detoured into the Fashion section. My mother loved clothes and always dressed beautifully. But I was always more comfortable helping choose a skirt or an Hermès silk scarf for her than struggling to find a compromise between my penchant for tatty jeans and T-shirts and her desire to see me dressed in 'something elegant for a change'.

Oddly enough, it was on these occasions, delving among the clothes rails, when the feminine alliance should have been closest, that I most missed my father's presence. I found myself longing for his endorsement of my desire – my need, even – to make my choice independently. I could have done with his support as Mother picked out some excruciatingly dull jumper and held it up against me, murmuring how well the colour suited me. But then guilt at my ingratitude would roll in and I would squeeze her arm as she proffered a cheque at the till, thanking her profusely for the latest disappointing addition to my already overfull wardrobe.

They were cosy, though, those weekends, without Father's ambiguous presence hanging over us. Increasingly, of course, I spent time on my own pursuits: the usual teenage things – discos, parties, or simply browsing the streets and record shops. Mother insisted that it wouldn't be fair to expect me to stay in and keep her company.

'I've got more than enough to keep me busy,' she reassured me as she set about spring-cleaning each room in turn or, tying an apron round her waist, rolled up her sleeves to batchbake for the next charity function. 'You go out and have fun!'

So I did; although I felt obliged – embarrassing though it sometimes was – to be home at whatever time, according to my age, she considered 'late enough for a young girl to be out, even on a Saturday'. Once, only once, she sighed: 'It would be different if your father were here to pick you up.' I stifled my own sigh – of exasperation – at her adamant refusal to drive after dark.

'Maybe,' I took the occasion to venture, 'Clare's father would give me a lift. They pass the end of the road anyway.'

My mother's lips pursed. 'No.'

She was like that; refusing to ask for or accept any sort of help from anyone. Unsanitary gurglings one Sunday morning advised that the drains were blocked.

'Wait till Daddy gets home,' I suggested.

Mother wouldn't hear of it. 'What do you expect me to do?' she demanded. 'Keep my legs crossed all day?'

I laughed. Then hastily straightened my face.

Unearthing some ancient sailing trousers and an anorak and reaching for the Marigold gloves, she covered herself from head to foot in waterproofing. Then, heaving aside the manhole cover outside the back door, she prodded the murky sewage with a broken branch. 'I think there are some rods in the shed,' she instructed.

I sought them out. Meticulously, she assembled them one by one, pushing the gradually increasing length down and along the underground pipe. I was despatched to lift off the drain cover further down the garden.

Mother raised her head. 'Anything coming through?'

Suddenly there was a sploosh, echoing and rumbling towards me, and a welter of thick brown porridge surged across the hole at my feet.

'You've done it!' I shrieked.

'Yes?' For an instant, something like pleasure crossed my mother's face as she stared enquiringly at me.

Much hosing later, with disinfected rods stacked neatly in their place again and scrubbed waterproofs hanging over the line, Mother emerged from the shower, smelling of soap and shampoo, her hair wrapped in a towel. 'There,' she said with a look of brave acceptance. 'One can always manage if one has to.'

If Father felt reproached when he returned that evening, he gave no sign of it. Mildly he remarked, 'You should have left it to me.'

I was about to say, 'That's what I said.' But Mother shushed me with a look.

I shifted restlessly in my seat as she served up spaghetti Bolognese, chattering about Mrs Duckworth's roses. Father commented on the traffic jams on the bypass. I wanted my mother to be angry, my father to acknowledge guilt. But as always, if they felt those emotions – or any others for that matter – they never showed them.

* * *

A motorbike swooped past me as I approached the brow of the hill. 'Bloody idiot!' I yelled, surprising myself at my vehemence. By the time I levelled off on to the narrow plateau, the bike was a blur disappearing down the other side.

I slowed. From my earlier study of the map, I guessed that the road ahead plunged straight into Cotterly; that I was less than a mile or so from my destination.

I pulled on to the entrance to a wheel-marked track into the wood and turned off the engine. I reached for my bag, found a cigarette and lit it. Stupid habit, I acknowledged, but one I'd taken up after the Mark episode. Mother didn't approve, of course. I tried not to smoke when I visited her. In any case, I usually restricted myself to two or three, just in the evenings. But today was different.

I inhaled deeply and wound down the window to allow the smoke to escape. The air that flooded into the car had a tang to it. On impulse, I pulled the key from the ignition and climbed out. My shoes sank into the soft ground. I leaned against the warm bonnet while I finished my cigarette, savouring the freshness of the air on my face. Then I threw the stub on to the ground and watched it extinguish as I shrugged my arms into my coat and hugged it round me. A walk would help clear my mind.

By keeping to the hump in the middle of the track, I was able to circumvent the worst of the mud. Ditches on either side were filled with composting autumn leaves. On their slopes, and in among the trees too, occasional clusters of primroses winked pale yellow eyes. I picked my way across the ruts and crouching down, coat-skirt tucked carefully behind my knees to prevent it trailing on the ground, gathered a small bunch. I held them up as a nosegay, breathing in the fragrance.

A cloud crossed the sun which, weak though it was, had been shining comfortingly on my back. I stood up, shivered, and marched on. I could see that the trees petered out a hundred yards or so further along and had an idea that maybe I would be able to look down on the village.

I was right. A huge muddied grass field fell away in front of me revealing a hotchpotch of dwellings in the distance. Which one of them, I wondered, was Wood Edge? I would have to ask directions.

I wondered suddenly if my mother was aware that the sealed envelope, inscribed so seemingly mundanely in my father's handwriting 'Weekend address', had been tampered with. Two weeks ago, a few days after Father's funeral, I had located it, discreetly tucked away at the back of the top right-hand drawer of the bureau where Father had whispered to me from his hospital bed I would find it, and steamed it open while Mother was having tea at the vicarage. I'd been invited along too but had pleaded a headache. Mother had nodded understandingly: 'But I feel I have to go – so kind of them to invite me.'

It had been a curious feeling staring at the address – the words on the page somehow transforming the ethereal quality of Father's 'absence' into the concrete reality of his presence elsewhere. Presumably Mother didn't know the details of it, else why was the envelope there? Had she, bar in dire emergency, always preferred not to; been devoid even of curiosity?

I copied it out, re-inserted the original into the envelope and stuck it down again as neatly as possible. I could only hope Mother wouldn't notice the hint of tell-tale wrinkling, nor indeed the lack of dust which I'd wiped away to erase the smudges I'd made in it.

She refused my suggestion, inspired at least in part by that concern, that she wait and let me help sort through Father's things next time I could get down from London. 'Nonsense,' she said. 'I can manage. And anyway I'd rather get on with it.'

I wondered what progress she'd made. Staring down now on the place where Father had spent so much of his time, I wasn't sure whether I was grateful or not to be excused the somewhat ghoulish task. Wasn't it all part of the last rites; of saying goodbye?

A wind ruffled briefly across the ridge and for an instant a vision of my father, laughing with me, filled my mind. I sank down on a tree stump, careless this time of my clothing, and found myself rocking, head in hands. Tears welled up. For a moment I felt like a child again – confused, angry, helpless.

I pulled myself together. This was ridiculous. I was, I reminded myself, twenty-five years old, owner – courtesy of a deposit I'd only briefly hesitated, damn it why not, to accept from Father – of a flat in Fulham, and a rising executive in a West End-based travel company. I hadn't been close to my father for years. If either of us should feel his loss at all, it was my mother.

And Flora. The thought took me by surprise. I pushed it away.

I stood up, glanced once more at the innocuous-looking buildings below, and turned. As I retraced my steps, a Land Rover lurched along the path towards me. Moving over, I waited for it to pass.

'Is that your car back there? Had a hell of a job squeezing past it!' Early to mid-thirties; expensive but well-worn jersey over check shirt; land-owning accent. Not aggressive; not even irritated; just mildly reproving.

He had driven on before I'd decided whether or not to apologise. I glared after him indignantly. Tough. It wasn't my choice to be here.

Back at the car, I jettisoned the already drooping primroses, cleaned off my shoes as best I could, and renewed my make-up. The books were still lying, dishevelled, on the floor. I heaved them back on to the seat, straightened their edges, and pulled on to the road. The car purred reassuringly and the sun, already on a downward path, reinstated itself in a patch of watery blue sky. I checked my watch as I started the descent. Well gone two already. If this one-horse place did have a pub, it would probably be closed by now. And I could have done with a sandwich at least – not to mention a drink.

I passed a farmhouse, and then a pair of cottages. As the road levelled out, a T-junction loomed before me. 'Cotterly ¼ mile', declared the sign pointing left. So this was it. I took a deep breath and turned the wheel.

CHAPTER 2

A lemon-coloured Citroën, old and battered, was parked on the grass beyond a broken-down gate, along the top bar of which the inscription 'Wood Edge' was faded but legible.

I had experienced no difficulty finding Flora's house. Despite my pessimism, the doors of the pub, easily spotted at the side of a small green, had been open; but the clamour of male voices, raised in exhortation at the flickering figures of rugby players on the television screen within, decided me to try the shop next door instead.

I waited impatiently while two small girls and a boy rummaged among the sweets on the counter, finally handing over precious ten-pence pieces. I purchased a bar of chocolate and made my enquiry.

'Wood Edge?' The short, middle-aged woman pushed to the drawer of the till, then, wiping her hands on her apron, ushered me to the door. She pointed along the road. 'The lane up to the right, 'bout a half mile along. Just past Manning's barn.'

I had devoured the last square of chocolate as I passed the huge corrugated-iron hay store and drew the car to a halt some fifty yards further on.

Now I climbed out, flung my bag across my shoulder and hoisted the books into my arms. I crossed the lane and stood in the entrance.

The house, like most of the others in the village, was of yellowish grey stone, mellowed with age. The garden sloped up towards it, unkempt grass lush with the first thrust of spring. Purple crocuses dotted banks supporting a path beneath the windows. Here and there, clumps of tight daffodil buds promised a golden flowering.

A robin hopped across the driveway in front of me as I crunched towards the front door, then darted to the branch of a straggling buddleia where it bounced round to face me, twittering. Sparrows rustled in the bushes and overhead a pair of wood pigeons flapped lazily towards some unknown destination. There was no other sound or sight of movement. For the first time, the possibility occurred to me that Flora might not be at home.

The front door, approached by three stone steps built into the abrupt rise, was firmly shut. There was no bell; just an old and tarnished brass knocker. I lifted it and banged twice. The sound echoed. I waited, then knocked again, this time with greater force. As the reverberations faded, there was silence.

I retreated down the steps and surveyed the frontage. One of the upstairs casements was ajar. In the country that probably didn't mean anything. What now? Presumably I could find somewhere to leave the books. A note through the door . . . I struggled with a sense of anticlimax.

Then: 'Come on, Columbus. We have a visitor.' The voice floated from somewhere along the side of the house. Footsteps sounded.

From under the ivy-clad overhang at the corner, a tallish and solidly built figure, in what I'd guess were her late fifties, appeared. She strolled towards me along the upper path, a somnolent cat, knitted into the design of her heavy jumper, undulating across her bosom as though rocked on a gently rolling sea. At her feet padded a ginger tom, tail erect, rubbing confidently against the green of her scuffed cords. This presumably was the companion I had heard her addressing; but addressing in a tone startlingly softer than the one she now directed at me.

'Yes?' Short; to the point; unsmiling.

The cat turned slit eyes towards me and stared. Flora's own were wide and brown and framed by waves of greyed hair among which glints of auburn provided curious contrast. In one hand she held an ancient trug, half-filled with mud-smeared potatoes and knobbly shapes that might have been swedes; in the other a garden fork. Wooden sabots hugged her feet which she planted firmly on the top of the bank.

I looked up at her; never in all my childhood imaginings had I visualised her thus.

I resisted an instinctive step backwards. 'You're . . .' I hesitated over the informality '. . . Flora?'

'Yes.' The same clipped neutrality.

I took a deep breath. 'I'm Charissa,' I said, glad of the extra stature I felt my full, and somewhat distinctive, name gave me. Then, as her eyes roved over me, 'I came to return these.' I held the bundle of books out towards her.

There was a pause, while she continued to size me up. 'So you are. Spitting image of your father of course.' The merest hesitation before, just a shade less abruptly: 'You'd better come in.'

Ignoring the proffered parcel, she turned on her heel and started round the house, Columbus falling into step behind her. 'Never use the front door,' she announced, leaving me to catch the words as they floated back on the air. It seemed I had no alternative but to follow.

In Indian file, the three of us made our way to a paint-chipped door. It gave access to a lobby cluttered with gardening paraphernalia. Flora deposited trug and fork, kicked off her shoes and pushed the kitchen door wide. A wave of warmth billowed to greet me.

Moving straight to the Aga at the far side, she lifted one of the heavy circular lids and slid the kettle across on to the hotplate beneath. Columbus bounded on to an elderly chesterfield and took possession.

Flora turned, leaning against the rail over which teatowels were drying, and looked at me, arms folded.

'Well, come in then.'

I took a step across the threshold. The room, unlike the exterior of the house, had a cared-for look; that is to say, not clinically scrubbed as my mother always kept her kitchen, but comfortably clean and ordered. And, yes, cheerful. A first glance took in an antique Welsh dresser hung with good quality china, a large oak kitchen table, the near end of which was home to a pile of shuffled papers, and a set of cupboards and work surfaces along the length of the window wall. Dotted here and there, but always looking as though they belonged, were the bits and pieces that gave the room its lived-in feel – table lamps, a busy Lizzie draped from the window sill, a magazine lying open.

'Push Columbus over,' Flora instructed, noting my hesitation. 'Oh, and . . .' she nodded towards the bundle I was still carrying '. . . put those down somewhere. By the bookcase will do.'

It stood against the wall immediately to the right of the doorway, out of vision until I entered and moved towards the sofa.

On its top shelf, and flanked by a rosebowl on one side and a pair of silver candlesticks on the other, stood a large framed photograph of my father. It brought me up short.

'Tea or coffee?'

I looked across at Flora. Her face was expressionless. 'Coffee, please. Black.'

Turning back, I stared at the picture again. It had been taken in the garden, presumably at the rear of the house; and, as was clear from the fit of my father's familiar brown tweed jacket, long before his illness began to take hold. He was standing beneath the branches of an apple tree in full fruit, laughing. That sparkle in his eyes . . . I hadn't seen it since . . .

I bit my lip. Flora – I glanced in her direction – was spooning coffee. I placed the books on the floor as directed and squeezed a place for myself beside the already slumbering ball of ginger fur.

The photograph drew my gaze inexorably. I forced myself to lower it and study instead the contents of the shelves. They held an eclectic collection, bundled in together with the familiarity of use.

Books of poetry rubbed shoulders with a Dickens or two, some Nevil Shute, tomes on subjects ranging from philosophy to the peoples of the Pacific, the odd cookery book, one on pruning roses. All interspersed with a range of current paperbacks. The equally varied selection I'd returned would slip back in comfortably.

I raised my eyes to my father's picture again. What was it, I wondered – at that moment more perplexed than resentful – that had not only drawn him here, but brought such a look of relaxed contentment to his face?

'It's a good likeness.' Flora had glided across the room in her stockinged feet and was standing over me, a mug in each hand. She passed me one, then swivelled a dining chair and sat down.

I nodded agreement, and waited for her to initiate further conversation. She didn't.

'Nice part of the country, here,' I offered eventually. 'Very peaceful.' I forced a light laugh. 'Makes a pleasant change to get away from London traffic.'

She inclined her head.

'Had quite a good run down,' I suggested. I prattled on about the time it had taken me, the weather . . .

I tried a different tack. 'I'm sorry,' I said. 'About my father's death, I mean.'

This time she did comment. 'So I should imagine.'

I stared at her. 'What I meant was . . .'

'Yes?'

Confusion stoked animosity. 'I meant *you* must miss him.' It came out angrily, attempts at civility swept aside.

There was a flicker of something indefinable at the corners of her mouth. Eventually she said, as though having considered the matter, 'Yes, I miss him.'

'I suppose – ' I managed to soften again as the thought struck me – 'I suppose we might have invited you to the funeral.'

'I came anyway.'

I felt my eyebrows shoot up. But then I hadn't really been aware of anyone but family among the congregation, and I wouldn't have known who half of them were anyway. I could hardly have been expected to notice a stranger – Flora – in their midst. And maybe, in any case, she'd slipped out before we turned to leave. Must have done, or surely she'd have recognised me more quickly when I arrived.

'Tell me – ' Flora changed the subject abruptly – 'why have you come?'

It wasn't a question I was expecting. I twisted my mind back. 'My father asked me to.' I nodded towards the books. Then defensively, pushed into elaboration by a lack of response, 'One doesn't refuse a dying wish.'

'Oh, no. One doesn't, does one.' Flora's tone was bland. She leaned back, that considering look on her face again. Then: 'Was that the only reason?' The question, though mildly put, felt nonetheless to prise into me.

The hurt of years surged suddenly in a wave of hatred. How dare she interrogate me! With great control, I rose from my seat, placed the coffee cup carefully beside the photograph of my father and looked her squarely in the eye. 'Of course. What other reason could there be? Thank you for the coffee. I must be on my way.' It was, I prided myself, a dignified little speech. I reached for my bag.

'Sit down.' Again quietly said; but, given the discomposing effect she was having on me, she might as well have delivered a karate chop to the back of my knees.

I sank back on to the cushions.

Taking her time, she asked casually, 'Do you

always run away from the truth?'

'I beg your pardon?'

She repeated the query.

'I don't know what you mean.'

'Then maybe – ' there was the faintest lift of an eyebrow – 'you have a thing or two to learn.'

'But not from you!' The retort, satisfyingly, seemed to fire itself without any conscious effort on my part.

Flora's expression didn't change, and my momentary sense of triumph evaporated as I felt caught up in a childhood game of 'stare as stare can'. I yielded and looked away.

'I really must go.' But the words sounded petulant.

Flora, unperturbed, got up. 'I expect you'd like something to eat first. I take it you're going back to London? How about some soup?' Her tone was matter of fact.

A sick feeling in my stomach identified itself at least partly as hunger. To my astonishment, I found myself accepting.

Unhurriedly, Flora set about the preparations. 'By the way,' she said, 'if you want to wash your hands there's one the other side of the lobby, or the bathroom's upstairs.'

I opted for the lobby. On my return, I wandered over to the window and stared out. Beyond the bushes and bare-branched trees bounding the garden, the top of the haybarn I'd passed earlier was outlined against the pink-tinged clouds of

24

early evening. 'Shepherd's delight,' I murmured automatically.

'We'll have a beautiful sunset.' The observation floated from behind me.

I turned. Flora was stirring a pan.

Grabbing for the relief of small talk, I said, 'I was admiring your crocuses.'

'None of my doing.' Abruptness had returned to her voice. She poured the soup into a bowl and transferred it to the table, indicating to me to seat myself.

This time, I decided, I would be the one to ignore a comment. I picked up the spoon. The soup smelled good. I tasted it. It was thick with fresh vegetables, just peppery enough to bring out their flavour. Flora placed a farmhouse loaf and the butter dish before me. 'Help yourself.' She took the chair opposite. Columbus, wakened by the activity, descended from his bed and sauntered, yawning and stretching, towards the table. He raised his front paws on to Flora's knee and leapt up. She fondled his ears.

I saw an opportunity for conversation again. Nodding towards the cat, I asked, 'How did he get his name?'

'Your father gave it to him. We found him down by the river, soaking wet. He said he looked as though he'd swum the Atlantic.'

'So he was a stray?'

'Yes.'

Her monosyllabic response left me scant scope.

'Was my father fond of cats?' I regretted the question as soon as it was uttered.

'He loved animals. Didn't you know?'

I took a mouthful of soup to delay replying. Columbus purred complacently.

I decided to go on the offensive. 'The fact that I didn't know him as well as I should,' I said carefully, 'is hardly my fault.' I stressed the 'my'.

'Does anyone say it is?'

She had missed the point. Or had she? Flora didn't strike me as unintelligent. Far from it. All right, then; if she wanted me to spell it out . . .

'Don't bother,' she forestalled me. Her eyes were glinting with something. Not anger – I could have coped with that; more an amused, or perhaps merely patient, tolerance.

I put my spoon down. 'Look,' I tried. 'I've come all this way . . .'

'And I'm supposed to be correspondingly grateful?' She paused. 'I can't think why. You could have consigned the delivery to the Post Office.' Again, that indecipherable expression. I heaved a sigh; this was getting us nowhere.

'I take it,' Flora continued consideringly, 'that I'm not reacting in whatever way you've decided would be appropriate to the . . . er . . . circumstances. Which, I would remind you – ' she fixed me with one of her unwavering looks – 'you have created.'

'*I* have created?'

'You chose to come.'

Her calm only fuelled my indignation.

'And what about the circumstances *you've* created!' I thumped the table and the tingle ran up my arm and into my shoulder. 'Don't you have any feelings about what you've done to us? Don't you realise how our lives have been devastated by your relationship with my father?'

A level glance met my furious one. 'I realise it's affected yours.'

So she acknowledged it. Something snapped inside me. 'Then what,' I heard myself explode, 'do you intend doing about it?'

Throughout the exchange, Flora had scarcely moved a muscle. Now she slowly lifted Columbus from her lap and deposited him on the floor. Then she leaned forward, forearms on the table. The knitted cat nestled into the dip between her breasts.

'So is that why you came?'

Taken aback, I glared at her. 'How do you mean? No, of course not. It was just – ' I shrugged – 'a figure of speech.'

'Was it?' She sat back again, fixing me with eyes that seemed to bore deep inside me.

'If anything – ' I cast around for a more accept-able explanation – 'it was curiosity.'

She nodded. 'That, too, I can well believe.'

The conversation was again becoming intoler-able. I swallowed the last of the soup, stood up and moved over to the window. The sky had darkened and a deep crimson, interlaced with streaks of purple, had replaced the earlier, lighter colouring. There were no shadows; just shades of grey.

I turned back, my hands grasping the edge of the sink behind me for support. Flora was still seated, immobile. In the subdued light, she no longer looked quite so formidable.

'Have some more coffee.' She rose to fetch it.

I sat down at the table again, aware of fiddling with my bracelet. It was the gold one my parents had given me on my twelfth birthday.

'Your father chose it,' my mother had said. 'I'm not sure it's really suitable for someone your age.'

Father had winked at me over her shoulder.

'I'll look after it,' I'd promised.

I had. Most of the time it sat in the brocade box I'd rather grandly, when I was younger, called my jewel case. It contained only a couple of other items of value. I seldom wore any of them. My decision today, to clasp Father's gift – I always thought of it as his – around my wrist, had been an impulsive one.

'Yes, I suppose possibly I was curious,' I admitted.

Flora had, I was sure, heard me, but she said nothing, merely returning with freshly filled mugs. Her chair scraped lightly on the tiled floor as she resumed her place. Then there was silence. As my ears accustomed themselves to it, I became aware of a clock ticking. I wasn't sure whether the sound came from within the room or somewhere outside it. I didn't care to raise my head to discover which.

I ran my fingers over the hard circle on my arm – and began to remember.

I remembered the taste of trout.

I remembered the time, long before Father's fishing days, when he used to joggle me around the garden piggyback style. I remembered visits to the zoo and clutching his hand as a lion raised its head and yawned, baring ferocious fangs; I saw him down on his hands and knees on wet sand enthusiastically constructing forts which he then pretended to defend from the incoming tide with Canute-like imperatives; I heard again his ostentatious applause when, having ignored my mother's remonstrations, he'd urged me up on to the pantomime stage and I returned to my seat beside him, flushed with pleasure. I recalled . . . oh, I recalled so many little incidents – delicious moments of companionship and laughter when I revelled in the certainty that my father found me the most wonderful little girl in the world.

'He did love me,' I murmured.

And he'd loved my mother, too. Or I'd thought he did. They used to sit side by side watching television, he with his arm draped over her shoulders as she knitted, or crocheted, or sewed. Sometimes I would try to squeeze in between them; then my father would lift me on to his lap and, as I snuggled against the warmth of his vast chest, his spare arm would slip back to rest around my mother.

He was, altogether, a big man, my mother slim

and neat. They made a handsome pair. And I was their princess.

'But then everything changed.' I realised I'd spoken aloud.

Slowly, carefully, hesitating over my words, I began to slot the jigsaw pieces of my experience together.

'It wasn't as if he just upped and left us. I could have understood that. Not why, but at least the fact of it. But he hadn't gone. Not physically anyway. Even when he was . . . away, his coat still hung in the hall; his razor stared at me from the bathroom shelf; his favourite biscuits were always there in the tin; Saturday's post stood propped on the bureau all weekend.

'But he *had* gone. Once he knew that I knew – what little I did know – he never quite seemed to meet my eye again. Oh, he tried to behave normally during those weekday evenings. Sometimes he helped me with my homework, occasionally we even played a game of chess or draughts. But he never . . . we were never . . . close again; never did things together any more, not in the way we used to. It was as though he'd handed me over to my mother.

'She was marvellous, so brave about it all. She never complained. Just got on with the business of running the house and looking after me.'

I paused. Columbus materialised as if from nowhere, and sprang on to my knee. I stroked his fur and he snuggled down.

'It was as though my father had died, yet I couldn't tell anyone, talk to anyone about it; I had to go on pretending he was still there. But he wasn't. Not my real father. The man who called himself my father was a weekday lodger, a stranger.'

Columbus was kneading my thigh with his paws in a slow, steady rhythm. I sat there, allowing my thoughts to tumble over one another.

'And now he really is gone.' The words seemed to float towards me across the table. They were spoken so quietly that if there had been any other sound I might not have heard them.

My control shattered. Great sobs, starting way down in the pit of my stomach, forced their way up through my chest, constricted as though by a steel band, and exploded outwards. My elbows involuntarily moved forward on to the table to support my head as it fell forward into my hands. I was vaguely aware of a scrabbling in my lap as Columbus, alarmed, leapt down.

'There, there. It's all right.' I neither knew nor cared whether it was me or the cat Flora was reassuring.

Eventually as the racking subsided, I raised my head. The room was in virtual darkness. Flora's shape loomed upwards. 'You need a brandy,' she said.

CHAPTER 3

The alcohol calmed my shivering. Flora had switched on the lamps as she fetched it, and the glow
they cast harmonised with the warmth spreading
inside me. As I drained the tumbler, she stretched
out a hand to the bottle and raised an eyebrow in
query.

'I'd better not,' I said. 'I've got to drive.'

'There's a spare bed made up if you'd prefer to
wait and make the journey in daylight.' There was
nothing in her tone to persuade me one way or the
other.

I didn't need to turn my head to be aware of the
blackness outside. I hesitated only momentarily;
then nodded. 'Thanks.' I drowned the waves of unease at my decision in a second generous tot.

It was all becoming increasingly unreal somehow – and Flora's down-to-earth practicality did
nothing to dispel that feeling. It was as though I'd
strayed into another world; one in which I was
neither approved nor disapproved of – merely
accepted; where I was neither guest nor intruder.
My mind, hazed at least in part by alcohol,

struggled with the problem of how to behave and gave up. It was simpler to sit back and let fate take over.

And it did seem to be something more ethereal than Flora to which I was relinquishing control. For a moment, I had a vision in my head of my father.

Flora placed both hands on the table and pushed herself to her feet. 'I have things to do,' she said. I was vaguely aware of her shrugging on shoes and coat; and then of the beam of a torch as she opened the back door and closed it again behind her.

I pressed the stopper back on the brandy, then rinsed my glass under the tap, staring out through the window as I did so. The night, I realised now that my back was to the lights in the room, was not as dark as I'd imagined. As my eyes accustomed themselves to the dimness, pinpricks of stars enlarged into dancing crystals. I started as a shadow streaked across my line of vision. A bat, maybe? Hardly. Not this early in the year.

But the thought had stirred an image; myself, cringing; and Father sweeping me up in his arms, laughing away my fears. 'They're only bats, silly,' I heard him say, his voice deep and comfortable. When could that have been, I wondered.

Now I could discern branches stirring gently and, in the distance, the shimmer of headlights. I watched them approaching, turning into the lane and lighting it up with powerful beams. There was a squeal of brakes and the sound of tyres swerving on gravel as the vehicle swept round and up to the house. The lights were extinguished.

I retreated towards the table. A metallic bang was followed by heavy footsteps. A broad shape passed the window. Then, with no more than a token knock, the same man who had spoken to me earlier in the day from his Land Rover pushed open the door and stood in the entrance.

He gave a swift glance round the room before addressing me. 'Flora in?' Then he looked at me more closely. 'Oh, it's you. Nearly ran into your car out there.' He shook his head tolerantly. 'Do you always park in damn fool places?'

I clapped my hand to my mouth. 'Oh, I'm sorry . . . no lights. I hadn't thought . . .'

'If you give me the keys, I'll move it.'

I scrabbled in my bag and produced them. 'That's very kind of you.'

'Self-interest. By the way, where's Flora?'

I hesitated. 'I'm not sure. I mean, she didn't actually say.'

He gave me a bemused look. 'Probably shutting up the hens.' He jiggled the keys in his hand. 'Right. I'll just go and do this.' He strode out.

Aware that my face was probably still showing traces of my recent outburst, I reached for my make-up. As I touched up, Flora returned.

'I see Andrew's here,' she said from the lobby. She stepped into the kitchen. 'Where is he?'

'Moving my car.' My words were accompanied by the sound of its engine starting up.

She nodded and went to the sink to wash her hands.

When he came back, she introduced us.

'Not . . . ?' He hesitated and looked questioningly at Flora.

'Yes. That's right. Hugh's daughter.'

His reaction on discovering my identity was totally different from Flora's. His eyes lit up in greeting as he moved forward to grasp my hand. 'Really?'

I responded gratefully.

Andrew turned to Flora. 'You didn't tell me . . .'

'I didn't know.' Flora stood leaning against the cupboard, arms relaxed at her sides.

'You mean . . . you just . . . ?' He swivelled his head from one to the other of us, seeking clarification.

'My father asked me to return some books.'

Andrew's face sobered. 'We all miss him,' he said. Then, as though realising the possible trickiness of his ground, 'What I mean is . . .'

'Thank you,' I said.

So he obviously knew the situation. It occurred to me that Flora wasn't the sort of person to try to hide it. Whatever else, there seemed a straightforwardness about her. I couldn't help wondering if things would have been different if my mother had cared less about what the neighbours thought.

'So what brings you, Andrew?' It was Flora who spoke.

He jerked his attention back to her.

It turned out to be a matter of mild curiosity about rumours concerning the egg farm. They chatted about it, Flora meanwhile opening a tin of cat food and spooning it into a dish. Columbus, awoken by the sound of scraping, stirred himself and then bounded across the room to its source. When he'd licked the plate clean, Andrew bent down, scooped him up and carried him to the door where he unceremoniously shooed him out into the night. 'Go catch some mice,' he said.

For the first time, I saw Flora laugh. 'What, with his stomach as full as that? At best he'll only have the energy to sit and ogle Joe Manning's tortoise-shell.'

Andrew's eyes crinkled acknowledgement. 'Mind if I help myself to a beer?' He was clearly very much at home.

'Go ahead.'

He poured himself one and came to sit beside me on the sofa, to which I'd retired while they were talking.

'Flora's bite's not nearly as fierce as her bark,' he informed me conversationally, grinning across the room to where she still stood. Her face was a mask.

He pulled out a packet of cigarettes, gestured it towards Flora who waved it away, then held the packet out to me.

I made to take one, then glanced at Flora. 'If you don't mind?'

'Not at all.'

Gratefully I lit up.

'So,' Andrew said, 'did you enjoy your walk this afternoon?' He gave Flora a quick résumé of our earlier encounter.

We pursued the subject briefly. Then: 'Didn't Hugh do a painting of the view from up there?' He looked enquiringly at Flora.

She nodded.

He turned to me. 'Has Flora shown you your father's watercolours?'

I hesitated, then opted for honesty. 'I didn't even know he painted.'

A flicker of surprise crossed his face, and then he said, 'Well, you must see them.' He looked at Flora for confirmation. 'Mustn't she?'

Flora went to fetch them, for the first time opening the door to the rest of the house. A rush of cooler air swept in, and on it the steady tick of what I guessed could only be a grandfather clock – the sound I'd been aware of earlier, no longer muffled by panelling.

I shivered involuntarily. Andrew grinned. 'Now you know why Flora lives in the kitchen.'

She returned moments later bearing a dozen or so examples of my father's work. As I studied them, one by one, I gasped. 'But they're amazing. Did he really do these?' I found it hard to comprehend. The paintings were delicate and robust at one and the same time; mostly landscapes, but here and there focusing with finely sketched lines on an animal or, in one instance, a young woman. I stared at this last – one of the only two framed ones. The girl was seated amongst meadow grass, arms hugged round legs over which full skirts were drawn tight, eyes turned towards a background of tree-dotted hills. Cornflowers bent, as though pressed by the same gentle breeze as ruffled her hair.

Andrew studied it over my shoulder. I felt him turn to look again at me. 'It's you!' he said.

I knew he was right.

Yet again those tears – those damn tears – started to well up.

Flora was the one who broke the tension.

'Are you staying for supper, Andrew?'

'I was hoping you'd ask me. Ginny's taken the boys off to visit their grandparents. Don't know where she gets her energy from, working all week and then rushing around at the weekend.'

I surreptitiously dried my eyes, then stacked the paintings. From the conversation I gathered Ginny taught music, wind instruments mostly and some singing, juggling her time between several different schools.

'Mind you, I'm all for it,' Andrew was saying. 'No point women sitting at home all day, wasting their talents.'

'I do.' Flora challenged him with a look that might or might not have been serious.

'Waste your talents?'

Flora allowed herself a small smile. 'That's for others to judge. I meant stay at home.'

Like my mother always had, I thought.

Andrew was laughing. 'Ah, but you're one on your own, Flora. You don't need the world like the rest of us mere mortals.'

He had, I realised with a sudden start of recognition, the image of my mother receding rapidly, put his finger on something.

'And what about you, Charissa?' He turned to draw me back into the conversation. 'Didn't your father say . . .' He stopped. 'Don't you work for a travel company?'

I nodded. 'At their head office.'

He encouraged me to expound.

Recruited from university, I explained; stints in different sections. 'I seem to have settled for the time being in the Complaints Department.'

His eyebrows shot up. 'Whoops,' he said, 'that must make you pacifier in chief?'

'Something like it,' I laughed.

I could feel myself relaxing as he pressed me to recount the contents of some of the more bizarre mail that landed on my desk.

Flora intervened to allot tasks in the preparation of the evening meal. As I peeled potatoes and Andrew chopped vegetables beside me, he whispered, while Flora was briefly out of the room, 'Don't judge Flora on first acquaintance. There's a heart of gold under that dour exterior.'

I didn't answer but concentrated on swishing the mud off the last potato.

'I hadn't intended to stay more than half an

hour,' I eventually said. Let him make what he would of that for a response.

'Oh? I'm not sure that I quite . . .'

'You haven't told me what you do.' My tone was artificially bright. 'Do you farm?'

He accepted the change of subject. 'Only at weekends – and even then only because I'm dragooned into it. No, no. I'm the second son. It was the army or the law for me. I opted for the latter.'

'You're a solicitor?'

'Small practice in town. Mostly land disputes; a few matrimonials. Not so dissimilar from what you do, I suppose, except it's fists rather than letters that thump on to my desk.'

I laughed, picking up the saucepan and turning.

'Goodness. You are like . . .' Andrew was staring at me.

'My father?'

'Well, yes.'

'Do you know,' I said slowly, 'until today, no-one's ever suggested that to me.' I passed the saucepan to Flora, who had returned to her place at the stove and was standing there, holding out a hand.

I recollected the scene, back in Fulham the following afternoon. Remembering Flora's Aga, the flat seemed dispiritingly chilly, despite my having turned up the central heating. I had a sudden urge to wrap my hands round a mug of cocoa. Rummaging in the back of the cupboard, I found an ancient tin.

It tasted good. I curled up in an armchair and switched on the television. A 1940s' black and white film was nearing its climax. I tried to concentrate, to pick up the threads of the story, but found it impossible to focus my attention. The turmoil of the last thirty-six hours was too immediate.

Throughout supper, which we'd eaten at the kitchen table, Andrew had kept up a stream of light conversation. The children, I discovered, were Tom and Justin, aged eleven and nine and 'noisy little terrors'. I blinked. Andrew must either have started young or be older than he seemed. Still, he was saying, it was good to see them enjoying life; and Ginny, he had to hand it to her, was a first-rate mother.

I learned that old Mr and Mrs Partridge had been on holiday to 'Oh, somewhere in the Balearics' and – he turned to me: 'This will sound familiar' – hadn't stopped moaning since they got back about not being able to tune in out there to the British weather forecast. 'Seems their only interest was in comparing hours of sunshine and making sure they were getting their money's worth.' Mrs Tuckett – 'Why couldn't she have chosen anywhere but here to retire to!' – had managed to get herself elected on to the village hall committee and had been so rude to Commander Lancaster that now there was some doubt that he'd allow his paddock to be used for the summer fête. More seriously, had Flora heard that there was a brucellosis scare at Upper Farm? Philip – his brother, I deduced – was only too thankful he'd switched over to arable.

It was all village talk and I was torn between disdain and reluctant fascination. Whichever, I was more comfortable sitting on the sidelines listening.

Andrew left at about ten, gripping my hand and hoping he'd see me again soon.

I helped clear away the dishes and wash up.

'Andrew's nice,' said Flora, as she dried her hands. 'Parents left everything but the old Dower House to Philip, of course. Andrew and Ginny...' She lapsed into silence. I shrugged mentally; it was no concern of mine. It was what I was gleaning about my father that tantalised me. Over a cup of coffee before bed, I brought up the subject of his paintings again.

'I really had no idea,' I said.

'I expect you'd like to have the one of you.'

'May I?'

'Of course.'

I expressed my gratitude. I wished I could make her out.

Flora was glancing at her watch. 'I'll show you your room. You'll need a hot water bottle.' She fished one out from a cupboard and filled it from the kettle simmering on the hotplate.

I was glad of it; the bedroom was icy. Flora produced a nightdress and toothbrush. 'Come down when you're ready in the morning,' she said.

Despite everything, or perhaps because of it, I

must have fallen asleep straightaway. I woke to the sound of hooves clopping along the lane. It took me a moment or two to orientate myself.

I got out of bed and, wrapping the eiderdown round me, pulled back the curtains. The room was on the opposite side to the kitchen, facing east. Frost glittered on the ground, and a faint glow behind the trees indicated that the sun would soon dispel the greyness.

I dressed and crept downstairs. The grandfather clock, ticking away sonorously, registered a few minutes past seven. For a moment I considered sneaking out to the car and driving off before Flora appeared. After all, I'd completed my mission. But then the childishness of such an action dissuaded me. I would at least wait and bid her a civil farewell.

Warming myself by the Aga, I heated the kettle and brewed a pot of tea. To my surprise, it was the back door that opened. 'Oh, there you are,' said Flora. She deposited a handful of eggs beside the sink. 'Breakfast?'

In the end, it was mid-morning before I left. Somehow Flora persuaded me to take a walk through the woods before I departed. 'You should,' she said. 'Your father loved it.' She didn't suggest accompanying me.

The lane petered out to a track, horseshoe imprints fresh there in the damp earth. Between the shadows of branches meeting overhead, sunlight glinted, dappling tree trunks and ground. I stood and breathed in great lungfuls of sweet-tasting air, gasping at yet relishing its coldness. It seemed to reach right through me, scouring out restraint. I stared up at the sky and shook my head in wonder. Every sense tingled.

Then I heard it – the sound of running water. Twenty yards further on, I came across a broad stream meandering up to the edge of the path and away from it again. I hunched down beside it, watching the flow of ripples round stones. I looked for fish but couldn't see any. Maybe it was too early in the year.

I'm not sure how long I stayed there. Eventually, cramp in my legs forced me to straighten up. Reluctantly I wandered back, pausing every now and again, as though I could capture and hold within me every whisper and scent.

When I got back to the house, Flora was in the garden picking daffodils. 'I thought you might like to take a few with you,' she said. 'They'll come out in a day or two.'

In the kitchen, the watercolour had been set aside from the others and lay ready on the table. Flora carried it out to the car and stood waiting as I took it from her and placed it carefully in the back. The daffodils I laid on the passenger seat.

'Well, goodbye.' I hesitated awkwardly beside the open car door.

Flora reached out and touched my arm. 'Take care,' she said.

* * *

The daffodils! I'd dumped them unceremoniously on the draining board when I first came in. I zapped off the television, jumped up and found a vase. Pity to let them die. I crushed the ends as my mother had taught me, and found myself wondering whether Flora would have done the same. I fingered the tight buds lightly. No hot-house blooms these; they smelled of the country and freedom. Impatiently, I brushed away something that was more than a physical sensation. I didn't wish to be reminded of Cotterly.

I'd driven up the hill out of the village in a state of confusion. It wasn't until I reached the motorway and was able, with my foot hard down on the accelerator, to put distance between myself and the source of my bewilderment, that I began to feel a sense of normality returning. Cars beat a steady rhythm along the uniform stretches of tarmac. This was the world I knew. As I crossed Hammersmith flyover, the buildings on either side enfolded me in the familiar again. Relieved to be home, I'd staggered up the stairs fully laden, balancing Father's painting between raised knee and chin as I turned the key in the lock. I'd left it just inside the door.

Now I wondered what to do with it. I almost regretted having accepted it. It was disturbing somehow – my father imposing an image of me on the landscape he loved. Had he sent me down there simply to make a reality of the fantasy he'd painted? Just once? Or did he have some deeper

45

intention? I'd assumed my visit was aimed at satisfying some need of Flora's. Having met her, that hardly seemed likely. What was he up to?

Dammit. I didn't know, and I didn't care. I'd done what he asked. That was the end of it.

I carried the flowers through to the sitting room, changed my mind about placing them on the coffee table, and instead made space on top of the cupboard in the corner. I picked up the phone, trailed its lead across the room, and perched on the arm of a chair.

'Clare? Are you in? Can I invite myself over? . . . Supper? Hadn't thought about it. I could bring a tin of . . . Right. See you in ten minutes.'

I was my old resilient self again. I threw on a coat, grabbed my contribution to the feast, and clattered down to the street. I loved London, particularly at night. Lights everywhere; the buzz of traffic; bright, exuberant voices of passers-by; traffic lights alternating red, amber, green. I walked the three blocks, humming to myself.

It was eleven-thirty when I returned, pleasantly weary. My old schoolfriend, temporarily grass-widowed by her boyfriend's attendance at a conference in Stockholm, had been a good choice of companion for the evening. She didn't believe in moping – whether over a broken ornament or, as she assumed in my case, a bereavement. Instead, she kept up a bright bubble of chatter and encouraged me to help her drain a large bottle of Spanish red.

I fell into bed. My last thought before falling asleep was that I'd forgotten to ring my mother. Too late now. I'd do it tomorrow.

CHAPTER 4

I wondered, next day, whether Mother would ring me at work. I rather hoped she might; I'd have an excuse to keep the conversation brief. I felt uncomfortable at the prospect of speaking to her. I'd never lied to her before. Not about anything of any consequence. However, I'd decided from the beginning that there was no need for her to know about my visit to Flora. The whole matter, I'd reassured myself, was totally unimportant, and the sooner it was done, finished, forgotten, the better.

But I'd come back with that painting. I wished I'd never seen it. I wished Flora hadn't been at home. I wished . . .

I struggled through the day, formulating platitudes to disgruntled customers and seeking advice on two particularly thorny problems from our legal people. I tried not to snap at the school-leaver who dropped a tray of coffee in the corridor outside, jangling my nerves. Even the physical exertion of an aerobics class after work did nothing to relieve my mood.

I slammed into the flat that night, tired and

sweaty. The first thing I would do was throw out those daffodils. I marched across the room and grabbed the vase. But Flora was right: they were already beginning to open, their bright gold centres offering themselves up. So vulnerable they seemed; so fragile. I replaced the vase. For heaven's sake, they were only flowers.

The phone shrilled. Skidding my sports holdall out of the way, I grabbed it; then wished I'd waited long enough to prepare myself.

'Hello, dear. Is that you?'

'Hello, Mother. How are you? Sorry I didn't ring last night.'

As always, she was understanding. She expected I'd been late getting back. Had I had a good weekend?

'Yes, fine. Gorgeous weather as well.' Then hastily, as I sank down into a chair, forcing myself to relax: 'How were Leah and Harold?'

My enquiry was genuine enough. I was fond of my mother's sister and her husband; and knowing she was occupied entertaining them over the weekend had somehow made me feel less guilty about my own activities.

She gave me a quick run-down on Uncle Harold's hernia operation; and amused me by lowering her voice – as though even now Mrs Potter next door might be skulking in the flower-bed, ear pressed to the curtained window pane – to confide that they were somewhat concerned about my cousin Elspeth. 'Taken up with a very questionable type, by all accounts.' She heaved a sigh. 'I can't tell you what a relief it is that you're so sensible.'

No, I thought. I certainly didn't give her any worries over men. Most of those I came across these days were firmly attached elsewhere, as often as not to my girlfriends.

'What about your weekend?' she was asking as I banished a sudden image of Andrew.

'Oh, lovely,' I heard myself respond. 'Paula's totally immersed in nappies . . . yes, twins, didn't I tell you? And James . . .' I garnished the tale with up-to-date information gleaned from a recent telephone conversation with my ex-university class-mate. The words slipped smoothly from my tongue.

Later, lying full length in the bath, I wondered, guiltily, at the ease of the deception. But then, Mother had never had any cause to doubt my loyalty. Nor was she by nature suspicious. I wondered how long it had been before she became aware of Father's infidelity. Now, the thought struck me, not only was I the one deceiving her – but over the very same person.

Flora. I wanted to put her out of my mind, but her image confronted me implacably. What on earth could my father have seen in her? 'Heart of gold,' Andrew had said. Even at her mildest, I'd seen no sign of it. On the contrary, she must have taken some sort of sadistic pleasure in stirring me first to anger and then to tears.

I lunged for the hot tap and turned it on full

pressure. The water scalded my toes and I scooped it round to merge with the cooler pool at my back. I added more oil and lay back once again, surrounded by a mist of steam which settled in a film on the tiles. I watched the small rivulets of condensation as they trickled down the mirror-hard surfaces.

Three months later – three months devoted, by dint mainly of immersing myself in work, to putting the past, that is to say anything to do with my father, out of my mind – I wallowed similarly in the 'tastefully-modernised-en-suite facilities' of a Georgian country house which some years ago had been converted into a highly priced hotel. It lay, as the blurb had it, 'betwixt Warminster and Bath'. Which meant it was in the back of beyond. But, given the rates we tightly renegotiated each year, it suited us as a base for day excursions or as an overnight stop on circular tours.

It had been on our books since before I joined the company. When time for another inspection came round, I found myself volunteering. We had our regular team of appraisers of course but, having just been moved – on gratifying and, I complimented myself, well-deserved promotion – to that department, I'd persuaded the head of section, my immediate superior, that some 'hands-on' experience would be useful.

'Why this hotel?' I taunted myself, flicking foam across my stomach and watching the tendrils of froth settle over my navel. I brushed them aside to reveal again the curving indentation. Above and below it, the outline of my bikini was still faintly discernible. I considered whether, this year, I might dare to return from some hotspot with only a lower triangle of pallor. Crazy, really, that I'd never as yet summoned up the courage. My flatmates, in the days not so long ago when five of us shared two floors of a house in Maida Vale, returned each summer uniformly brown from their hip-bones upwards. 'God, you're so inhibited,' one of them – Becky, no doubt – had teased me on more than one occasion, rolling her eyes in mock despair. Maybe I was. A bit, anyway. Something to do with being an only child? After all – I looked down now approvingly at my boobs – nothing to be ashamed of there.

I knew I was distracting myself from my own interrogation. Why this hotel? Why here? Why not Carlisle or Aberdeen or Norwich? Reluctantly, I confronted myself.

'So it's Flora country. Give or take. So what?' I sank deeper into the water until my chin rested on its surface, the hair at the nape of my neck instantly saturated. It wasn't as though I had any intention of going anywhere near her again. Maybe I was just taking the opportunity to prove the point – by ignoring, as I would, the turn-off to Cotterly on my return journey this afternoon. That was it.

Or was it? Just as clearly as I visualised myself driving straight back to London, I saw myself detouring at least as far as the hilltop above the village. Unable to dissolve either image, I hoisted myself impatiently up through the vapour and towelled vigorously.

It was a relief to descend to breakfast and concentrate on the details I needed to note for my report.

I attempted to write it in the garden, settled on a slatted bench with the file on my knee and the sun on my back, out of sight of the wide sweep of the tarmacked entrance. A faint burr of voices and the slam of car doors mingled with intermittent chatter of small birds and the hum of a foraging bee. I did my best to focus on the task in hand, but my mind refused to co-operate. I stared at the tip of a church spire, visible above rhododendrons which formed an effective hedge between me and the long stretches of countryside beyond.

I don't know why I thought of Mark. Churches? Marriage? A starling flying towards its nest with a full beak? Had I missed the only boat, I wondered. Did I care?

I'd been right to finish the relationship, of course. Mother had been devastated. 'But he's so nice. And stockbrokers don't come two a penny, you know. You'd have been very comfortable.'

'He never actually asked me to marry him,' I said.

'He'd have got round to it . . . He adored you . . .'

I couldn't tell her what had sparked our break-up.

We'd been lazing in bed – his bed – one Sunday

morning, debating how to spend the day.

'Let's go and visit your parents,' he'd suggested. 'Wouldn't mind doing justice to a traditional Sunday lunch.'

I hesitated. I'd taken him home several times during the fifteen months I'd known him, usually choosing a weekday evening when the Market was quiet and he could get away promptly. We'd reach the Surrey dormitory town at about a quarter to eight, earlier if the A3 traffic was light, and drive back, fortified by my mother's cooking, in time to fall into bed at around midnight. 'It suits my parents better,' I'd explained. 'They tend to be busy at weekends.' I'd elaborated this excuse to explain my father's absence on the one or two occasions I hadn't been able to avoid our calling in on a Saturday or Sunday.

I stroked the soft hair on Mark's forearm as he put it round my bare shoulders and pulled me towards him. 'Or, of course,' he teased my ear with a flick of his tongue, 'we could just stay here . . .'

I snuggled up to him. Then I pulled away.

He reached out for me again. I resisted. 'I've got something to tell you.'

He grinned up at me.

'Seriously. It's about my father,' I said. 'And my mother too, I suppose. And – ' I took a breath – 'someone called Flora.'

I expanded, Mark prompting me with the occasional question; when I'd said as much as there was to say, I drew up my knees and rested my chin on them. 'I've never told anyone before,' I said.

In the silence, I could hear two people calling to each other in the street below. Suddenly Mark flung back the sheet and leapt out of bed. 'For Christ's sake,' he said. I turned my head; and giggled. Standing there stark naked, he looked, I decided, like some indignant Greek god straight out of a Renaissance painting.

I waited for the declamation.

It came. But not in the form I was expecting. 'Why the hell didn't your mother let him have a divorce?'

I sagged, staring at him. 'What do you mean?'

'What sort of bitch is it that . . .'

'You've got it all wrong.'

'The hell I have.'

'But . . .' I felt my tongue on my lips. My mouth was dry as ice. I got up, enfolded myself in a dressing gown and tied the belt. In the kitchen I automatically flicked the switch on the kettle. 'Coffee?'

'No! Well, yes. Please.'

He followed me and put his arms round my waist as I reached up into the cupboard. 'I'm sorry. I didn't mean to upset you.'

'Milk?'

He loosed his hold and fetched the bottle from the fridge.

We carried the coffee through to the sitting room. I took the big easy chair while Mark fetched a towel and wrapped it round himself, sarong-style. He perched on the edge of the sofa, leaning towards me, his broad bare feet planted squarely on the thick-pile rug.

'OK,' he said. 'So that's not how you see it?'

'Of course not!'

He raised his arms in mock surrender. 'All right. All right. Have it your own way.'

'I should never have told you.'

'Whyever not! It explains a lot. I mean, why your parents are so . . . polite with each other.' He hesitated. 'Some of your attitudes too, perhaps?'

'*My* attitudes! What are you talking about?'

'Forget it.'

But I wouldn't. I made him spell it out. Challenged him. Provoked him. I was aware of what I was doing but unable to stop myself. It was a blazing row, with no holds barred on my part. Every last thing I could find to throw at him, real or imaginary, I flung in an oral stream of rage that seemed unstemmable.

On a tide of exultation, I stormed through to the bedroom, threw on my clothes and, gathering up what possessions of mine I could carry, swept out, crashing the door behind me.

Frigid, he'd called me. Distrustful of men. Well – I waved away a fly that had settled on my notepad – I supposed he was right. About being distrustful anyway.

Clare, good old Clare, robust as ever, had scorned the accusation of frigidity when I confided

56

a vetted version to her. 'That's what all men say when they can't have things their own way.' It made me feel better – a bit. But there was a nasty, logical little corner of my mind whispering that if you don't trust someone entirely, then maybe you do hold back. And that – I swiped angrily at the fly again – was no doubt what I'd been doing ever since. Attempts to patch things up with Mark hadn't worked; nor had any relationship since then progressed beyond the first few dates.

And I'd never again risked telling anyone, not even Clare, about Flora. With a sudden start it dawned on me that it wasn't just men I didn't trust. I didn't trust anyone. Not even my mother? I certainly didn't trust her to understand about my visit to Cotterly. A wave of loneliness engulfed me.

'Shit!' I said it aloud, but there was no-one to hear.

I stood up and, grasping my briefcase, marched back into the hotel.

I dreaded the moment when I would be faced with the decision whether to head straight back to London or to turn off and take the valley road.

As I drove, I resorted to a game of counting red cars – why red ones? – as they passed me heading back the way I'd come, like plucking petals from a daisy: I will turn off, I won't turn off, I will . . . In the event, it was a grubby blue Volkswagen trundling along at a steady thirty that fate commissioned. Several times I prepared to overtake, only to drop back hastily as a van or lorry appeared over the brow of a hill or round a corner. Distracted by the frustration, I lost track of my counting game, relaxing my consciousness of precisely where I was even. As I flicked my indicator yet again, the junction sign loomed at the roadside. I glanced in my mirror at the line of vehicles holding back behind, anticipating my pulling out. The indicator ticked remorselessly... and obediently I allowed the Astra to follow the grid markings on to the centre of the road. On the passenger side, the queue ground past as, committed, I waited to cross the oncoming traffic.

It was madness, of course. I regretted the impulse as soon as I'd acted upon it. Even now I should have been half a mile further along the main road, heading sensibly back to London. If I'd kept going, I'd have been back by late afternoon, in time to arrange to meet someone later for a Chinese or even to change and wander over to the South Bank to pick up a last-minute 'return' for tonight's show.

Oh, well, instead – the thought restored me – I could call on my mother and drive up to town early the next morning. I should have thought of it anyway. After all, I hadn't really given her as much time as I might have done these last couple of months. Not that she'd complained. That wasn't her way. 'You have your own life to lead,' she'd said. 'I can manage.'

She had certainly shown herself wonderfully resilient in the face of widowhood. 'At least,' she'd confided with a brave smile on the day of Father's funeral, 'black suits me.'

The weekend after my mission to return Flora's books, when guilt prompted a visit home, she ran out to greet me as I pulled up in the driveway, sheltering us both from the rain under a huge golfing umbrella. She was wearing a black and silver polka dot blouse.

'New?' I queried as we settled round the fire and Mother poured tea. Flames hissed quietly around the artificial coals.

'Why, no. I've had it quite a while.' She leaned across, proffering cake. 'In fact I discovered I had quite a number of suitable bits and pieces tucked away at the back of the wardrobe.' Almost – I tried to suppress the thought before it could surface – as though she'd been waiting for this day. Not that anyone, least of all me, would blame her if she had. It had hardly been – I searched for the right word – a satisfactory marriage.

Even so, it was not like my mother to let an opportunity for a new outfit pass. Surely she wasn't needing to economise? Whatever else, Father had always provided amply. An image of Flora loomed up as an appalling possibility struck me. Casually, helping myself to a piece of Battenberg, I asked, 'Has Father's will been sorted out yet?'

Her answer was reassuring. It would all take time, but according to the solicitor, 'such a nice young man ... taken over from old Mr Robinson who retired last year ...', everything was very straightforward. 'He's left everything to me, of course.'

I breathed a sigh of relief.

'Apart from some small bequest to – what was it now? – some wildfowl trust, I believe. Wildfowl, I ask you!' She picked up the teapot, nodded towards it and looked questioningly at me.

'Oh. Yes please.' I passed my cup and saucer.

'Eventually it will all come to you of course . . .' Mother transferred her attention to the milk jug. Then she looked up brightly. 'If you need anything at the moment . . . ?'

'No, no. I'm fine.'

The telephone rang – someone checking the Meals-on-Wheels rota, it became apparent. Mother could oblige on Tuesday, but Wednesday was her library run, and Friday . . . She certainly kept herself occupied, I reflected. What with her good works and her keep-fit classes and her keen membership of the local fuchsia society. I'd asked her once whether she'd ever considered taking a part-time job; like so many other mothers, I'd suggested. She'd stared at me in bewilderment. 'But how would I ever find the time? And in any case there's no need.' There wasn't, of course. Feminist ideas, I reflected, hadn't percolated through to Mother – not as far as she personally was concerned anyway.

She was still chatting. I leaned back, idly surveying the room. The furniture was arranged as it had always been, each chair and table nailed by habit to its decreed position. The usual pile of magazines sat to attention on the shelf beneath the occasional table, and my parents' wedding photograph, set at its precise angle, continued to grace the top of the bureau. It was all comfortingly familiar and reliable. In contrast, the gap where my father's pipe-rack had always stood seemed, as soon as I identified it, as substantial as the physical object itself.

'You've made a start on sorting Father's things, then?' I observed when my mother eventually replaced the receiver.

'I've done more than that. I've been through the entire house. Easier done straightaway. It's all in the garage waiting to go down to the charity shop or be collected for the Scouts' jumble sale.'

I nodded. 'Well done.'

She looked at me doubtfully. 'I can't imagine there's anything you'd want? I told Harold to take anything he could use . . .'

'Quite right.'

I took my bag upstairs and dumped it on the bed. The bedspread was the one I'd so painstakingly crocheted with oddments of wool while I was still at junior school. I'd resisted regular suggestions by my mother that it was about time to throw it out. The colours had faded and in places the wool had worn thin, springing into holes. Gingerly I fingered them. They could be darned – if I was prepared to take time and trouble.

'I think,' I said to my mother before I left on the

Sunday, 'I'll take that old bedspread back with me. If that's OK with you?'

'I'll be glad to see the back of it.' She laughed. 'You are funny. Is there anything else you want?'

I lied. 'No, I don't think so.' For some reason I didn't feel inclined to own to having already stashed three fishing rods and a red tin box in the boot of the car.

They were still there, wedged against the slope of the back seat; offering, in some way, an excuse for the route I was now taking. All I needed – I grinned wryly – was a pair of green wellies and a Barbour. I indulged the entertaining image of myself so dressed; standing by the open boot, rods in hand – smiling for a cameraman from one of the up-market glossies. I laughed aloud. My mother would love that. Her daughter: '. . . relaxing at the weekend on Lord Whatsit's estate,' she'd read out delightedly from the blurb alongside.

'And you could have had it all,' I mentally parodied her, 'if you'd married Mark.' Yes, well, I didn't.

There was a sweep of bare earth to the side of the road where it curved to approach a bridge. I pulled on to it and wound down the window. The silence flowed in, cocooning me more effectively than pressed metal and reinforced glass ever could. Two children, glancing sideways in momentary curiosity, rattled past on bicycles. They paused on the hump of the bridge and, standing astride their crossbars, peered over its low parapet. Their voices piped towards me, then wafted away into the stillness. When I glanced again, they were weaving their way up the hill beyond. And were gone. The occasional car swooped or, according to its driver's temperament, crawled past – like flies across the pages of a book. I lit a cigarette and leaned back. There was no hurry.

No hurry for what exactly? What was I planning; what did I expect to happen? It was as though the valley were a stage and I a member of the audience – the sole member of the audience – waiting for the curtain to rise. Had I come to observe, or – as at the pantomime so many years ago – to take part?

I jerked round in my seat, for a split second experiencing the almost physical presence of my father beside me – his smiling warmth, his bulk. The vision melted and I shivered, turning back and trying to ignore the sense of Mother behind me frowning disapproval.

Abruptly I switched on the ignition and, pausing only to grind out my cigarette, pulled the wheel sharply over as the car moved forward. I was going home; the time for fantasy was long gone.

The screech of brakes as I nosed at right angles on to the road was real enough though. I slammed on my own and watched helplessly as the other car veered towards the hedge opposite and buried its bonnet in the branches ten yards or so further along.

Somehow it didn't surprise me at all that it was a familiar figure who clambered out across the passenger seat of the Volvo. Father, I reflected later, could be said to have had his way this time too. There was no opting out of this scene.

Still clutching the wheel, engine running, I watched as Andrew peered across the bonnet of his car at the offside wing. I wondered, guiltily, how much damage had been done.

He shrugged, then turned and walked un-hurriedly towards me. 'Could be worse,' he announced. He bent to peer in. 'Good God, it's you.' His eyebrows lifted, and he laughed. 'You're an absolute menace with this thing, aren't you?' He patted the roof just above my head.

I shifted in my seat. 'I'm terribly sorry . . .'

The grin was still there. 'Don't worry. I doubt there's anything a bit of touch-up can't put right. In any case, I was probably driving too fast.'

'Even so . . .' I reached for my bag, intent on producing insurance documents.

He cut across. 'Been to see Flora, have you?'

'No.' I kept my tone carefully neutral. I produced my wallet, opened it and took out the certificate. 'You'll want to make a note of this.'

'I doubt it. Here, let me get the thing off the road – ' he straightened up – 'and then we can consider.'

He bounded across to his car, climbed in and reversed. Branches sprang back into place; up-rooted strands of grass clung to his front wheels. He steered the car efficiently on to the rough beside the Astra and crunched up the handbrake.

I got out and went to meet him. Together we surveyed scratches to the paintwork and an ugly three-inch-long dent just behind the headlight. I ran my hand over it. 'Soon knock that out,' said Andrew.

'Are you sure?' I looked at him uncertainly. He stood there, as relaxed in a suit by the side of the road as in a pullover lounging in Flora's kitchen.

'It's honestly not worth making a thing about. Can we drop it?'

I gave in – gracefully, I hoped. 'OK,' I said. 'But I owe you.'

'Good. Then come back and have a cup of tea.' He waved his arm towards a boxful of files on the back seat of the car. 'Help me put off the evil moment when I have to start wading through all those.'

CHAPTER 5

'My curiosity,' said Andrew, leaning back and crossing his legs, 'is getting the better of me. If you didn't come to see Flora . . . ?'

We were sitting in his garden, the sun throwing a patchwork of light through the branches of a horse-chestnut on to our afternoon-tea scene. It was all very Rupert Brooke somehow – fine china set out on a silver tray, garden trestle and chairs casually occupying an oasis of close-mown grass bounded by flower-beds and an orchard.

I'd had time, as I followed the Volvo along the route I'd taken in February, to prepare myself for the inevitable question. By the time we reached the T-junction, turning right rather than left this time, I'd decided to be honest. More or less.

I explained my visit to the hotel; and the start of my drive back to London. 'I suddenly saw the sign,' I said. 'It was just one of those spur-of-the-moment things.'

'But you didn't go to Wood Edge?'

'No. Where you "found" me – ' I grimaced at the

euphemism – 'was as far as I'd gone. I was turning to go back.'

'Why?'

I shrugged and reached towards the table. 'May I help myself to a biscuit?'

'Sorry.' He leaned forward and passed the plate. I selected a Bourbon. Andrew picked out one with a dollop of jam at its centre. 'Come to think of it,' he said, pausing to swallow, 'you probably wouldn't have found her at home anyway. I've an idea this is her week for going to see Donald.'

'Donald?'

He threw his last piece of biscuit to a blackbird that had been eyeing him hopefully, and watched as it scooped the titbit up and flew off. Then he glanced across at me. 'Her brother.'

'Oh.'

In the silence that followed I smoothed my skirt and tried not to consider that I could, and should, have been halfway back to London by now. Andrew, sitting sideways on to me, appeared totally at ease. He'd taken off his jacket and tie as soon as we arrived. One arm was flung over the back of the garden chair; with the other hand he balanced his cup and saucer on his thigh.

'I'm not sure,' I said, bringing myself back to the moment, 'that I had any idea of calling on her anyway. I think I might have gone up to the meadow. The one above the village. You know, the one at the end of the track.'

'Where I nearly ran you down.'

I smiled. 'Hardly. But yes, that one.'

Andrew put his cup down and pulled out a packet of cigarettes. He passed me one. I held the end to the flame as he flicked the lighter. Settling back, I watched the fronds of smoke rise and waft gently towards the house.

It had, I remembered Flora saying, been built as a dower house. Not that long ago, maybe seventy years or so by the look of it; but long enough for the bricks to have mellowed to a deep golden grey, to unstripped parts of which ivy clung; like old memories, I thought. Inside, as Andrew had proudly shown me when we arrived, the place had been totally redecorated and the kitchen gutted and fitted with modern units. 'Ginny says,' Andrew had laughed, 'that if she's to be deprived of a big kitchen, at least she'll have an efficient one.'

I remembered Flora's kitchen. And Andrew in it.

'Did Flora give you the painting?' His voice, against the stillness of the summer air, startled me.

I swivelled my attention back. We both knew which one he meant. I pictured it, still propped at the back of the hall cupboard; thrust there in discomfort that first evening back at the flat. 'Yes, she did.'

'I thought she might.'

I brushed a leaf from my skirt and squinted up at the sky. 'So Flora has a brother?' I said eventually.

Andrew accepted the change of subject smoothly. 'She doesn't talk about him much,' he said.

I took a sip of tea and raised my eyebrows politely.

'Visits him every month, though. He's in some sort of a home in Sussex.'

'Really.'

'Caught by a sniper in Malaya. Brain damage. That's about all I know.'

'And he's been like that for . . . what . . . forty years?'

'Coming up for. He was there towards the end of it all, I think.' Andrew took a final pull on his cigarette. 'Almost died twelve or so years ago. Pity he didn't, poor fellow.' He leaned sideways and pressed the butt into the flower-bed, sweeping the earth over it. Sitting up again, he looked across at me. 'That was how Flora and your father met, of course.'

I stared. 'Go on.'

'You don't know this?'

'I don't really know anything.'

I flinched slightly under his gaze as he breathed in and paused.

'They phoned through to the Horse and Dragon. Typical Flora. Wouldn't have a telephone then – and still won't. Just one of her quirks,' he explained in response to my raised eyebrow. 'Making some sort of statement about her space, I guess. Anyway – ' he returned to his tale – 'your father happened to be downing a half of Guinness at the time, grasped the situation and, having driven round to Wood Edge with the message, offered to drive her over.'

'All the way to Sussex!' I shot upright.

Andrew surveyed me calmly. 'I wasn't there so I can't recount the tale blow by blow. But yes, he certainly – so I understand – ended up taking her the whole way.'

'And, I suppose, held her hand through it all.'

'He was that sort of man.'

I subsided. 'But that,' I said after a moment or two, 'doesn't excuse his . . . getting involved with her.'

'No . . .' Andrew spoke slowly. 'I don't imagine it does.' He reached up and took a considering swipe at a trailing branch. Changing patterns of sunlight waved across his arm and face. 'I hadn't realised how angry you were with him,' he said.

'Are you surprised?' I demanded.

'I don't know. I take people at face value. If they're pleasant to me, I'm pleasant back.'

'And if they're not?' I made the effort to calm down.

He grinned. 'I walk away.'

'Does that apply to your clients?'

He considered. 'No. But that's different. I'm talking socially. Bit of an emotional coward, I expect that makes me.' He eased forward and cupped the teapot in both hands. 'Stone cold. Is it too early for a drink, do you think?'

'I won't, thanks.' Suddenly restless, I rose to my feet. 'I know what I should like to do.'

'Go up to the meadow?' Andrew leaned back

and regarded me lazily. 'Shall I come with you?'

I wandered across to the flower-bed, ostensibly inspecting a clump of marigolds. I'd rather he didn't. One of the heads came off in my hand as I stroked it. Guiltily I leaned down and placed the circle of orange petals carefully on the earth. 'Sorry,' I said. The apology dissipated among the scents rising from the border. I turned. 'What about your paperwork?'

He waved it away.

Squeezed into a pair of the older boy's rubber boots – Ginny's flatties had turned out to be even smaller – I clumped after him up a narrow path behind the house.

'Watch the nettles,' he called, too late, as I sucked my wrist. At the top he waited, holding out a hand to steady me over the stile. We skirted the upper part of a crop field. 'Oats,' he announced over his shoulder.

I feigned interest. But as we approached the ridge, I felt my spirits lifting. Up here the as-yet-green heads swayed delicately and a light gust lifted my hair almost imperceptibly from my scalp. As I straightened up from a stumble across a crumbling clod of grey-brown earth I instinctively halted, raising my face to the sun and breathing in – and in some more, until my rib cage felt it would burst.

'Are you all right?' Andrew was silhouetted twenty yards further on, staring back at me.

I let the air go. 'Fine.' I hurried to catch up. 'You forget . . .'

'Forget what?'

We'd reached the gate. Ahead a broad swathe through trees led to the road.

'Now I recognise where we are,' I said.

The hardness of the tarmac under my feet, as we strode left along it, restored a sense of reality. I clung on to it as we turned off along the track I'd walked before. The primroses were long over, their leaves, together with last year's mulch, buried under a tangle of fresh greenery. Further into the wood, in the shade of branches locked overhead, bluebells sheltered from the sky, radiating their own deep indigo.

'Forget what?' Andrew and I had been walking side by side in companionable silence.

I blinked. 'Oh . . . I don't know. Everything I suppose.'

I was aware of his glancing at me. Then, as though having considered, he said, 'I love this part of England.'

'Have you always lived here?'

'Basically, yes. Did a bit of travelling and was at law school in London. Then articles there. Didn't need my arm twisting to leave it, though. I just don't seem to be the ambitious type.' Again he turned his head to look at me. 'Are you?'

I considered. 'Well, yes . . . Reasonably so, anyway.'

We strolled on. My foot scuffed the ground sending a flurry of dust and small stones billowing ahead of us. A sudden commotion erupted in the undergrowth and a squirrel leapt towards a tree trunk and up it, bounding away through the branches.

We reached the end of the track. The gate, now, was shut. I leaned up against it, staring into the meadow.

'It's OK. Only horses. No bulls.'

'What makes you think I'd be worried?'

Andrew laughed, steering me through and across to the base of a large oak standing on its own. I perched myself on a root, facing away from the rooftops of Cotterly. Andrew sank to the ground beside me.

I slid my legs out of the borrowed boots and wriggled my toes, relishing the coolness around my ankles. Picking nodules of dried-out earth from around the base of the tree, I crumbled them between my fingers. Two horses, one a deep brown, the other a mottled grey, cropped peacefully in a lower corner of the field. Every now and again they swished their tails at flies. At one point, the grey abruptly cantered forward a few paces, then stopped and dropped his head again to continue grazing. It was as though the moment of activity had never been.

I broke the silence. 'Do you ride?'

'Not any more.' The answer rose lazily. 'We had ponies as children. Mine was a skewbald. Stubborn as hell except when she was pointing for home.' He laughed, and rose on one elbow. 'Do you?'

'Me? No. Unless you count donkeys on the

beach.' I remembered the occasions – two of them; Father hoisting me up . . .

'I suppose we were pretty spoiled. Lots of freedom. We used to go off all day with a packet of sandwiches, build dens in the wood, fish a bit . . .'

'My father fished.'

'Not that sort of fishing. The trout stretches are all heavily controlled. Apart from anything else our pocket money wouldn't have stretched to the fees. No, worms on bent pins, that sort of thing. Kept the cat supplied with minnows – and the occasional roach. I sometimes wonder about all those kids trudging along pavements . . .'

'I was one of those kids "trudging the pavements", as you put it.'

'So is my sympathy wasted?'

I had to laugh. 'Not entirely. But it wasn't as dreary as you make it sound.'

I didn't feel inclined to elaborate. Andrew lay back and closed his eyes. I hugged my knees and stared over the hedges towards the horizon. This was where Father had painted me, or rather his image of me. Sitting like this. But a little further over. I estimated the spot, then rose and padded across to it, the grass coarse against the soles of my feet. I squatted down, surveying the scene.

My nose twitched at the sickly-sweet odour of horse dung, a large dollop of which, disturbed by buzzing flies, steamed gently close by. The smell mingled with the scent of baked earth and grass, fine dust from which hovered in the air, tickling the back of my throat. A plane, jetting towards London, scored the sky, its slipstream flaking out into a cotton-wool trail. I could just make out the tiny silver shape at the head, winking the sun's reflection. In less than half an hour its passengers would be disembarking at Heathrow; real people again with lives to lead, no longer cocooned in a sliver of metal suspended in mid-air.

I straightened up and strode back towards Andrew. 'I really should be making a move,' I said.

'I'm sorry.' He bounded to his feet. 'I've kept you too long.'

'It's only that I'm planning to stop off overnight at my mother's – ' I looked up from pulling on a boot – 'and it's a good hour and a half's drive.'

'Of course.' He steadied me as I pushed my foot into the second one.

'Pity you haven't seen Flora,' he said as we wandered back.

'Why?'

'Because you ought to talk to her, get to know her.'

'How so?'

'You tell me.' He turned and placed a hand on my shoulder. 'You're kidding yourself, you know, if you pretend you don't want to.'

I released myself and walked on quickly.

When he caught up, I said, 'Will Ginny be back?'

'Possibly. And the boys. Why?'

'I'd like to meet her.'

'She'd like to meet you.' I felt him looking at me. 'You're changing the subject.'

I didn't answer.

'Oh, well,' he said eventually, 'it's your life, I suppose.'

We'd reached the road. Ahead of us it dipped towards the village. As we turned off it to retrace our steps across the field and down the path to the house, I said, 'I can't see it would do any good to speak to her. It's all in the past now.'

I marched on. 'In any case,' I said, as we descended to the garden, 'Flora wouldn't want to see me.'

'You don't think so?'

The house was empty. I retrieved my shoes and made towards the car. The Volvo stood next to it, the scrape disconcertingly visible.

'I'm sorry,' I said, grimacing towards the damage. Then, unnecessarily formally, 'You've been very kind, and I've enjoyed my afternoon.'

He held the car door open. 'See you again perhaps.'

The revving of the engine drowned my muttered, 'I doubt it.'

I was angry. I knew I was angry, for reasons I couldn't quite put my finger on, and I drove badly, narrowly missing a grey Metro as I swooped round the corner and changed gear for the climb away from the source of whatever it was that was bugging me. Its driver was a fair-haired woman. Two smaller heads bobbed in the back. I guessed it was probably Ginny. If so, I was relieved to have left; I was in no mood for polite conversation with a stranger.

Would Andrew tell Flora of my visit? What did it matter? My stupidity in returning here at all was embarrassing anyway.

I didn't stop at my mother's. It was too late, I told myself lamely, knowing the real reason was that I wanted to be alone. Safely back in Fulham, I switched on the hi-fi as I started to fling the contents out of my suitcase. A recording of popular arias was, for some reason, already in the machine. As soon as the baritone came in, I lunged for the off-button. I threw myself down on the sofa and pulled the crocheted rug, still awaiting attention, up over me. Forty minutes later, the burning smell of a forgotten pizza drifted through from the kitchen.

I was only just beginning to feel more relaxed when, halfway through the following week, the postcard arrived. The handwriting was large and sprawling. I turned it over. The brief message filled the space. 'I'll be at home next weekend if you want to come. F.' I didn't really need to check the postmark, but I did and it left me in no doubt. How did she have my address? But then she clearly knew a great deal more about me than I her.

No, I didn't want to go, damn her. Whatever gave her the idea I'd want to have anything more to do with her? In any case, I'd already arranged to spend the whole of the bank holiday with Mother.

I'd been neglecting her shamefully, I'd reminded myself again early on Monday when the need to replace laddered tights had me nipping into Selfridges, one of her favourite London shopping haunts. I'd said as much when, fortified by the normality of a frenetic day at the office, I rang her that evening.

'It has been a while,' she acknowledged. 'But you mustn't worry about me.'

'But I do.'

'I wouldn't want you to feel you have to come unless you want to.'

'Of course I want to. It's just that we're so busy at work at this time of year and I'm utterly exhausted by the time I get home.'

'Then you need a break.' She promised me roast pork with crackling, and a lazy time in the garden.

Mother's idea of relaxing outdoors usually involved back-breaking weeding, but I said, 'Lovely. See you on Friday, then.' I sketched out plans in my mind. We would go into the town together on Saturday morning as we always used to – I might even pick up a bargain in one of those little side-street boutiques – and in the afternoon drive over together to Windsor or Henley. Mother would enjoy that.

Poor old Mum. She'd had it tough. She needed my support; deserved it. After all, who was it who, virtually single-handed, cared for me through my growing-up years? I was looking forward to doing what I could to cheer her up. Over a cup of coffee, I glared again at the postcard and thrust it behind the toaster.

And there it would no doubt have curled and yellowed until eventually I threw it out if Mother hadn't opted to postpone our arrangements.

But she did. At mid-morning on the Friday. When I'd already watered the plants, packed a bag, and brought the car into central London ready for a quick getaway at the end of the day.

Aunt Leah, she apologised down the wire in that slightly off-key voice I recognised as meaning she had already made up her mind, was begging her to accompany her on that coach trip to Wales she was so looking forward to. 'Harold was going with her,' she continued as though, despite having made the booking for them, I didn't know, 'but he's decided now – now, I ask you – that his tomatoes are at a delicate stage and he can't leave them. She'll be so disappointed if she has to cancel . . .'

At any other time, I'd have grinned to myself; Uncle Harold had built up a lifetime's subtle resistance to being organised. With wry amusement, I'd have imagined him in his greenhouse conspiring with his plants to produce the necessary excuse.

Today, exasperated, I flung my arm out in a gesture of frustration. A plastic container rattled to the floor, scattering paper clips. 'Damn,' I said.

'Oh dear, I'm sorry. Is that upsetting your plans?'

Clearly it was upsetting my plans. 'No, of course not. I just knocked something off my desk.' I bent to retrieve the half-dozen clips that had landed within reach. 'That's fine. Have a good time.' I tried to sound cheerful.

Alone in the flat that evening, ensconced with an Indian take-away and a bottle of wine picked up on my way home, I attempted, without much success, to still the voice of self-pity. The room, despite my having flung open all the windows, was hot and airless. The sound of children's voices, and of a mother calling them in to bed, hung on the humid air like a long drawn out echo. Everyone I knew had taken the opportunity to get out of London for the holiday. Somewhere on the M4 a coach – one of ours, just to rub salt into the wound – was heading towards the Severn bridge. I felt thoroughly abandoned.

I refilled my glass. The bottle, I noted, was already more than half empty. Looking into it, as I held it up to pour again, I could see the inside of the label. Where the wine level cut it, the image shifted sideways. Refraction of light, I murmured. For a moment I was back in the science lab at school. All those bunsen burners and rows of chemicals in glass jars with enormous stoppers. And the smell – musty, yet sharp and sickly at the same time.

I'd never been very good at science. But I did remember about refraction of light. Perhaps because my father, poring over that piece of homework with me, had cited fishing to illustrate its application.

'Maybe you'd like to come with me sometime?' he'd suggested.

But my mother, looking up from her embroidery, had shaken her head. 'Don't be silly.' Then, to me, 'You wouldn't want to, darling, would you?'

I stared into the bottle again, twisting and turning it to first maximise and then eliminate the distortion. 'Interesting,' I announced a shade over-solemnly.

I woke next morning with a dull head, aware of having slept restlessly. I heaved the duvet, three quarters of which had ended up on the floor, back on to the bed and went in search of orange juice. I was out of it. I plugged in the kettle, reached for the coffee jar, then changed my mind and tore the cellophane off a box of teabags. The windows were still open from the night before. The day promised to be another hot one, but for now it was cooler and I shivered. Crossing to the kitchen window to close it, I saw a woman opposite shaking a tablecloth into the air above her half of the two small squares of garden that divided us. I smiled, but she turned back inside without acknowledging me.

I slopped water on to a teabag and thrust a slice of bread into the toaster. I pulled out the card from behind it. 'Well, why not?' I said.

CHAPTER 6

The temperature rose steadily as I drove, the early summer heatwave showing no signs of breaking. The heat pressed in through the wound-down windows whenever I was forced to slow.

The twists and turns of the last few miles were now sufficiently familiar to allow me to anticipate the road ahead. The feeling of confidence this gave me began to wane as I drove through the village, up the lane, and turned in through the gates of Wood Edge. I parked beside the yellow Citroën. The handbrake squealed as I pulled it on.

I eased myself out of the car, my crêpe shirt peeling away from the back of the seat and clamping itself in damp creases across my spine. I brushed back the wisps of hair sticking to my forehead.

'You look as though the first thing you need is a shower.' Flora had materialised behind me as I burrowed into the car to retrieve bits and pieces from the passenger seat.

I emerged and held out a bunch of irises. They matched the blues and yellows in her dress, which hung low necked and loose from comfortable shoulders. 'Rather like bringing coals to New-castle,' I apologised, looking round at the garden about to burst into unordered bloom, 'but I didn't think chocolates would survive.'

She led the way into the house and stopped at the bottom of the stairs. 'The bed's made up. You remember where the bathroom is.'

The shower was a hand-held one in the cast-iron bath. I pulled the curtains round and doused my-self. For a few minutes, everything but the blissful relief of tepid water on parched skin was drowned out. I towelled my hair, brushed it back loosely and, dressed in fresh cotton, slowly descended to the kitchen.

Flora had meanwhile prepared a tray – a pile of salad sandwiches and a large earthenware jug of juice in which segments of apple and orange floated.

I followed her outside and round to the back of the house. She placed the tray on the ground under the apple tree and I helped set up deck chairs in its shade.

'I'm not at all sure why I've come,' I said, having drained one glass of grape and pineapple and accepted another.

Flora acknowledged my statement with no more than the merest movement of her head. She leaned back, seeming in no hurry to press me to talk. In an odd way I found it comfortable sitting here with her, lunching companionably. Apart from the dis-tant whirr of a tractor, there was no sound other than the discreet ones of our eating. But it was a deceptive silence. As my ears accustomed themselves to the quiet, I began to be aware of a background murmur: a flutter of wings; the protest of drying-out timbers as a bird landed on the shed roof; the sigh of grass under its feet as it hopped down, searching spy-eyed for insects; the click of its beak on the hardened soil. Bees, busy about their pollinating duties, strummed a steady harmony.

I put my plate down on the ground beside me. 'That was delicious,' I said. 'Was the lettuce from the garden?'

She nodded.

She was watching my face and, with nothing to occupy me, uncertainty returned. 'I thought it must be.' I laughed awkwardly. 'Lot more taste than those limp things one gets in London.'

I stared into the branches overhead. 'Why did you invite me?' I wondered what I was hoping she'd say – and what I was afraid she might say.

'Andrew told me you'd been down. He got the impression you felt you wouldn't be welcome. I thought you might appreciate reassurance.'

I lowered my gaze and tried to read her expression. It told me no more than the words themselves. 'I think you've just put the ball back into my court,' I complained.

'Not really.' Flora regarded me without rancour. 'It's always been there, hasn't it?'

'In my court?'

'In the sense that it was up to you. You would

have been more than welcome here at any time.'

I looked at her. Did she mean it?

'It was hardly that simple . . .' I said.

'Your father and I both realised that.' Flora picked up the jug, checked my glass, then refilled her own and sat back.

There was an extraordinary stillness about her. So unlike my mother who, even when she sat down, had to keep her hands busy. I wondered where she was now. Probably scouring some tourist attraction, determined not to miss any small corner on the itinerary. Just as she did with her duster; there was no place for cobwebs in her house. Everything clean and orderly.

Flora had been a particularly untidy item.

'Even if I'd wanted to, I couldn't have come.' I remembered my father's one hesitant suggestion and knew it was true.

Flora's hands cupped her glass. Her fingers were round and softly lined. An emerald gleamed on her right hand, its gold band nestling into the supple skin. 'So why is it different now?'

I sipped my drink and wondered.

Flora rose to her feet; not particularly elegantly – I was beginning to realise that wasn't her style. 'I think I'll clear these things away.' She collected up the plates, leaving the jug and glasses.

'Can I help?'

'You stay there and relax. You've got things to think about.' She brushed crumbs on to the grass and strolled off towards the house.

I was glad of the time to myself. My mind jumped and twisted; but came up with no satisfactory answers.

'Here, Columbus!' I'd forgotten about him until a ginger shape undulated silently round a bush directly in my line of vision. The cat hesitated, tail erect, and stared. Then he padded across and rubbed the length of his body across my shin. I patted my knee. 'Come on, then.' Again that considering stare. 'Well?' He leapt up and balanced facing me, stretching out his neck and making little exploratory movements with his head. I responded, jutting out my own chin – laughing as I mirrored him.

'You're honoured.' Flora had glided back. 'He normally saved that sort of communion for your father.' She settled in her chair again.

Columbus lay down on my lap, his head turned towards Flora, ears standing up in little triangular points. I stroked his fur, soft under my fingertips. I could feel the heat of his body and cautiously eased my legs in search of cooler air. I wasn't altogether sorry when, a few moments later, he spotted movement behind the tree and jumped down. I watched him chase a sparrow which spluttered upwards to safety.

'If,' I said, coming back to the thought that Flora had left me with, 'Father hadn't insisted on my coming – ' I could have sworn I saw her lift an eyebrow but the movement, if it was one, was so slight as to seem, the next moment, to have been

imagined – 'if he hadn't begged me to, anyway . . .
what I mean is . . .'

Flora's face was expressionless.

'OK,' I said. 'Maybe something in me wanted to.
To see where he disappeared to every weekend; to
find out what you were like; to try to understand, I
suppose. But it was more than that.' I reached into
my bag, pulled out a packet of Dunhill and lit up,
almost without realising what I was doing. I took a
deep pull, looking upwards and concentrating on a
cluster of apple buds. 'I guess it was that I just
couldn't bear to refuse him. Not that one last time.'
I turned my head to gaze defiantly at Flora. 'I did
love him, you know.'

She nodded. 'I'm sure he knew that.'

'He did? Then why didn't he do something . . .' I
was less disconcerted now by Flora's silences. I
lapsed into one myself.

It was Flora who broke it. 'So many questions,'
she observed as though she could see them crowd-
ing through my mind. 'Haven't you worked out
answers to any of them?'

'How could I?' I was indignant.

'Maybe you've never really tried to.'

'There was no point.'

There hadn't been. The silence on the subject of
Flora, the disruption to my life, had left me with
only fantasies – and insubstantial ones at that. It
hurt, I realised, that neither of my parents had
talked to me about it at all. I supposed they had
wanted to protect me. Instead they'd locked me in

limbo – observing but not understanding, not involved. But I *was* involved. A surge of anger took me by surprise.

'No-one ever talked about it; about you,' I said. 'We were so happy.' I fought the tears pricking the back of my eyes. 'Then suddenly, "wham". And neither of them said anything. No explanations. Nothing. My mother pretended to all the neighbours that everything was fine. What could I do? I hated pretending.' I ground my cigarette butt under my foot, then picked up the flattened end.

Flora observed my predicament. 'Chuck it in the bushes.' She inclined her head towards something green with tiny white flowers.

I threw.

'I'd have liked to be able to throw *you* into the bushes,' I said, carefully continuing to stare at the point where the butt had landed.

'Bit difficult when I was out of reach.'

'Exactly.' I felt myself unexpectedly grinning. I waited for something more, but nothing came.

I ruminated. 'What I don't understand,' I said, 'is why they carried on as they did. As though everything was perfectly normal. It was eerie. I mean, if they'd so much as referred to it even, at least it would have been out in the open. I'd have known where I was.'

'But, as things were, you didn't.'

I shook my head. 'But then, after a while, you adjust to it.'

'Did you adjust?'

'I just said so, didn't I? Well, yes. I mean, I didn't have any choice. Not as far as day-to-day living was concerned anyway.' I slithered a piece of apple from the bottom of my glass and bit into it. 'We developed a routine, Mother and I.'

'Sticking plaster?'

I looked at her. 'Wounds heal,' I said.

'Not necessarily. Not if they don't get enough air.'

I considered. 'Father said that once.'

It had been a deep graze – I'd come off my bike on the gravel path leading up to the recreation ground. By the next day my knee was red and throbbing.

'Here, let's get that thing off,' Father had insisted, easing at the large pink square covering the torn skin.

I could hear Mother's squeal now: 'She'll get dirt in it.'

'No, she won't.' Father had been firm. 'In any case, better that than leave it to fester.'

Almost without thinking, I touched my knee. It had got better, and the scar all but disappeared.

Flora sat there, hands in her lap.

'I suppose,' I said, 'you think you know what's going on inside me better than I do?'

'I only know what you tell me.'

I protested. 'You know a lot about me. Father must have talked.' Making the point: 'You knew my address in London.'

'I thought we were talking about your feelings.

I've only been able to guess at those. I know your father was concerned.'

'Then why didn't he talk to me, do something?'

'It seems to me,' Flora observed lazily, 'that we've just gone full circle.'

I blinked; then acknowledged it. 'So,' I said, 'what *was* the reason?' Exasperated now at her silence, I prodded. 'You must have some idea.'

'Would you accept any explanation I gave you?'

'Why shouldn't I?'

Her failure to answer irritated me. I turned on her. 'I think you're enjoying this.' I got up and paced across the grass. The sun, as I moved out of the shade, slapped on to my head and back. I turned and stared at her, my arms folded. Then I felt my shoulders sink.

'I suppose you're right,' I said. 'You'd only be defending him. At least, I'd be afraid that's all you were doing, But then – ' I scuffed at the grass – 'maybe I want you to defend him.' The admission startled me.

'And if I did?'

I laughed ironically. 'Why, then I could blame it all on you. Make you the fall guy.'

'Would that solve things?'

'Damn you, no. And I don't know why it wouldn't because it ought to. I am angry with you. Of course I'm angry with you – ' I was shouting now – 'but it doesn't take away that feeling in here . . .' I thumped myself just below the breast-bone: 'It's like a tight knot. And it frightens me.'

90

I stood there, rigid and bemused. 'God, you're a cow,' I said at last.

Flora's expression didn't so much as flicker.

'I'd better go,' I said.

Still no acknowledgement.

'Oh, hell,' I said, wandering back and collapsing in the chair. 'You know I don't want to, don't you?' I stared at the sky.

'It seems to me,' said Flora slowly, 'that you have every reason to be angry with me. But that's the easy bit. What's complicated is—'

'My anger with them? My father, I mean. I'm not angry with Mother – how could I be? None of this mess was her fault. She's the one who's suffered.'

'What a straightforward picture you paint.'

'Ha! You see, you are defending him!' I scored triumphantly. Then wished I hadn't. I needed Flora on my side.

The thought took me aback.

'I think it would do us both good to go for a walk,' she said.

We deposited the glasses in the house and started along the lane.

'Your father and I often used to walk up here,' said Flora.

I allowed the image to take shape. Would my father's arm have been round her shoulders, I wondered. Would they have held hands? Somehow I doubted either. Flora wasn't the sort who invited protective gestures. And her ability to establish contact didn't rely on physical touch. On both counts she was totally different from my mother. Not that my mother was particularly demonstrative. A kiss of greeting and of farewell . . . I wondered what I was saying.

Flora was strolling, hands in the pockets of her voluminous skirt. I looked at her. 'Didn't you mind,' I said, my thoughts expressing themselves aloud, 'being "the other woman", only seeing him at weekends?'

She smiled. 'One adjusts,' she quoted. 'But no, it was different for me. I did know where I stood. I was content to settle for the arrangement.'

Why, I wondered. I debated whether to ask her.

Flora had glanced in my direction. 'It wasn't such a hardship, you know. I'm quite content with my own company most of the time.'

'Even so, you make it sound as though you had no say in it all either.'

'On the contrary. I could have said no.'

'What would have happened if you had?'

Flora hesitated as though about to say something and then changing her mind. 'We'll never know, will we?' she said.

I considered. 'You mean my father would have been forced to choose between you and my mother?'

'That's one way of putting it.'

And which of them would he have chosen? Why, my mother of course. And then – I tantalised myself with the pretty picture – everything would have returned to normal and we'd have been happy again.

But somehow I knew I could no longer believe it was that simple – any of it. I took a swing at the long grass beside the path, pulling away some of the seed head as I did so. I inspected the soft green shreds as they lay in my palm, then brushed them off.

We walked on, past the curve in the stream where I'd paused when I came here on my own. Flora kept up a steady relaxed pace. The first breezes of late afternoon stirred the trees. Abruptly we emerged from them.

Flora stopped. 'Do you feel like going further?'

'Perhaps not today,' I said.

I put down the book I had been idling through and stared across the kitchen at the play of sunlight just catching the top edges of the window.

Flora had announced, some ten minutes earlier, that she was off to feed the chickens. She hadn't invited me to accompany her, and I hadn't liked to suggest it. Why not? It would have been something to do, and different from picking grey cardboard cartons of sanitised eggs off supermarket shelves. I rather thought I'd enjoy the experience of coming into close contact with a real live hen or two.

I glanced at my skimpy Bond Street sandals, wishing I'd had the sense that morning to throw in a pair of trainers. The lane had been one thing; I wasn't too sure how they'd stand up to the rough end of a country garden. Only one way to find out. I made my way across the lawn and through a gap between raspberry canes. To either side of me stretched disciplined rows of vegetables: cabbages, carrots, purple sprouting, swelling onion sets, rounded lettuces. A grass path, flattened by constant use, ran through the middle. Ahead was a hedge which, glimpsed earlier from a distance, I had assumed marked the boundary, just as its counterparts to left and right did.

I picked my way towards the tall, narrow gate set into it and pushed it open to find myself standing in the entrance to a large netted-off chicken run. To the left stood a wooden hen house, low slung with a ramp up to its small, square entrance. Egg boxes projected from one side. In the far right-hand corner of the run, a clutch of flustered chickens scuttered to and fro along the fence while Columbus lay, haunches bunched and quivering, front paws stretched out sheepdog style, monitoring any escape manoeuvre. Lording it from his perch on the handle of a rusting garden roller, a black-tailed cockerel jutted out his neck as if about to crow approval, then thought better of it, and raised a claw to scratch his head feathers. In the centre of this tableau, Flora crouched, a protesting hen grasped firmly between her skirted thighs. On hearing the gate creak, she half turned her head.

'Looks as though it's broken its leg,' she said, clasping the bird and rising. I stepped gingerly towards her across the dung-spattered earth.

94

Flora allowed the leg to dangle. 'See what I mean?'

'How did it do that?'

Flora allowed herself a quiet chuckle. 'Probably squabbling over the cock. Here, can you take it?' She pushed the bundle towards me. 'Keep your hands over its wings – that's right – no, don't squeeze the poor thing – just hold it firmly. I'll collect the eggs. Then we'll take it into the house and see what we can do.'

I stood there uncertain, holding the struggling bird well out in front of me while she checked the boxes.

'Oh, for heaven's sake, Columbus, leave them be,' Flora scolded, straightening up; and as the cat reluctantly relinquished his self-appointed guard duty and the hens scattered, we proceeded back through the gate and along the path. I was less aware of the crumbs of loose earth that had worked themselves under my instep than of the smell of grass and the pulsing warmth permeating the smooth feathers.

I held Arabella while Flora constructed a splint from pieces of thin ply neatly split, with a penknife, from the side panel of an old orange box. She padded them out with cotton wool and bound the dressing with a pipe-cleaner – one of my father's, I registered absently – retrieved from a kitchen drawer. I was sent to rummage in the shed for a large cardboard box. We settled the invalid on wadges of newspaper and ensured there could be neither egress nor ingress – Columbus was watching the operation consideringly – with a square of netting retrieved from behind a clump of gooseberry bushes. Space for the box was made in the lobby between the boot rack and the trug.

'Time for a drink, don't you think?' said Flora.

I peered into the box. Two beady eyes stared up at me reproachfully. 'Will it mend?' I asked.

'Can but hope.' Flora was all matter-of-factness again.

She opened a bottle of wine. We sat down and sipped from generously filled glasses.

'I suppose I'd better start thinking about supper,' said Flora.

'Would you like me to do it?'

Flora looked at me with just a hint of a quizzical expression. 'If you like.'

I decided I did like.

She directed me to the fridge and a pair of man-sized chops. I discovered mushrooms; and located elderly jars of herbs in the corner cupboard. I guessed Flora might have fresh ones in the garden and was relieved she said nothing – I wouldn't have known how to use them.

I had my back to her as I prepared vegetables and set pans on the Aga.

'I see,' she said, and I realised she must have picked up the thin volume through which I'd been browsing earlier, 'you've been reading the War Poets.'

'Only glancing really.' I'd picked it off the shelf for something to look at. It was one my father had had me bring down. I topped and tailed a leek and rinsed out the remnants of soil lurking among the layers. 'I only read a couple.' I sliced the leek. 'They're very moving.'

As I ran the tap again, I said, 'Andrew told me about your brother. Well, not much. Just that he was . . . wounded; that you visit him. He thought that was probably where you were last weekend.'

'Yes.'

I was about to say I was sorry, but Flora, surprisingly without prompting, went on. 'One of life's unfairnesses. He was so young.'

I kept my eyes turned to the sink.

'It was Malaya, of course. He could have deferred National Service until after his degree. Had a place at Cambridge to read law. But being Don . . . so full of energy – couldn't resist the physical excitement . . .'

Turning off the tap as unobtrusively as I could, I heard Flora's voice swing back to pragmatism. 'Pity,' she pronounced. The cushions in the chesterfield sighed as she rose. 'Does your glass need topping up?'

'I think I'm OK,' I said.

I made the sauce and left it simmering alongside the vegetables while I attended to the meat. 'Wasn't it,' I said, 'because of your brother that you and my father met?' The chops sizzled as I flipped them over.

'That's right.' The familiar neutral tone.

I put down the spatula and turned to face her. 'I gather he drove you over; understandable enough in the circumstances, I suppose; but what happened after that?' As calmly as I could, I said, 'I'd like to know.'

Flora met my gaze appraisingly. Not for an instant did she attempt to avoid it. I waited.

'Did you know,' she said at last, 'that your father had a close friend who was killed in Malaya?'

I shook my head, uncertain whether or not she was dodging my question.

'Simon, his name was. They'd gone right through school together. Like Don, Simon decided to do his National Service straightaway; your father was persuaded to qualify first.'

'He did his afterwards, though,' I said. 'I remember him mentioning it. In Cyprus.'

'That's right. He'd expected – wanted – to go to Kenya but ended up in a desk job in Nicosia. Hardly saw a shot fired. Even missed the worst of the riots.'

'That was lucky,' I said.

'He didn't see it that way. Felt guilty at getting off so lightly.'

I was beginning to make the connections – Simon, Don . . . 'But by the time he met you,' I said, 'he must have put all that behind him.'

'Oh, he had. To all intents and purposes anyway.'

'So?'

'So I think to start with he just wanted to do what he could to help.'

'Struck a chord, you mean?'

Flora nodded. 'He called in next time he was down to ask after Don. Then . . .' she paused, calculating '. . . it must have been a couple of months before I saw him again. Quite by chance. I was in the village when he drove through.'

'And he stopped to say hello.' I felt cynicism rising.

'It was just before lunch. He invited me for a drink. We talked.'

'About how his wife didn't understand him, I suppose!'

Flora met my glare calmly. 'No. About fishing mostly. And his childhood.'

I decided not to bother apologising.

'He was brought up in the country,' I volunteered. 'In Gloucestershire somewhere. I remember visiting there when I was small. The cottage . . . a beautiful thatched one . . . was up a lane and backed on to fields.' That of course – my mind flashed back – was where the memory of bats came from. 'Then, when Grandpa retired, they moved to Devon. Ended up in a very dull little bungalow. But it was practical.'

Mother, I recalled, had considered it a vast improvement, and not only because it was within half an hour's drive of Plymouth's shopping centre. She never could abide, she'd said, all those crawly things. As a house-warming present, she'd given my grandparents an electric fly-catcher – one of those which glowed blue and hummed quietly and incessantly. 'It simply wasn't worth bothering in that dreadful old place,' she'd commented to my father. He hadn't said anything, I recalled now; just gone across to the sideboard and helped himself to a whisky. I remembered because neither of my parents normally drank except when we had visitors; occasions which had always been very formal, with Mother polishing and baking for days beforehand. Strange really – except of course that Mother enjoyed showing off her culinary skills – that even after Father's . . . defection she had continued, though considerably less often, to do her duty as hostess. Or was it Father doing his? All part, for both of them, of the social pretence?

'Come to think of it,' I said, 'it must have been soon after they moved that Father took up fishing.' I thought about it. 'Actually, no. It must have been after Grandpa died. But then that was only two or three years later. A day or so before my ninth birthday,' I recalled. I grinned sheepishly. 'I was afraid I wouldn't be able to have my party.'

'And did you?'

'Oh, yes. But Father couldn't be there, of course. He'd had to go down to support Gran.' I'd been decidedly put out about it, I remembered.

I mused on. 'She – Gran – went into a nursing home eventually. Mother and I visited her once or twice when we were down there on holiday.' I inspected my toes. 'It was all a bit uncomfortable; making excuses for Father not being with us. She was a lovely old lady.'

'She was indeed.'

I looked up and stared.

'I met her many times.'

'You mean Father took you to meet his mother? That she knew? How could he . . . ?'

'She was a very down-to-earth, practical woman.'

'But she never said anything to us.'

'Would you have expected her to?'

I have an idea I must have been standing there with my mouth open. Flora unexpectedly shifted her gaze and nodded past me. 'Do you think those chops are done?'

'Oh, my God.' I snatched up the pan and wished I'd had the thought to grab the ovencloth first. I deposited it on a cooler surface and sucked my fingers.

CHAPTER 7

The meal I served up was hardly of the standard I would have wished. If I was hoping that, if only for politeness's sake, Flora would be generous about it, I was to be disappointed.

'Not one of your better efforts, I take it,' she observed wryly as she cut into the meat. 'Still – ' there was a hint of a crease at the corners of her eyes – 'it's only burnt on one side.' She took a mouthful. 'Umm. The sauce is good though.' From Flora, that, I decided, was approaching high praise. In any case, now that I was becoming accustomed to it, I wasn't sure I didn't prefer her directness to the conventional courtesies. In an odd way, it was reassuring.

The fridge yielded up home-made yoghurt to follow. As we settled down with our coffee, I challenged her. 'How did you know I'd come this weekend?'

Flora looked up. 'I didn't.' Said simply; factually.

'You appear to have been catering for two,' I persisted.

She shrugged. 'I could always have eaten the second chop tomorrow.'

I smiled acknowledgement to myself, capit-
ulating. I had to hand it to her: she had an answer
to everything. When, it occurred to me, she chose
to. She hadn't, I realised, curiosity reasserting itself,
answered my original question. I pointed this out.
'So you had a drink together in the Horse and
Dragon,' I prompted.

For a moment there was just a hint of exasperation in her voice. 'What do you think happened?
We found we enjoyed each other's company. He
started to pop in whenever he was down. We
talked.'

'He didn't talk much at home.'

'No.'

I tried to imagine my father in deep conversation. It wasn't that he was given to flippancy; just
that it was my mother who prattled on. Nothing
consequential was ever said in our house. I strained
the reaches of my memory. Trivial information was
what he imparted – if he was ever asked for it: an
amusing incident at work; a frustrating one when a
client simply would not accept that the Inland
Revenue couldn't be persuaded round to his point
of view *all* of the time; the state of his colleagues'
wives' health – a subject Mother enjoyed specu-
lating on at length; once in a while the odd
reminiscence prompted by something on the television. 'I remember . . .' he'd say; or, turning to
Mother: 'Do you remember . . . ?' Most of my glean-
ings about my parents' lives before I was born, or
old enough to remember, were picked up that way.

Sometimes I'd probe and he'd expand; but more often than not, Mother, after a few minutes of heavy tolerance, had – it dawned on me now – interrupted with some current parochial titbit.

It had been different when, during my child-hood, we went to stay with Gran and Grandpa. That is to say with Father's parents – my other grandfather had died when Mother was a baby. 'And even Leah barely out of nappies,' so Nan, as she insisted on being called, constantly pointed out. 'Don't you forget,' she'd say, wagging a bony finger, 'I brought them up singlehanded – and never a spare penny by the end of the week.'

Mother would frown impatience over Nan's head. 'Never mind, things are different now,' she'd reprove her – and sigh with relief once we'd deposited her back at the sheltered housing in north London where, even then, she'd already taken up residence. She must, by now, be one of their longest incumbents.

Mother had given the same impression of endur-ing a trying but necessary duty when Father's parents visited. But when Father took a long week-end and we went to stay with them, the atmosphere was less laden. There, if I came in with grubby hands and knees from playing in the garden with Ben, the fox terrier, Gran's eyes would widen. 'My goodness, you have been having fun,' she'd approve; and Mother's instructions to go and wash would mute to no more than a background drumbeat. Sometimes, too, Gran – deliberately, I felt sure – kept my mother chatting in the kitchen while I crept into the book-lined sitting room where the two men would be sunk in leather-covered armchairs, Grandpa's gammy leg stretched out stiffly, his stick resting against his knee.

Yes, I remembered, Father could talk. Companionably, easily; at times seriously, at others laughing; sometimes arguing a point vehemently . . . I would seat myself on the little cane stool that stood to one side of the fireplace, listening not so much to the content of their discussions as to tones of voice; watching their faces.

They seemed to know I was content doing so. Occasionally Grandpa would glance across at me. 'And what do you think, pet?' I'd shrug and grin; and both of them would smile and return comfortably to their conversation.

'I was thinking about when we used to visit my grandparents,' I said. 'When Grandpa was still alive.'

Flora put down her coffee cup. 'Oh yes?'

'Nothing really.'

I reached for a cigarette – my third since supper, I registered, noting the contents of the ashtray at my elbow. I hesitated. Then, 'What the hell?', I thought, and lit up. Flora observed the small pantomime, but made no comment.

'How long was it,' I asked, 'before you . . . ?' I wasn't at all sure I should be asking, still less that I actually wanted to know; but something was driving me.

Flora looked at me consideringly. 'Being charitable,' she said, 'I assume what you're really wondering is how easily your father – how shall we put it – abandoned his marriage vows?'

The curious, old-fashioned expression which somehow didn't fit on Flora made me smile. But I was grateful to her for protecting me with it.

'Not too quickly, nor easily,' she went on. She hesitated. This time I was the one who waited. 'To start with, it was rather like having Don back. They were the same sort of age; not dissimilar in looks. Don and I were inseparable as children – probably because there weren't many others around; and in any case there was less than eighteen months between us. He's the younger one, but that worked very well. By the time he was six, he climbed trees better than I did.'

I struggled to imagine Flora as a small girl shinning along branches. It wasn't easy. She was so solid. One felt she could never have been other than as she was now.

'About a year after war broke out we were sent to live with an aunt in Bristol.' Flora's eyes creased in ironic amusement. 'Other children had been evacuated from the cities, and Don and I . . . Anyway, I think that drew us even closer.' She leaned back and stared, softly, towards the window. 'It was a tall, narrow house with only a square of garden. Different certainly from what we'd been used to.

Aunt Celia was a real character – my father's senior by twelve years. She seemed ancient to us. She had a passion for opera. Until '39 she'd taken herself off to Milan for a couple of months every year – hat boxes, trunks, the lot. Regarded the war as an exasperating inconvenience.

'The whole of the top floor had been turned into a music room and reference library. Heaven knows how they got the piano up there – just as well it was only a baby grand. The walls were covered in posters and photographs of the famous, some of them signed, and there were shelf-fuls of old programmes and sheet music as well as endless books. As often as not she'd be up there when we came in from school, singing away to her own accompaniment.

'She had a huge record collection too, and one of those old wind-up gramophones which she kept in the drawing room downstairs. On Sunday afternoons we had to sit round while she played a selection and quizzed us – not just which opera, which aria, but which performer. Whichever of us, Don or I,' Flora smiled at the memory, 'scored least had to get supper. Not,' she laughed, turning her attention back to me, 'that that was such an arduous task. The maid had always left everything prepared.'

I must have raised an eyebrow.

'Sunday was her day off.'

'Lucky her!' What was the matter with me? Why couldn't I just keep my mouth shut?

Flora regarded me mildly. 'It wasn't so unusual in those days to have help. And Annie had been with Aunt Celia since the year dot. She was too old for any sort of war work and it was a living for her.'

Reproved, I lowered my eyes.

When I looked up again, I said, 'You must have learned all there is to know on the subject?'

'I imagine I could make a fair attempt at humming any aria you cared to name,' she said drily. 'Except Wagner. Don and I came across a whole set of *The Ring* – a fair pile of old 78s – gathering dust in the attic. Aunt Celia said she'd put them there so that if we were bombed they'd take the initial impact. It was a joke of course – she had an air of invulnerability about her. As though no harm could possibly come to any of us, even though a pair of houses further along the road had taken a stray hit. And, of course, it didn't. Not during the war anyway.'

I stayed silent, acknowledging the reference to Don.

After a while, I said, 'What happened after the war?'

Flora interpreted my question in the context I'd intended. 'Oh, we stayed on there.' Almost imperceptibly the creases at the corners of her eyes hardened. 'It was easier,' she said. There was a finality in her voice, prohibiting further enquiry. I accepted it. It was, after all, none of my business. But it did tell me I'd touched a soft spot; that Flora was human too. I found the knowledge reassuring.

She'd reached for the lamp switch and the sudden brightness startled me – I'd hardly noticed the light fading. Columbus, who had been curled up on her lap, stirred, stretched his back into an arch and shook himself. Then carefully, putting one foot in front of the other, he lowered himself to the floor, sauntered to the back door, and stood there expectantly.

'Try the window,' suggested Flora; but when the cat didn't move, she indulgently pulled herself to her feet and went to let him out. I rose too. The sudden light in the lobby disturbed Arabella who struggled in the box and flapped her wings against its sides. Flora made soothing noises and the bird settled down. 'I'd better go and shut up the rest of them,' she said.

'Can I do that?'

'All right.' She gave instructions.

I followed Columbus out into the twilight. He was sniffing the air. As I ambled along the path, he lolloped up behind me, then slowed to match his pace to mine. His fur brushed my leg with each step.

Inside the run all was still, the roller a grey, deserted silhouette. I dropped the wooden shutter to the accompaniment of a faint rustle from within. The bolt slid into place smoothly.

Columbus had, by now, prowled off. I closed the gate behind me and stood staring towards the house and beyond. The evening was comfortably warm, and a cloudless sky suggested we were in for high temperatures again tomorrow. Without buildings to hem in the staleness of the day's heat, the garden scents floated free. The nearly-full moon was clear if not yet shining. I found myself wondering what it looked like in Malaya, or Cyprus, or Italy. Odd to think that the world was turning under my feet. I took a step to my left, to what I judged to be the west. Am I back where I was micro-seconds ago, I wondered. If one kept running westwards fast enough, would time stand still – or even go backwards? Logically, I argued to myself, knowing I wasn't too certain of the strength of that logic, it should.

I was staring up into the sky, still debating the point with myself, when I heard Flora calling.

'Are you all right?'

'Yes, of course. Fine.' And yes, come to think of it, I was. I hurried back into the house.

CHAPTER 8

The deck chairs strung out in front of the cricket pavilion next day glinted red, green or blue and white stripes in the bright sunlight, none the less so for the colours being, in most cases, faded.

'You will be staying till tomorrow?' Flora had said that morning as she lifted the lid of the freezer.

'I . . .'

'I'll assume you will.'

Being taken over, I noted; having decisions – well, one anyway – made for me. But somehow, in this instance, it wasn't an uncomfortable feeling. If anything, the opposite.

Without further discussion, Flora set me to the task of buttering sandwiches. 'Ginny and I always do the teas for this match,' she said.

I watched her surreptitiously as she worked, unhurriedly but efficiently, beside me. There was none of the fastidiousness of Mother's methods, none of the pernickety tidying up as she went along. And yet, suddenly, everything was neatly packed, the debris of jars and chopping board and crumbs cleared away in one clean-sweep operation.

Around mid-morning, just as we finished, there was a rap on the window. Two fair heads peered in. 'Mum sent us to see if you needed any help,' said the taller boy.

Their likeness to Andrew left me in no doubt as to their identity. 'You must be Tom and Justin,' I said, as they wandered round into the kitchen. Flora had disappeared to fetch her sunhat, leaving me to introduce myself. 'I'm Charissa.'

The older one held his hand out solemnly. 'How do you do.' Justin followed suit shyly.

'Do you like cricket?' It sounded as limp a conversational gambit as it was. They both nodded. I was relieved when Flora returned. She handed me one of the two elderly straw boaters she was carrying. 'You'll probably be glad of this.' We set off, laden with baskets.

The cricket field lay behind the Horse and Dragon, which had already opened its doors. White flannels mingled with colourful cotton dresses. Non-players, in open-necked checked shirts, nursed pints. Small children danced round underfoot.

Ginny – it was indeed she I'd glimpsed last weekend – was already in the rickety pavilion laying out cups and plates.

'Hello,' she greeted me, extending a hand. 'Andrew's told me all about you.' Her voice was warm and friendly. And she looked stunning in that casual way that no amount of grooming can emulate.

'Is he here?' It was no more than a polite enquiry, I assured myself.

'I hope so. He's opening.' Ginny waved a teaspoon, seeking a missed saucer. 'A spare one. I must have miscounted.' She dropped it into a wooden box. 'There, that's done. Let's go and grab somewhere to sit.'

The field was already assembled. To the side of the scoreboard, Tom sat importantly at a table, the record book open in front of him. Justin, beside him, hitched up his shorts and gravely checked the pile of numbered squares set out beneath the board.

To either side of me, Flora and Ginny started clapping. One beat behind everyone else, I joined in as the opening batsmen strolled out. Only once before had I attended a match, when Mark dragged me out into Berkshire to admire his performance as captain of the Old Boys' side. It had been a very different crowd there, spooning strawberries and supping fruit cup in the lee of impressive old school buildings. Self-conscious girlfriends – occasionally a very new wife – drawled competitive anecdotes of Hunt Balls and holidays in Hawaii. I'd managed to keep my end up – just, and not a little uncomfortably.

Andrew took up his position. The umpire, hands in the pockets of his white coat, nodded to the bowler who steadied himself for his run up. I determined, if possible, to cover up my no-more-than-rudimentary knowledge of the game.

It turned out not to be too difficult. There was an

easy assumption that I understood the rhetorical comment, the exclamations of delight or disappointment.

'Who are they playing?' The match had been underway for some time and I felt a need to demonstrate interest.

Ginny answered me. 'Chadham. The next village along. This is the main match of the season – well, this and the August bank holiday one. We usually beat them; but that young spinner of theirs is a bit dangerous . . . oh, no!'

Andrew, receiving a ball from him, had swiped it high into the air. All peripheral movement stilled as the entire field, players and spectators, watched the one fielder run backwards, then forward a few paces, to position himself beneath it. In slow motion, it seemed, the ball drifted down to earth – or almost. The waiting hands fumbled for a moment, but held it.

'Oh, well,' said Ginny, glancing over her shoulder to where her small son was busy rearranging the scoreboard, 'he made sixteen. Could be worse. Come on then, Philip,' she called as the next man strode out, nodding to Andrew as he passed him. Philip was shorter than his brother, but broader, his chin jutting, his walk determined. He took his place at the wicket and, having blocked the first ball, hit the second up and over the boundary.

'A six. Oh, well done,' enthused Ginny.

Andrew, having disposed of his pads, strolled up and stood behind Ginny's chair.

'Bad luck,' said Flora.

Ginny tipped her head back and smiled up at him. 'Idiot!'

'Hi,' said Andrew to me. 'Enjoying country pastimes?'

When they broke for lunch, Philip was still in, his score just short of a half-century. 'Big brother showing me up as usual,' commented Andrew rue-fully. 'Right, then. Food.' He loped off towards the pub in search of Ploughmans.

Ten minutes later he emerged, triumphant, with a trayload. Flora and Ginny excused themselves and wandered off, plates in one hand, drinks in the other, to chat elsewhere. I watched them go, Ginny's hips swinging gently beneath a light skirt, Flora ambling comfortably.

'Hope you like pickled onions,' said Andrew, set-tling himself beside me. The cuffs of his soft cream shirt were folded back loosely, his trouser legs slightly rucked where the pads had been fastened.

I turned my eyes towards the platter on my lap. 'Can't say I'm mad keen,' I admitted.

Andrew laughed. 'Sorry, I should have asked. Here, tip them on to my plate.' He scooped them up, then tucked in with relish. 'Demonstrating my unsophisticated taste,' he suggested through a mouthful.

'What's sophistication?' I challenged.

'Ah, now there you have it.'

He looked at me, amusement creasing his eyes, waiting for me to explore the subject further.

Trouble was, I wasn't sure I knew quite what I'd meant. Except that for an instant any definition I might have given the word seemed to have been stood on its head.

Andrew seemed to sense my dilemma. 'Far too philosophical a topic for a lazy Sunday,' he offered. 'Tell me instead what's going on in the great metropolis.'

I tore off a piece of French bread and cut into the cheese. 'It's hot,' I said.

He laughed. 'I can imagine.'

We chatted about inconsequential details. I almost wished, I realised after a while, that he wasn't quite so easy to talk to – I wasn't at all confident my tongue might not run away with me. I turned the conversation back to the cricket field.

'Philip,' I asked, latching on to him arbitrarily as a subject. 'Does he have a wife?' I looked around as though I might spot one among the crowd.

'Not exactly.' Andrew took a slurp from his glass then set it down on the ground beside him again. 'He did have, but she upped and left him after only six months. Can't say I blame her – he's a bit dour at the best of times. Even so, it's been hard on him. As far as I know, though, they haven't done anything about a divorce.'

'He's not the confiding type, then?'

He shrugged. 'Ginny gets on better with him that I do.' He looked across to where, amid a crowd of others, she was now in apparently amused conversation with his brother. 'She seems to have the ability to get a smile out of anyone,' he said. For a moment I wondered if he was implying she was something of a flirt; but his face, when I glanced at him, gave no such impression. Instead, the corners of his eyes and mouth twitched in self-deprecation.

I began to feel self-conscious, sitting on my own with him, and Flora's reappearance, accompanied by Tom and Justin, was a relief. The boys badgered Andrew for money for ice-creams. He delved into his pocket and produced a 20p and some coppers. 'Is that enough?'

'Course not.'

'Then go and ask Mummy.' He grinned, and sent them scampering across the field.

'First cricket match you'd been to, was it?' said Flora over supper. Damn her, she didn't miss a trick.

'Second,' I was pleased to be able to correct her. 'This one was fun,' I said, and meant it. I'd enjoyed helping with the teas, too. Flora had simply introduced me, here and there, by my first name. Only an elderly colonel had acknowledged making the connection with my father. 'Liked him,' he growled. 'Sorry to hear...'

'Everyone's very friendly,' I commented now.

Flora smiled. 'There speaks a townie,' she said. 'Village politics hum under the surface. But real ill-will is rare. It's pettiness for the most part.

'For which you have no time?'

'Not a lot.'

'Andrew,' I said, my mind turning over the comment she'd just made. 'He and Philip don't seem to get on too well?'

'They rub along all right I think. Philip's a bit puritanical – doesn't smoke and never drinks anything stronger than the occasional beer. Takes life seriously.' She smiled. 'Regards Andrew's easy-going attitudes as verging on the profligate, I shouldn't wonder.'

'You prefer Andrew and Ginny, don't you?' I ventured.

'I certainly don't have anything against Philip. But he tends to keep himself to himself. Busy, though – and he's not afraid of hard work. Physical hard work.'

I thought of Andrew lounging in his garden; and nonchalantly chewing a blade of grass out on the boundary that afternoon. Not that he hadn't moved fast enough to scoop up any ball heading his way. 'You mean Andrew *is*?'

'No, I wouldn't say that. He helps Philip out a lot at weekends. But he's more of a thinker. Probably why he and your father got on so well.'

'They did?' Out of nowhere, as I considered the statement, the recently remembered image of Father and Grandpa together loomed in my mind.

Flora reached across for my plate. I was only half aware of her moving around, substituting a fruit bowl for empty vegetable dishes.

I peeled an orange. Flora bit into an apple.

'When did Father start painting?' I asked.

'Oh, I don't know. About ten years ago, I should think. Why?'

I wiped juice from my fingers. 'Andrew seemed to think I needed to talk to you about him – but I'm not at all sure why, or what good it can do.'

Flora leaned back.

'All it does, whenever he's mentioned, is hurt.' Something inside me seemed to be twisting up. I stretched my shoulders to relieve the sensation. 'Everyone,' I said, hearing my voice rising, ' – well, you and Andrew anyway – close to my father. But not me. I only ever knew a shadow. Yet he feels so real here – almost as though I could reach out and touch him. But I can't. It's too late.'

'Maybe not entirely.'

'Of course it . . .' I slumped in my seat. 'Is that why – ' I spoke thoughtfully now – 'he wanted me to come here? But why this double life? One person at home, quite a different one here.'

'I'd have thought he was essentially the same person wherever he was.'

I rearranged the peel on my plate. 'Just showed a different side, you mean? According to the place and the people?'

I wasn't sure whether Flora nodded. I lapsed into silence and found myself staring across the room at his relaxed and smiling photo. What was going on behind those eyes? Why – and I had to acknowledge it was that way round – had he stayed with my mother, not cut the ties entirely? On the other hand, why couldn't he have been happy at home?

What was it Flora offered that my mother, or my mother and I, lacked? I began to feel sick.

I excused myself and, to avoid disturbing Arabella I said, went upstairs to the bathroom. In the mirror I contemplated myself, recognising his eyes, his nose, the slightly square shape of his chin. I reached out a hand to touch the glass. When I stepped back, the mist of damp fingerprints stayed for a while, then contracted and vanished.

Angrily, I reached out again, clawing opaque streaks down the glass. My whole body quivered with the rage overtaking me. I turned away, clasping my arms around myself, hunching myself in; trying to contain a force that felt as though it must explode. Sinking down on the edge of the bath, I clung to control, commanding myself to take deep breaths. Gradually, gasping at first, then gulping, I steadied my intake to regular lungfuls.

There was a knock on the door. 'May I come in?'

I pushed myself to my feet, tidied my hair as I glanced in the mirror, and pulled back the latch. Unsteadily, I grasped at the bath again, and lowered myself back on to its side.

Flora took the few steps towards me. I stared, unfocusing, in the direction of her ankles. 'At this rate,' I heard her say, 'I'm going to have to get in a whole case of brandy.'

I smiled weakly and raised my head.

'Come on downstairs,' she said, and held out a hand to help me up.

* * *

She steered me into the sitting room and settled me in one of the large Victorian chairs I'd previously only glimpsed through the doorway. From behind solid wooden doors at the base of a glass-fronted bookcase, she took out brandy goblets and a crystal decanter which she carried across to the coffee table. The measures she poured were generous. 'Here. Have a good slug of this.' She seated herself opposite and raised her own glass.

I took a sip and leaned back, cradling the bowl in my hands. The lamp at my elbow – the bulb a concentrated orange glow in the dimming evening light – flickered a spectrum of violets and reds across the facets. Another sip, larger this time, and I felt the tension in my muscles easing. I heard myself giggle. 'Sorry,' I murmured. I risked a glance at Flora. That same steady gaze was turned in my direction, attentive but undemanding. I snuggled against the cushions. The overwhelming emotion I'd been experiencing just a short time ago seemed far away.

I said so. 'I can't think what came over me,' I apologised.

Flora nodded.

I glanced around the room. The mellow furniture, the likes of some of which I'd only previously seen in bow-windowed antique shops, rested as comfortably beneath the low ceiling as a cat on a hearthrug. I wondered what my mother would make of it. I wondered what she'd make of me. The realisation dawned that I didn't care. Guiltily I twitched my gaze back to Flora, and for a stark second experienced myself considering what it would be like if she were my mother. I jerked myself away from the fantasy, then slumped. 'I'm just so tired of having to be strong,' I heard myself say.

Flora's eyes widened the merest fraction, expressing interest rather than surprise.

I blushed nonetheless. 'I can't think why I said that.' I inspected my glass; then ran my finger round the rim. The surface of the brandy swayed slightly.

'Perhaps *I* can.'

I looked up, startled. Her eyes, warm and brown, held mine. I turned my head and stared out of the window. Gentle puffballs of cloud, scarcely discernible in the greying sky, drifted peacefully. A moth fluttered against a pane. Somewhere a tap dripped on concrete. Inside the room the sharp smell from my glass mingled with the slight mustiness of elderly upholstery.

I fought the lump in my throat, took a swig of brandy, and choked on it. When I'd recovered I forced a laugh about it. 'That's what you get for being sorry for yourself.'

'Nonsense.' She was smiling.

'I *was* being sorry for myself. And that's ridiculous. I mean, what about you?' I was aware that the alcohol was getting to me, but I was determined to put into words the thoughts strumming through my mind. 'You cope. You've lost Father too. Not that I'm saying I approve of . . . but, it's a fact . . .

and Mother . . .' I tailed off. 'It's all a muddle . . .'

'Isn't it just.'

I checked her, suspiciously.

'Why are you being so nice to me?' I demanded, my mood swinging abruptly. 'You know I resent you. You know I'm so angry I could . . .' I leaned forward, reached for the decanter and topped up my glass. Settling back, I glared defiantly over it.

The corners of Flora's mouth quirked. 'Have some more brandy.'

'Now you're making fun of me.'

Her face straightened. 'That I most certainly am not.'

I took refuge in silence. It probably looked like a sulk. It probably was a sulk. I was a child again, and I didn't know how to respond.

Flora made no attempt to rescue me. After a few minutes, she heaved herself to her feet. 'I think I'll go and tackle the washing-up.'

I sat there for a while, twiddling my glass. In my head I debated whether to bury myself in a copy of the *National Geographic* lying nearby; but my hands, occupied in their repetitive rotational task, seemed divorced from any instruction my brain might be sending.

Eventually I managed to force a connection, and the act of setting the glass on the coffee table jerked me out of my stupor.

I scrambled up and went through to the kitchen. Flora's ample back was towards me, dimples exposed in the plump flesh of her elbows as she busied herself at the sink. I collected a teatowel as I passed the Aga, and picked up a handful of dripping silver. Flora acknowledged my presence with a small sideways smile.

'You said – ' I polished the blade of a knife with unnecessary care – 'you understood why I . . .' I watched her hand as she held a plate under the running tap and then transferred it to the draining board.

'That you feel alone, with all the cares of the world on you?'

'I didn't say that exactly.'

'No?'

'What I meant was . . . What I think I meant was . . .' I sighed. 'I don't know what I meant.'

'How frustrating.'

There was a mixture of amusement and concern in her voice that made me look up.

'I certainly haven't got . . . what was it you said? . . . all the cares of the world on me. On the contrary,' I gave a short laugh, 'maybe the problem is that apart from my mother – and she seems to be managing fine – I haven't anyone to care about.'

'Or anyone to care about you?'

I paused in the middle of drying the last dinner plate. The cornflower pattern around the rim merged to a haze.

Flora removed the plate gently from my hands. 'We really shouldn't be having this conversation while you're handling my good china,' she observed matter-of-factly. 'Come and sit down.'

'You make me feel like a small child,' I said, once safely ensconced on the chesterfield beside the silently snoozing Columbus.

'Good. It's about time you stopped being so determinedly grown-up.'

I stroked the cat's fur, considering the statement. Images of myself in the company office in London, where I knew I was heading upwards fast, flashed across my mind; and I saw myself in my flat – mortgage statements, household bills, insurances, all neatly filed, under control.

'But I am grown-up,' I pleaded.

'Well bully for you.'

I opened my mouth, and shut it again. The clock in the hall ticked its regular rhythm, a slower and steadier echo of my own pulse. 'I wish I were,' I said finally.

'Ah well, we're all striving towards that.'

To my amazement, I realised her eyes were twinkling. Abruptly she rose to her feet, moved across to the dresser, and pulled open a drawer. 'When did you last play tiddlywinks?'

'Tiddlywinks! I've no idea.'

She rummaged around and produced counters and a large, shallow dice shaker. 'This'll do.' Sweeping papers from the kitchen table on to a chair, she sorted the counters into piles. 'Which colour would you like?'

Neither of us was too sure of the rules. 'We'll make up our own as we go along,' announced Flora. Counters, flicked with more enthusiasm than skill, skidded and leapt around the table. Competitiveness yielded to hilarity; and reverted as each of us concentrated on homing our final counter. When Flora's red one plopped into the bowl, I raised my arms in mock surrender. 'OK, you win.' I flipped my last, lone, blue one high into the air. Flora extended a hand, caught it, and dropped it neatly in with the others. I inclined my head in exaggerated acknowledgement.

'Cocoa?' enquired Flora.

In my dreams that night the counters were dual coloured – blue on one side, red on the other – and Flora was adept at flipping hers over so that in the end they all lay on the table red side up. 'I've won,' she chortled. And suddenly she wasn't Flora any more, but the Queen of Hearts screeching, 'Off with her head.' Waking from the nightmare, I stumbled across the dark landing to the loo, and discovered I had started my period.

A disturbed night, a mild hangover, and the dull ache in my abdomen did nothing, when I emerged from my room next morning, to restore the frivolity of the previous evening's mood.

Over breakfast, I conjured up excuses as to why I needed to get back to London by early afternoon, and clung to them even more determinedly when Andrew drove over to suggest midday drinks at the Dower House.

Leaving him and Flora chatting in the kitchen, I

went upstairs to pack. I stripped the bed and folded the sheets, relieved that they weren't marked. Good thing I woke when I did, I reflected ruefully. I remembered the fuss Mother had made when once, as a teenager, nature had caught me out. 'It's not your fault,' she'd insisted as she abandoned her toast mid-bite to whisk up stain remover in a bath of cold water and immerse the offending linen in it. While I hovered, her rubber-gloved hands rubbed and dubbed. 'You mustn't feel guilty about it,' she'd said, scrubbing ever more furiously.

Like a toddler who'd shamed the family by 'having an accident' in front of some austere maiden aunt, I'd crept back to my room, and for the next few years – in fact, as long as I lived at home – always kept my knickers on at night 'just in case'. As I piled the pillowcases and towels neatly on top of the sheets, I wondered how Flora would have reacted. At least I didn't have to undergo the embarrassment of finding out.

I checked the room to make sure I'd left nothing behind, then paused at the head of the stairs. I could hear murmurs from below, a man and woman laughing together. Across the landing, Flora's bedroom door stood ajar. Sunlight, streaming in through the window ahead and to my right, shone across the passageway and through on to the heavy woven bedspread flung tidily but softly across the high double bed. It slanted across the corner of a tall old-fashioned chest of drawers, lighting a sprinkling of dust on the mellowed wood surface; and it fell in a gentle cascade down on to the well-worn Indian patterned wool carpet.

Maybe it was a cloud passing across the sun which caused a sudden movement of shadow. But the sense created of a presence in the room – my father's – was disturbingly real. I grasped the banister rail and closed my eyes for a moment. When I looked again, all was as it had been; and Andrew was calling to ask whether I needed a hand with my bag.

CHAPTER 9

Less than a week later – the following Friday evening – I stood in the doorway of another bedroom; the one my father had shared with my mother.

After half an hour of chit-chat during which she gave me what seemed like a minute-by-minute account of her tour the previous weekend, she had shooed me upstairs. 'You'll want to freshen up,' she'd urged.

To reach my room, I had to cross the length of the landing and pass the door, standing slightly open, through which the smell of Chanel No. 9 always wafted. I knew with certainty as I climbed the stairs that I was not going to be able to walk straight past. Almost hypnotically when I reached it I paused and, with my holdall in one hand, pushed the door wider. Although what sun there was – uninterrupted blue skies having given way to cooler, showery weather – had now moved round to the other side of the house, the still strong light beamed in through the embroidered nets and between the looped rose-patterned curtains. It illuminated the gilt detailing on the expensive floor-to-ceiling fitted units, the two identically framed flower prints on the walls, and the matching bedside tables with their matching bedside lamps; and it fell on the twin divans over which squared-off fitted counterpanes had been smoothed with military precision.

I stared at them, long and hard, and then dragged my gaze away to scan the minutiae of the room. Apart from the fact that my father's bedside table was bare but for the lamp, and that his bits and pieces – an ebony-backed clothes brush, the enamelled box for his cufflinks, a tortoiseshell shoe-horn – which used to stand on the top of one chest of drawers, had been replaced by a vase of dried peonies, everything was exactly as I'd always known it. It took no more than a quick glance to check. A small carriage clock and a book – one by a popular romantic novelist, I noted, screwing my head sideways to identify it – lay beside Mother's bed; evenly spaced along the window sill squatted half a dozen daily-dusted ornaments; and on the dressing table, a line of cosmetic jars and the large Chanel bottle stood guard over hairbrush, comb and hand mirror. Beneath the Lloyd Loom chair, Mother's backless slippers snuggled daintily, and – as I knew it would when I peered round – her dressing gown, a pale oriental silk, hung in careful folds behind the door.

Mother, I thought wryly, was resistant to change; once she'd organised things as she wanted them. And this – I startled myself with the thought – had

130

always been *her* room, the second bed – even the original double one which the two singles had replaced – no more than a concession to her married state; and now no doubt, by some sort of convoluted thought process, to her widowhood. I cast around the clutterless room again, aware that within the cupboards and drawers, every item of clothing was hung or stowed in disciplined tidiness.

I hugged my knitted jacket round me.

A click of heels sounded in the hall below. 'Well? What do you think?'

I turned and peered over the banister. 'Sorry?'

'Your room. What do you think?'

'I . . . My room? I haven't been in there yet.' I muttered something about the bathroom.

'Oh.' She was disappointed. 'Well, do go and have a look.'

Guiltily, I crossed the landing and threw open the door. A Laura Ashley-esque blaze hit me. The room had been redecorated in co-ordinating forget-me-not designs, sprigged on the wallpaper and clustered tightly on the curtains. The bed was swathed in a cover of the same material. On the carpet, between the end of the bed and the wall, a rug in the same tone of blue hid the patch – scarcely discernible anyway following Mother's repeated ministrations with a variety of cleaners – where I'd once had a disaster with a bottle of ink. My sun-faded bookcase had been painted white to match the kidney-shaped dressing table and fitted

131

wardrobe. On the top shelf, above the rows of children's books now arranged in size order, sat my china-headed doll, her old-fashioned dress newly washed and pressed.

Mother, eager for my reaction, had followed me upstairs and now stood at my elbow. 'So?'

I spun round. 'It's lovely!' Full of remorse, I gave her a hug.

Mother smoothed her dress back into place. 'I thought you'd be pleased.'

More seemed called for. 'It's absolutely gorgeous. You'll have me coming down every weekend just to enjoy it.' But I hoped she wouldn't take me too literally; and when I suggested celebrating with a bottle of wine, what I really meant was that I felt in sudden need of a drink. For a brief moment, it occurred to me to wonder whether Father had ever similarly had an urge to reach for the whisky bottle.

Back in the flat late on Sunday, I sought out the old bedspread, the removal of which, Mother had explained, prompted the redecoration, and sat down with it. It had been a pleasant enough weekend; and if there had been further flashes of comparison with that other place, Father's other world, I'd hurriedly banished them.

With a glass or two of wine inside her, Mother – or was it me? – had relaxed. To my amazement, she even agreed next day to let me stick a Marks and Spencer's pie in the oven 'to save trouble'. We'd

chatted companionably. Not – agreed – about anything of great moment; but about things like the
WI summer schedule and her part in it, and the
possibility of her visiting an old schoolfriend
now living somewhere in Yorkshire – 'Such pretty
countryside round there. If I can be spared from
my various engagements of course,' she added. She
regaled me with an anecdote about the man who
had come into the charity shop where once in a
while she helped out, bearing – in addition to a
council rubbish bag stuffed with torn shirts and
trousers 'not fit even for a jumble sale' – a bird cage
complete with budgerigar. 'What did he think we
are, an animal sanctuary?' She was more affronted
than amused.

'I miss your father dreadfully, of course,' she said
at one point, as I held a gardening basket while she
dead-headed the roses.

Dampness, clinging to the wilted blooms after
the overnight rain, steamed gently in sunlight
breaking intermittently through the high cloud. I
sniffed appreciatively. The scent seemed stronger
than that from those which were still vibrant. Or
maybe it was just their proximity, lying discarded
on the wickerwork in my hands.

'You're being very brave about it,' I ventured.

Mother snipped; then straightened and turned.
'Do you think so, dear? Well, one does try. And of
course,' her face assumed an appropriate expression, 'I have my memories.' She snapped shut the
secateurs and pulled off her gloves. 'Time for a cup

of tea, I think.' It was a change of subject, not an invitation to confidences.

Now I stuck a finger through a hole in the crochet and waggled it at myself. What memories? And how much did she miss him? I grimaced at the disloyal thought. But there had been moments – as when Mrs Webb from next door popped in to say that Jack, Mr Webb, would be round later that afternoon to fix the window catch – when it seemed Mother almost glowed with widowhood. When Mr Webb appeared with his tools, she had dispensed tea and apple cake and charm; and, did I imagine it, or did she really look smug when he turned to inform me in scarcely concealed reprimand: 'We all have to look after your mother now.' All a far cry, I thought sceptically, from the days when, refusing to acknowledge her situation, she would have sent me to the DIY shop round the corner for a packet of nails. Little did Mr Webb know. And why was I calling him 'Mr Webb' as though I were still a teenager?

Restless, I got up and fetched my sewing basket. Somewhere I had a wool needle. Delving among the reels and thimbles, I found one at last and, pulling the blanket on to my lap, located and threaded a loose end. There were, I discovered on inspection, a lot of them. Still, I could at least make a start. But my resolution faltered by the time I'd darned in three or four. I pushed the mending to one side and switched on the television.

Over the next couple of weeks, I threw myself into mind-occupying activity. I rang friends, some of whom I'd hardly seen since moving into my solitary flat a year ago, filling my diary with arrangements to meet for drinks in favourite West End or King's Road pubs and accepting invitations to a couple of parties. I persuaded the amenable into joint outings to the theatre – the latest musical on one occasion, some revival at the Barbican on another – and into sharing the fun of late-night shopping sprees. On the first of these Thursday evening excursions, urged on by one of my ex-flatmates who took vicarious pleasure in encouraging other people's extravagance, I impulsively treated myself to a top-of-the-range hi-fi system as a replacement for my temperamental basic version; which in turn gave me an excuse to pick out, during spare lunch hours, all the newest CD releases. What with that, several additions to my wardrobe, and a variety of frippery for the flat – including a ludicrously expensive ceramic planter – my credit card statements next month were going to resemble railway timetables. But what the hell, I thought. My salary justified a splurge once in a while.

And in case that wasn't enough, I fitted in at least one extra session a week at the gym. During one of my work-outs, as I rested, panting, on the rowing machine before moving on to the stair-master, the trainer sauntered over. 'Are you sure you're not overdoing it?' he commented.

'Probably.' Between breaths I summoned up a grimace of acknowledgement. 'But it certainly distracts the mind.'

'Feeling pressurised?' he interpreted. 'How about signing up for one of our new aromatherapy treatments?' He smiled helpfully. 'Similar result. Just a less exhausting way of achieving it!'

Dismissing cynical thoughts about salesmanship, I booked one on the spot.

It was bliss lying there, surrounded by the smell of jasmine and lavender and frankincense, the hands of the therapist – a tall girl with long fair hair loosely tied back – smoothing essential oils into my skin and gently massaging away the tensions.

'Stressful job?' she enquired as her thumbs discovered and pressed down on painful spots on my shoulders.

'You could say so.' Not strictly true, of course. Demanding, yes. But then that was what I liked about it, what I wanted, found reassuring.

'Other things too, perhaps?' Her hands had moved to my lower back.

'No, nothing.' Then, not wanting to appear unresponsive, 'Well, my father died recently.' That covered a whole range.

I had the sense, as I stared horizontally at the wall, that she was nodding sagely. 'Fresh air,' she recommended.

Perhaps it was that which prompted me, in a fit

of devil-may-care, to take up, only days later, a long-standing invitation to sail with Clare and her boyfriend.

It would be stretching a point to say I enjoyed it. I sat on the bunk with my stomach churning as the thirty-two-footer ploughed round the North Foreland. Leo, revoltingly cheerful, poked his tanned face down through the hatch. 'You'd feel a lot better up top,' he suggested.

Obediently, I struggled up on deck.

'Here,' he said. 'Take the helm while Clare and I fix the sails.' Uneasily, I did my best to follow instructions and maintain a course.

'You're doing fine,' encouraged Clare, as they returned and flopped down in the cockpit. 'Nothing like being in control to stop the queasiness.'

'I don't feel in control,' I moaned as the boat heeled and I put out a hand to steady myself.

They laughed, and suddenly I was more aware of the sun on my face than the cold spray splashing on to my arms and shoulders. Even so, I was very happy to leap ashore and do my inexperienced bit with ropes when at last we returned to the mooring.

Wandering back along the quay, Clare put a pally arm round my shoulders. 'Coming again next Sunday?' She was half-teasing, half-serious. Leo, swinging a holdall, caught up with us. 'The thing about the sea,' he declared, 'is you can't fight it. You have to go with it.'

'Just listen to the philosopher!' Clare gave him a playful punch.

I turned to them as we parted. 'Thanks,' I said. We exchanged kisses. Clare's exuded the warmth of long friendship. 'See you again soon,' she promised. Leo's made me long for the solidity of an older brother. That evening, and for no apparent reason, I wept gently.

Just as dawn was breaking next day, I woke, startled, convinced that both Andrew and my mother were standing at the end of my bed. Mother was saying I couldn't let Andrew in with me; it wouldn't be right. Andrew just stood there, unmoving, his expression blank. Then he faded away. I shook myself to full consciousness and peered at the clock. Time for another two hours' sleep. I lay back, irritated by the image still etched on my mind. Eventually, and despite a cacophony from London's stirring sparrows, I drifted off into some illogical and unrecallable argument with my mother.

It was around mid-morning that, surrounded by office files brought in by a junior, I picked up the phone and heard the receptionist's perfunctory announcement: 'Personal call for you.' For a bizarre moment I thought it might be Andrew. After all, he knew where I worked.

But, of course, it wasn't. Why should it be? A female voice, at once familiar and yet not immediately identifiable, checked: 'Charissa?'

'Yes. Sorry, who is it?'

'It's Elspeth. Your black sheep cousin. Bet you

weren't expecting to hear from me.'

'Elspeth! Hello. How lovely . . .'

'I hope you'll think so when I've told you why I'm calling.'

I laughed, tension spilling out of me. 'Go on. Tell me.'

'Thing is, Peregrine and I—'

'Who?'

'The man in my life. That's to say the *ex*-man in my life . . .'

'Oh.'

'Well, that's the point. He is ex. Decidedly. And I'm in London. I was wondering – ' her voice assumed a child-like plaintiveness – 'you couldn't possibly put me up for a few days?'

She seemed to be holding her breath as she waited for my answer.

'It's only a small flat,' I countered. Then, trying not to sound too dubious, 'You'd have to sleep on the sofa.'

'No problem. Bare boards would do. Thanks, Carrie, you're a star.'

She was waiting outside my door when I got back, a drooping bundle flopped on a battered suitcase at the head of the stairs. She sprang to life as I rounded the final turn. With a squeal of delight, she rushed down towards me, almost tripping over the hem of her long skirt.

Balanced preciously mid-flight, I was engulfed in a rapturous embrace. 'Carrie. It's so good to see you.'

'You too,' I muttered into her shoulder.

She followed me in, heaving her suitcase. 'Wow. It's gorgeous. You should just see the pit I've been living in. This is heaven.' She bounced experimentally on the sofa. 'Bliss.'

'You like it?' I observed superfluously.

I looked at her. She was dressed from head to toe in creased black cotton relieved only by a jangling collection of beads, her short dark hair nonetheless expertly cut and groomed. Her eyes shone with appreciation as her glance roved round the room. It didn't seem to me to justify quite that degree of euphoria.

Abruptly she turned back to focus on me. 'How long has it been? Three, four years? It was that summer. You were studying for Finals. Put me up on my way to some rock concert or other.'

I remembered. She'd burst upon our, by comparison sedate, student household in a whirl of art college colour and energy.

'You insisted on doing the cooking,' I recalled, and laughed. 'Something totally inedible with unpronounceable vegetables.' A thought struck me. 'You're not still a vegetarian?'

''Fraid so. Still can't bear to eat dear little lambs and things.' She lounged back and grinned. 'But my recipes have improved.'

'That's something.'

She jumped up. 'I'll do supper tonight, shall I?' Then, jutting her chin at my dubious expression: 'Just you wait and see.'

140

'You're right,' I acknowledged later over a plateful of some nameless concoction. 'It's delicious.'

'Not bad for supermarket ingredients,' she conceded. 'Tomorrow, I'll really go shopping.'

We smiled at each other, comfortably companionable in re-awakened family closeness.

'So,' I said, 'tell me. You've had a bust up with . . .'

'. . . Perry. Yes. I must have been mad. He's turned out to be a complete bastard, dregs of the dregs.' Her face, which had straightened, turned impish again. 'So I've come to sit at the feet of my sensible cousin, and learn.'

'So what –' I ignored her latter statement – 'does someone have to do to become the dregs of the dregs?'

Elspeth fiddled with a spoon, inspecting its handle. 'It's not so much what he's done, as what he hasn't done. What he's never done. Just sitting around all day. Only stirring to collect his Giro.' She shrugged. 'Your average drop-out, I suppose. *You* know.'

I didn't really. I guessed I must have led a pretty sheltered life.

'But then,' she looked up, 'he took a swing at me.' She lowered her eyes again. 'About two weeks ago. I tried not to take it too seriously . . . he *had* had a skinful – though usually that mellowed him . . . Anyway, I didn't want to overreact – but then somehow . . . Well, I began to see him differently. I guess I've just given up hoping he'll ever get his head together.' She picked up a fork and pushed lentils around her plate with it. 'Trouble is, I kept on thinking . . . if I loved him, was supportive . . .' Her eyes suddenly brimmed. 'Oh shit.'

I got up and went to put an arm round her shoulders.

'You know what makes me so furious,' she said. 'Not him. Me. How could I have been so naive?' She fumbled among the folds of her skirt to find the pocket and extracted a delicate lace hanky. 'I really despair of myself for being so stupid.'

I abandoned her for a moment to fetch a box of tissues. 'Don't be silly,' I said over my shoulder. On impulse, I opened a cupboard and reached for a bottle of Martini – the strongest thing I could find. Flora-like, I bore it to the table.

By the end of the evening, tear-stained but talked out, Elspeth pronounced herself much better. We made up a bed and I left her, as I thought, watching some late-night chat show on the television. But as I smoothed cream on my face, there was a tap on my door.

A head peered round. 'Just realised I've been so busy talking about me I haven't said how sorry I am about Uncle Hugh. I did like your father, you know. Very much. I should have written. Anyway I just wanted . . .' Her expression changed in an instant to a self-effacing grin. 'Won't disturb you again.' She backed out with exaggerated quietness, closing the door with a slow click.

'See you in the morning,' I called through the woodwork. 'Sleep well.'

I saw her, but she was oblivious to my tip-toed skirting of her and her scattered possessions seven hours later. I left a note and a spare key on the kitchen window sill. There was a smile on my face as, rather as she had done the night before, I pulled the outer door to with scarcely a sound.

'Lovely day, isn't it?' said the old lady on the ground floor, stooping to pick up her milk bottle.

I nodded agreement. I'd forgotten how refreshing it was to have someone else around.

When I got home, delighted with a deal I'd sewn up, Elspeth rushed to fling open the door as I turned the key in the lock.

'Da, daa!' she announced, flourishing her arms wide.

I peered past her in mock suspicion.

'Enter!'

'Wow,' I said. 'You've been busy.'

'Least I could do.'

I touched the heads of a huge vase of gladioli dominating the sideboard. 'They're beautiful.' Their scent filled a room now tidied within an inch of perfection, throw-overs straightened, cushions plumped up, wood everywhere gleaming. She led the way through to the kitchen with another expansive gesture. Another posy, this time of violets, coloured the already-laid dining table, and beside the flowers stood an uncorked bottle of Côtes du Rhône.

I sniffed appreciatively in the direction of the shining cooker.

'Supper in half an hour,' confirmed Elspeth. 'May I – ' she picked up the bottle and gave a small bow – 'offer you a glass of wine?'

'You're mad,' I laughed. 'Yes please.'

It was after we'd eaten and sunk down on comfortable chairs that she suddenly said, 'By the way, I found a watercolour in the hall cupboard.' She looked at me and her expression faltered. 'Oh dear. Have I been poking around where I shouldn't? But you did say I should hang my things there.'

'It's OK.' I wasn't sure whether I was reassuring her or myself. 'I'd just . . . forgotten about it. That's all.'

She brightened. 'Can I get it out?'

She was back in less than a minute. Reseated, she balanced it at arm's length on her knee, her head tipped sideways in a critic's pose. She looked across at me. 'Well? Aren't you going to tell me about it?'

'What do you think of it?' I stalled.

She pursed her lips. 'It's good. If it's the work of an amateur, it's very good. I like . . .' She elaborated with technical comments to which I only half listened.

'Sorry,' I heard her saying. 'I'm being an art student show-off. But you did ask.' She leaned forward. 'Come on, it's you, isn't it? Who painted it?'

I decided on honesty. 'My father.'

'Really?' Elspeth was intrigued. 'I'd no idea he had an artistic streak. Not to mention talent.' She explored the detail. 'When did he do this?'

I wondered. When precisely had he sat in the meadow above Cotterly with his easel and paints, imagining me there? 'I don't know,' I said.

Elspeth's face registered bemusement.

'He did it from memory.' Then anticipating the next question: 'Down in the West Country somewhere.' I was aware of looking away as I spoke. When I turned back, Elspeth's attention was apparently on the painting again.

'Umm,' she said non-committally, and for an instant I had the unnerving sense of having said far more than I'd intended. 'Well,' she decided, 'it certainly deserves to see daylight. Where shall we hang it?'

'Your mother rang,' said Elspeth that Friday evening as I dumped my briefcase on the floor and collapsed into a chair. 'I told her I was your cleaner.'

'I don't have a cleaner.'

'Exactly what your mother said. So I persuaded her I meant I was from the carpet valeting people.'

'Why did you do that?'

Elspeth looked hurt. 'What's wrong with having carpets shampooed?'

'No, you idiot. Why didn't you say it was you?' I reached for a cigarette and offered one to Elspeth. She shook her head.

'Oh, I see what you mean. Well, I thought she might think I was leading you astray if she knew I'd dumped myself on you.'

I laughed.

'No, really. She doesn't approve of me. You know that.'

Suddenly I felt light-headed. 'Is that a compliment to yourself or not?'

Elspeth stared. 'Good God, you have changed.'

I drew contentedly on my cigarette, wondering.

'Anyway,' she said, 'it wasn't only that. I haven't put Epsom – ' she referred to her parents – 'in the picture yet. And you know what your mother's like. She'd be straight on to Mum.'

'Aren't you going to tell them?'

'I suppose I'll have to. But not yet. Don't feel I can face the told-you-so's.' She sprang up. 'I could use a gin. How about you?'

My drinks cupboard had expanded during the few days that my cousin had been in residence. I wasn't unhappy about it. Relaxing against the cushions, I heard the fridge door open and the click of ice cubes dropping into glasses. Then a sharp crackle as the spirit hit them and a hiss as Elspeth unscrewed the cap on a bottle of tonic water.

'Here.'

She handed me the glass. I raised it. 'To . . . whatever you like.' I hesitated before taking a sip. What would I choose to drink to, I wondered. Simplicity; lack of complications in my life?

Elspeth had extracted her slice of lemon and was sucking on it. Instinctively I winced. She noticed and laughed.

'Sorry,' I felt called on to apologise. 'Different taste buds . . .'

'Different a whole lot of things.' She pondered. 'You'd tell your mother about Perry, wouldn't you? I mean . . . you'd never have got involved with someone like him in the first place . . . but even so . . .'

But even so, I thought, as Elspeth leaned forward to help herself from the pack of cigarettes lying on the table, there are a lot of things – suddenly – I'm not telling her. I passed the lighter.

Elspeth lit up. 'The trouble with playing the rebel – ' her cheeky grin had returned – 'is one has a reputation to maintain.'

I mimed looking over the top of imaginary glasses. 'Oh, yeah?' And what, I wondered, about one's reputation as a loyal daughter?

'Actually,' I confided – maybe the alcohol was having an effect – 'I'm not sure I don't envy you.'

'Really?' Elspeth was wide-eyed.

'All the emphasis on doing the right thing, on appearances . . .'

'How do you mean?' Her expression was curious, almost cautious.

I fiddled with the top button of my shirt. 'Oh, I don't know . . .'

Elspeth drained her glass and set it down with as much care as if it had been the finest Waterford crystal. 'You're referring,' she said, 'aren't you, to your father's affair?'

I stared at her. 'You know?' I sank back. 'How long have you known? Have you always known?'

'Since I was about fifteen. I overheard Mum and Dad discussing it. Demanded to know the whole story. They swore me to secrecy.'

'But you could have said something to me.'

'Uh, huh.' She shook her head. 'That was part of the deal. I wasn't to let on I had a clue. Not to anyone. In fact, I don't think Mum was even supposed to have told Dad. Let's face it, your mother was positively paranoid about anyone knowing.'

'Too right. I mean, I haven't even been able to talk to her about it. Ever.'

'What!'

I shook my head.

'That's weird.'

I supposed it was. I looked across at my cousin. She had hitched her legs up beneath her skirt to sit cross-legged on the sofa, elbows on knees, chin cupped in her hands, eyes wide and curious. Hers was not the detached attentiveness of Flora, but one of eagerness to be involved.

'You look like a Buddha,' I joked.

'Not solemn enough.' She grinned, wriggling her bottom into the cushions. 'Come on then, tell.'

So I did. About the sudden realisation and my mother's one-sentence confirmation; about watching her ingenuity in deflecting the inquisitiveness of neighbours; about my own pretence with my schoolfriends. And, above all, about the strange, strained politeness with which my parents treated each other.

'Sometimes I wanted to scream,' I said.

I suddenly recalled an incident: Mother standing at the stove; Father squeezing past, his hands automatically settling on her hips to steady her as he did so; and then his apology as she shook him off. 'I can see his face now,' I said. 'It was as though all the expression went out of it.' I considered. 'You know what it reminds me of? That blank look, in films, of prisoners about to be tortured.' I giggled. 'Not that she had a thumbscrew hidden away anywhere that I know of.'

The telephone pealed into the silence. 'Oh, God,' I said, 'that's probably her.' I looked at my cousin. 'What am I to say about you?'

'Oh, tell her if you want to.'

'Hi. Yes, hello, Mother. Carpets? Oh, no, just Elspeth being idiotic. Yes, in London for a few days. She's very well. No –' I grinned at Elspeth over the receiver – 'definitely more respectable these days. We're having some great chats. And she *has* spring-cleaned the flat while I've been out – it's positively gleaming.

'What's she doing in London? Mother, for heaven's sake.' I tried to keep my voice light-hearted. 'Can't someone visit the big bad city without you going into interrogation mode?'

149

I saw Elspeth's eyebrows shoot up, and put a hand over my mouth to muffle my choke of laughter.

'Yes, yes. One or two.' I mimed to Elspeth raising a glass to my lips.

'Oh, all right then. Bye.'

I put the telephone down and grinned. 'She says she'll ring back when I'm sober.'

'You're not exactly pissed.'

'Pity,' I said. 'I might really have told her what I think.' I stared in horror at Elspeth, then, collecting up the empty glasses, escaped to the kitchen. I gazed blankly out of the window for a while before refilling them. What had I meant? What did I 'really think'? For an instant the window blurred, as though I were staring at the crazed result of a smashed windscreen.

I shook myself back to reality and picked up the bottle, resisting the urge to pour doubles. I was vaguely aware of Elspeth speaking on the telephone.

'I've ordered pizzas,' she announced as I returned. 'Extra helpings of ham and salami . . . ugh . . . on yours. Lots of protein. It'll do you good.'

'Great.' Even to my own ears, my response lacked conviction.

'You need looking after.'

I took a slurp from my glass and then stared into it, struggling to swallow past the lump in my throat and fighting watery eyes. Eventually I looked up and grinned sheepishly. 'They say gin makes you depressed.'

'And they also say,' she said, exuding know-ledgeability, 'that depression is – ' she drew quotation marks on the air – 'the outward expression of suppressed anger.'

I forced a weak smile. 'That sounds very technical.'

'I read it somewhere.'

I let out a muted scream, more grimace then sound.

Elspeth nodded amused approval. 'Go for it.'

I repeated the experience, with a little more volume this time – though with a restraining thought for the neighbours.

Elspeth was grinning.

I laughed. 'You're right. I'm bloody angry.' Suddenly my eyes were clear again and I was aware of an emptiness in my stomach. 'I'm also starving. Where's that pizza man?'

In bed, I cosseted my anger, undefined though it was. That is to say, I rolled it around inside me rather as one rolls something sweet around one's mouth, extracting every last gram of pleasure from it. It tasted good – unlike the bitterness of the rage I'd exploded at Flora.

It occurred to me, lying there ruminating, that for the first time in as long as I could remember, the shadow of guilt had lifted. Like a curtain going up, I thought, and behind it there, there, was my anger.

Knowing where precisely to direct it, and why, was another matter.

CHAPTER 10

I sneaked past Elspeth's huddled form next morning, brewed myself a coffee, and retreated to my
room. What, under the glow of shaded lamps, had
seemed like some sort of cathartic revelation, now,
in the harsh light of day – a spot-on description if
ever there was one – appeared no more than embar-
rassingly self-indulgent nonsense. I felt decidedly
foolish.

But Elspeth, when I forced myself to emerge and
join her for an ad hoc breakfast, wasn't having it.

'Come off it,' she announced through a mouthful
of muesli when I apologised for my idiocy. '*In vino
veritas*,' she quoted. 'And if whoever said that was
drunk at the time, it only proves the point. Anyway,
you weren't.'

'Mother seemed to think I was,' I recalled.

'Only because you gave as good as you got for a
change. She's not used to that.'

I felt myself relaxing. Perhaps I hadn't done or
said anything too shameful last night. And Elspeth
had already known about Flora.

'The only person I ever told,' I said, following

my train of thought, 'was Mark.'

'That stockbroker boyfriend? I heard about him. Part of your perfect cousin image!'

'Disaster. We had the most terrible row. That's what led to the bust-up.' I explained – loyalty to my mother reassuringly reinstating itself – how he had totally misunderstood; had taken Father's side; been scathing of Mother for not giving him a divorce. 'As though it was all her fault. I couldn't believe he could be so insensitive. I just hit the roof.'

Elspeth scraped up the last spoonful of oats and sultanas, then took her dish across to the sink and rinsed it. 'Actually, I've never understood why they didn't split up.'

I pondered, coolly now. 'Funny isn't it, it never really crossed my mind it was a possibility. Sounds crazy, but in some way it was as though the arrangement actually suited them both. I mean . . . if it hadn't . . . surely one of them would have pro-voked a row? Instead they went out of their way to avoid any sort of upset. Egg-shell carpets.' I looked up. 'Yeah, that's how it was.' I thought about it. 'Mind your feet, Charissa,' I mimicked. It was my mother's voice.

Elspeth assumed an always-keen-to-help expression. 'Shall I scatter some around now so you can jump up and down on them?'

I couldn't help but laugh. 'Think of the mess.'

'Umm. Nice.' She stuck a finger into the marma-lade pot, scooped up a blob of jelly and sucked on it. 'You know, I can't imagine Mum putting up with it. But then she doesn't have to. Had the foresight to marry someone who was quite content to sublimate his sex urges in the vegetable patch.'

'Elspeth! That's a bit . . .'

'Come on. Dad's lovely. But he's hardly the most urgent stud in the field. Probably why I went for Perry – he's certainly got what it takes in bed.' She narrowed her eyes and rolled her hips. 'Ooh, don't remind me, or I'll be back there like a shot.'

'You wouldn't?'

Elspeth tilted her head down, wide eyes teasing me from behind her eyebrows. They were deep brown, smooth, and precisely matched. This morning I found their perfection irritating.

'You wouldn't! You need a job. Take your mind off it.'

'Quite right. First thing on Monday morning. I'll do the rounds of the agencies. See who's crying out to offer me thirty grand!'

'You do that.' I got up from the table. 'Come on,' I said, suddenly restless, 'let's go somewhere.'

We settled on a walk by the river and drove the mile or so to Putney, parking on the south side in front of the boathouses. The tide was up and lapping close to the top of the slipways.

Elspeth swung along the towpath, seemingly unhampered by her breeze-blown light cotton skirt catching against her knees and ankles, while I strolled in practical jeans and T-shirt. Her dulled patchwork jacket contrasted with the designer sweatshirt I'd flung across my shoulders and tied loosely in front.

Away from the confining airlessness of the flat, I would have liked to pick up on our breakfast-time conversation, but couldn't decide how best to reintroduce it. I stared out across the water. In the centre of the river, an eight in bright red strip was thrusting towards Hammersmith, the spray from their oars flicking up and catching on the misty, cloud-diffused light – like so many ever-changing, ever-moving, dew-spangled cobwebs, I thought. Twenty yards ahead of us, close in to the shore, a flotilla of ducks drifted peacefully. I shifted my gaze from one to the other, wondering at the contrast.

As the rowers disappeared round the bend, I nodded in the direction of the ducks. 'Maybe families can be too cosy,' I said.

As though in response to my thoughts, one of them suddenly flayed his wings and, assisted by furious splashing, lurched out of the water to flap upstream. We watched as the turning current began slowly to drift him back.

'I wonder if I would have put up with it,' I heard myself say.

Elspeth, pausing to unwrap a bar of chocolate she'd disinterred from the depths of her pockets, looked enquiringly at me.

'My father's weekend disappearing acts.'

Elspeth broke off a slab and offered it. 'You did. In your own way.'

'Oh, come on. What could I have done about it?'

'Trampled a few egg shells, I suppose.' Her eyes glittered mischievously. 'When I think, I practically had to go out and lay my own . . .'

I took a playful swing at her, and she dodged sideways, laughing. 'Well then,' I challenged. 'What would you have done?'

Serious once more, she considered. 'Not sure. But I couldn't have stood not being confided in. One way or another I'd have had to make them talk to me about what was going on.'

I wandered over to the edge of the water. It rippled gently against the sides. Every now and again a gust, or the tail end of an already distant boat's wake, swirled it against the concrete. Further along, a toddler on reins was valiantly thrusting his arm out to throw handfuls of bread which as often as not landed short. Frustrated birds hovered close to the edge, daringly swooping elongated necks to snatch at the crumbs.

I stuck my hands in my pockets and traced a doodle in the loose gravel with my toe. I tried to imagine myself at home, demanding information from my parents. What then? Why, then they would have banged the door, their bedroom door, shut in my face. It was no business of mine. And quite right too. But later – the fantasy seemed to be acquiring a direction of its own – Father would have come up behind me in the kitchen and put his hands on my shoulders and said that yes, I was old enough now, I should have it explained to me . . . and I would have turned and buried my head in his shoulder as I did when I was little and smelled the tweed and felt the roughness of it against my face and cried because what I wanted more than anything else was to be held tight . . .

My foot, of its own accord, had scuffed out the pattern it had been drawing. I looked up. Elspeth had retired to lean against a nearby tree. The bar of chocolate in her hand was considerably depleted. She held out what remained as I re-joined her. I shook my head. 'No thanks.'

'You must miss your father.'

I was taken aback by the observation, as though she'd somehow intruded into my own private world. 'What is there to miss?' Underlining the point, I gave full rein to a cynical snigger. 'I couldn't give a damn about him.'

Elspeth licked her fingers, scrumpled the chocolate paper and stuffed it in her pocket. 'God, I thought I was supposed to be the mixed-up one.' She turned to face me. 'You're as bad as your parents – no, probably worse. About avoiding issues, I mean.'

I stared back at her, ignoring passers-by who were looking curiously in our direction. This was Mark all over again. Not understanding. Attacking me. 'But that *is* how I feel.'

'Come off it.'

There was no urge to cry, no anger bubbling up. Just numbness. I was in Flora's kitchen. She was standing by the Aga, Columbus prowling round her ankles. A teatowel slid from the rail and drifted with eerie slowness to the floor. The pattern on it was faded and, in its crumpled heap, totally indistinguishable. I heard her voice: 'Do you always run away from the truth?'

'That's more or less what Flora said.' I could hear the resignation in my voice.

'Flora?' Elspeth's voice rose in astonishment. She stared at me. In the stillness, a rowing coach's megaphoned instructions echoed across the water. 'You've met her then?'

I stood there dumbly.

Elspeth's expression changed to a purposeful one. 'Cup of something,' she decided. 'Come on.' She jollied me back towards the High Street. 'Hey, look at that,' as a bare torso above crotch-clinging Lycra hurtled past; 'Whoops, catch us on the way back,' as she sidestepped a bicycling child seemingly in training for the Tour de France.

We hesitated outside a pizza house but chose instead an unassuming coffee shop which, surprisingly for a Saturday morning, was comparatively empty. We seated ourselves at a round, cloth-covered table beneath a Monet print. The window nearby provided a comforting barrier between us and the world.

Elspeth ordered. As the black-skirted waitress busied herself whipping up the cappuccino, Elspeth leaned across. 'I'm sorry. I shouldn't have said all that.'

'It's OK.'

Elspeth cocked her head on one side, considered, and then apparently decided to accept my reassurance. 'Well, then? Flora . . . ? You know I'm bursting with curiosity.'

'My father asked me to return some things to her. When he died. Some books.'

'So you did?'

I nodded.

We leaned back to allow our coffee to be delivered.

'Well, go on,' urged Elspeth as soon as privacy was restored.

Once I'd started, I wondered why I'd held back the previous evening. It didn't seem such a disloyal tale after all. Maybe because Elspeth was both intrigued and approving. Her eyes widened with incredulity as I described Flora.

'So she's certainly not some bimbo?'

'Hardly. I've never met anyone . . . I still don't know quite what to make of her.'

'But you like her?'

I thought about it. 'I suppose so. Yes and no. That's to say, I'm beginning to get used to her.'

Elspeth stretched out a hand and nudged my cup closer to me. 'You're letting it go cold.'

Obediently I took a sip. 'I think, though, I'm starting to understand what attracted my father.' I unwrapped the complimentary biscuit lying in my saucer.

'What, you mean other than her Renaissance curves?'

I glared at her. 'Don't you think of anything but the basics?'

Elspeth seemed about to make some further witticism, then to change her mind. 'Sorry.'

I carried on with my story. 'She's so totally different from my mother: so laid-back, so relaxing – ' yes, it was true – 'to be with.' I did my best to describe her robustness, that extraordinary calm of hers that allowed me to explore, and even articulate, what I was feeling at any given moment, that strange sense of an awareness on her part which was at once both disconcerting and, in some way I couldn't quite define, reassuring; trying to justify perhaps my having allowed a relationship – of sorts – to develop. And by implication, it occurred to me, my father having done so too.

'I wouldn't have gone to see her a second time,' I said, 'if it hadn't been for Andrew.' I explained about our encounter on the valley road in May, and what followed that afternoon. But even as I recounted how his subsequent intervention had prompted Flora to invite me to go down again, honesty forced me to acknowledge – to myself – that it had been I who accepted the opportunity she offered. Because I was cross with my mother for letting me down. Strange really; ironic even.

'So what made you decide to go?'

I shrugged, pushing aside my private thoughts. 'Andrew seemed to think I ought to talk to her.' Well, yes, I supposed that was the reason, too. Indeed, maybe Mother's selfi— well, thoughtlessness anyway, had merely provided the excuse I needed.

'And did it help?'

'We played tiddlywinks,' I said.

'You what?'

'And then I dreamed she was the Queen of Hearts. Lewis Carroll's,' I clarified.

'Curiouser and curiouser.' Elspeth widened her eyes in mock amazement.

I laughed. Then sobered. 'A bit of a looking-glass world, I suppose.'

'And I'm the Mad Hatter. Have some more tea, well, coffee, Alice.' Elspeth summoned replenishments.

I stared through the window at the people passing to and fro in the street outside. An elderly couple paused, exchanged comments, then pushed open the door. The draught of air brushed over me. I watched them hesitate, decide on a table, then move across and settle in their seats.

Elspeth brought my attention back by snapping her fingers under my nose. 'Hey, where have you gone to?'

'Nowhere. I was thinking.'

'What about?'

'Nothing. It's just – ' I gave myself a mental shake – 'it's as though . . . it's like two different worlds. And I'm not quite sure which is the real one.'

'Now you're being dramatic.'

'Am I?' I was surprised.

Elspeth grinned. 'You're trying to pigeonhole everything. It doesn't work.'

I thought about it. 'You mean all of it's real.' I recalled Flora's comment about my father being the same person wherever he was. And I had a sudden image of my mother, stacking jars into cupboards and closing the doors. 'I suppose you're right,' I said. I lifted my cup. I hadn't really wanted this second one. 'Come on, drink up,' I urged. 'Let's go.'

On the way back in the car, Elspeth said, 'So what about Andrew? He sounds quite a hunk.'

'A very much married hunk, in case I forgot to mention it. With two young boys. His wife's sweet.'

'So what were you doing having a cosy little tea party with him all afternoon?' I glanced sideways and caught her raising an eyebrow in pretended reproof.

I turned my attention back to the traffic. 'Being grateful he wasn't making a fuss about the dent in his car.'

'And how much more grateful are you hoping he's wanting you to be?'

'I'm not! And he's not looking for it. It's totally platonic. Anyway, I hardly know him.' I considered. 'But there is a sort of affinity.' I thought some more. 'Something to do with my father.'

'You said they got on well together?'

'So Flora says. And, yes, from the way he talks about him, they must have done.' Though, come to think of it, he and I hadn't mentioned him much.

'Are you jealous?'

I braked sharply to avoid a car elbowing in from the left. 'Jealous?'

'Well, it sounds a bit like a father and son relationship.'

'But I'm still his daughter!'

I sensed Elspeth grinning as I changed gear and pulled forward into a gap. 'With a dream of a big brother. Is that it?'

It was, I realised. And suddenly the jigsaw pieces slotted into place, offering a warm picture: one in which it would be OK to tease and be teased; where, if need be, there was a shoulder to cry on. In some way he belonged to me. There was no need to have even a sneaking conscience about Ginny. Ours – my imagination let rip – was a different relationship.

I smiled. 'I guess so.'

'Lucky you.' Later – many weeks later – I recollected the slight sideways look I was aware she gave me, the slight rise of her intonation, and wondered whether there had been more than a touch of irony in her comment. But at the time I took it – gratefully, smugly even – at face value.

'Yes I am, aren't I?'

Although my scenario didn't explain where Flora fitted in – despite her being somehow at the hub of it all.

CHAPTER 11

Elspeth departed as abruptly as she'd arrived – a scrawled note propped against the coffee jar explaining she hadn't waited or I might have talked her out of it. Yes, she'd gone back to Perry. Stupid, but there it was. Some guff about the heart being stronger than the head. But a million thanks. She'd added a PS under her flamboyant signature: 'Re. Andrew et al – go for it! And keep me posted.'

I didn't know whether to laugh or cry. It was Wednesday evening and I'd returned from work hoping to be able to congratulate her on the success of a job interview she'd been due to attend that morning. Had she even gone for it, I wondered.

The flat seemed suddenly devoid of colour. I wandered from room to room, my movements seeming to echo in the emptiness. On impulse, I went into the hall and flung open the cupboard there. A neat row of hangers dangled above the space where her clothes had hung. I bent and picked up a gilt button, triangular shaped, difficult to replace. Returning to the kitchen, I threw it into an ornamental bowl on the window sill and slumped down at the table.

It had been fun having her around. And such a relief to be able to talk about Flora. She had cropped up ever more naturally in our conversations since our outing last Saturday. In the course of them, the guilt about my visits to Cotterly had waned and been replaced by more than a touch of resentment that I'd been prevented from going there in the past. I could see my mother's point of view, of course. Or I supposed I could. She'd been protecting me.

Elspeth's expression had been somewhat cynical when I pointed this out.

'What's that look meant to mean?' I'd demanded.

She hesitated.

'Go on.'

'Could be . . . it was herself she was protecting.' She refused to elaborate.

'That's nonsense,' I said eventually.

But the thought nagged at me from time to time.

Now I found myself staring through the open door to the sitting room, my gaze held by Father's painting on the wall opposite, where Elspeth had talked me into hanging it. My fist, seemingly of its own accord, was, I realised, thumping the pine surface in front of me; and to my amazement I heard myself, a moment or two later, silently drumming out the words 'I . . . want . . . my . . . father'. Jerking up, I rubbed the tingling edge of my hand. Then I smoothed both palms across the wood, eking out some sort of comfort from its evenness.

Eventually I rose and switched on the kettle.

By the time my mother rang, ten minutes later, I was composed. 'No,' I told her in a voice that surprised me with its firmness, 'I'm sorry, but I can't come down this weekend.' I stared at the painting again before offering an explanation. 'I'm visiting friends in the West Country.'

It was irritating that I couldn't contact Flora direct. I hesitated a moment then dialled Directory Enquiries. Two minutes later I was speaking to Ginny.

'It's a bit of an imposition,' I apologised, 'but I wondered whether you or Andrew could check with Flora whether it would be convenient . . .' I suggested I ring the following evening to get her reply.

'No, no. Give me your number. We'll call you back.'

It was Andrew who did so. The degree of pleasure I felt on hearing his voice disconcerted me at first, but then I decided it wasn't unreasonable to feel warm towards a proxy family member.

'Flora says she'd be delighted.'

'That doesn't sound like her,' I risked.

I sensed him grinning at the other end of the line. 'Ah, you're beginning to know her. All she actually said was "Fine", but I thought my version—'

'Thanks.'

He chuckled. 'And bring some sensible footwear this time.'

'Her instruction or yours?' I was beginning to enjoy myself.

'Ginny's. The boys may need their boots themselves!'

His tone remained lighthearted but I suddenly panicked that I was assuming too much. I backed off into formal thanks for his trouble.

'No problem. See you on Saturday. Supper here.'

'Great.'

I stifled doubts, once I'd replaced the receiver. I'd committed myself now.

Flora's greeting, when I arrived mid-afternoon, was as to-the-point as ever. 'Oh good, you're here. I need to go into town. Your car or mine?'

I looked doubtfully at the Citroën.

'We'll take mine,' she decided, and had squeezed into the driving seat before I had time to form, let alone offer, an opinion. I climbed in beside her as she started the engine. Columbus, who had been standing, tail erect, by the back door, skittered to safety as she slammed the car through a three-point turn on the gravel.

Behind the wheel, an almost boyish alter ego of Flora's peeked its head out. That same one, I thought later, that had had her clambering up trees as a child. The road we took, straight on past the Dower House, was even narrower than the one I was becoming accustomed to travel. Clinging on as she plunged round bends and over blind rises in the road, I eventually could bear it no longer. 'Are we in that much of a hurry?' I begged.

She eased off the accelerator. 'My driving

168

alarmed your father, too,' she observed. 'Usually he insisted we take his car.'

Strange, I thought. I'd never visualised them together anywhere but at Wood Edge or wandering through the village. Even though, I remembered now, she'd mentioned them visiting my grandmother.

Flora glanced sideways at me as she jolted the car over a hump back, an amused glint in her eye. 'I'm quite safe, you know.' I decided to believe her.

We swung to a halt in the market square. I followed in her wake round a series of small shops, my growing, albeit still somewhat grudging, respect for her reinforced by other people's obvious liking. I stood by as the baker chose to reject a slightly burnt loaf and picked out for her instead one that was perfectly browned, and while the proprietor of the hardware store insisted on digging down among endless boxes to find just the right half-dozen nails she needed to secure some loose boarding on the shed.

Our final visit was to the feed merchant to stock up on chicken supplies. 'And how is your wife?' Flora asked the old man as he hoisted the bag into the boot of the Citroën. It was all the invitation he needed. We listened patiently to a seemingly endless account of medical tests and treatment. Eventually he limped back towards his shop, whistling.

'Did him good to get that lot off his chest,' I commented as Flora shut the boot.

She looked at me and smiled. I smiled back.

A thought occurred to me. I nodded towards a small tearoom opposite. 'How about . . . ?' I suggested. 'My treat, of course.'

'Nice of you, but I'd honestly prefer a large mug at home. Wouldn't you?'

In the kitchen, I thought. With the windows flung wide. I nodded.

Flora was lowering herself into the car. I moved round to get in beside her, then paused. 'Just a minute.' I ran back to the bakery. 'Cake,' I explained as I rejoined her with my package.

'Aren't you wondering why I invited myself down this weekend?'

Flora was pouring tea. She didn't look up. 'I expect you're going to tell me.'

I laughed. 'You're impossible. I can't win with you.'

'Are you trying to?'

'No. Yes. That is to say I think I was, but no, not any more.'

'Good.'

I shook my head in amusement. Flora seated herself and looked across. 'So then, tell me; why have you come?'

Faced with the question, I was suddenly unsure. 'Maybe I just like being here,' I said.

'Fair enough.'

'And maybe I needed someone to talk to.' I ruminated. 'Someone who would understand.'

'Thank you.'

I raised my eyes to meet hers. They were warm and straight.

'Though why I think you should I don't know.'

I pulled the cake I'd bought towards me and picked up the knife placed ready beside it. 'Shall I?'

Flora nodded.

I cut into it. It was soft and spongy and reminded me of birthdays long gone. Cream oozed from the sides. I made two more incisions, then eased one of the pieces free. I swivelled the plate and pushed it towards Flora. She helped herself. I turned it back and took the other. Floury crumbs powdered my lips as I bit into it. The cream was smooth on my tongue.

'My cousin's been staying with me,' I said as I dusted off my fingers.

'That would be Elspeth?'

I looked across at Flora, surprised yet not surprised. 'Strange,' I said, 'how you know so much about . . . us.' I rotated the mug standing on the table so that its handle pointed away from me, and cupped it in both hands. 'And Elspeth knew about you. That feels even odder.' I took a mouthful of tea and held it for a while before swallowing. 'All those years . . . pretending . . .'

Flora waited. Then: 'Was that the hardest thing?'

I wondered. 'Maybe. I mean, I don't know. It was like a grey shadow. A fog, sort of. Talking to Elspeth has lifted that. It doesn't all feel so shameful somehow.'

'You felt ashamed?'

'I suppose I must have done.' I forced a laugh. 'Sins of the fathers and all that.' I took another mouthful of tea. 'Or maybe I thought it was my fault. Funny, really.' One of those seemingly trivial bits of information one picks up crowded into my mind. 'Don't they say children always blame themselves when parents divorce? Or even just row?' I considered the point. 'But mine didn't do either.'

I looked up. 'Was Dad ashamed of his relationship with you?'

'I hope not.'

I considered. 'I can't imagine he was. Well, not in regard to you anyway. Maybe he felt bad about Mum though.'

Again I looked straight across at Flora – it was still amazing me how easy it was to talk openly with her like this. 'If, say, Mum weren't there – if she'd died or something – would you two have married?'

I knew, suddenly, the answer I was hoping for; and I got it. 'I expect so,' she said. 'Certainly we'd have wanted to live together.'

Ridiculously, incomprehensibly, I experienced an urge to leap up and hug her. Mentally, I pulled myself together. With my finger I traced the pattern – a series of wavy lines – on the mug I was still holding.

'Mind you,' I suggested, 'wouldn't that have meant you leaving Cotterly? Would you have minded?'

'I think it's more likely your father would have moved down here.'

'But his job . . . ?'

'He'd have been more than happy to resign his partnership and look for something different locally.'

'Like what?' I was intrigued.

'Anything that kept him out of an office, I imagine.'

'You mean he didn't enjoy being an accountant?'

'Not overmuch.' Flora's tone was dry. It warmed as she elaborated. 'He'd have been much happier involved with art or history, or with nature preservation perhaps. Hands-on work with the National Trust would have suited him down to the ground.'

It hadn't ever occurred to me. After all, he'd never given any indication he wasn't quite content donning his dark grey suit or his pinstripe each weekday morning. Not to me; and not, I imagined, to Mother either.

'Then why . . . ?' But I guessed I knew the answer. I had only to think of Mother and her chequebook. 'And a divorce would hardly have resolved that problem,' I acknowledged, confident that Flora knew I'd grasped the point. 'So he was stuck?'

'In his profession, yes.'

My mind moved on. 'But not necessarily in his marriage?' I checked. 'After all, you *could* have moved up to some little Surrey village. Or maybe he could have transferred to a firm here and still been able to afford to provide for Mother?'

I took Flora's silence as acknowledgement.

'Didn't he ever . . . didn't you both ever . . . think about that possibility?'

'He certainly thought about it.'

'Then why didn't he . . . ?'

But how could he? I tried to imagine him suggesting to Mother that they part openly. Had he ever done so, I wondered. And if so, how must she have responded? Refused to discuss it, presumably. Being a divorced, or even separated, woman simply wouldn't come into Mother's scheme of things. Even if technically, legally, it had been forced on her, she'd never have acknowledged it. Just as she'd never acknowledged Flora's existence – other than on that one brief occasion to me and, presumably in a moment of weakness, to her sister.

I felt an overwhelming surge of anger – more frustration than anything else. And not only to do with Father and Flora. Mother created her world. And that was how it was. No amount of huffing and puffing would stir it. I had an image of the three little pigs; only in my scenario, for some reason, they were the ones outside the house with their cheeks blown out. Well now she was a respectable, and respected, widow. That should satisfy her. Everything neatly resolved. For her.

Flora had risen and was moving around the kitchen, collecting up mugs and plates, putting the remains of the cake in the fridge. I imagined my father here with her. Comfortable. Relaxed. How it should be.

'Was it very hard for you when he died?' I heard myself asking.

'It's always hard when someone dies.' She paused in the act of reaching up to close a cupboard door and looked at me over her shoulder. 'You're not alone, you know.' It was said gently. She turned and leaned against the work surface. 'Though you've more to grieve for than I have.'

'Me?'

'All those lost years.'

I met her eyes; then lowered my own. There was dust on my shoes, I noticed. I bent and brushed at it.

'I'm not sure I want to be reminded.' My voice was scarcely above a whisper. For a moment I thought she might come and put an arm round me. But she just stood there.

'I really enjoyed seeing Elspeth again,' I said eventually. 'Of course she couldn't have stayed at the flat for ever. Too cramped. I suppose I was hoping she'd find somewhere close by.' We'd have been able to meet often. Talk.

'I'd never really got to know her before. We used to visit as children, of course, but that was different. We're such a small family. Father an only child. Mother with only one sister. Elspeth and I are all each of us has got. Of our generation, I mean.' I hadn't thought of it like that before, but it was true. 'And now she's gone back to this boyfriend of hers.'

'Ah,' said Flora.

'What do you mean – "Ah"?'

'Another desertion?'

Did she mean Father? 'It's hardly the same.'

'True.'

'Yeah, but maybe it touched a nerve or something.' I stared at my feet again, stretching my legs out to align the toes of my shoes. 'Actually it was she who encouraged me to come down. Made it sound OK somehow.' I tucked my feet back out of sight. 'Mind you, she seems to think – ' I laughed uncertainly – 'that I've got a thing for Andrew.'

'And have you?'

'Do I like him? Yes. But only as a friend, of course.'

'Just as a friend?'

What was she suggesting? I was tempted, defensively, to point out I wasn't in the business of stealing other people's husbands, but resisted the barb. Let her work out, if she wanted to, the reason for my silence. In any case, I was feeling ever more confused about the rights and wrongs of it all where Flora was concerned.

'By the way,' she reminded me, 'you do know Ginny's invited us for supper, don't you?'

The sun, that late June evening, was still some way above the horizon as we strolled through the village. It was a twenty-minute walk, but I'd agreed with Flora's suggestion that we leave the cars behind. She was sure Andrew would give us a lift home.

Although she had informed me it wasn't necessary to dress up, I changed into the light linen trousers and cream shirt I'd brought with me in anticipation. A football bounced across the grass as we skirted the green. Flora skittered it back, raising a hand in acknowledgement of the shouted thanks. Pop music blared incongruously from one of the cottages. Further along the lane, only our footsteps added to the natural rustles and sighs. Flora obviously wasn't concerned to make conversation, and I was more than content to walk in companionable silence.

It was Andrew, looking up from under the bonnet of his car as we turned in at the gate, who broke it. 'Hi.' He waved grease-streaked hands. 'Sorry about this. Come on round.'

We were, we discovered as we followed him, to eat in the garden. Flora looked dubiously at the sky. 'Hope the rain holds off.'

'Bound to,' decreed Andrew. 'Can't have mere weather spoiling Ginny's spread.'

She had by this time emerged from the house to greet us. 'I certainly hope so,' she contributed. 'The boys are camping in a friend's garden.'

'Toughen 'em up if it pours,' said Andrew. 'I remember . . .'

Ginny grinned. 'Now, don't you start . . .'

The banter between them set the tone for an informal evening. In some ways I was sorry the boys weren't there. Life seemed to be full of new experiences just at the moment and taking part in a family evening – such a long time since I had done, and never from an adult perspective – would have been another. On the other hand, no doubt Tom – and certainly Justin – were too young to be expected to sit through what turned out to be a leisurely meal. It made sense that they had been found an alternative occupation. Just as, I recalled, I had been at their age, and indeed later; except that in my case alternative occupation had meant banishment upstairs with homework or a book and instructions to put the light out at the decreed hour.

'What do you think, Charissa?'

I hedged, my attention having wandered.

Andrew, if he realised, rescued me. 'About . . .'

The conversation was general, and relaxed. It ranged widely but lacked – I recognised with a start – the self-conscious intensity so often experienced among my younger, London friends, and to which I, no doubt, contributed as much as any of them. No-one, this evening, was concerned to set the world to rights; there was none of the anxious checking of pecking order on some overall career ladder; no scarcely concealed bragging about who'd been where, done what, and knew – intimately of course – whom. If there was any competitiveness, it was light-hearted and short-lived, as when Andrew teased Ginny about her ignorance of some well-known historical date.

'OK,' she countered. 'So who won Wimbledon the year before last? That's at least more recent.'

Andrew made a stab at a likely name.

'Wrong!' Ginny sing-songed her triumph.

'Do you know?' Flora turned to me.

I supplied the correct answer.

'You follow the tennis then?' And we were off, discussing this year's tournament.

In due course, Flora's pessimism about the weather proved justified. We pulled on jumpers and hugged jackets closer round us as the meal progressed; and just managed to spoon up the last of the raspberry soufflé before the first heavy drops plopped into our laps. Amid a hilarious scramble back into the house, I found myself jammed in the doorway with Andrew. Flora was ahead of us, Ginny a few steps behind caught in the downpour.

'Come on, you two. Don't just stand there,' she urged.

Andrew grinned and squeezed out backwards, easing the tray he was carrying so as not to tip it.

We deposited everything on the kitchen table and stood there, shaking off the wet.

'It seemed a good idea at the time,' laughed Ginny. 'Here – ' she handed plates and a cheese-board to Andrew – 'take those through and I'll make the coffee.' Flora picked up the biscuits and followed him.

'Can I give you a hand?' I asked Ginny.

'Thanks.' She showed me where to find the coffee cups and I started laying up a tray. Ginny stacked the dishwasher while we waited for the coffee to brew. I passed plates and dishes to her. It was the first time we'd been alone together.

Making conversation, I asked about her job.

It had started off being very part-time, she told me. Just one school and a few private lessons. 'But now I'm dashing around virtually full-time. Only during term, of course.' She straightened up from slotting plates into the bottom rack and threw her arms wide. 'Only another ten days and then I have two months off. Bliss.'

'You don't enjoy teaching, then?'

'Oh, yes. But it's nice to have time with the boys. I did toy with the idea of playing professionally – I've a friend with the Philharmonic – but it didn't feel right to palm Tom and Justin off with au pairs. Particularly not when they'd already lost their father.'

I stared at her, any joggings to my memory about thwarted career preferences blotted out before they'd even taken shape. 'Lost their father?'

'Jonty. He died. Didn't you know? Some stupid pile-up on the autobahn. That's why we came back to England.'

'I'm sorry, I hadn't realised.' I made a mental adjustment: so Andrew was her second husband.

'It's OK. Years ago now. Well, about five actually.'

'But the boys are so like Andrew!' It was out before I'd stopped to think.

Ginny stared at me. 'Well, that's not really so surprising. Family genes . . .' Then she threw back her head and laughed. 'Oh, my God. Hasn't anyone explained? I'm Andrew's sister.'

CHAPTER 12

Back at Wood Edge, when Andrew had dropped us off, I rounded on Flora.

'Why didn't you tell me they were brother and sister?' I demanded.

Flora was slipping her feet out of her shoes. She looked across at me. 'I wondered whether you'd realised.'

'Of course I hadn't. How could I have done? I assumed . . . I mean, there was no reason to query it. A man and woman living together with two children. What else was I supposed to think?' I could hear my voice rising. 'Why didn't you explain? I felt an absolute fool. Does one always have to check everything?'

Flora bolted the back door. 'Better than jumping to conclusions.' She sounded weary. 'Time for bed, I think.'

I ignored the comment. 'And is there anything else I ought to know? Like . . . Andrew's gay, or something?'

The suggestion raised a smile from Flora. 'No,' she said. 'I think you can rest assured on that one.

181

Come on,' she moved towards the stairs, 'let's leave it till the morning. We can talk about it then if you want to.'

I lay in bed, staring at the ceiling. The rain pattered on the ivy under my window. The comfortableness – for me anyway – had gone out of the evening following Ginny's disclosure. I don't know what my face must have registered at the moment of it – a total mix of emotions, I suppose, and, yes embarrassment. Why, I don't know. It was hardly my fault I'd been under the misapprehension.

Ginny had been quick to pick up on this. 'Don't worry,' she'd said. 'It was stupid of them – ' Andrew and Flora presumably – 'not to explain. Trouble is, everyone in the village knows. Dammit, we've all grown up here. I guess they just didn't think. Come on.' She picked up the coffee pot. 'Let's take this through.'

I was tempted to ask her not to say anything, but I hesitated and the moment was lost as she pushed open the door with her shoulder and went ahead. In any case, what did it matter? It didn't make any difference to me one way or the other. And indeed, without the explanation, what might Andrew already have read – and, more to the point, continue to read – into what had been, after all, only friendliness?

I braced myself for Ginny to share the joke. But as she distributed coffee and the after-dinner mints I'd brought along as a contribution and still said nothing, I realised she wasn't going to. Not publicly, anyway. No doubt she and Andrew had chuckled over it as they prepared for bed. Bed? I disengaged them. Separate rooms. It was a strange thought.

I imagined them saying goodnight on the landing. 'I thought she went a bit quiet,' Andrew might have surmised. I knew I had done. I'd tried to join naturally in the conversation; but all the time I was conscious not only of avoiding addressing Andrew directly but of worrying whether Ginny was watching me, quietly monitoring. I didn't want to give any of them the wrong idea.

I'd busied myself unwrapping a mint when he'd mentioned a walk across to Chadham in the morning. Yes, I admitted, carefully folding the green foil, I had remembered to bring trainers with me. No point in appearing incompetent on top of everything else.

Flora excused herself from any intended expedition. Ginny pleaded chores.

'So it's just you and me,' Andrew had announced cheerfully. 'Don't *you* let me down. Anyway, do you good to get some fresh air into those London lungs of yours.'

There was no escape. Desperation produced inspiration. 'What about Tom and Justin? Maybe they'd enjoy it too?'

There was some discussion as to whether they could be retrieved at a reasonable hour. But in the end it was agreed. 'And I'll drive over with Flora, and we'll all meet at The Three Bells for a pub lunch,' decided Ginny.

I wasn't looking forward to it. Maybe, I thought hopefully, it would still be raining in the morning. I turned on my side and curled into a ball. After a while, I resorted to resolutely counting sheep.

Andrew turned up just before eleven. I'd decided, on coming down to breakfast, not to make any further issue of last night's revelation, and Flora didn't raise the matter. Instead she and I spent the first half of the morning – inevitably, given my hopes for an excuse to cancel the excursion, an irritatingly fine one – cleaning out the hen-house. There was, I discovered, a lot of satisfaction to be gained from shovelling out damp, dung-laden sawdust and wood chippings and replacing them from clean-smelling sacks. Memory jogged, I enquired after Arabella.

Flora pointed. 'There she is. Limping a bit still – but making the most of her injury.'

It wasn't difficult to identify her among all the other uniformly brown Rhode Islands. As though realising she was the focus of our attention, she stopped and lifted her gammy leg, turning a beady eye pathetically towards us. I laughed. 'I see what you mean.'

We were returning to the house when the Metro pulled into the drive. 'Saving our strength,' explained Andrew, tipping forward the front seat to let the boys out.

'Goodness, I didn't know you were planning that strenuous a route,' said Flora.

Andrew acknowledged he wasn't. He'd thought we'd take the bridle path as far as the piggery, cut across the hill and then follow the river. He grinned at Tom. 'Only about ten miles.'

'What?' I was the one who reacted.

'Just teasing. Probably more like four.'

I blanked my face, resisting being drawn. I turned my attention to Tom and Justin. 'Hi,' I said. 'How was the camping?'

I pressed them to chat about it as we set off ten minutes later. Tom was determinedly cool about a leaking tent, Justin innocently wide-eyed about having woken up in the middle of the night to find himself lying in a puddle. They'd had to bang on the back door to be let in, and been wrapped in blankets and given cocoa and cake. 'And then we all slept on a big mattress on the playroom floor!'

Andrew had listened in amusement. 'Which was much more exciting than merely dossing down under canvas,' he commented to me over Justin's head.

Justin looked uncertain. 'No,' he decided at last. 'Course it wasn't.' And he galloped ahead to join Tom who was poking around in the hedge inspecting, it turned out, the remains of a nest.

We'd been walking back in the direction of the village. Halfway along the lane, Andrew steered us off the road and through a gate on to a broad track dividing two fields of swaying barley. The ground was soft and damp beneath our feet, the air freshly cleansed.

The path led on between more fields, then meandered across a swathe of untended hillocky grass to a planked footbridge over a stream. As we wandered along, Andrew chatted as naturally as ever – regaling me with village anecdotes, commenting on some item in the news, weighing up England's chances at Headingley. Now and then he turned his attention to his nephews, confirming a species of bird or deliberating with them on the state of the grain waving alongside us.

Gradually I relaxed. I was being totally paranoid in my self-consciousness, it dawned on me. If Andrew had always assumed I knew he was unattached, what was different now? What was different, I acknowledged – and had the grace to smile at myself – was my recognition that, even so, he treated me as no more than a pleasant companion. It was my perception of the situation that had been rocked, not his. If there was a frisson of disappointment in the realisation, I nudged it away; replaced it with tentative relief; almost regretted matters were not as I had believed. Far better to be certain of him as a friend than risk possible complications and tensions. I still wondered whether Ginny had told him of my misapprehension.

Beyond the watermeadows, the path curved through trees. Now we reached a point where farmyard smells preceded the sight, round the next bend, of outbuildings. As we passed them, I tried not to wrinkle my nose too obviously. Justin had no such inhibitions, accompanying his snout face with snuffling grunts. I laughed. Andrew mimicked him. 'Come on, Porky,' he said, and led the way up a barely identifiable track through the trees opposite. We emerged into the rough grass and low gorse of a hillside rising gently above us. 'Race you to the top,' he challenged, and the three of them charged off, shorter bare legs searching for gaps between stubby bushes while long trousered ones ploughed indiscriminately through them.

'Oh, oh, my ankle. I've twisted it.' Andrew hopped to a halt and made play of rubbing his lower leg, allowing the boys to catch up. Tom, I sensed, recognised the ploy for what it was but pounded past anyway, giving no similar quarter to his younger brother. Andrew, hobbling ostentatiously, managed a close third. Flopped on a grassy knoll at the top, they watched me floundering up to join them.

We sat there in a group for a while facing back the way we'd come. The midday sun shimmered warmly through a chiffon of high white cloud.

'They're great kids, aren't they?' I said when they'd wandered off on some exploration of their own.

Andrew nodded, then grinned. 'I gather you thought they were mine!'

I waited for embarrassment to rise. But it didn't: Andrew was so clearly sharing his amusement with me.

'Sorry,' I said.

'No need.' He looked over to where they were bent over something on the ground. 'I'd not have any urge to disown them.'

That wasn't quite what I'd meant.

He glanced back at me. 'I assumed Flora would have explained. Mind you,' he gave me a quizzical look as he rose to his feet in response to a summons from Tom, 'I'd barely graduated when that one was born. I'm not sure I'd have welcomed fatherhood quite that soon!'

I laughed an apology as he started to move away to investigate. 'Maths was never my strong point,' I excused myself. But even so – suddenly recalling our conversation in the meadow – what about those subsequent years of legal training; and hadn't he mentioned doing some travelling . . . ? I supposed I should at least have wondered.

The three of them were investigating something the boys had uncovered. 'Dead adder,' Andrew reported on returning.

I pulled a face.

'*Dead* one,' he stressed.

I still made a note to watch where I put my feet.

Later, walking along the wide, grassy river bank, I raised the subject of Ginny. 'She only told me her husband had been . . . had died. In an accident.'

Andrew nodded. 'They were living out in Germany. Jonty was an engineer. He was returning from some site inspection – then . . .' He gave a sympathetic shrug. 'The flat they were in went with the job, so she just packed up her bags and brought the children home.'

'And moved into the Dower House?'

'Obvious thing to do. It had been standing empty for a while, so we all got down to it. You should have seen the grass – ' he laughed suddenly, dismissing the mood of a moment ago – 'it was about a mile high. Philip directing operations as usual, of course.'

'So you obviously weren't living there then.'

'I was still up at the farm. The old man had died about a year earlier, but Mother was still there. Keeping the peace!'

'That bad?' I took my light-hearted cue from him.

'No, I'm joking.' He grinned. 'I think. Then, when she went . . . That was something of a shock. She'd had a bit of heart trouble for a while but none of us thought it was that serious.' He picked up a stone and lobbed it absently into the water. 'I think I'd have moved out anyway – after all, the farm was now Philip's – but in any case we'd hardly buried her before he announced he and Julia were going to get married. I reckoned it would be a bit crowded.'

The ripples created by the stone had now fanned out towards the bank and subsided. I turned to Andrew. 'So you moved down with Ginny?'

'It seemed logical at the time. We'd been left the house jointly. Don't know what the old man thought we'd do about it. One of us buy the other out, I suppose. But he didn't want to break up the

189

farm, and that was his only other asset. Anyway, I didn't fancy a flat in town, and Ginny seemed to approve of the idea. Has a thing about it being good for the boys to have a man about the place.' He waved to Justin who was shouting information about his latest discovery.

'Yes,' I said, 'but what Ginny needs is a proper man . . .' My jaw dropped as I assessed the words dangling in the air between us.

Andrew threw back his head in an outburst of mirth.

'Oh . . . ! I didn't mean . . . the way it came out wasn't . . .' But his hilarity was infectious.

'It's OK. I understand exactly what you mean.' He was still chuckling. Then his face straightened. 'You're right, of course. I'd assumed she'd have found herself someone else . . . have remarried . . . long ago – certainly by now; that our sharing the house was only a temporary arrangement.' Unchar-acteristically, he scuffed at the turf. 'To be honest, though for heaven's sake don't repeat this, I feel a bit stuck. Because of Tom and Justin mainly. They've got used to having me around . . .'

'Difficult.'

'Not that Ginny hasn't had some very present-able men taking an interest from time to time. One in particular. He was widowed too, with a small daughter. Met him at some teaching conference or other. Would have been ideal, I'd have thought. But I guess none of them, in her eyes, matches up to Jonty.' He gave a shrug. 'Problem, isn't it?'

I agreed it was.

We strolled in silence for a while. The boys wandered back to join us, Justin demanding to know how much further it was. He was hungry.

'Only about half a mile,' Andrew reassured him.

The river had broadened out and here, at its widest point, a couple of anglers were trying their luck. We all stepped back and waited as one of them prepared to cast. Fascinated, I watched the line loop forward and back and forward again as he directed it to some chosen spot.

'Much luck?' enquired Andrew as we passed.

'Not a lot.' The man smiled ruefully. 'Can't seem to discover what they're taking today.'

We nodded sympathy, and paused to listen politely as he listed the flies he'd already tried without success. The names triggered my memory.

'He should be using a Golden Retriever,' I said as we moved away.

'Should he?'

I laughed. 'I've really no idea.'

'What's a Golden Retriever?' demanded Tom.

'It was a fly my father used. He did a lot of fishing when I was about your age.'

'I remember him talking about it,' said Andrew. 'Years ago when he first knew Flora. But then, of course, he took up painting.'

'I suppose,' I said, 'they're not such dissimilar interests.'

'Well, you need a canvas stool for both!'

I decided not to be pedantic about the type of

fishing. 'I was thinking more of the colours and shapes.'

Andrew, witticism over, looked thoughtful. 'And the artistry.' He turned and stared back at the fishermen. I followed his gaze.

'Look at the way they're brushing the lines across the water,' he said.

I nodded; there was something extraordinarily soothing about the steady gentle movement.

'Come on.' Tom was standing with his hands on his hips. 'I'm starving.'

We spotted the parked Volvo as we approached The Three Bells. Flora and Ginny had, we discovered, already established claim to a table at the bottom of the garden, close to the water's edge. Just as well, as the pub, enjoying a prime trading position next to the bridge, was becoming more crowded by the minute.

I accompanied Andrew to the bar to fetch drinks and to order. When we emerged into the sunlight, he weaved his way ahead of me, ushering me to sit between Ginny and Tom and positioning himself, I noticed, beside Flora rather than next to the boys. It was Ginny now who was giving them her attention, Andrew very much the indulgent uncle who'd done his stint. I felt a surge of sympathy for them. Tom in particular had reached an age where he must be beginning to be aware that Andrew could never fill the gap in their lives. It wasn't just Ginny – remembering my gauche comment to Andrew –

who needed a 'proper' man; the boys surely needed to see her in such a relationship. The thought echoed eerily in my head, and my mind flashed back to those good times before the emotional stand-off between my parents.

Now it was Ginny I found myself observing. Was she as content as she appeared? Had she had the odd fling since Jonty died, I wondered. Or, like me since my break-up with Mark, had she kept men at a chaste distance? I crossed my legs, disconcerted by the stirrings my train of thought produced. I avoided too obviously looking at Andrew who was deep in conversation with Flora.

I excused myself and went in search of the Ladies. There I took the opportunity to pull a comb through my hair, taking my time smoothing and ordering it. I renewed the light make-up I was wearing not – I convinced myself – out of vanity but as though the act of blotting on more foundation could somehow blank my feelings from my own consciousness as well as hide them from others.

Obviously I had not been as successful as I'd hoped. 'So Elspeth was right?' Flora had observed later.

Temporarily idling in a London-bound traffic jam early that evening, I recalled the comment. Phrased as a question, it was more of a statement – a bland one, giving no lead as to how I might respond.

Ginny had dropped us off – Flora, Andrew and myself – back at Wood Edge; Andrew had chatted for only a few minutes before glancing at his watch and announcing he'd better get up to the farm and 'heave a bale or two; show willing at least'. We'd watched him drive the Metro away, and retired into the house before Flora dropped her remark.

I'd laughed off the suggestion that – in Elspeth's words – I 'had a thing' for Andrew, and Flora let it go; but as I sat now, tapping my fingers on the steering wheel, I wasn't sure whether I resented her perception or was glad of it. So different from Mother who only ever saw what appeared under her nose – and even that only if she wanted to. It occurred to me now – as I pushed the car into gear and inched forward – that what I'd put down to an admirably trusting nature was a symptom, rather, of a lack of awareness and understanding. I half regretted brushing aside the opportunity Flora had offered to confide my confusion.

But only half. Some things were best tucked away and ignored. Even if I was having to reassess my image of Andrew as a proxy brother now that Ginny so undeniably had prior claim, she didn't seem averse to sharing him. Indeed – the thought lifted my spirits – I seemed to have acquired a whole new family; even – I recalled Justin shyly reaching up to give me a kiss as I prepared to alight from the Volvo – down to the third generation.

A thrill of anticipation flowed through me as I recalled I'd more or less committed myself to going

down to Cotterly again next weekend. Not inten-
tionally. Not even explicitly. Mention had been
made over lunch – distributed round the table
by the time of my return to the pub garden – of
Saturday's annual fête. Justin had been gleefully
anticipating Andrew's head in the stocks; then,
when he saw the face I was pulling, reassured me I
could be one of those on the throwing end of the
wet sponge.

'But only if you contribute a cake to Mum's stall,'
Tom had intervened.

'I can't make cakes,' I protested.

'Right. It's the stocks for you.' Andrew led the
hilarity.

Caught up by it, I pretended panic: 'Will a
bought one do?'

They'd made play of considering the matter.

'Let me know if you're coming,' Flora had commented later as she walked me to my car. So easy,
so untroubled.

The traffic was moving now in one of its
intermittent half-mile free flows before grinding to
a halt again. But it didn't pause long, and as I
relaxed and my thoughts began to turn to the tasks
waiting for me at work, it gradually unsnarled itself
and I sailed, with scarcely a thought, past the junction where, had I been so inclined, I could have
turned off to my mother's.

CHAPTER 13

I did go down to Cotterly the following weekend; and the next, and the next. And as my involvement there developed a momentum of its own – Flora stopped changing the sheets between each visit and I began leaving odd items I wouldn't need during the week in what was rapidly becoming 'my' room – I pushed aside any concern for my mother. I fobbed her off with excuses for still not having time to visit her: a work conference, a sick girlfriend, a christening – in the guise of Paula's convenient twins.

Call it rebellion. The delayed adolescent variety maybe. But I'd worried about her for too long. Now it was my turn. I had a lot of ground to make up. If she hadn't kept me away from Cotterly all these years . . .

Anger bubbled just below the surface, offering justification for the attitude I was taking; and any guilt that threatened only added to it. I stamped on the smallest hint of conscience – I wasn't going to let Mother spoil this new-found freedom in my life. It was Father I wanted to think about; Flora and

Cotterly, friendships at the Dower House I wanted to enjoy.

And I intended to do so. Starting off with the fête where, after a few minutes' awkwardness, I felt my inhibitions drain away. Difficult to hang on to self-consciousness when a nine-year-old – Justin – grabs your hand and drags you off to a blindfolded attempt to pin the tail on the donkey! By the end, I was lobbing the anticipated sponges with as much gusto as anyone.

'I'll get you for this,' promised Andrew as water dripped down his face.

'Catch me first,' I chanted over my shoulder as I headed away to fish for lucky numbers.

I was clutching a small teddy bear as, late in the afternoon, Flora and I strolled back to Wood Edge. I sat him on the kitchen table and lowered myself on to a chair to face him. I wiggled his front paws. 'Well, little fellow,' I said. 'Did you have a good time today?'

'Yes, thank you,' I ventriloquised. 'How about you?'

'Me too,' I responded solemnly; then looked across at Flora who was observing my antics with dry amusement. I swivelled away from the toy, laughing at myself. 'Like playing with dolls, isn't it?'

'Um . . m . . m.' Flora exaggerated her agreement, raising an eyebrow as though maybe she saw more in my remark than I did. She started unpacking her basket – a crumpled cardigan, a tin of beans she'd won at the hoop-la, an empty cake plate or two. 'What are you going to call him?' she asked, still delving.

'Call him? I don't know.' I glanced back at the toy. 'Teddy, I suppose.' I stroked the man-made fur. It prickled my fingertips. 'I had a teddy when I was little,' I recalled. 'The only male,' I reflected, 'among all the females.'

'He must have had a high old time.' Flora's mouth twitched. It wasn't the first time, I recognised, that her humour had surfaced in this way. I considered her as she moved towards a cupboard. No-one would ever call her sexy . . . and yet . . .

'He didn't get a chance,' I came back swiftly. 'I always took him into bed with me.'

'Naturally.' Flora was still amused. Her face straightened a touch. 'So what happened to him?'

'Oh, I don't know. Mother threw him out, I suppose.' A sudden lump materialised in my throat. I swallowed.

Flora noticed, looking enquiringly at me.

'Ridiculous,' I explained, 'to be sentimental over a child's plaything.'

'If that's all it's about.'

Well, it was, wasn't it? But Flora had this knack, with her comments, of touching something deeper. Disconcerted, I pushed the bear to one side, making a mental note to offer it to Joe Manning's little granddaughter next time he brought her round to collect some eggs.

Later that evening, Flora fetched out Father's paintings again. We spread them out across the kitchen floor and took up a vantage point side by side on the chesterfield. I scooped up Columbus as he made to pad cautiously across this strange new carpeting and held him on my lap, soothing him into quietness.

Flora, sitting there comfortably beside me, started to identify their locations: the old mill over at . . .; the view along the river from The Three Bells – 'recognise it?'; 'and this . . .'

There was one I particularly admired. 'Just over the hill,' she said. 'Why don't we go up there tomorrow?'

It was the first of several expeditions over the coming weeks, walking or driving, to those places where he'd set up his easel. I sat with Flora beside streams, on grassy hillocks, above farmyards, relishing the sounds and smells of the views he'd reproduced in washes of greens, blues, yellows; drinking it all in as she described how, lounging beside him, she would immerse herself in a book while he concentrated with his brush and his box of tints; how, in companionable silence, they would break off to share a picnic. I understood about the silence. Once Flora had painted her word picture, shared her experience with me, I too was content to sit and stare. The sense of their togetherness, neither demanding of the other yet giving freely, was almost overwhelming. Back at the house, in more pragmatic mood, she would pull a rag from the box in which she stuffed them and hold up a holey sock, remarking ruefully, 'He never would trim his toe nails.' Or, in the garden, shake her head over rampaging roses: 'I told him they needed pruning right back.'

It was all part and parcel, as he increasingly figured, easily and naturally, in our conversations, of my building up a picture of my father; resurrecting the man I'd known as a child – warm, affectionate, full of laughter; fleshing out aspects of him I'd glimpsed but never had the opportunity to explore – well-read, intelligent, interested in everything from art to politics to the latest scientific discoveries; introducing a sensitive side I'd never recognised. So powerful was his image becoming that sometimes I would look up suddenly, half expecting him to be standing in the doorway. When Andrew appeared without warning one day – Flora and I had been engrossed in sorting through a clutter of photographs – I gave an enormous start on seeing a figure outlined in the entrance to the kitchen. Even after reality had replaced fantasy, my heart continued to thud.

'Sorry,' said Andrew, 'I should have knocked.' He glanced curiously at me.

'What was that about?' asked Flora after he'd gone. 'You looked really shaken.'

'It's crazy,' I said. 'It was just that for an instant . . .'

Flora nodded. I was glad she didn't put out a hand to comfort me; emotion was too near the surface.

I got up and transferred the kettle from the simmer plate to the hot one. 'It's no good,' I said, realising it needed filling and doing so. 'I really must get you an electric version.'

'I don't need one.' Flora sounded mildly amused.

I turned to her. 'Yes, but *I* do. This slow thing – ' I gave an apologetic grimace – 'drives me mad.'

'Only because you're used to the other. What you've never had, you don't miss.'

I doubt it was anything but a straightforward comment. She'd said much the same thing when I'd tackled her about her lack of a telephone. 'But it would be easier for people to get in touch with you,' I'd insisted. 'Quite,' she'd observed.

It was the answer I could have expected. Even so, I'd shaken my head. One just had to take Flora as she was. In so many ways.

Now I strummed my fingers on the Aga rail. 'The problem arises,' I said, 'when you start to discover what you *have* missed.' I gave the body of the kettle an experimental tap with a fingertip. 'Ow,' I said. I reached for mugs. 'Can you bear instant?' At least she didn't eschew that particular convenience.

'There are moments,' I mused, as I waited impatiently for steam to rise, 'when I begin to think being here, talking about Father, only make me feel worse. Everything – you, this house, the country-side in some strange way – is a constant reminder.'

'I understand,' said Flora.

The kettle had at last come to the boil. I poured

water into the mugs, watching the browned liquid frothing as the levels rose. I added milk and carried them across to the table.

'It's never easy,' Flora observed, as I reseated myself, 'facing up to loss of any sort.' A curiously remote expression brushed across her face. 'Maybe particularly to lost opportunities, the might-have-beens.'

'At least when I'm in London, I can forget about it all.' It was partially true anyway.

'Yes, but ignoring it –' Flora's attention was fully back with me again – 'distracting oneself, doesn't solve anything.'

I considered. 'Just drives the hurt underground, you mean?' I stared into my mug. 'I'm not sure it wasn't a good deal more comfortable there,' I remarked.

'Trouble is,' said Flora reflectively, 'a whole lot else tends to get pushed down with it.'

'Like?'

Flora picked up her coffee and took a sip.

'Like the frustration I felt about it all, I suppose,' I answered for her. 'Festering alongside. It certainly,' I recalled, 'erupted when I met you.' A thought struck me. I looked at her. 'Was that why you were so bloody to me to start with? Were you deliberately prodding it to the surface?'

Her eyebrows puckered a rebuttal. 'Nothing so calculating.'

'You mean,' I said, and I laughed, 'I was just *being* a pain! So self-righteous.'

She smiled. 'You could say so.'

'I *needed* someone to be angry with,' I not so much apologised as clarified.

Flora inclined her head.

'I mean . . . all those years of feeling so damned helpless.' I ran my finger round the rim of my mug. 'And then you made me feel even more inadequate. Talk about taking control.'

'Did I?'

'It certainly felt like it. I certainly lost mine. And then – ' I recalled the tears – 'all the hurt bubbled up too.'

'I remember.'

'Still a fair old amount milling around down there, though,' I said. 'I guess that's the problem. Reminders prick at it. That's what I meant . . .' I thought about it. 'But it feels different now. Not so . . . sharp, not so overpowering.'

'Maybe you've found space to let in other things – good experiences, happier ones – to help cushion it.'

I hadn't thought of it like that. But then, wasn't that what was happening?

I allowed my mind to range – past and present, around Cotterly and beyond . . .

'Did I tell you,' I said suddenly, homing in after a while on the occasion, 'that I gave a dinner party last week?' It had been part of the outfall from my frenetic pre-Elspeth activity – strange the way things work – and only the second formal one I'd ventured since moving into the flat.

Flora nodded. 'You mentioned your plans.'

I launched into a cheerful account.

By now Flora was becoming familiar with much of my life in London. Perhaps precisely because she was more inclined to listen than to talk, it had been, and continued to be, easy to chatter on. Mostly about trivialities, but at times I found myself confiding the sort of things I'd have glossed over with my mother: a friend's unwanted pregnancy – even the abortion she'd opted for; the smoking of the occasional joint at student parties – and the odd time since, when we first came down. And somehow I found myself telling her about Mark; and, more to the point, what had led to my break up with him.

Flora gave one of those enquiring little looks of hers when I explained.

'I know, I know,' I said. 'With hindsight I over-reacted. But in any case that was *then* . . .'

'Do you regret it?'

'No.' My response was unhesitating. I thought about it. 'Whichever way you look at it,' I said, 'it showed him up to be pretty insensitive. Too sure of his own judgement by half.'

Flora made no comment. Yes, well, I supposed Mark hadn't been the only one taking a one-sided view. After a while she said, 'And have there been other boyfriends since?'

I shook my head. 'Been much too busy.' It wasn't too far off the truth. 'Decided there and then that from now on I was going to concentrate firmly on my career.'

'Oh, I see.'

Did she? Did I?'

'I'm ambitious,' I explained. I pursued it: 'Is there anything wrong with that?'

'Nothing at all.'

'As long as I don't let it squeeze out everything else?'

'You said it, not me.'

I accepted it. 'What about you?' I asked, spotting an opening. 'Didn't you have ambitions when you were my age?'

Flora answered lazily. 'I can't say I did. Not in the way you mean, anyway. I did start nursing training but then gave it up to look after Aunt Celia when she became ill.' She gave a wry smile. 'Can't say I was sorry – starched uniforms never suited me.'

I did my best to visualise her in an old-fashioned striped dress and stiffly perched cap. 'No,' I laughed. 'I don't imagine they would have done.' I thought of her behind the wheel of the Citroën. 'You'd have been more at home on a motor-racing circuit,' I chanced.

'Very possibly,' she agreed. There was just a hint of a twinkle in her eye. But she allowed something, deliberately or otherwise I wasn't sure, to divert her attention then and I hadn't pressed her.

Nor did *she* attempt to draw *me* – as we pottered in the garden or into town or around the village, or sat companionably reading books – into talking about Andrew; not in any personal sense anyway. He continued, during those July weekends, to be totally at ease in his friendliness, and I was more than happy to take my cue from that.

Not that we saw much of him except in the evenings. Haymaking was underway and he spent a lot of time, when he wasn't roped in for some cricket fixture, helping out at the farm. On one occasion I walked up there with Ginny. I'd only ever glimpsed the farmhouse from a distance, half hidden by trees at the far end of a long gravel drive. It was an old, low-slung building, dotted about with barns and outhouses. Straw spilled from open-sided ones and littered the ground under the wheels of tractors and a conglomeration of implements. The warm smell of fresh bales mingled with oily fumes and the racket of machinery.

Tom and Justin came running across the yard to greet us. Philip, whom I'd only ever seen at the cricket match way back in the early summer, and at a distance at the fête, emerged from a barn. Ginny introduced me and he gave a curt nod of acknowledgement. He waved a handful of tools. 'Bloody baler's stuck.' We declined a lift in the Land Rover and instead strolled up to the top field where we stood around as he and Andrew, stripped to the waist, struggled to free the workings from a tangle of twine.

'Very restful watching other people work,' teased Ginny.

206

Philip gave a disgruntled, 'Humph.'

'You could always fetch us a flask of tea,' Andrew suggested tolerantly.

So we wandered back to the farmhouse and into the hopelessly untidy kitchen dominated by a huge old-fashioned range and an enormous oak table whose surface was pitted and cracked – and from the depths of whose cupboards Ginny unerringly unearthed what was needed. By the time we climbed back to the field, the baler was operational again and we sat in the sun for half an hour or so, watching its steady progress and lulled by its hum. We had both of us, while the boys followed behind it, lain back and closed our eyes. I came to to find Andrew standing over us. 'Come on, lazybones,' he said, sprinkling a handful of hay over each of us.

I blinked up at his silhouette, then put a hand to my eyes to shield the sun.

CHAPTER 14

By the time of a fourth, or rather fifth, consecutive weekend visit, the car purred along seemingly on automatic pilot. Even the largely landmarkless stretches of motorway were assuming familiarity. I'd taken to going down on the Friday evening, and today I congratulated myself, as though the density or otherwise of the traffic was any of my doing, on clearing the massed exodus from London two or three miles earlier than usual. The sun, as I turned off the A road, was already an enormous orange ball dipping towards the horizon, and I had to screw up my eyes on westward-pointing twists of the road against its permeating glare.

I glanced at my watch. It confirmed I had made good time; that the evenings were already starting to shorten. Learning and logic presented themselves: we were, after all, almost six weeks past the summer solstice, even if – vagaries of the English climate permitting – the best of the weather was yet to come. August next week. Oh, God. Mother's birthday. I supposed I'd have to make a thing of it. Last year Father had taken us both to the theatre. I had found it a somewhat stilted occasion, though Mother had seemed as relaxed as she ever was. At the time, I had viewed his attempts to be jolly with cynicism. Doing his duty, I had assessed disparagingly. Now I was looking from a different standpoint. If he'd felt uncomfortable, maybe it was at the hypocrisy of it all, something which seemed to worry Mother not one jot. Indeed, she had taken her time getting into the car, making sure the neighbours had been given the opportunity to look up from their gardening or car-washing and take note of my father's dinner jacket – she had insisted he wear it – and her own little couture number.

I had reached the top of the hill now, and a sense of pleasurable anticipation filled me as I began the descent to Cotterly. It was almost, I thought idly, my mind hiving off towards more immediate matters, as though my mother had been more than happy with how things were.

I hesitated at the junction, then decided to turn right and drop off straightaway the length of material Ginny had asked me to pick up from John Lewis's.

'Just as well,' said Ginny when she realised I hadn't already been round to Wood Edge. 'Flora's not back yet. She's been over to see Donald. The Citroën's on the blink so Andrew's gone to pick her up from the station.'

'Oh, right.' I waved through the kitchen window to the boys who, defying the gathering dusk, were knocking a cricket ball around.

'Said I'd do supper. Bunged a casserole in the oven. Hope that's OK. Glass of wine?'

'Great.'

I stood sipping it in the open doorway as Ginny pottered at the stove. 'I'd almost forgotten about Donald,' I said. 'Flora never mentions him.'

'I think maybe she prefers not to.'

'The one time she did,' I said, 'I got the impression they were very close as children.'

Ginny heaved up the lid of the deep freeze and extracted a packet of peas. She grimaced. 'Flora won't approve of frozen, but she'll have to put up with it.' She emptied them into a pan. 'Difficult to know what does go on inside Flora. I have an idea ... just odd remarks she's made ... that she was a bit of a mother to him. Feels responsible in some way perhaps.' She pulled a stool from under the table, picked up her own glass and sat down. 'You know her parents virtually abandoned the pair of them?'

'No, I didn't. She only said she and Donald went to live with an aunt during the war. And then she looked after her later.'

'Eccentric old duck, by the sound of it. One way and another, Flora's been very much on her own. Case of sink or swim; Flora presumably decided to swim.'

'I take it she was never married?' Somehow I hadn't found – or made – an opportunity to ask her.

'If she was she's never told anyone. Such a waste. Though maybe she's just too independent.' Ginny raised her head and looked me straight in the eye. 'We all thought it was wonderful when your father came along.'

I stared into my wine – the very palest of pale yellows. Its aroma drifted upwards, dry, bitter-sweet. Then I looked up. 'I think I do too.'

'She deserved him.'

And he her, I thought. It was confirmation rather than revelation. Aloud I said, 'I'm glad you liked him.'

'Andrew knew him better.' Ginny's tone became matter-of-fact. 'They're very alike in so many ways, of course.'

I nodded. Not so much in looks – though there was a similarity if one thought of Andrew as a slimmed-down version. No, more in terms of personality.

'I couldn't have two more different brothers,' Ginny was chuckling. 'Philip's a real chip off the old block. Tough, practical, never says much . . .'

I laughed. 'I noticed,' I said.

'. . . whereas Andrew is more . . .' She searched for the right adjective.

'Sensitive?' It was how Flora had described my father.

'I guess so.' She turned to me. 'You like him, don't you?'

'Well, yes . . .'

'Good.'

211

The potato water, coming to the boil, spilled over and spluttered on the grids. Ginny swivelled and leaned across to turn down the gas. She glanced up at the clock on the wall. 'They should be back any moment.' She got up. 'Call the boys in, would you?'

I turned my attention to the two shadows chasing among the trees.

If I'd been disconcerted by Ginny's question, any residual self-consciousness dissipated amid the conviviality of supper-table conversation. Ginny hustled the boys off to bed as soon as we'd finished eating, and after a decent interval Flora and I excused ourselves as being, both of us, tired after our journeys.

'How was Donald?' I ventured, as we sat over a final cup of coffee.

'Same as ever.'

'If I'd realised, I could have suggested giving you a lift back.'

'Thanks, but I prefer the train. Gives me time to unwind.' It was a rare glimpse, despite the ever-increasing easiness in our relationship over the last few weeks, beneath Flora's surface.

I found myself covertly observing her as the weekend progressed: her stillness, her calm – as though she'd come to terms, or at least learned to cope, with whatever life had thrown at her; accepted the world – and people – for what it, they, were. I wished I had that same capacity.

Not that she was any the less acerbic when

occasion warranted it. Over a batch of washing-up, I passed some disparaging comment on Elspeth's decision to go back to Perry.

'And who are you to judge what's best for her?'

I inspected the handle of a jug I was drying. Eventually, I looked up and grinned. 'Maybe I'm jealous.' Flora's training in taking little, least of all my own perceptions, at automatic face value, I observed wryly to myself, was beginning to tell.

She rewarded me with a raised eyebrow and a small smile.

When Andrew called round on the Saturday evening to suggest a drink at the Horse and Dragon, Flora cried off. 'All I want to do,' she said, padding around as so often in bare feet, 'is curl up with a book.' We left her to it.

It was, it dawned on me as we wandered down the lane, the first time I'd been alone with him – for more than some incidental five or ten minutes – since the afternoon we'd had tea in his garden.

'Ginny doing the mothering bit, I suppose?' I said.

Andrew confirmed it. Our pairing this evening, it helped remind me, was only an accident of circumstance.

But even if reality demanded I recognise we were just two friends thrown together for a drink, nonetheless it was hard to dismiss, as I walked beside him, the aura of a date. I struggled not to let the fantasy run away with me – but the urge to indulge it, silently, within myself, was stronger.

Elspeth, as Flora had noted, had of course been right all along, I acknowledged. I recalled, in almost physical clarity, our drive back from the river at Putney, my smug insistence that my only interest in Andrew was sororial. But since then the situation had changed, or rather my understanding of it; yet still I'd been avoiding admitting just how much I fancied the man – damn him. Why? There was no reason at all, was there, why we shouldn't . . . ? Even Ginny, if I chose to interpret her comment that way, had given us her blessing.

I slowed involuntarily. It gave the opportunity to view him as he strolled ahead – the easy, casual swing to his walk. It was hard to resist an image of him in bed, his arms around me, his legs entwined with mine.

He'd stopped and turned. 'What's up?'

I bent and fiddled with my sandal; adjusted the strap. 'Just a stone.'

No reason at all – I reverted to my train of thought – except that Andrew had given no indication he had any interest in that direction. In one way it was a relief; the whole idea of involvement, now I was so much as considering it, was pretty unnerving . . .

He waited while I caught up with him.

The moon was a white semi-circle in a not yet darkened sky. I pointed it out. 'Strange,' I said. 'You only expect to see it at night.'

Andrew halted and put his hands – friendly ones – on my shoulders, bringing me to a standstill. 'Now you see it,' he said, 'and – ' he swivelled me through 180 degrees – 'now you don't.' He turned me back again and dropped his hold.

'Very cryptic,' I remarked. 'What was that supposed to mean?'

He shrugged.

'Oh, God. You're as bad as Flora.' I laughed, more for my own benefit than his. I wished he hadn't done that.

We reached the pub. Andrew exchanged greetings, joined in the banter, the discussions. There was little opportunity for any sort of personal chat. The place filled up – a hubbub of farming talk, dogs bounding underfoot . . .

It was getting on towards closing time when we emerged.

'Sorry,' said Andrew, as we crossed the green. 'Not much fun for you.'

'On the contrary,' I countered gamely. 'All part of country life.'

'You enjoy it then?'

'I must do, or I wouldn't keep coming down.'

'True.' But I sensed him looking sideways at me, studying me.

Back at Wood Edge, only the light in Flora's bedroom was on.

'I could make us a cup of coffee,' I offered.

'Not a bad idea, if I'm to drive home.'

We sat opposite each other at the kitchen table,

cradling mugs. The warmth between my palms was reassuring.

'Will you be down again next weekend?' Andrew asked.

It reminded me of Mother, and her wretched birthday. 'Can't,' I said. I hesitated for a moment, then explained.

'When's *your* birthday?'

'November,' I said. 'Why?'

'No reason. Just wondered.'

We sipped coffee in companionable but, for me, frustratingly undefined intimacy.

'I was just thinking,' Andrew spoke surprisingly diffidently, 'I have to be up in town at the end of the week. Case coming up in court. If you were free on Thursday evening . . .' He laughed. 'Save me from staring into some hotel *soupe du jour*.'

The extraordinary knotting sensation just inside the base of my rib cage seemed lifted straight from the pages of the romances I'd lapped up as a teenager. But: 'Sure,' I managed casually. 'Why not?'

I allowed the arrangement to drift into my conversation with Flora next morning. We'd just finished picking a bowl of raspberries and, collapsed in deck chairs, were dipping into them with our fingers.

'Oh, yes?' Non-committal as always.

She leaned back and tilted her face up to the sun. 'Where's he taking you?' she offered eventually.

I licked juice from my palm, where it had run

down. 'I rather thought I might take *him* some-where.'

'Very modern.'

'Well, I can afford to.'

She turned an eye lazily towards me. 'I'm not doubting it.'

'Maybe we'll go dutch,' I conceded.

'Uh, huh.'

'Are you trying to tell me something?'

'My dear girl, I'm not trying to tell you anything. It's your life. You're the one who has to sort it out.'

I wished I wasn't.

On the drive back, I made a mental list of things to do. First and foremost I had to contact my mother.

'It's your birthday next Sunday,' I announced to her over the phone on the Monday evening. I tried to sound enthusiastic.

'I was wondering whether you'd remember.' There was more than a hint of reproof in her voice. I supposed I deserved it. 'Will you be joining us?'

'Us?'

'Leah and Harold didn't want me to be alone. They've invited me over there for the weekend.'

Oh, shit. I really was in the dog house.

'I'm sure they'd be delighted if you came down for the day.'

Guilt, guilt, guilt.

'I'll ring and arrange it with them, shall I?' I said. 'Look I really am sorry about this last month—'

'My dear, you have your own life to lead.'

Similar words to Flora's, only somehow the message was totally different.

It was Uncle Harold who answered my call. 'Your aunt's out,' he told me.

I explained why I was ringing.

'Of course,' he promised. 'We'd love to see you.'

'I feel terribly guilty. I didn't mean to land you and Leah—'

'Our pleasure. And listen . . .' He hesitated a moment. 'No need to feel so responsible for your mother. She's well able to look after herself.' He chuckled. 'I should know. I'm married to her sister.'

It was the first time I'd ever known him make any comment about her; or his wife for that matter. It startled me. But I could have hugged him. 'Thanks,' I said.

That settled, there was nothing to stop anticipation mounting at the prospect of my assignation with Andrew. Even the excitement of a major new project in Scotland in which I was heavily involved failed to breach the nine-to-five barrier as, over both the following evenings, I concentrated on spring-cleaning the flat which had received little more than a cursory swipe with a duster since Elspeth's departure. I paid particular attention to the bathroom, purchasing specially some new product that promised – somewhat over-zealously, I discovered – an instant gleam on the tiles.

I checked the drinks cupboard, and got in the best coffee and a box of gourmet biscuits. In Boots, during a snatched lunch hour, I slid a pack of condoms discreetly alongside my other purchases before handing them to the assistant. Every girl, I reassured myself, should have some in her dressing-table drawer, just in case; it wasn't as though I planned to carry them around in my handbag.

On the Thursday, I made sure I left the office promptly. We'd arranged that Andrew pick me up at the flat, rather than direct from work. 'There's a rather chic little French place only two minutes' walk away,' I'd suggested when he phoned. 'Would that do?' More to the point, it gave me the chance to shower and change.

And I'd chosen my outfit with care. Understated sophistication, I congratulated myself as I surveyed my image in the full-length mirror.

Andrew was gratifyingly impressed. 'And there was I thinking you might appreciate a pair of wellingtons for Christmas!'

'I might too,' I laughed. 'I'm very adaptable.' But my response came across as *too* jolly; *too* good-mates-together-ish. Too Cotterly.

And thus the evening continued. Even though the food was excellent – we both settled for seafood followed by *canard au poivre* – there was no edge of flirtation to our conversation, nothing to distinguish it from the easy chat and innocent exchanges that had become the norm between us.

At the end of the meal, Andrew flatly refused – did I appreciate it or not? – to let me pay my share. 'My bit, anyway, can go down on expenses,' he pointed out.

He escorted me back to the flat.

'Coffee? A drink . . . ?' I ventured as we climbed the stairs to my door.

Andrew looked at his watch. 'Better not. But thanks, it's been a great evening.' He waited while I turned the key in the lock. I hesitated, door half open.

He leaned forward and dropped a kiss on my forehead. 'Well, goodnight then. See you soon.'

'Goodnight,' I said. As an afterthought, as his head disappeared below the line of the banister rail, I called, 'Good luck tomorrow. With your case.' I didn't know whether he'd heard me.

Half an hour later, in my ultra-clean bathroom, I sponged my eyes and told myself not to be so stupid. But the sense of desolation after the build-up I'd allowed myself was hard to bear. Just as well for Flora that she chose not to be on the phone. The urge to ring and cry on her substantial shoulder would have been irresistible.

Though whether I would have been doing so from disappointment or relief – or perhaps a mixture of both – I was none too sure.

CHAPTER 15

It's amazing what a good night's sleep can do. And against all the odds I was out for the count as soon as my head hit the pillow. Maybe the rather fine Chablis had something to do with it.

Whatever, daylight brought perspective, and to add to it my morale was lifted sky-high during the morning when the MD himself – that elusive figure rarely glimpsed other than as a pair of pinstriped legs disappearing upwards in the open-plan lift – put his head round my door to congratulate me on my part in a recent coup.

Pity I can't handle my personal life as effectively, I reflected when he'd gone. But the thought couldn't detract from the satisfaction of the praise I'd just had heaped on me.

I swivelled in my chair, idly tapping the end of a pen between my teeth. How was Andrew's case going, I wondered. Yesterday's conference with Counsel, he'd confided, had not left him feeling over-optimistic. And it was one, he'd explained, which he felt strongly about winning – and winning well. He'd clearly been concerned about the outcome. 'One shouldn't let it get to one personally, but . . .'

I wished now I hadn't let my own disappointment at the way the evening had been going distract me from taking a greater interest. Though, come to think of it, he had been the one who'd changed the subject – to a consideration of the relative merits of chocolate mousse versus some exotic strawberry concoction.

I forced my attention back to the papers on my desk and the computer screen at my elbow. But concentration soon wavered.

Maybe I should ring him over the weekend and ask how it went. I almost managed to convince myself it would be no more than a friendly gesture; might have succeeded if a sudden image of Flora with her eyebrows raised hadn't loomed. 'Do it if you want to,' I could practically hear her saying, 'but don't kid yourself . . .'

So my motivation wouldn't be pearl-white pure. Always the truth; the bloody truth.

'OK, Flora,' I mentally interrogated her, 'so what should I have done last night? Dragged him into the flat? Tied the sodding man down?'

I saw her standing there with her back to the Aga, arms loosely folded. 'Would it have helped?'

'Oh, stop being so damned realistic, Flora.'

I scrumpled a sheet of paper and chucked it, hard, at the wall opposite. It was almost as satisfying as banging my own head against the brickwork – I supposed there was brickwork under there –

and I felt a whole heap better for the gesture. Which, I decided when I surveyed the mound of files staring at me, was just as well.

I took a pile of them home with me at the end of the day, poured myself a stiff Scotch – and a second one – and gluttonised on the biscuits as I worked my way steadily through sales figures and budget projections.

I drove down to Epsom on the Sunday to arrive at Leah and Harold's neo-Georgian semi on the dot of twelve. I'd gift-wrapped the sort of brooch I knew my mother would love and which I wouldn't be seen dead wearing. It was, to my mind, ostentatious to the point of vulgarity, but had cost a fair amount in one of those little jewellers in the Burlington Arcade. The assistant, about my age, had been poker-faced as I picked it out. 'For my mother,' I explained; and the look that passed between us allowed her to smile collusively.

My mother and aunt, ensconced amongst the sitting-room chintz, were enjoying a leisurely glass of Pimms when I got there. I handed Mother the parcel. As anticipated, she was delighted with its contents, all my misdemeanours apparently either forgiven or forgotten.

'You are so good to me,' she gushed. 'I was just saying to Leah how lucky we are to have daughters.'

'How *is* Elspeth?' I enquired. 'It was great to see her – ' I knew Mother would have passed on the information – 'when she was in London. You know she stayed at the flat?'

She'd called only last week; she'd seemed absolutely fine. Leah's tone suggested that, whatever my mother had chosen to imply, my aunt had already been placed on the defensive.

'She was certainly on good form a month or so ago,' I confirmed.

My mother chipped in. 'But I'm sure your aunt will be happier when she settles down with a proper job like yours.'

I searched for an excuse to opt out of Mother's point-scoring. 'Where's Uncle Harold? Shall I go and say hello to him?'

Inevitably he was busy with his watering can at the bottom of the garden. 'They're discussing their daughters,' I felt able to confide after I'd kissed his cheek and exchanged pleasantries.

He winked. 'Say no more.'

Lunch was cold salmon, laid out in splendour with all the trimmings.

'Umm, home-made,' I commented appreciatively as I spooned mayonnaise on to my plate.

Uncomfortably, I found myself the centre of attention, Mother preening opposite me as I was pressed to spell out my – in her view – giddy ascent up the career ladder.

'I'm not doing too badly,' I demurred.

'And modest with it. Just like her father.'

I stared at her, sitting there complacently, delicately dissecting a portion of salmon. What did she know about him? What, for that matter, did she understand – care, even – about me? Instead she dangled us like glittering accessories. I speared a piece of tomato.

She was chattering on about him now, impressing on the assembled company his many attributes as a husband – as though her sister and brother-in-law didn't know about his weekend . . . excursions.

Leah leaned across and patted my mother's hand. 'So hard for you to lose him so young.' I glanced at Harold. He had one of those see-all-say-nothing expressions on his face. It didn't change when he caught my eye, but something – some sort of empathy – passed between us.

After a decent interval, Leah focused on me again. 'And how about boyfriends?' I stifled irritation. Presumably Leah saw such probing into my current personal life as no more than a natural extension of 'And how are you getting on at school/how are you enjoying university?'

'Oh, Charissa has plenty of admirers,' Mother intervened.

I did my best to fend them off. 'No-one special.'

Mother, no doubt torn between disapproval of my cousin actually living with Perry and the fact that her sister's child did at least have a man in her life, assumed a would-be-knowing air. 'Ah, but maybe there is someone. You've been very evasive these last few weeks . . .'

There was sufficient ring of truth to have me struggling not to shift in my seat.

''Fraid not. Sorry to disappoint you.'

It occurred to me that even if there'd been anything to own to about Andrew, I couldn't have done so. How would I explain him? 'Just someone I met through Flora,' would I say nonchalantly?

I swallowed the last mouthful of salad and laid down my knife and fork. 'That was delicious,' I said firmly.

I escaped at about four, promising Mother I'd try to get down to see her soon – perhaps one evening. 'Or maybe you could come up? Do some shopping; meet me for lunch?'

She brightened. 'Yes, maybe I will.'

Leah pressed the remains of a gooseberry tart on me. 'You working girls,' she said. 'You never look after yourselves.' I accepted it gracefully – a case of appreciating the deed more than the thought, yet at the same time touched by it. Harold patted my shoulder. 'Good to see you.'

What on earth, I wondered, winding down the car window to wave goodbye, had made Elspeth feel the need to shake this particular dust from her feet? But then maybe it was just too cosy, her parents too compatible; no real space for her? In my own case, there'd been more than enough room for me – in my mother's life anyway. And with hindsight it felt decidedly less comfortable than it had at the time. The whole situation – even allowing for all that I was coming to understand about my father – had not, I increasingly sensed, been anything like as clear cut as it seemed. Though what I based that feeling on, I wasn't at all sure.

I recalled Uncle Harold's words: 'Your mother's well able to look after herself.' I guessed she always had been. And was it possible I'd been an unwitting pawn in her doing so; had she been using me in some way I couldn't quite identify? It was an uncharitable thought, but one I had difficulty shaking off as I steered my way through the London maze.

I'd taken the opportunity, as I helped carry coffee cups through to the kitchen, to ask my aunt for Elspeth's telephone number.

We'd left my mother reclining in today's-my-birthday state on the patio, peering from under half-closed lids at Harold's ministrations to the compost heap. 'You'll need to turn it more,' she'd advised in a voice whose pitch carried across the distance and beyond. Harold had raised a hand, and carried on as before.

'She left in a bit of a whirl,' I explained as I stacked. 'I forgot to get it from her.'

'Be nice if you two saw more of each other.' Leah sounded wistful.

'We certainly get on well. ' I debated whether to say more and decided against it.

Now, flopped on the sofa and with the television offering nothing to take my fancy, I considered ringing her. The only communication since she went had been a scrawled note of thanks – no address – on a postcard of Blackpool Tower which, judging by its yellowing corners, she'd unearthed for the purpose from the back of some drawer or other.

Maybe she could sort me out, I thought. I was certainly beginning to feel I needed it. Pulling the phone on to my lap, I dialled her number. But there was no reply. I replaced the receiver and sat for a long while staring into space.

I'd never have imagined a phone call from Gavin, whom I'd known since university days and who saw himself as hopelessly – and it was accepted between us it *was* hopelessly – in love with me, could be fortuitous. But this time it was.

Feeling the need of a breather from Cotterly – from Andrew and my own stupidity – I had, late on Monday evening, dropped a note in the post to Flora excusing myself this coming weekend. Making excuses all round, I thought as I thumped the stamp on to the top right-hand corner of the envelope.

Gavin at least was safe, and I greeted the sound of his voice on Tuesday afternoon with more than usual enthusiasm. Working as he did on some mysterious edge of the media world, he'd managed once again to get hold of a pair of complimentary theatre tickets – and on this occasion they were gold-dust ones.

I accepted his invitation with alacrity. 'Wonderful. I've been longing to see it. And I'll throw some supper together for us afterwards,' I offered in return.

I was in comfortably mellow mood the following evening as, still discussing the performance we had just been to, I transferred the lasagne I'd prepared earlier from fridge to oven and set about putting a salad together. Gavin uncorked the wine. When the phone rang, I reminded him where the glasses were and went through to answer it.

The by-now-so-familiar voice took me by surprise. 'You can't do this to me!' The lightness of Andrew's laugh had an undertone to it. 'I've been trying to get hold of you all evening.' I glanced at the answerphone. It was flashing. But before I could apologise for not having yet checked my messages he went on, 'Flora tells me you've cried off?'

I floundered. 'Hardly cried off. It wasn't a firm arrangement. I just found . . . various things I really need to catch up on this weekend.' Why wasn't I coming up with a really big lie, like some three-line-whip company reception?

'Nothing you can't cancel then?'

I tidied back a stray strand of hair. 'What do you mean?'

'My own fault for thinking it was a good idea to spring it on you – I've booked for the open-air concert at Harringdon.' Harringdon, I recalled, was a stately home in vast grounds some twenty miles south-west of Cotterly. 'Ginny,' Andrew was saying, 'thought it would be your sort of thing.'

'And hers too.' I shifted the phone to the other ear.

'Well yes, normally. But she's committed to taking the boys up to Leamington, to Jonty's parents.'

'So just you, me and Flora?'

'Actually I thought it would be nice . . . just the two of us . . .'

Through the doorway to the kitchen I could see Gavin inspecting his drink.

'Can I ring you back tomorrow? This isn't . . . I'm in the middle of cooking supper.'

'This late?'

'We've been to the theatre.'

'Oh.' There was a pause. 'Sorry. Obviously not a good time to have phoned.' Another hesitation. 'Fine. Give me a call.'

'Sorry,' I apologised to Gavin as I returned to slicing cucumber.

I went. Of course I went.

I had laughed away Gavin's pouting accusation that he had a rival. 'Dozens of them,' I countered lightly, reflecting that whatever he chose – consciously or unconsciously – to pretend about his feelings towards me, he'd run a mile if ever I gave any indication of returning them. Sad, really. He'd probably go through life the eternal bachelor; too scared ever to get involved; chasing a love, or loves, he knew – thank goodness – to be unattainable.

I found myself confiding this assessment to Andrew as, on the Saturday evening, we laid our picnic out around us. The concert was not due to start for another half an hour, but even so we had left it fairly late to secure a space to spread the rug. In the end, we'd climbed right up to just below the tree line from where we could look down over the heads of the crowd to the covered podium erected for the occasion.

Flora, bless her, unfazed by my vacillations over going down that weekend, had packed a generous basket and, having assured me earlier, while she was doing so, that sitting on hard ground for two hours or more was definitely for the young, waved us off benignly. 'I take it you're producing the champagne?' she'd instructed Andrew. He'd assured her – with amused little-boy solemnity – that it was already in the boot.

Now he popped the cork. 'So,' he said, reaching for the glasses, 'am I allowed to ask who you were gallivanting with on Wednesday? Or is it none of my business?'

It was tempting to portray Gavin as some dream man. I might well have done so with someone else. But it didn't feel right to play the tease with Andrew. Apart from anything else, I wasn't at all sure how far he was teasing me. So I told him.

'I expect you're right,' he said when I'd summed Gavin up. He offered a home-made sausage roll – Flora's goodies were more practical than delicate – and considered me quizzically.

'What's that look supposed to mean?'

'Sometimes you're very perceptive . . .'

I was confused. 'Is that a straightforward compliment, or . . . ?'

'Just an observation.'

I puzzled over the comment as Handel's *Water Music*, a little later, floated towards us. Andrew appeared totally lost in it, knees hunched, his chin resting on them. I had an urge to stroke the curve of his back where his shirt hugged it. Why, I wondered, did I find men's shoulders so irresistible? I kept my hands to myself and turned my attention to the stage.

But it didn't want to stay focused there. *Sometimes* I was very perceptive. But not always, was he implying? What was I missing; was he trying to tell me something? If so, what? Impatiently I dismissed the questions. I was reading altogether too much into a simple statement.

I'd have liked to shift my position – the ground, as Flora had anticipated, was far from soft – but felt obliged to wait for the piece to end. When it did so, Andrew turned and smiled, taking the opportunity to refill my glass.

Wandering back to the car park, with the smell of fireworks hanging in the air, I hugged my jacket tighter. Andrew, swinging the basket in one hand, slipped a warm arm about me.

We drove to the Dower House: 'There's the remains of the champagne to finish,' he pointed out.

It was strange having the house to ourselves. I felt I should be creeping around so as not to disturb those already slumbering. And there was something eerie about the boys' boots lined up just inside the back door.

'Reminds me of the time I borrowed them,' I said, pointing. An age ago and, yes, there'd only been the two of us here then too. The garden – I peered out through the kitchen window – was in total darkness now. My image, or rather the outline of it since my face was in shadow, stared back. For some reason the lack of defined features disconcerted me.

'Come on, let's take these through. ' I swivelled back. Andrew was standing there, glasses in one hand, the bottle, retrieved from the basket dumped on the side, in the other.

We settled side by side on the sofa, Andrew stretching towards the coffee table to pour. He turned to look at me as I sipped.

'Thanks for coming down,' he said.

'Thanks for persuading me.'

It was perfectly obvious, as he removed the glass from my hand and set it down, that he was going to kiss me. But it was a very light one, scarcely brushing my lips.

'I've been looking forward to doing that for a long time,' he said. He considered me for several moments more, then leaned back. 'Tell me,' and now his tone was conversational again, 'was it worth abandoning your chores for? The concert, I mean.'

I assured him it had been. We discussed the programme; compared the interpretations of this orchestra with those of others; agreed that the atmosphere more than compensated for the lack of concert hall acoustics.

Eventually I looked at my watch. 'The time! I'd better get back.'

Andrew glanced at his own. 'Too late. Flora will have bolted the door and gone to bed by now. Simpler if you stay here.'

Why I was so taken aback I don't know. I should have seen it coming, been prepared.

'Come on.' He rose to his feet and pulled me up. Automatically I responded.

Then: 'Don't worry,' he said, 'I'm not planning to seduce you. I'll go and sleep in one of the boys' beds if you like.'

If I liked. I didn't know what I'd like. 'But what will Flora say? I mean . . .'

'I don't imagine she'll say – or think – anything.'

No, she wouldn't. I saw her again, in the garden: 'It's your life. You have to sort it.' In any case, I wasn't a sixteen-year-old any more.

The carpet on the landing was jade green. On the walls – I tore my eyes away from the mesmerising colour – rural prints alternated with flower drawings . . .

Andrew's bedroom itself was typically masculine – in so far as I knew what constituted that: I had only Mark's room, other than my experience of student chaos, to compare it with. But the general impression was one of sturdy practicality. A Victorian tallboy and wardrobe, and an upholstered chair in one corner, were scattered about by evidence of sporting interests – a conglomeration of racquets, an elderly hockey stick, photographs on the wall of a rowing eight and what was presumably a school cricket team – and with seemingly hastily tidied shoes and items of clothing. A row of heavy books lined up on what had once been the mantelpiece hinted at the contents of his briefcase slung on the carpet beneath it. The bed, under the window, was a wide single, covered with a plaid rug that suggested long ownership.

Andrew drew the curtains together and then, as I stood there uncertainly, began unbuttoning my dress. 'You won't want to sleep in this,' he said. I slid it from my shoulders and eased it down, stepping out of it and dropping it on to a nearby chair. As I did so, he turned back the bed covers. 'Come on. Hop in.'

Still in my cream camisole and knickers I did so, shivering involuntarily at the coolness of the sheets and watching – there wasn't really anywhere else to look – as he pulled his shirt over his head, then unzipped his trousers and kicked them off.

'Move over.' Casually he slid in beside me, twisting to switch off the bedside lamp before easing his length alongside mine. 'Here.'

Now he had his arms around me and instinctively our legs eased together. I lay there, nestling up to him, the pulse of our breathing seeking and finding matching rhythms.

And then I realised he was asleep.

Tentatively I reached up and touched his hair. It was fine-textured but thick and my fingers slid through it without brushing his scalp.

After a while, I turned over and snuggled my back into his chest.

I was awake before him too. Stretching out a hand, I pulled the curtain open seven or eight inches, allowing the light to stream in. It glinted on the mirror propped on the tallboy opposite. In the shadow, away from the main beam, my dress lay sprawled where I'd abandoned it, the sleeve of Andrew's shirt caught against its skirt.

In sleep, his face was fully relaxed. I longed to touch the hint of stubble around his chin, to experience the roughness of it. Instead, lightly, I allowed my hand to rest on the soft hair of his chest, feeling the rise and fall beneath it.

''Morning.'

I turned my head; his eyes were open. Raising himself casually on one elbow, he leaned forward and allowed his lips to rest on mine for a few seconds before: 'Breakfast. Scrambled eggs do you?'

I dressed and joined him in the kitchen. He'd thrown open the back door and the fresh morning air contrasted with the stale warmth of the house.

'You can cook then,' I observed as I stood watching him stir a pan.

'Man of many talents, me.' He dished up. The eggs steamed gently alongside buttered toast, and I discovered I had an appetite.

When we'd finished and pushed our plates aside, he reached out and placed his hand over mine, pressing it against the hardness of the table. 'You OK?'

'Yes. Of course.' I returned his gaze.

His remained steady. 'What I'd like,' he said, 'is for us to go away somewhere together for a couple of days.'

I'd have withdrawn my hand if I could.

'Think about it. I know a great little place in Somerset.'

'When?'

'Is next weekend too soon?'

'Won't Philip need you?'

His mouth quirked. 'Is that a "yes"?'

I wished I knew.

'Come here.' His hand gripped mine even more firmly as he drew me to my feet and round the table towards him.

This time he kissed me in a way that left no room for doubt as to what was in his mind.

CHAPTER 16

Why, mid-week, was I overcome by total panic?

I had at first hesitated, on the Sunday, to tell Flora of our plans but since, predictably but nonetheless to my relief, she hadn't turned a hair when Andrew drove me round at about ten, I risked it.

Actually, what I said to her when Andrew had left – 'Tractor duty calls,' he'd grimaced – was that he'd *suggested* we spend a weekend in Somerset, the implication being, I hoped, that I hadn't yet agreed.

Which in a way was true. When does a failure to say no become a yes?

Flora, down on her hands and knees adjusting the wire-netting at the edge of the chicken run, looked up. 'And?'

'I just thought I'd mention it.'

Flora, task completed, heaved herself to her feet.

'Well? What do you think?' I prodded as we negotiated the path back between the vegetables. I waited while she inspected the runner beans.

'I think,' she said, having satisfied herself that they were coming along well, 'that you'll probably enjoy it.'

When does lack of disapproval constitute approval? At least I'd been open with her; more to the point, it occurred to me, had been able to be up-front with her. Where Mark was concerned, I'd always been very circumspect in discussing our relationship with Mother. And I hadn't been close enough to my father to test the water with him. I found myself looking up at the sky as though maybe he was up there somewhere, observing. No thunderstorm broke so I chose to believe he was smiling.

But London's leaden skies, as I hunched home through summer drizzle a few days later, undermined my confidence. 'You're being ridiculous,' I tried telling myself as I shook the damp from my coat and hung it to dry from the shower rail. 'It's what you want, isn't it?'

Elspeth, over the phone half an hour later, made the same point.

I had managed to get through to her at last. After the usual long-time-no-sees, how-are-yous, I'd poured out the story of events since her visit.

'But I thought,' she said, bemused, 'that's what you wanted.'

'It is. I think.'

'Then buy yourself some sexy underwear and go for it.'

'Yes, but . . .'

I heard her sigh at the other end of the line. 'OK, so what's the problem?'

'I don't know,' I wailed, all my insecurities reasserting themselves.

'Look,' she said. 'The man's drop-dead gorgeous, you've been after his body –' I winced at her one-track focus – 'for ages, and what's more it now turns out he's as free as the air.'

'Maybe that's the trouble,' I heard myself say miserably.

'What!' I could practically hear her brain whizzing. Mine, meanwhile, seemed stuck in neutral.

'You mean you'd be happier having an affair with him if he were still married?'

'Not "still". He never was.'

She brushed the correction aside impatiently. 'You know what I mean.'

'It's beyond me . . .' Her voice broke into my paralysis. 'I thought it was moral scruples holding you back?'

'It was.'

'Carrie . . .' Her exasperation was almost tangible.

'Well I thought it was.' Maybe it had just been an excuse; I remembered my assessment of Gavin.

Elspeth assumed a calmly authoritative tone. 'Just go. Have a ball –' she giggled briefly – 'in more ways than one. And stop making such a mountain out of it.'

'You're right,' I said.

I rang Andrew and confirmed I could leave work early on Friday.

As the mid-afternoon train to Taunton settled into

its steady rhythm, a fatalistic calm overcame me – that sense of a journey begun from which there was no turning back. I looked for Andrew as I alighted around six. He waved as he disengaged himself from helping an elderly woman sort out the mechanics of the left-luggage lockers.

'Don't know why they always pick on me,' he said, giving me a quick hug and taking my bag.

We drove north out of the town, through the initially flat surrounds and up on to the Quantock hills. The cooler, fresher air blowing into the car streamed across the side of my face and hair. I wound the window up a little and pulled out a pack of cigarettes.

'Not yet,' said Andrew.

He slowed and drew off the road, the sills of the Volvo scraping gently against the heather. The smell of it as we got out was sweet and earthy.

We walked up a steepish track, the stone chippings rough beneath our feet. A handful of others, some strollers, some anoraked walkers with backpacks, dotted the hillside. But the paths were splayed out so that we only passed within speaking distance of one couple who returned, with a courteous nod of the head, Andrew's ritual 'Good evening'.

At the top, we stopped and looked down across the landscape stretching right around us. Andrew positioned himself behind me, his body against mine, his arms folded round me. 'Isn't it glorious?' he said. Slowly he turned me through the panorama of the Bristol Channel – the coast of Wales blurred but discernible through the opaque light of early evening – across the smoothly curved hills of the Brendons and the Blackdowns, on over the gentle undulations of the Somerset–Avon borders, and back again to the far-off glint of dipping sun on water. We stood there for a while. Not speaking. Close. Then he let his arms drop and we wandered back to the car.

'Now you can have a cigarette,' he said.

'I'm glad you took me up there straightaway,' I said, an hour and a half or so later.

We were having dinner in the panelled dining room of the renovated manor house which had turned itself into a small hotel. It was tucked against the hillside, back from one of those narrow roads running down to the vale, and we had arrived with just enough time to shower and change.

Our table allowed a view through the mullioned windows across the stretch of fields to the ridge beyond, now grey in the almost faded light. 'Tomorrow,' said Andrew, pointing, 'we'll walk right across there.' He outlined the route he planned, identifying it by names with which he was clearly familiar – something or other stone, the trig. point at . . ., drop down to the pub at wherever for lunch . . .

'You love this area, don't you?' I said.

'It's my retreat. Always has been. Usually I just

drive over for the day. Then I simply walk; imagine I'm Coleridge or Wordsworth . . .'

'I didn't know there was a poet in you.'

He raised an eyebrow and smiled. 'Call me an incurable romantic.'

And one, it became clear to me over the next two days – as he headed confidently along the often narrow criss-crossing tracks, forking unerringly left or right – who knew every twist and turn of this particular stretch of countryside . . .

Just as equally, I discovered that night, he knew his way around a woman's body.

Lying naked with him in the huge soft bed – why for crying out loud did I choose, at this moment, to let it remind me of Flora's? – I responded to his touch. Yet even as his hands explored, I felt myself tightening. Knowing he couldn't help but be aware of it only made it worse.

'Don't you dare tell me to relax,' I said.

I sensed him grinning beside me. 'I wouldn't dream of it.'

Then he raised himself on one elbow, his expression – caught by the moonlight hovering between the drawn-back curtains – one of careful, amused neutrality. 'I didn't know I was dealing with a virgin.'

'You're not.' Indignantly.

'A reconstituted one, then.'

'Sod you!' But I was laughing too.

And suddenly what we were doing was fun – pleasurable fun; but with an underlying tenderness on Andrew's part which raised it above the merely playful.

And if in the course of it he felt any sense of urgency, he disguised it; until the moment when he moved on top of me, and by then mine was as great as his.

As my return train on Sunday evening pulled heavily out of the station and settled down to its steady throb, images – like a series of photographic slides projected on a screen – flashed in indiscriminate succession across my mind: Andrew striding ahead along some narrow path trodden around a hillside; strolling hand in hand with me between avenues of beeches; steadying me down steep slopes; lazing idyllically beside me amongst the heather. So still we'd lain on one occasion that a group of deer had ventured close. Alerted by a rustle, I detected at first only a pair of deep brown eyes and pricked ears peering over the rise. I sat up, slowly, uncertain what I was seeing.

I shook Andrew gently. 'Look.'

Four or five of them, delicate, curious, were paused, regarding us. Then they cantered away, stopping once to look back before disappearing into the fold of the valley. We saw others at a distance, always in groups, leaping at speed. In contrast, the wild ponies showed no concern at our presence, cropping peacefully as we passed within feet of them.

Civilisation intruded from time to time in the

form of the occasional Land Rover lurching across the landscape or, even more incongruously, a noisy spluttering motorbike; but each was soon gone and the countryside returned to its unspoilt tranquillity.

My personal slide show switched back to the hotel: that first morning, awakening to a blanket of mist extending an eerie dampness right up to the windows; Andrew teasing away my disappointment. 'Good,' he'd said. 'No rush to go down to breakfast.' And this time his love-making was intense and passionate.

Memory lingered; then shifted to the dining room: tables being cleared of already departed guests' crockery and crumbs; steaming coffee; Andrew tucking into fried bacon, eggs, tomatoes, mushrooms, while I settled for a boiled egg and toast. The sun had by now broken through and it caught on his hair as he lifted his cup and, holding it in both hands, stared unwaveringly across it at me.

'Don't,' I'd begged, aware of the waitress discreetly gathering up tablecloths. 'You're making me self-conscious.'

The Inter-City rocked across points and I smiled to myself, surreptitiously. The woman sitting opposite looked up from her book and checked her watch. 'We must be approaching Reading,' she suggested. I nodded agreement.

Half an hour later we drew into Paddington. I hesitated only a moment before heading for the taxi rank. The weekend deserved to be finished in style.

Strange, I thought, as I lounged back in the cab's depths, aware yet not aware of the lights and buildings without, how the rest of the world can remain so unaffected by one's own change of spirit. By rights, pedestrians should be dancing in the streets, horns trumpeting *Gloriana* rather than blaring warnings, street lamps flashing Technicolor.

I hurried up the grey stairs between off-white walls to the flat. Scarcely had I switched on the lights before the phone rang.

'Hi.' Warmth.

'Hi.'

'Just checking you got back safely.'

'Of course. But yes, thanks, no problem.'

'OK. Goodnight, then.'

'Goodnight.'

I replaced the receiver and stood staring at Father's painting hanging on the wall in front of me. 'Yes,' I confirmed. 'Yes.'

Then I made coffee and went to bed.

I tackled problems at work next day with renewed energy. And there were plenty of them as the backwash from this year's operations combined with the flood tide of next year's planning.

I even had cheerfulness to spare when Mother rang to remind me I'd suggested lunch.

'But not this week,' I pleaded looking round at the paper littering my desk and figures flickering on the computer screen.

We settled for the following Wednesday. 'Things should be calmer by then.'

'Unless of course,' a plaintive note crept into my mother's voice, 'you feel like coming and spending the weekend at home?'

'Mother, you'll *love* a trip to the West End. It'll be perfect timing: the crowds will have gone and you'll be able to take first pick of the stores' new winter stock.'

Martin from Sales came in just as I replaced the receiver 'You look happy,' he observed, almost accusingly. 'What's your excuse?' I laughed and offloaded a couple of files into his arms in return for those he dumped on me.

Elspeth inevitably was agog when I finally got round to punching out her number. 'Well?'

'Great,' I confirmed. 'Thanks for giving me a shove.'

'So he came up to expectations?' As ever, she was unable to resist the sexual innuendo.

I played along. 'Yes. And how.'

She mooned with me over the deer and the ponies – 'how sweet' – before reverting to practicalities. 'So when are you seeing him again?'

'This weekend of course. I'm going down to Cotterly.'

'Ooh. Lots of lovely hay to roll in.'

'Now there's a thought.' Laughing.

'My God, you're a different woman. I approve of this man. When do I get to meet him?'

Clare demanded an answer to much the same

question when I spoke to her. 'Don't feel like coming sailing again, do you?' she'd rung to suggest.

'Can't,' I said thankfully, recalling my previous experience. 'I'm off to the West Country again.'

'You've got a man down there.'

I admitted it contentedly.

'You dark horse, you. How long has this been going on?'

I gave her a thumb-nail resumé – though omitting any mention of Flora.

'Well drag him up to London. I must,' she said, referring implicitly to my lack of anything but the most fleeting male involvement over the last couple of years, 'inspect this phenomenon.'

I gave the required promise but afterwards sat tapping my fingers on the chair arm, reflecting on the complications of allowing my two worlds to merge. I almost rang Clare back to warn her not to mention Andrew to her mother lest – in some fantasy scenario in Sainsbury's – word of his existence should get back to mine. But then Clare, if I did so, would probe for explanations . . . Better to let things ride lest I open up what could develop into a yawning chasm.

Little did I know that, without any help from Clare, that particular ground was, in any case, about to start rumbling.

CHAPTER 17

Circumstances at Cotterly were not, Andrew and I both accepted, conducive to passionate activity. I stayed at Wood Edge, and he and I contented ourselves, for the most part, with goodnight embraces in the shadow of Flora's buddleia – 'Very third form,' he commented, 'but never mind' – before he departed to his own bed at the Dower House.

Not that we attempted to hide the change in our relationship entirely. If I'd thought that maybe we should do so, Andrew made it clear he had no such intention, greeting me in Flora's kitchen and under her enigmatic eye with an obviously delighted hug. At the cricket ground too – it was the important bank holiday return match against Chadham which had decreed, any other considerations apart, our, or anyway Andrew's, presence there – he showed no inhibition, steering me around possessively. Ginny responded warmly to the new situation, and even Philip deigned to extend a muttered 'Hi' as he strode past.

But that was hardly sufficient to prevent our eagerly anticipating another opportunity to be alone together. Next weekend, we agreed, Andrew would come up to the flat.

I mentioned this to Flora over breakfast on Monday morning. She was spreading marmalade on a slice of toast. 'You know,' I added, 'don't you, that I *am* aware that I've been treating you a bit like a hotel recently?' I gave a little grimace of apology.

The corners of her mouth twitched. 'Just a touch maybe.'

'I'm sorry. I've been more than a little self-absorbed, haven't I?'

She gave a hint of a smile. 'Oh? I thought it was Andrew your attention was fixed on?'

I grinned back. 'I suppose it comes to much the same thing. Anyway – ' I didn't give her a chance to interrupt – 'I just wanted you to know I appreciate it. Everything.'

Flora picked up her cup and stared deep into it. Then she looked up and directly at me. 'It's my pleasure having you here.'

Those eyes, which at times had bored uncomfortably into me, were now softer than I'd ever known them. They reminded me of the deer, regarding me over the heather. Impulsively I pushed my chair back, rose and, skirting round the table, leaned over and hugged her. 'Oh, Flora,' I told her, 'you are lovely.'

She reached up and patted my arm. 'You're your father's daughter,' she said simply. Then she disengaged herself, got up, and started clearing away the dishes.

Later, on the way back to London, I thought about that remark of hers. It had so many inter-pretations . . . and I liked them all.

I was still in a first-rate mood when I sought Mother out in Dickins & Jones' restaurant. She had already settled herself at a central table from where she could watch for my arrival, and was sur-rounded by Oxford and Regent Street carrier bags. She lifted her cheek to accept my greeting.

'Had a successful morning, then,' I observed as I sat down.

'Wonderful. And I've just seen a marvellous little dress downstairs. A red one. Maybe we can look at it on the way out?'

'Good idea.' I surveyed her mustard two-piece with the toning yellow and black patterned scarf tucked in at the neck. 'I'm glad you're feeling able to break out into bright colours again,' I approved.

'You don't think it's too soon?' She reminded me for a moment of a rather anxious hen.

'Of course not.'

Reassured, she sank back and we ordered. As we ate, she chatted on, just – I thought – as she always had done over those bland, emotionless meals with Father. I listened patiently, attempting to pay con-structive attention to the diary of her day-to-day events.

'But of course,' she said suddenly and unex-pectedly, 'you're not interested in any of this.'

'Mo . . . ther.'

'You have your career to think about, I do realise—'

'You're being unfair.' Though I knew she wasn't.

She reached into her bag and extracted a tissue. Delicately she dabbed at her nose.

'Even so, that doesn't explain . . .' Her tone became plaintive. 'You haven't been home for ages. The garden's looking lovely; I'd hoped . . .' She straightened. 'But that's not the point.' She stared at me accusingly. 'There's something going on. I know there is.'

'No—'

'You can't fool me. Why all the secretiveness about what you're doing at weekends? You're . . . involved with some man, aren't you? And if you can't tell me about it – ' her voice rose in triumph – 'it can only be because he's married and it's some surreptitious affair you're having.' She'd clearly spent time arriving at this conclusion.

Relief – or partial relief – caused me to laugh. That and the irony of the half truth.

'No, Mother, I promise you . . .'

I'd expected her to be reassured. But she wasn't. It was as though she were speaking from some pre-determined script and wasn't about to be deflected.

'I don't believe you. It *is* a man, isn't it?'

I stared at her. Her face was pale.

'OK,' I compromised. 'Yes, there is a man, but—'

'I knew it!' She glared at me, and delivered the coup de grâce I realised, in a flash of clarity, she'd been working up to: 'You're just,' she pronounced, 'like your father.'

The clink of knives and forks and the burr of normal conversation from other tables accentuated the silence as I took in Mother's remark.

'Do you realise,' I said at last, surprising myself by my calmness, 'that's the first time you've referred to . . . Flora . . . since . . . well, since the very beginning?'

Mother dropped her gaze, discovering a need to adjust her napkin. 'It was better not to.'

'How was it better?'

'I really don't think we should talk about it.'

'I think we should. Tell me, what do you know about her?'

'That tart!'

I bit my tongue. 'Are you so sure?'

'What else could she be? All your father wanted was – ' she gave a shrug of distaste – 'well, you know.' She turned on me. 'And I suppose that's all you're after too. Your generation with your high-flying careers and liberated ideas. You think you can have it all, think you're so clever . . .'

'I can't believe – ' I could hear an evenness in my tone as I ignored her attack – 'that was all Father thought of.'

'Oh, can't you?' Her voice was rising again.

'In that case,' I said, putting to her the question that had teased me so much recently, 'why did you choose to stay married to him? Why didn't you divorce him?'

'And let him get away with it!'

I looked at her.

'Anyway, there was you to think of. I wasn't going to let you anywhere near that . . . female.'

'You certainly managed to prevent that.'

I leaned back to allow our plates to be removed. Mother waved away the dessert menu. 'Just coffee,' she instructed.

I downed mine as quickly as I could.

'This man . . . ?' said Mother.

'He's not married. And that,' firmly, 'is all I'm going to tell you about him at the moment.'

Mother looked hurt. 'I'm only concerned for your welfare.'

'I must be getting back.' I gathered up my things. 'I'll settle up,' I said, and departed.

I wondered afterwards whether she'd bought the red dress.

I went over the conversation as I lay in my bath that night. Only concerned for my welfare! That's what she'd always led me to believe. It just didn't ring true any more; hadn't done for some time, I realised. Probably why I'd been able to stand up to her; and why – it dawned on me now – I felt no guilt at having done so.

I submerged, allowed my hair to float, felt the water rise over my ears, cheeks, eyes, nose. I sat up again and reached for the soap. I foamed it over my legs, arms, shoulders, body, then slithered down into the warmth once more and lay there, contemplating.

I'd always done – and been – what she wanted. Now I was branching out. And she didn't like it. Well, tough.

Wouldn't let me near 'that female', wouldn't she? But Father had known . . . had cared . . . I saw again the parcel of books; his thinned face. 'Return them to Flora. Yourself. Please.' That final surge of effort on my behalf. Although I could wish he were here, now, to advise how to extricate myself from the complications it had led to.

I got out of the bath, rinsing off under the shower as I did so, and towelled. The mirror over the basin was steamed up. I wiped a window in it and stood staring at what I could see. Down to waist level only. I thought of Andrew, his hands travelling over me; except that for a fleeting moment what I saw, in my mentally enhanced reflection, were not his hands but my father's. Appalled, I thrust off the fantasy and hurriedly threw on a dressing gown.

Later, I managed to laugh. No doubt Freud would have read something into it; I was damned if I was going to. My more down-to-earth concern, nagging intermittently over the next few days, was whether Mother, if I let her, might somehow mess up my relationship with Andrew. His connection with Flora, should it ever come out, was the obvious reason to keep my guard up, yet instinctively not the only one.

Even so, my wariness didn't extend to supposing she'd go so far as to fall off a ladder in order to put a spoke in my wheel.

* * *

It was a week to the day after our lunch together that her local hospital rang. Over the intervening weekend, in the shelter of Andrew's good humour, I'd brushed my misgivings aside. On the Saturday morning I'd dragged him round the Portobello market which, despite his spending time in London, he'd never visited, and in the afternoon we strolled through Hyde Park. It was one of those days when showers threaten but, apart from a few tentative drops now and again, never quite materialise. Nonetheless, a September edge to the wind reminded that summer was effectively over. Glad of our jackets, we lounged for a time on the bank of the Serpentine, then cut across the grass to Speakers' Corner and wandered between the orators before hailing a taxi home.

At lunchtime on Sunday, after a second heady night in bed, we met Clare and Leo for a drink. I'd been apprehensive about it, but Andrew skilfully fielded any conversation that could have led to Flora. 'Dishy,' Clare pronounced when she rang me afterwards for a post mortem, 'and didn't he and Leo get on well?' I remarked that it was pretty much guaranteed when two guys discover a mutual passion for rugby. 'Men!' we laughed.

The call on Wednesday jolted me from my sense of well-being. It came late in the afternoon, at that point when I was assessing how much I could hope to deal with before packing up for the day and what would have to be left until tomorrow. I was irritated at being thwarted in the completion of one task by repeated apologies from a secretary that the person I needed to speak to was 'still in a meeting'. Knowing him, more likely taking an extended lunch in some hotel bedroom, I thought viciously.

'This is the Accident and Emergency Department,' a voice announced.

My pencil automatically completed the word I was writing, then held itself poised above the reminder note I'd been jotting.

'We have your mother here.' Then, swiftly reassuring: 'Nothing too serious.'

An exchange of questions and answers elicited the information that she'd fallen, and a cautious diagnosis that she'd probably only sprained a ligament in her knee. They wouldn't know until someone had a chance to look at it next day. But yes, since she'd banged her head in the process, they'd certainly be keeping her in overnight. 'Just to be on the safe side.'

'I'd better come down and see her,' I said.

There was sufficient pause to suggest it wasn't absolutely essential before: 'I think she'd probably appreciate it, if you can.'

Promptly at five-thirty, I made my way to Waterloo. I'd debated whether to go back to Fulham and get the car, but decided that since the hospital was only five minutes' walk from the station it wasn't worth the rush-hour hassle. As we clattered towards Surbiton and beyond, I reflected on my previous rail journey, less than three weeks ago, and the contrast in my destination.

By the time I arrived, Mother had been moved to a ward. She sat propped up in a hospital nightie, looking pale beneath the remains of her make-up. There was a noticeable bruise on the side of her head.

'Well,' I said, over jolly, 'what have you been up to?'

A large nurse turned from adjusting the covers on the next bed and busied herself puffing Mother's pillows. 'We've been climbing up ladders when we shouldn't, haven't we?'

'It was only the stepladder. There was a blockage in the garage guttering . . .'

I almost said, shades of Father, 'You should have waited and let me do it.' Then remembered – guiltily – that I'd made it clear I wouldn't be down for a while. 'Why didn't you pop next door and ask Jack Webb?' I substituted.

'I should have done.' She reached out and clutched my hand. 'I'm so sorry.'

'Well, there we are. We all live and learn.' The nurse, satisfied, turned away. I watched her move across the ward, a bustling Florence Nightingale dispensing tolerant maternal reprimand at every bed.

'What actually happened?'

Mother explained happily.

'. . . luckily Mrs Mackenzie was walking that Pekinese of hers – I was really quite dazed, you see . . . think maybe I knocked myself out – and she called an ambulance. Of course it caused quite a stir in the Avenue . . .' Mother perked up no end as she recalled the collection of neighbours gathering round solicitously as she was stretchered on board.

'I expect it's very painful?'

Mother touched her forehead and winced.

'And your knee.'

She pulled aside the bed covers to show me how swollen it was. 'Of course, I'm afraid I'm going to be a terrible nuisance. I shan't be able to move around much for weeks. They've told me so.'

I soothed away her apology. No need to concern herself. We'd sort out help during the week and naturally I'd come down at weekends.

'Oh, but you have so much on these days.'

'It's OK.' I softened the unintentional edge in my response: 'Just one of those things. After all,' I laughed, hoping it didn't sound as mirthless as it felt, 'you hardly did it on purpose.'

I directed her attention to more immediate practical matters, apologising for my short-sightedness in not bringing the car. Gallantly she insisted she could manage with the minimum and I caught the hospital shop just as they were about to lower the shutter. Toothbrush, toothpaste, hairbrush, face cream, I ticked off; and for good measure some light reading.

'Lemon barley?' suggested the volunteer helper.

I hesitated. 'Why not.' Though why Mother should want it here when she never drank squash at home . . . Still; all part of the hospital ritual. One might as well conform.

Mother was duly appreciative when I reappeared, and expressed contentment with my reassurance that I'd ring next day to monitor progress. 'Though I should be grateful,' she said, apparently in all innocence, as I gathered up my bag and jacket, 'if you'd just check the house before you go back to London.'

'But . . .' I suppressed a sigh. 'OK. Fine.'

Back at the house a taxi ride later, I stowed the abandoned stepladder in the garage, then toured the empty rooms, ensuring all the windows were firmly latched. Everything was, as I knew it would be, firmly in its place – apart from a used cup and saucer on the draining board. I rinsed and dried them while waiting for the kettle to boil for coffee. It was already gone nine, and I hadn't eaten. I found some Edam and tomatoes in the fridge and made myself a sandwich. My bed, as always, was made up. No point, I decided, in trekking back to London tonight.

I slumped down in a sitting-room chair with what was going to have to pass for supper, aware as I munched of odd creaks and occasional gurgles in the water system I'd never noticed before. But then this was the first time I'd been alone in the house – anyway in the evening or at night. I switched on the fire, more for the companionship of its flicker and gradually reddening glow than out of any real need to supplement the central heating.

Even so, I suddenly felt despondently isolated.

So much for my expectations for the coming week-end. I had planned with Andrew that he'd come up to London again, that maybe we'd drive out to some stately home or other, go to a bar or a club in the evening perhaps – someone at work had mentioned a new one just off Shaftesbury Avenue. It had been left vague – on the assumption that time was our own. That easiness was now placed on hold; and, it seemed, would remain so for some time to come.

I supposed I'd better warn him. Reaching for the phone, I dialled his number. But it wasn't either he or Ginny who answered.

'Flora?' I queried, the unexpected making me uncertain.

'Uh, huh.'

She was sitting in with the boys, she explained. Andrew and Ginny were out to dinner with friends.

It was not the moment to remind me there were other people in Andrew's life. I even had to jerk myself around to the re-recognition that Ginny was his sister, nothing more.

'You sound disappointed.'

'It was just that I wanted to explain to him . . .' Matter-of-fact to start with; then spilling out.

'Very inconvenient of her,' observed Flora when I'd finished. I imagined her face and dry smile. 'I expect you've decided she did it deliberately?'

I laughed, relaxing. 'I wouldn't put it past her.'

If Flora was raising an eyebrow, I couldn't see it.

'So will you ring Andrew tomorrow, or shall I pass on a message?'

'You could tell him I called,' I said. 'Give him the gist.'

I put the phone down and leaned towards the friendliness of the fire. I could almost feel Flora in the room with me. If I turned my head, she would be sitting there on the sofa, resting comfortably, her hands folded softly in her lap. I stared into the flames for as long as the sensation lasted. Even when I roused myself at last and got up, the sense didn't totally desert me.

For a moment when I woke I was confused by the wallpaper, the sprigs on it dancing before my still unfocused eyes. I reached out a hand to silence the buzz of the alarm and found I had turned the wrong way; the bedside table was on the opposite side. Beyond it – I was now fully awake – my china-headed doll, whose clothes Mother had so meticulously washed and pressed, stared back at me. The eyes had once been deep blue in a rose-cheeked face; now the glaze had faded and cracked, giving her a weary look.

My grandmother – that is to say Father's mother – had given her to me. 'I used to play with her when I was a little girl,' she'd told me.

I had been over-awed; Mother impressed. 'You take great care of it,' she'd admonished me.

Grandma had chuckled: 'Yes, but not so much that you can't enjoy her.'

In a way I was surprised that Mother continued to give prominence, in her tidying and reorganisation of my room, to a gift from Father's side of the family. Yet in another way, not. Father's solid professional background had been for her a conflicting source of both pride and envy. While bemused by many of their attitudes and regularly disparaging them within the privacy of the family – 'those dreadful old chairs, the rows of musty books, that wilderness of a garden' – nonetheless she would lose no opportunity to mention outside it 'my father-in-law, a retired professor, you know'. With studious offhandedness – I recalled from my childhood – she would refer to 'their place in the country' as though it were some aristocratic family seat. I'd always regarded Mother's . . . pretentiousness, you could only call it, as one of her foibles. Now I cringed in hindsighted embarrassment.

Why, I wondered, had Father married her? She'd certainly been very pretty, beautiful even – indeed, she was still an extremely good-looking woman – and an efficient home-maker. No doubt about it, she could certainly cook. But what about his other appetites; and I wasn't just meaning . . . in deference to her, I found myself, even in my own head, taking refuge in the euphemism 'marital bed'. I guessed all that had stopped years ago. Maybe long before Flora? Who could tell.

It was far from being only that, though. Mother wouldn't even have recognised, let alone understood, his other needs – the stimulation of companionable discussion, the shared enjoyment of music, poetry, art. It wasn't that she was unintelligent; merely blinkered. And it was just at that point when I might have begun to be able to offer him such companionship . . . Maybe – the thought skimmed almost unread across my mind – she preferred him to find that with Flora than with me.

In the distance a church clock was striking. Reminded of the time, I threw back the bed covers, and was out of the house within twenty minutes. Who'd be a commuter? I should have called the hospital; I'd do so as soon as I arrived at the office.

When I rang a second time towards the end of the afternoon, they confirmed the damage to her knee was no more than a sprain. But they were – to my relief – willing to keep her in a second night when I pleaded the predicament of my job commitments. I relaxed, and on my way back to the flat made a mental list of things I needed to do that evening.

The light on the answerphone was flashing when I walked into the flat. It was Andrew. He'd tried to get me at work, he said, but . . . True, I'd been in and out of meetings all day. He was sorry to hear about my mother; he hoped she was all right.

I poured myself a hefty gin and settled down with it before returning his call. I gave him a quick run-down of the situation. 'She's going to be on crutches for several weeks. I'll just have to go down at weekends and give a hand.'

'I suppose now – ' whimsically – 'isn't the moment to introduce myself?'

'No.'

'You're probably right. Not when she's got a pair of sticks handy to clout me with.'

I laughed.

Andrew assumed a self-mocking tone. 'I think I hate her.'

'Join the club.'

There was a surprised silence at the other end of the line. My response jolted me too. For a moment I had an image of Andrew, at ease in his garden that first time, looking up into the chestnut. 'I hadn't realised,' he'd said of my father, 'how angry you are with him.' And now with Mother?

'Cheer up.' He'd recovered and was speaking again. 'I'll just have to find an excuse to come up mid-week.'

Comforted by the prospect, I washed my hair and started packing a bag. At least I might have the chance to catch up on some reading.

Ticking off my list, I tried ringing Leah – I should have done so yesterday – but there was no answer.

CHAPTER 18

I tried hard to remember, as I fetched and carried for Mother, that my incarceration with her was not the result of some devious plan to prevent me being with Andrew; and that, moreover, she was genuinely in pain. It was tough going at times, but I fixed a smile on my face and made a conscious effort not to allow her repeated apologies – which served more as reminders of her dependence – to irritate me. After a while, both became less forced as though the outward show of cheerfulness actually diffused, in part at least, the resentment it was covering.

With the aid of a nurse and a hospital porter, I'd eased Mother into the back of the car on Friday evening, feeding the crutches into the well as she settled her leg across the seat. 'Now make sure you don't put any weight on it,' she was instructed. Smiling complacently in my direction, she assured them she'd rest it. 'After all, my daughter's here to look after me.'

Getting her out at the other end was more of a problem. In the end I summoned help from next door and together, amid a mass of contradictory instructions, we manoeuvred her into the house and on to the sofa.

I brewed tea while Mother held court. 'Of course,' she was pointing out as I re-appeared with a tray, 'I can't see how I'm going to get up the stairs.' I supposed I should have anticipated the difficulty.

Meg Webb took over. By the time the spare-room divan had been bumped down to the dining room, the table lifted to one side to make space, and eager helpers departed, it was already half past eight. Mother feigned little interest in food.

'Well, I'm starving,' I insisted. And no doubt Mother should be grateful, I thought, as I returned from fetching a take-away for us both, that I hadn't taken her at her word.

Later I steadied her to the downstairs cloakroom to which I'd already transferred her toiletries, and hovered outside the door. The sounds of her struggling with her crutches mingled with those of the cistern flushing and taps being run.

There was a thud, dulled by the carpeting.

'Are you all right?'

'I've dropped a jar.'

One of those heavy glass ones by the sound of it.

'Don't worry, I'll pick it up.'

She became more adept at moving around as the weekend progressed; particularly after I'd heaved and shoved furniture to give her clearer passage.

I contacted a home-help agency, whose number

I'd managed to obtain from the local surgery. Yes – to my relief – they could arrange for one of their 'girls' to come in each day. I jotted down details and handed them to Mother. Later, as I pushed a trolley round the supermarket, stocking up with ready-meals, it occurred to me to wonder why she hadn't made the calls herself. It wasn't as though she'd lost her wits or her voice.

'Why don't you ring Leah?' I suggested on my return, recalling that I still hadn't managed to get through to her.

'They've gone to Brittany for a fortnight; not due back till next Saturday.'

'Really?' Mentally, I registered that Uncle Harold's tomatoes must be over for Leah to have succeeded in dragging him away; also that it cut off the only possible source of reprieve from next weekend's duty.

By Sunday, the novelty for Mother of reclining on the sofa – relieved though it was by a string of lengthy phone calls advising all and sundry that she was, so regrettably, out of action – was beginning to wear off. She lumbered after me into the kitchen to supervise my preparation of lunch.

'You never were very domesticated,' she observed as I opted for the easy way of chopping carrots – into circles rather than the appetising slivers she would have created.

'True,' I conceded. I made a joke of it. 'But then, I couldn't possibly hope to compete with you.'

Mother frowned, ignoring my comment. 'Spent

far too much time with your head in books.'

'Oh, come on . . .' I flipped the saucepan on to the stove, shook in salt.

'You'll never catch a husband if you can't cook.'

'Is that how you caught Dad?' It was out before I'd considered.

She heard it as repartee only. 'He certainly appreciated my culinary skills.'

I didn't doubt he had. Though I experienced no difficulty visualising him tucking into Flora's sturdy meals either. The plain roast I was about to serve up – plenty of cold meat left over for Mother tomorrow – was more akin to what he'd become used to at Cotterly than here.

I opened the oven door and peered in. The meat was, in my view, sizzling satisfactorily. Mother's face registered doubt that my cursory check could be sufficient.

'Right,' I said. 'We've time for a drink.' I preceded her and poured as she negotiated herself back to the sitting room. I adjusted an occasional table at her elbow. 'Cheers,' I encouraged.

It wasn't until after we'd eaten – from trays on our laps – that she got around to what was really on her mind. She adjusted her leg, supporting it with both hands as she did so, and smoothed her skirt down over it.

'This man you're seeing . . .'

Mentally I sat up, on guard.

'. . . aren't you going to tell me anything more about him?'

'There's nothing to tell.' I felt much as I had done as a child when parental enquiries about some private quarrel in the playground demanded self-protective stone-walling.

She pressed.

I gave in at last. 'OK, he's thirty-three, he's a solicitor.' Then in a defiant rush: 'Single, heterosexual, and as far as I know has no convictions for either murder or rape.'

Mother's eyebrows jerked primly upwards. 'I wasn't suggesting—'

'Good.'

'And does he have a name?' She'd recovered.

Schoolgirl again; resentful; and at the same time irritated: 'Andrew.'

'Andrew what?'

'For heaven's sake, Mother, you'll be asking me next what his father does.'

'My, we are cross.'

Yes. And all the more so for letting her rile me.

She allowed me time to calm down.

'So how did you meet him?' Her sweet reasonableness was all the more threatening, the temptation to fling the truth in her face almost overwhelming.

But not quite. I thought frantically, resorting to fabrication. 'Through work.' That surely was innocent enough.

She opened her mouth to probe further.

'For crying out loud, Mother, will you stop cross-examining me?' I got up. 'How about some coffee?'

As I made for the door, her complaining tone pursued me. 'I just don't understand the need to be so secretive.'

I switched on the percolator and stared out through the kitchen window. She'd been right, the garden was looking lovely – a disciplined mass of early autumn colours. Next door, the other side from the Webbs, Mr Potter's head was just visible above the hedge. The click of his shears was almost – though jarringly not quite – in synch with the bubble of the gradually darkening coffee. Somewhere a lawnmower was humming. I wasn't sure whether the ordinariness, the predictability of it all, was comforting or confining.

Attempting conciliation when I rejoined Mother, I picked up my parents' wedding photograph. 'You've never told me,' I invited, 'how you and Father met.'

Mother demurred. 'It's such a long time ago. You wouldn't be interested.'

I teased it out of her piecemeal: his firm's annual dinner; he, a junior partner overseeing the arrangements; she, as assistant to the catering manager at the hotel they'd chosen, deputed to agree the menu with him. Somehow, since by the time they'd finished discussing it in the bar she was off duty, they'd moved on to the dining room. 'To do some advance sampling, he said – and insisted I join him. I was,' her expression challenged me and her hand went up to titivate her hair, 'more than . . . averagely attractive in those days.'

'You still are.'

'You think so?' Mother preened.

Don't you dare, I thought, say it's a pity I haven't inherited your looks. She had done once. It had taken me a long time – had I yet? – to get over the image of myself as a gawky teenager.

'He complimented the hotel food. I said I could do even better.' She gave a girlish trill. 'So he invited me round to his flat to prove it. I keep telling you, the way to a man's heart . . .'

I could just imagine the sort of cynical witticism with which Elspeth would have greeted that comment.

'We were married less than six months later. Look.' She picked up the photograph I'd put down on the coffee table and summoned me to study it with her. 'Such a beautiful dress; and my bouquet – a mass of Easter roses, with . . .' She listed, largely from memory now the detail was faded, the various additional flowers that had gone into its creation.

'Father looks pretty good too.'

The irony was lost on her. 'Yes he does, doesn't he. Such a handsome man. And so much more mature than some of the boys I'd been out with. All my friends envied me.'

'So when,' her determination as she turned her attention back from the memories was irrepressible, 'are you bringing this Andrew to meet me?'

'Mother.' Exasperated. 'If you're anticipating wedding bells, forget it. I'm not thinking in those terms – about him or anyone else. Marriage isn't the be-all and end-all.'

She looked affronted. 'Marriage is everything, and you'd do well to remember that. Why,' she demanded, 'do you think I put up with—' She broke off.

I held my tongue, waited.

'I'd made my marriage vows. In church,' she added self-righteously.

And he his, I thought.

'If your father bent them a little . . .' She began to look flustered. 'Men have different needs . . .'

I let her escape; passed the *TV Times*, flicked on the set. 'I think I might go for a walk,' I said.

Three houses down, I was waylaid by Mrs Mackenzie. Mother was doing fine, I assured her. Yes, if she could 'pop in' now and then, Mother would certainly appreciate it. 'And I'd be very grateful.'

I wandered on, debating at the end of the road whether to turn left or right. Head in the direction of the call box, ring Andrew? But there was no point; I could speak to him tomorrow.

In the end I walked up to the recreation ground and leaned on the railings, watching children on the slides. It was here that I'd come a cropper from my bike. I recalled recounting the incident to Flora, and her response. Well now it was indeed a different wound receiving an airing; but how to get the grit out of it when I could do no more than sense the irritants still chafing under the skin?

* * *

Andrew was as good as his word and found a reason – or at least an excuse – to come up to London for an evening.

'I've told my secretary I have to look something up at the Law Library tomorrow morning,' he said.

'And have you?'

'No.'

I giggled and snuggled up to him on the sofa.

He looked indulgently down at my upturned face. 'Difficult, at this moment, to imagine you commanding your troops at the boardroom table.'

'Not quite the boardroom.'

'Whatever.'

'I change character with my clothes,' I offered.

Andrew leaned away from me, considering my about-town-girl's casual, but well-cut, leggings and expensive silk shirt, in favour of which I'd discarded my daytime suit.

'No party frock; no Alice band,' he teased.

I pummelled him playfully.

He caught my wrists. 'How about a thoroughly adult kiss . . .'

He got his breath back before I did. 'So how is Mother?'

Firing on all cylinders, I remembered. 'She's fine. That is to say, managing. Has a good moan about the home help every time I ring, of course: missed a bit of dust here, muddled the magazines, left a smear on the silver. *You* know.'

'Not really.' He was amused.

'Had a go at me over the weekend about being so undomesticated.'

Andrew looked around him. 'I wouldn't say that.'

'We're talking about *her* standards,' I said.

He eased himself against the cushions. 'But you get on well with her?'

I hesitated. 'I used to,' I said cautiously.

Had Andrew picked up the disconcerting habit of saying nothing at moments like these from Flora, or was it his lawyer's training?

'She's changed, though,' I volunteered eventually. 'Or maybe I have. Since Father died. Since I got to know Flora. I don't know – ' I waved the subject away – 'we just don't see eye to eye in the same way any more.'

If I thought, even so, that Mother would have the sense, or at least the restraint, to leave the subject of my 'extra-mural' activities alone, I was wrong.

The second weekend started off well enough. Balanced on her crutches, she was watching for me at the window as, after what seemed a particularly short respite, I turned into the driveway. I waved, pulled on the handbrake and disgorged myself. Smiling, I held up my house key – no need for her to bother hobbling to the door to open it.

'The kettle's just boiled,' she announced as I greeted her in the sitting room.

I dumped my bag on the floor, then, seeing her expression, picked it up again to take it back into the hall.

'I'd rather have a drink,' I said. 'The traffic—'

'There's only sherry.'

'That'll do fine.'

She did most of the talking that evening. I marvelled at the fact that, housebound as she had been, she nonetheless found so much to relate. Patiently I sat through discourses on Mrs Mackenzie's nephew's difficulty in selling his house, on an upset between the vicar and someone I made the mistake of owning to not recalling – 'Yes of course you know who I mean, they live at . . . she had a son who . . .' – and on what the world was coming to when young lads break into the newsagent's in the High Street and rifle the till. It was, if I were honest with myself, not so very different from the village chatter I found so absorbing at Cotterly.

She'd heard about the break-in, Mother was saying, first from young Jane Simpson who'd called in to collect the charity collection envelopes she, Mother, now couldn't of course distribute, and then again from the girl at the hairdresser's when she'd rung to make an appointment. 'For tomorrow morning,' the recollection reminded her. 'If you can get me down there.'

'We'll manage,' I assured her.

And we did. Afterwards I drove her, splendidly coiffed, to a local beauty spot where we lunched, amid much solicitous concern from the manager and several waitresses as they assisted her to a table, at the lakeside restaurant there.

It was, yet again, over Sunday lunch that Mother renewed her probing. It wasn't until some time later that it occurred to me that, on each occasion, the prospect of my imminent departure might, in one way or another, have determined the timing.

Her approach was subtle to start with. 'It is so good of you to come down – I don't know how I'd have managed without you.'

I accepted her appreciation at face value.

'Of course,' she said, reaching for the salt, 'I realise you'd rather be with . . . Andrew.'

'No problem. He understands.' What else was I supposed to say? I could hardly deny it.

Her tone sharpened just a shade; her smile remained, though, deceptively disarming. 'You should have invited him down for the day.'

'Mother, I've explained—'

'You haven't explained a thing.' Her eyes totally negated, now, the smile she was holding firmly in place.

I sliced into a roast potato. 'I have my reasons.'

'And what can those be, pray?' I didn't need to look up to be aware of the accusing stare directed at me.

When I didn't answer, her patience snapped. 'This is just what I went through with your father. I knew something was up. I waited and waited. At least when he eventually admitted it, I knew where I was. Anything is better than not knowing.' It wasn't until later that I recognised the irony of her remark.

'But what I do, my relationships, don't affect you in the same way.' Plausible enough but – as I was only too well aware – on this occasion untrue. I pushed food around my plate.

Mother calmed her voice. 'Just give me one good reason, then, why you can't be honest with me.'

'I can't.' Dejected; helpless.

'Then *tell* me.'

She'd done it again. Pushed my back up against the wall.

I squirmed. 'You'd be hurt.'

I forced myself to raise my eyes. She was staring at me, lips pursed in cynical disbelief.

I took a deep breath. 'OK, then; judge for yourself.' I was on a rollercoaster. It was cresting the ride. I plunged. 'Because he's a friend of Flora's.'

It was a different sort of disbelief that her face registered. It transformed into bewilderment; then incomprehension.

'Of Flora's?'

Maybe I should have got up, put an arm round her, attempted to comfort her, reassure her. But I was rooted to my chair.

'How,' she enquired in a tightly controlled voice that chilled me, 'do you come to know Flora? I take it you have met her, then? This isn't just some extraordinary coincidence?'

I nodded. Miserably. Where was all that anger at her rôle in everything? Her coldness was like ice on a flame. It was my disloyalty – nothing else – that stared me in the face.

I had to get away. Yet even as I experienced the urge, my practicality asserted itself. I reached for the plates. 'I'll clear these,' I said.

As I did so, and made coffee for her, the questions battered me: 'When did you meet her; how did you meet her; so is that where you've been spending your time?' I answered them, shortly, to the point. By the time she'd finished she had all the factual details.

'I have to go,' I said. 'I've left a tray set out for your supper. Can you manage?'

'I suppose I'll have to.'

Was that what she'd said to Father? Wasn't that what she'd done? Managed. How had he felt? What did I feel?

I went upstairs to collect my things. When I came down she was standing, propped on her crutches, at the foot of the stairs. 'You do realise,' she said, freezing me mid-flight, 'that it's because of you that your father deserted me.'

The exaggeration of his actions hardly registered. 'Because of me?' I stared at her. 'What do you mean?'

What was she going to say? What sin had I committed? Had Father hated me after all? I reached out for the banister rail.

'You tore me apart when you were born. Literally. You have no idea . . . Hardly surprising – ' she looked at me scornfully – 'I couldn't have any more children. But your father always wanted a son. I couldn't give him that.' She glared. 'Things were never the same between us again. He never forgave me.'

'That's not true. I'm sure it's not true. He'd never have held it against you. He wasn't like that.' I sank down on the stairs. 'And even if it were, it's not fair to blame me.'

'I'm not blaming you – ' cold reason – 'just telling you. What I don't understand – ' and now her voice rose – 'is how, after all I've gone through for you, you could do this to me.'

'Do what? What is it I've done? Except want to love you both.' Tears were streaming down my face.

'Love us both!' Her lip curled. 'You never loved me. Loved your father, maybe. Smarmed up to him. *And* he encouraged it. Well, you were the only one – *his* baby.' She swung herself round on her sticks, swaying.

Automatically I leapt up, and down the last few stairs to steady her. She shook my arm away and lurched towards the sitting room, leaving me standing.

'Perhaps,' I said, surprised at the control in my voice, 'it would be better if you asked Leah to come over next weekend.'

'Yes, of course. I mustn't keep you from Andrew.' Her words floated over her shoulder as she negotiated the doorway.

The heavy thud of rubber ferrules across the carpet preceded a pause and then the sigh of cushions as she sank down.

I left, clicking the front door quietly behind me.

I wanted to stop at the end of the Avenue, but forced myself instead to drive on for several streets before pulling the car in to the kerb. I rested my arms on the steering wheel and let my head fall forward on to them.

What a mess. What a bloody awful mess.

CHAPTER 19

I'm not sure at what point I decided, rather than take the A3, to drive via Epsom.

Aunt Leah took one look at my face when she opened the door, and pulled me inside.

I skirted round suitcases in the hall.

'Sorry,' she said, 'we've only just got back.'

I wasn't up to apologising for the intrusion.

I followed her through and allowed her to steer me to an armchair. 'Tea, Harold, please,' she called; and I heard the sounds of movement from the direction of the kitchen.

Leah crossed the room to close the patio doors. A sparrow, pecking at insects on the crazy paving beyond them, fluttered anxiously away at the disturbance. She returned and sat down opposite me, leaning forward. 'I've just had your mother on the phone,' she said, satisfied I'd had time to settle, 'so I've an idea what this is all about.'

I remembered odd occasions as a child when I'd run to Auntie Leah for sympathy. She'd always been far less reserved than my mother. 'You're the only person I can talk to,' I said – though now it wasn't just her manner but how much she already knew that made it possible.

'It's all to do with your father and this . . . other woman, isn't it?'

I nodded.

Leah reached beneath a side table and handed over a box of tissues. 'Looks like you could do with a good cry. Go ahead; you'll feel much better.'

Harold appeared with a tray. I raised a smudged face and gave him a watery smile. He patted my shoulder and retreated, waved out of the room by Leah.

'I wasn't going to tell her,' I hiccoughed at last.

'That you've been in touch with Flora?' She countered my surprise: 'It's all right. Your mother's just poured it out to me.'

I smiled sheepishly. 'I'm sorry. Now you've got me doing the same thing.'

She passed me a cup of strong tea. 'I must say, it might have been better if you hadn't told her.'

'I tried not to. But she kept on and on at me. About Andrew.' I let it all come out – the main facts anyway.

'Well, you can't really expect her to like it, can you?' Leah observed when I'd told the tale.

'No, of course not. But it's not fair of her to blame me. I mean for Father going off with Flora in the first place.'

Leah frowned. 'How do you mean . . . ?'

'She said my father wanted more children, a son; that he never forgave her . . . that's why . . . But it's

283

hardly my fault she wasn't able to.' I rushed on. 'Well, in a way it is of course if – ' I quoted her – 'I tore her apart—'

'Is that what she said: that she *couldn't* have more children?'

I nodded.

Leah put out a hand and touched my knee. 'It's not true,' she said. 'I don't know why she said it, but I can't let you go on believing it. You weren't an easy birth by all accounts. Though – ' her face creased in memory – 'no worse than my first one.'

'Your first one?' I did a double take.

'I had a stillborn little boy before Elspeth.'

'I didn't know.' Then, as the thought occurred to me: 'Does Elspeth?'

'Oh yes. Although we don't dwell on it. We were so thankful when she arrived – after all the miscarriages as well.'

'I see.' I looked at my aunt with fresh eyes. 'I'd no idea you'd been through all that.'

She looked reflective. 'We'd have liked at least one more. Girl or boy, it wouldn't have mattered; but then when I lost another at three months, well, we decided to call it a day.' Abruptly she straightened up. 'But that's our story, not hers.'

'So it's not true . . .' I prompted.

'Of course not.' She sounded impatient; or cross; or both. 'She didn't have a particularly easy time when you were born, but – ' she hesitated – 'well, there was no medical reason that I know of why she shouldn't have had another half-dozen.'

'So why – ' I could hear the hint of a wail in my voice – 'is she saying there was?'

Leah's face expressed concern. Then she rose. 'I'd better go and see what Harold's up to; get him to take those cases upstairs. You stay there; pour yourself another cup of tea and relax.'

I heard her chatting to him, the sounds of heavy objects being heaved up the stairs. I wandered over to the piano, an upright above which hung a selection of family photographs. Idly I lifted the lid, picked out a one-fingered tune: 'Oranges and Lemons'. I'd had lessons once but had never mastered the left hand.

Leah reappeared. She smiled. 'Long time since that's been played. We got it for Elspeth . . .' She sat down. 'How are you feeling now? Better?'

'Yes thanks.'

Harold poked his head round the door. 'I'm just popping down to the garden centre.'

Leah shook her head as the door banged. 'Your uncle and his plants. I don't know – even when he's on holiday he's thinking about them.'

'How was your holiday?'

She launched into the account I'd invited.

'So what,' I pleaded, returning – when that and various other small-talk subjects had been exhausted – to what was uppermost in my mind, 'am I going to do about Mother?'

'Let it be. She's upset; you can't be surprised.' Leah patted my knee again. 'Give it time. She'll come round; after all, she doesn't want to lose you.'

I waited for Harold to return before saying my goodbyes. I reached across the armful of plant pots he was emptying out of the boot and pecked his cheek. Leah reassured me about Mother. 'Don't you worry about next weekend. I'll see she's all right.'

It was still only early evening when I got back to the flat. I padded around, restless; not wanting to think about the day's events. The phone, reclining white and silent on the inlaid occasional table I'd picked up in a local antique shop, seemed almost sepulchral – as though any jerk into life could only herald ghosts from the past. Only common-sense restraint prevented me lifting the receiver and laying it to one side.

Determined to occupy myself at least physically, I remembered the crocheted blanket I'd rescued and promised myself I'd darn. So far I'd only made token attempts. Now seemed as good a time as any to tackle the task in earnest. It was fiddly; it might even distract my mind.

So many colours. As I'd built it up all those years ago from a central violet square, the remnants of wool I'd scrounged had at first each completed at least one row of the expanding rounds. But as the blanket grew, the lengths available had forced a more haphazard patterning – until the border; for which, I recalled, I had sacrificed the opportunity to add the latest pop music tape to my collection, purchasing instead with my pocket money two huge balls. Bright turquoise. A cheerful colour.

I set to with needle and patience. The concentration required did at least calm me. Mother had been hurt, I reminded myself. She was angry and she'd been lashing out. I secured an end and snipped. That was all there was to it. Forget it. I picked up a yellow strand and threaded it, stifling the 'yes, buts', the subsidiary questions; repeated my mantra: 'she was hurt ... forget it'. It worked – or seemed to.

But the act of breaking off to investigate the fridge allowed wider-ranging thoughts to sneak back. Why was she *so* angry; angrier, as far as I could tell, than she had been with Father? And why blame me for something which – even if it were true – I could hardly be held responsible?

I did my best to push the questions aside; made myself a sandwich – packet ham and coleslaw; munched an apple. Thoughts continued to intrude. Did *she* feel guilty for not giving Father more children? Why Father; why not herself too? Didn't mothers want children? And, if Leah was right and she could have had more, why didn't she?

I threw the core, still with half the fruit on it, in the bin. What did she mean by 'all she'd done' for me? What about all I'd done for her – all that support I'd given her, all that loyalty? And, yes, I had shown her both. At the expense of Father. I hadn't been allowed to love him. Not since Flora came on the scene anyway. Until then I had. Was she referring to those contented early years when she accused me of 'smarming up' to him; the way she'd said it . . . it was almost as though she were . . . well, jealous. Of me? Ridiculous!

Once again I found myself pacing, aimlessly tidying books, plumping cushions, eventually staring out of the kitchen window into the darkness, eerie under a sky yellowed by the glow of street lamps. Turning abruptly, I knocked a bowl from the sill. Grateful that at least it hadn't broken, I scrabbled on the floor, retrieving oddments for which it served as a receptacle. Among them I recognised Elspeth's button. I'd forgotten about it. Some time I'd ring her. Andrew too. But not tonight.

A headache, threatening all evening and gradually increasing from a nagging in my temples to an all-over throb, drove me to give in to an early night. I swallowed a paracetamol and tried to deaden the pain in the softness of the pillow. After a while the analgesic took effect and I fell asleep.

My dreams were the usual muddle. At one point I discovered myself on a boat – Leo and Clare's maybe? – bucking through heavy seas. At first there were others on board – who? – then suddenly they were gone and I was struggling with the helm, sails billowing out of control. Cliffs appeared on the port side; my earlier companions were strolling along them. I waved frantically but they ignored me. I was approaching rocks . . .

I shook myself awake, went to the loo, and searched out a glass of orange before returning to bed. This time, Mother – or was it Flora? – was kneeling by a flower-bed, trowel in hand, attending to a small plant. I stood behind her, watching.

I refused to allow my personal problems to accompany me to work. I dressed in my smartest outfit – the suit I'd worn, as it happened, to go and see Flora that first time – and spent time perfecting my make-up. I strode, rather than walked, into the office, and settled down with determination to be the efficient professional I was. Amazing what it did for my morale. Here at least I knew what I was doing.

I managed to summon up a similar confidence when I spoke to Andrew in the evening. 'Good news,' I told him. 'Leah's agreed to play nurse next weekend.'

'Great. How's she doing, by the way?' He meant Mother.

'Fine,' I said airily. I thought back to our lunch by the lake and regaled him with that. 'Surrounded by fussing staff – she was in her element.'

And how! I remembered, cynically now, the way she'd described her wedding – she the centre of attention, the princess. Yet so much for the happy-ever-after: her prince had let her down. But who ever spared a thought for him; except maybe the fairy godmother? Flora? The analogy skewed tradition. I brushed my ruminations aside – life, I was realising, didn't fall into neat, convenient patterns.

Later I picked up the blanket from the chair on which I'd abandoned it the previous evening and sewed in a few more ends.

I debated for several days whether or not to ring
Mother. In the end I decided to. The ringing tone
seemed to go on for ever before she answered.

'How are you?' I tried to make my voice normal.

'As well as can be expected.' End of reply. Silence
frosted down the line at me.

'I've spoken to Leah. She says she'll pop over on
Saturday, and Sunday as well if necessary. Check if
you need anything.'

'I know. We've been in touch.'

'Look,' I said, 'I'm sorry—'

'I think it's better if we don't talk about it.'

I shrugged. 'OK then. Well, I'll ring you next
week, shall I?'

'If you like.'

I wished I hadn't bothered. Except that at least I
had the satisfaction of having tried.

I sat for a moment, then rang Clare. 'How about
lunch tomorrow?'

Perched beside her in the sandwich bar next day,
I allowed myself to be more forthcoming about
Andrew: where he lived; how I'd met him. 'I was
visiting a . . . a cousin of my father's.' Well, it was
close enough, without rubbing Mother's nose publicly in the mire. Still protecting her, I recognised;
and wasn't sure how I felt now about doing so.

'By the way,' Clare remembered as we parted,
'we were thinking of having a drinks do on
Saturday. You'll both come, won't you?'

* * *

It was a good gathering of mostly familiar faces. Familiar to me anyway. Andrew had all of them – apart from Clare and Leo – sprung on him for the first time. I'd warned him what I'd said to Clare; how I'd explained Flora. 'At least I don't have to ask you to watch your tongue as carefully.'

He mixed in well, without apparent effort. On one occasion I caught him, out of the corner of my eye, leaning against a doorway, glass in hand, making easy conversation with friends Clare and I had known since university days; and later involved in deep discussion with a banking boyfriend of one of them. But not so deep that he couldn't break off to absorb others into a chatting circle.

I was proud of him. An odd thought – except that maybe I'd felt some anxiety about introducing him to my own crowd. I wasn't sure which concerned me most – their reaction to him, or his to them.

I certainly had no reason to worry about the former. 'Nice chap,' commented Douglas, having weaved his social way around the room and eventually ended up at my side. Lalage and Em, even more gratifyingly, were wide-eyed: 'Where *did* you dig him up?'

'From Bumpkin land,' I laughed; and for an awful moment saw my mother in me, preening.

We stayed on, with a select few, for one of Clare's curries. It was well after midnight by the time we made our way home.

'Well,' I asked as we sat at the kitchen table,

mugs in hand, 'what did you make of them?'

'I liked them.'

I checked him. Yes, he meant it.

We post-mortemed companionably. But after a while, Andrew's attention seemed to waver. He reached out and grasped my wrist. 'Something's not right,' he said. 'You're being over-cheerful.'

'Must be the alcohol.'

'No. You haven't been yourself all weekend.'

Hadn't I? I thought I'd been managing very well. I pulled my hand away and stood up, gesturing. 'Refill?'

He followed me, put his arms round me as I plugged in the kettle. 'What's wrong?'

'Nothing.' I knew I wasn't convincing. I spooned coffee, wished the water weren't so slow to come to the boil.

'Mother,' I said. 'We had a major row. She's hardly speaking to me.'

'Oh, so that's it.' I felt him relax, his hands slide up to my shoulders. Then he released me. Moments later he gave me a gentle push. 'Go and sit down.'

He poured, brought the coffee over, and settled in his chair. 'Well? Are you going to tell me more?'

I sipped tentatively. 'I told her about Flora,' I said. 'I mean, about my seeing her.'

'That was brave of you.'

I looked up. Andrew had his eyebrows raised.

'Hardly. She squeezed me into a corner. I didn't have any choice.' I explained in more detail. 'So,' I managed to laugh as I finished, 'it's all your fault really.'

'Thanks.'

I put out a hand, flicked my fingers against his. 'I don't really mean that.'

He grinned. 'That's a relief.' Then he sobered. 'What now? Will she come round?'

'Leah seems to think so.'

'Your aunt?'

'I went to see her afterwards. Thing is there was more to it than that.' I recounted the accusations Mother had hurled at me. 'But Leah says it's not true anyway. So why,' I pleaded across at Andrew, 'does she want to blame me?'

He looked sympathetic but uncomfortable. 'I don't know.' He concentrated on his coffee. 'I'll tell you one thing,' he said at last. 'I'm sure it wasn't because of you your father . . . left – in so far as he did. On the contrary, you were the reason he stayed.'

'How do you mean?' I stared at him, startled.

'He never said as much. Not in so many words.' He lit a cigarette, passed me one. 'Maybe I shouldn't say any more?'

'You should. Go on.'

'You have to understand I'm only reading between the lines, and anyway it's all hindsight – I hardly knew him at the time.'

'Stop being so bloody cautious.'

'OK, well, speaking as a lawyer, he was in a quandary if your mother wasn't amenable to a divorce.'

293

'Which she wouldn't have been.'

'I rather gathered. He could have tried "un-reasonable behaviour" on the grounds that . . . that they hadn't been . . . close. For a long time.'

'You mean little or no sex?'

'Well, yes . . .'

'It's all right. I'd worked that one out. So why didn't he?'

'Something about that generation maybe. Certain types of dirty linen they're reluctant to wash in public. Or protecting you, perhaps.'

I digested this.

'But what was to stop him simply moving out?' I remembered my discussion with Flora. So, I thought, he'd have had to go on totting up figures, but he could have done. 'And in any case, can't you then demand a divorce after five years even if the other one is unwilling?'

'I got the impression your mother must have made it clear that if he did, she'd make it damned difficult for him to see anything of *you* in the mean-time. That's what I meant when I said you were the reason he stayed.'

'Oh.' I let this sink in. 'But could she have done?'

'You were living with her. He'd have had to argue it in court if she were adamant. I think he must have decided that the hassle involved . . . not just for him, but for you caught in the middle of it all . . .'

'It might have been worth it.'

Andrew gave a shrug of helplessness. How Father must have felt.

I thought about it.

'Yes, but she couldn't have stopped me once I was eighteen ...' But would it have made any difference if he'd cut the ties completely then? By that time, mine to her were tightly knotted. It had taken a further seven years and a plea from Father, at that unrefusable moment, to persuade me to go down to Cotterly. And just look at Mother's reaction now she knew about it. How was that in all that time I'd never considered his point of view, never realised the struggle for him?

I fell silent. Poor Dad – *and* Flora. Poor me. Mother wielding the whip hand. But not much fun for her either. What had she got out of it? I felt the answers were all there, but at this time of night my mind seemed incapable of unscrambling them.

Andrew had seen me glance at my watch. Now he checked his own. 'Come on,' he said. 'Bed.'

He made no attempt to make love to me that night; but his arms around me were reassuring.

CHAPTER 20

Rather as it had done all those years ago when Mother acknowledged the fact – but no more than the fact – of Flora's existence, my mind churned through the questions now raised. What I could deduce reinforced the sense I'd developed recently that so much of Mother's behaviour had been inspired in some way by self-interest. Elspeth's suggestion – that she'd been protecting herself – now rang horribly true.

The various comments that had been passed, and my own thoughts over the last few months, particularly the last few weeks, bubbled in my head as I tried to make sense of my parents' marriage – and my rôle in it. One thing was certain, I wasn't going to get any help from Mother in sorting it out. And it was too late to talk to Dad about it.

I was moody; Andrew was patient, listening but reluctant to offer opinions. 'How can I? I've never met your mother.'

'What is it about her?' I demanded. 'It's almost as though everyone's scared of her.'

He laughed then. 'I can't imagine Flora being

afraid of anyone,' he said. 'Maybe you ought to talk to her some more. She of all people is the one you could check things out with.'

But I wasn't sure I wanted to. Not at the moment. Instead I rang Elspeth. 'Your button,' I said.

It didn't take much to get on to the subject of Mother. I told Elspeth about my visit to her parents too. 'You really should come down and see them.'

For once she sounded more mellow on the subject. 'Maybe I will.'

I took advantage of her weakening to press the point.

'Hey,' she said. 'Playing happy families with me and mine isn't going to sort out your mess.'

Is that what I was doing? I hadn't thought of it like that.

'I might have more chance of sorting it out if I understood it,' I said. 'I mean, why on earth did Mother—'

Elspeth interrupted. 'Hang on. If this is going to be a long session, I need to get comfortable.'

I heard sounds of her moving across a room, the scrape of furniture, a scrabbling as though she were settling into a chair. I visualised her, feet tucked up, a drink at her elbow. What sort of room was it, I wondered. Pictures and posters on the walls, ethnic drapes everywhere?

'Where's Perry?' I asked when she came back on the line.

'He's out. Got himself a job as a barman. Great, isn't it – anyway it's a start.'

Bearing in mind his predilection for alcohol, I wasn't sure how enthusiastic to be. Luckily Elspeth didn't seem to require a response. 'Go on then, shoot.'

By the time I put the phone down, some things at least seemed to have clarified. Elspeth was blunt on the subject of Mother and babies. 'Seems perfectly obvious to me she can't have wanted any more. For one reason or another. Maybe she pleaded health, but I'd guess she was far more concerned about her figure. And what a marvellous excuse her story gave her – if in any case she didn't fancy sex – to avoid it.'

'What makes you think . . . ? Anyway, there was always the Pill.'

'Exactly. Probably told him she couldn't take it for some reason; persuaded him nothing else was safe.'

'You're guessing.'

'Well, of course I am. But it makes sense, doesn't it?'

I had to admit it did.

'Wonder is,' Elspeth was saying, 'he put up with it for as long as he did.'

'We don't know how long that was.' I tried to remember how old I'd been when the double bed disappeared. It was a distant memory; I couldn't be sure.

'Shouldn't be at all surprised,' Elspeth pressed on, 'if she wasn't delighted when he transferred those attentions to Flora.'

That fitted too. As long as his doing so didn't disturb outward appearances. And, if Andrew was right, I'd been instrumental in making sure it didn't.

Why did I feel there was more to it than that? Something to do with me personally; something I'd seen in her eyes when she'd accused me of being responsible . . . I'd put a tentative name to it earlier. Now I brushed it aside; I was letting my imagination run away with me.

Over the following weeks, Andrew and I began to develop a routine – one weekend in London, the next at Cotterly. I ignored Mother's antagonism and, out of duty to the invalid, visited her several times, on one occasion calling in on my way back from Cotterly and, once or twice on a weekday evening, making the effort to go down specifically. We settled – as her leg, she reluctantly admitted, improved and she was able, eventually, to exchange her crutches for a stick – for cool politeness. Just as she and Father had done, it occurred to me one Saturday morning as, after spending the night at home with her, I departed and drove westwards.

And here I was, like him too, headed for Cotterly. Though not just for a weekend. My holdall, left discreetly in the boot overnight, bulged with heavy jumpers and the sort of clothes suited to an autumn week in the country.

It had been as much Andrew's idea as mine. Ten days ago, a memo through the internal post had landed on my desk – the Personnel Officer reminding me I still had three weeks' leave owing.

So I had! I'd been so carried along on the conveyor belt of events recently that I hadn't given it any thought. I'd commented to one of my colleagues who happened to come into the room as I was reading it. 'You look as though you could do with a holiday,' she'd remarked. 'Seemed a bit stressed these last few weeks.'

As though my body, even now, acknowledged the strain more readily than I did, I woke next morning, the Friday, with a stuffed-up nose and a grinding headache. I struggled through the bathroom routine and into my clothes, then sat on the end of my bed attempting to apply make-up. 'Ugh,' I grimaced, and dumped the hand mirror I'd been holding face down on the duvet.

I rang the office. 'I feel awful.' Later in the day I phoned Andrew. 'Better cancel this weekend,' I croaked.

But he insisted on coming anyway. 'Can't have you languishing all alone.'

'You might catch it,' I worried.

'I'll risk it.'

I insisted at least he sleep on the sofa, and he accepted the sense in that.

He arrived that evening armed with brandy, and fresh lemons, and a jar of local honey; and brewed up his cure-all potion in the kitchen while I snuggled, red-nosed, under the covers. He raided the fridge and produced rice-and-something: 'Call it risotto.'

I protested I wasn't hungry.

'Nonsense.' He sat on the edge of my bed and wielded the fork. 'Come on. Open up.' Obediently I accepted a mouthful.

'OK, OK.' I pulled myself up and took the plate from him. I laughed. 'You're just like my father,' I said. 'I remember when I had chicken pox . . .'

By next day I was over the worst of it. I sat on the sofa, wrapped in the crocheted blanket. Andrew lounged opposite me. 'You need a break,' he said.

'Funny you should say that.' I told him of the reminder I'd received. 'Trouble is, I'm not sure where appeals at this time of year, and anyway. . .'

Andrew stood up and came to sit on the arm of the sofa, behind my head. He put a hand on my shoulder.

'Thinking ahead,' he said, 'how about planning to go skiing together over New Year?'

'I've never skied.'

'First time for everything.'

I hesitated. Then laughed. 'Oh well, as long as you promise to carry me home if I break a leg or two.' I tilted my head upwards, expecting to encounter the usual tolerant amusement.

Instead he had an eyebrow raised. 'And what if I'm the one in a heap in the snow?'

'You won't be.'

He smiled, but somehow I had the feeling my response hadn't been the one he was looking for. But he made no further comment. Maybe I'd imagined it.

Later, realising such plans still left me a week to spare, we discussed a more immediate break from work. 'I wouldn't mind,' I said, 'just coming down to Cotterly. Spend some time with Flora . . .'

'Good idea.' He thought about it. 'If you make it the week after next, Ginny and the boys will probably be up in Leamington with her in-laws. Half-term. We'd have the Dower House to ourselves.' He parodied a leer. 'With a bit of luck they'll stay up there the whole time.'

Now, as I drove westwards a week later, I eased my foot on the accelerator, allowing myself time to look around, to take in the scenery. The trees, massed hues of late October golds and browns, edged the road, their leaves, defying autumn's rustle, deceptively secure.

It was about this time last year, I recalled, that Father had been taken ill. We – or anyway I – had assumed, if I'd really noticed, that his weight loss was just a mark of summer fitness. The doctor had sent him to the hospital for tests; they'd be keeping him in for a few days while they did them. I hadn't known then that he'd never come out. I'd gone with Mother to visit him each weekend; towards the end, additionally gone down mid-week. She'd always been there. Except once; and then I'd sat by his bedside not knowing what to say – saying nothing of importance.

I brushed the memory aside and concentrated instead on anticipating the week ahead. Andrew had confirmed that Ginny would be away until at least the following Thursday. My mind flashed back to the previous time I'd stayed at the Dower House . . .

I went there first but finding no sign of Andrew drove on round to Wood Edge. His car wasn't there either.

Columbus, busy with his ablutions by the back door, broke off as I drew up, watched me alight and waited as I approached. He stood up, arched his back and jutted his head to greet me. I bent down and stroked his chin. The door was unlocked. I knocked as I entered, Columbus following me in.

'Hell-o,' I called from the empty kitchen, wondering for a moment whether Flora, too, was out.

Then I heard the pad of her footsteps on the stairs. She appeared with a cloth and a tin of wax in her hands. 'Been giving that old chest a bit of a polish,' she explained.

'I've been round to the Dower House,' I said. 'I thought maybe Andrew was here.'

'He's had to go in to the office. Some crisis or other. Called round on his way to ask me to tell you.'

I stifled disappointment. 'Oh, fine.'

'Tried to ring you last night, I gather, but you weren't in.'

'I was at my mother's.'

'How is she?' Flora had only heard, from me, the basic facts of Mother's accident. Whether Andrew had told her more, I had no idea. I'd avoided doing so on my previous visits. Or hadn't found the opportunity. I wasn't sure which.

Suddenly I was angry about all the subterfuge. Well, not subterfuge exactly; more a pandering to Mother and her precious feelings. Why hadn't I given Andrew the phone number there? It was no good: Andrew existed; Flora existed; in my life anyway; and at some point Mother was going to have to accept it.

In an unexpected rush, I voiced these thoughts to Flora.

She received them with equanimity, opening a cupboard door and stuffing away the cleaning materials as she did so. 'Put the kettle on, will you?' she suggested over her shoulder. I lifted the lid of the hotplate and shifted it across.

There was something extraordinarily reassuring about Flora's kitchen table. We sat at it as we so often had before. She was wearing that same jumper – the cat one – that had so mesmerised me the first time I met her. I commented. 'Do you remember the first time I came?'

'Of course.'

'A lot's happened since then.'

She nodded, smiling.

My thoughts floated. 'On the way down,' I said, 'I was thinking . . . it's just about a year since Father went into hospital.' I looked up; the corners of Flora's mouth had straightened. I put out a hand, touched hers. 'I'm so sorry I never came down when he was alive.'

She patted mine. 'We understood.'

'Did you? I wish I did.' Why hadn't I stood up to Mother? Why – back to my earlier thought – was I still only partially doing so?

I stood up, carried my mug over to the window, stared out. Then I shook the questions aside and turned. 'How about I take you out to lunch?'

We drove over to The Three Bells at Chadham. At this time of year the beer garden had an abandoned look – umbrellas stowed away, the tables bare but for a stray leaf or two. We settled in a corner of the bar and I fetched a menu over.

'Your father always enjoyed their Fisherman's Pie,' said Flora.

We both settled for that.

'You used to come here with him, then?' I said.

'From time to time.'

I raised my glass. 'To you and Dad,' I said.

For a moment, I thought I detected a hint of mist in her eyes. If so, she recovered. 'To all of us,' she countered.

Who did that include, I wondered. What was Andrew doing at this moment? I had visions of a stale cheese sandwich and a plastic cup of coffee balanced amid a mound of papers. When we'd been in town on one occasion, he'd pointed out his firm's offices – the upper floors of a Victorian building reached via an unobtrusive doorway squeezed between an estate agent and a flower shop. We hadn't gone in. I wished in a way we had; I could have visualised him, now, more clearly.

Father had taken me into his office once. I suppose I was about ten or eleven at the time. Memory of the circumstance had faded, but the open-plan interior was as sharply defined in my mind as the familiar façade of the modern town-centre block. On our way to his own separate room with its huge desk and leather chair, we'd passed an army of clerks. Father had proudly – yes, it was proudly – introduced me to those who looked up, and to the one or two of his partners whose paths crossed ours. A secretary had brought us coffee and biscuits on a tray, and chatted to me about school while Father made phone calls. I'd felt very important sitting there in my blue check dress and my blazer with the crest on the pocket. I smiled now at the memory.

'Penny for them.' Flora was looking quizzically at me.

'I was thinking about Andrew,' I said. I repeated my image of his utilitarian lunch as I sank a fork into the steaming potato topping of my own appetising one.

It was gone six when he finally appeared.

'We've had a deliciously lazy time,' I informed him.

'Lucky you.' He looked tired.

Guiltily I dropped my teasing. 'Did you get everything sorted?'

Hopefully. In any case he wasn't going to think about it again till Monday morning.

We stayed and chatted with Flora until eventually she shooed us out: 'There's a play I want to listen to on the radio.' If it was an excuse she was offering us, we were grateful.

We drove in tandem to the Dower House. I parked the Astra in the spot normally occupied by Ginny's Metro. As I helped carry supermarket bags into the house, I suddenly felt less comfortable than I'd anticipated.

'Told Ginny not to worry about getting food in for us,' Andrew had said as he swung the boot open. 'She had enough to do getting herself and the boys off.'

'A male chauvinist with a conscience!' I'd quipped, and immediately regretted it. 'Sorry, that wasn't fair. It was just . . .'

What was it 'just'? I tried, lamely, to explain as we unpacked the shopping. 'It's a bit convoluted,' I said. 'Something about my mother being so much the mistress of her kitchen, of the whole house.'

Andrew looked bemused. 'I suppose there's a connection there somewhere.'

I knew there was. I could feel it; but couldn't quite put it into words: Mother in control, Father tolerantly allowing it; Ginny running the Dower House, Andrew not objecting; a huge question mark on everyone's rôles and, in particular, where I fitted into each household.

Andrew was unwrapping two large steaks. 'Wake up,' he admonished lightly. He nodded towards the lettuce I was aimlessly balancing. 'You knock up a salad while I grill these.'

We ate on our knees in front of the television – some inane comedy, but it relaxed me. Later I sat, or rather snuggled, through *Match of the Day*, wedged against Andrew's shoulder, secure in the warmth and faintly musky smell of him.

Once or twice he shook his head indulgently. 'There's a real baby in you somewhere, isn't there?'

'Umm,' I agreed, contentedly complacent.

Bearing refilled wine glasses, he followed me up to the bathroom and perched on the edge of the bath as I soaked. I lay there, sipping luxuriously, aware of his eyes roving over me – and enjoying it. Then he reached for the sponge and soaped me gently all over. 'All I need,' I laughed when he'd rinsed me off with the same smooth movements, 'is a plastic duck.'

I knew in an instant I'd said the wrong thing. His expression changed. Abruptly he reached for the towel. 'Come on. Out.'

I heard the shower running as I got into bed and lay there, casting my eyes over the evidence of him in the room. When he climbed in beside me a few minutes later, he seemed somehow preoccupied. I cuddled up to him, ran my fingers up and down his forearm, offered my face for a kiss.

Suddenly he turned on to his back, raised his arms behind his head and lay there, staring up at the ceiling. The hair in his armpits was soft and fuzzy. I'd have liked to reach out and stroke it.

Instead: 'What's the matter?' I asked. Then

teasingly, knowing it wasn't that: 'Did I pinch all the hot water?'

No response.

'Well something – ' still attempting light-heartedness – 'seems to have poured cold water on your ardour.'

'Maybe.'

I sat up, tried to read his expression. It was – the recognition shook me – that withdrawn one I'd seen so often during my teenage years on another face. Panic, irrational but all the more powerful for being so, spread upwards from my stomach. 'For God's sake – ' I could hear the scream in my voice – 'you look just like my father.'

He turned his head then, making as though to move his arms down. I thought for a moment he was going to put them round me, reassure me. But then he settled them back again, resumed his position.

'Maybe that's the problem,' he said, addressing some spot above him.

'What problem?'

'That I'm *not* your father.'

'Of course you're not.'

'But you seem to want me to act as though I were.'

A lump, huge and choking, materialised in my throat. 'That's not fair . . .' Now I too lay back and stared upwards.

I was aware of Andrew twisting his head sufficiently to see me out of the corner of his eye.

'Look' he said, 'I don't mind playing the supportive father rôle occasionally, but in bed Daddy's little girl is hardly my idea of a turn on. It's a woman I want.'

Was it hurt or anger that made me snap back? 'You mean a mother, I suppose?'

'No.' The evenness in his voice was chilling. 'A woman.' He swung over on his side away from me.

I lay there. 'Men!' I reassured myself. In a minute he'd roll back, apologise. I waited. Still, after about ten minutes, he hadn't done so. But the tension in his body told me he wasn't asleep.

Tentatively I put out a hand, resting it on his hip; then, turning on my side, allowed it to creep round to his chest.

He didn't move.

I curled the hair there against my fingers, then let them wander slowly down over his belly; teased my way lower, unhurriedly and gradually coaxing a physical response. Still he said nothing, gave no sign of even being aware of what I was doing.

Then at last he turned on to his back and without comment, roughly almost, pulled me astride him.

I stared into his face. The softness was gone from it, yet his expression was not so much hard as challenging. OK then; if that was what he wanted. I took charge, discovered an unexpected exhilaration in so doing – until, at the very last moment, he reached up and, in one rhythmic movement, rolled us both over till I was beneath him and he was thrusting deeper and deeper . . .

Afterwards he lay with his head buried in my shoulder. Then he raised himself and looked down at me. I opened my mouth to speak but he put a finger over my lips. 'Don't say a word.' After a moment or two he rolled off and we lay there, side by side, our clasped hands bridging what space there was between us.

CHAPTER 21

I slid out of bed next morning before Andrew had woken, eased into my silk wrap, and crept downstairs. In the kitchen I pulled up the blinds and started to prepare coffee and toast.

The garden had that autumn cleansing look about it – a spattering of leaves on the grass heralding a full-blown clear out. Today, for some reason, I felt less empathy with the leaves, clinging on, than with the branches overburdened with yellowing foliage.

Busy searching in the cupboard for marmalade and laying up a tray, I didn't hear Andrew come downstairs; nor even was I aware of him entering the room. It was only when I turned to fetch butter from the fridge that I caught sight of him.

I jumped. 'Oh, you startled me. How long have you been . . . ?' I broke off, my gaze drawn downwards, my eyes widening. He had slipped his arms into a bathrobe but hadn't bothered to tie it. I stared, then laughed.

Andrew glanced down, raising an eyebrow. 'Long enough, obviously.' He looked back at me, acknowledgement crinkling the corners of his eyes and mouth. 'I've been enjoying watching you.' Then, provocatively, as I stood there still gaping: 'Well? What are you going to do with it?'

Our eyes met. I remembered last night.

'Right.' I advanced towards him, recognising, perhaps for the first time, my power. 'OK, *Daddy*, I'll show you.'

And I did. Right there in the kitchen, with the breeze brushing a strand of creeper against the window and the smell of hot toast, popping up unheeded from its metal cage, permeating the air around us.

That afternoon, anoraked and booted, we walked. Across fields and through woods, most of the tracks familiar to me now. The flowers of summer had gone but in their place we found late fruits: acorns, conkers – and sweet chestnuts, their prickled green husks littering the ground beneath broad-branching trees. We heeled them open and squirrelled away pocketfuls to peel and munch as we strolled on.

I shared my thoughts of the morning about autumn's rôle in the scheme of things. 'It's almost,' I suggested, 'as though man and nature are at odds. Man *spring*-cleans ...'

We debated the matter; agreed that most of winter's grime was man-made. 'Just think of snow,' said Andrew. 'It's cars and feet, mainly, that create slush.'

We elaborated, sought further examples, argued back and forth; noted – as we passed a tractor ploughing in stubble – how farmers, in part at least, conform inevitably to nature's schedule; progressed to consideration of the merits and demerits of human resistance to the dictates of seasonal daylight.

I paused then and turned to him. We were walking along a ridge, the countryside spread out on either side. 'I suppose,' I said, 'these are the sorts of discussions you had with my father. You know, I used to be quite jealous of you.'

There was a fallen tree trunk beside the path. Andrew steered me across to sit on it. 'Tell me.'

I picked a burr from my sleeve. 'In a way perhaps I still am. Maybe that's why I've been so confused.'

Andrew put an arm round me and gave an encouraging squeeze.

'It's not easy,' I said. 'I'm not totally clear about it myself. I guess I was hurt – and angry – that you had the sort of relationship with him that I'd missed out on. It seemed so unfair. But it wasn't so bad when I could convince myself that made you some sort of a brother...'

I looked across, checking his reaction; grateful he didn't allow his expression to flicker.

'Then,' I forced myself to continue, 'after Ginny explained, when things ... started to develop ...'

He permitted himself a smile then. 'Difficult,' he acknowledged.

I put out a hand and rested it on his thigh, my

fingertips circling the matt roughness of his trousers, feeling his leg firm beneath it.

I got up and wandered away a few yards. I stared over the fields, then up at the sky – uneven snatches of blue between the cumulus. Was he right? Had I then turned him into some sort of father figure? I grimaced: just as incestuous, if I had.

I felt rather than heard him come up behind me. He put his arms round me, rested his head against the back of mine.

'You know,' he said, 'your father was only ever a casual friend – an older one, I grant you – to me. Yes, I enjoyed talking with him – our minds worked in much the same way; but no-one, male or female, could ever have usurped your place.'

He rocked me very slightly, moving with me. 'I guess maybe I've been the jealous one. Of him. Maybe . . . what I was saying last night . . . was my fault. Perhaps I've been trying to *be* him for you; replace him.'

I jerked my head round.

'No, not for your benefit. Well, only partly. More because it seemed a way to . . .'

I tried to turn, but he held me tight. 'But I don't want you to be my father.' It was true – now, anyway.

I felt his body relax against mine. Then he moved a hand down, dived it up and under my anorak, and settled it suggestively. 'Neither,' he said, and a lightness had returned to his voice, 'do I.'

Without displacing his hold, I twisted round to

face him. Stretching up, I closed my teeth on his earlobe, making brief play of biting it. 'Good,' I said.

We wandered on, hand in hand, mutually companionable.

'You're looking more rested already,' said Flora over bread and cheese.

It was Monday lunchtime. I'd lain in bed that morning as Andrew dressed. Luxuriating between the covers, I'd watched as he pulled his tie round his neck, flicking the end over and round and through, then peering in the mirror to tighten and adjust it.

'There's something very sexy about a man putting on a tie,' I observed.

He turned, narrowing his eyes. 'Watch it.' He glanced at the bedside clock, then reached for his jacket. 'Saved by the bell,' he grinned.

I heard the door slam and listened as the car drove off. After a while I stirred myself, padded round the house tidying here and there, and eventually pulled on jeans and sweatshirt: holiday wear.

I found Flora in her garden and spent the morning giving a hand. Together we collected up the remains of fallen apples and repiled logs she'd had delivered. We each of us carried an armful in, stacking them in the alcove by the drawing-room hearth to dry out. 'Maybe I'll light a fire later,' she said.

Now, as I reached across to slice off a hunk of

Cheddar, she made her comment about how much better I was looking.

I considered it. 'Country air,' I acknowledged.

'You had a good day yesterday, then?'

'Umm.' I balanced a piece of cheese on my bread, then looked up. 'Andrew and I had a bit of a heart to heart; sorted a few things out.'

'Oh?' Neutral enquiry.

'About Father,' I said. 'Well, in a way.' Leaving out the intimate details, I gave her the gist. 'Andrew,' I grimaced, 'seemed to think I'd been playing little girl.'

'And *had* you?'

I thought about it. 'I suppose I had. Lately anyway.' I found myself staring across the kitchen at Father's photo. I raised an eyebrow towards it and laughed ruefully. 'Maybe,' I acknowledged to Flora, 'I took you too literally when you said it wasn't too late to get to know him; imagined in some way I could find him again in Andrew.'

I munched thoughtfully. 'But that was hardly what you meant, was it? It was about seeing him more clearly, understanding him.' I nodded in the direction of the photo again. 'I wonder what he'd have to say if I could talk to him now? Probably agree with Andrew that it was about time I grew up.' I addressed the face in the silver frame: 'You'll be glad to know I think I am doing.'

Flora smiled.

'Was that –' my mind made a leap – 'why he got fed up with Mum?'

After all, in some ways she was quite childlike. I saw her, prettily domesticated, never a hair out of place; accepting Father's arm round her – in those early days anyway; never, that I'd been aware of, reciprocating; always the one on the receiving end of support – and even affection? As though she didn't even know how to respond perhaps; to give? An involuntary shiver rippled my spine. Like mother, like daughter – potentially? I gave mental thanks for what I hoped was my reprieve.

I looked across at Flora, then down again. 'Life's been a bit tricky with Mother these last few weeks,' I decided at last to confide. 'Did Andrew tell you . . . or maybe you've gathered? . . . I let on . . . well, it was more that she dragged it out of me . . . that I've been coming down here.'

For once Flora's face, when I glanced at it, showed undoubted interest.

'She was very . . . upset.' I crumbled an oddment of bread. Then I looked up. 'Can I tell you about it?'

'If you'd like to. Here – ' she reached over to the dresser and passed an ashtray – 'I expect you'll have a use for this.'

I smiled gratefully. 'Mother doesn't approve of me smoking.'

'Up to you, as far as I'm concerned.'

'Thanks.' I fetched my pack of cigarettes from the other side of the room and lit up.

'Maybe it's my fault. Maybe I should never have come down.'

Flora gave me a sideways look.

'What,' I demanded, 'is that supposed to mean?'

She pursed her lips. 'We do enjoy our guilt trips, don't we?'

'I thought you were going to be sympathetic?'

'I'd find it easier if you just gave me the story straight.'

I took a breath, accepting the reprimand.

'Right.' The last time I'd said it – in that way – had been in Andrew's kitchen. Yesterday morning. I smiled at the memory.

I collected my thoughts and, encouraged by nods of unsurprised acknowledgement or occasional confirmation from Flora, embarked on the tale. I told her what Mother had said; recounted my conversation with Leah; recapped on Andrew's explanation of Father's dilemma. Finally, I repeated – with some delicate blurring of the reasoning – Elspeth's blunt conclusion. 'She seemed to think,' I said, 'that Mother was probably quite relieved when Father started . . . spending time with you.'

Flora looked across at me. 'Is that what you want to believe or not?'

'I want the truth.'

She nodded, checking my expression. Then: 'I'm as confident as I can be,' she said, 'that Elspeth's right.'

I experienced a huge sweep of relief.

'Don't misunderstand me,' she continued. 'I'm not opting out of responsibility as far as its effect on you is concerned; but let's say I'd have felt a lot less ... comfortable about it if your mother hadn't—'

'Encouraged it?'

Again that assessing look. 'I suppose you could say that.'

I cracked a laugh. 'It gives a whole new twist. There was she, practically thrusting Dad's weekend bag at him; and I've been feeling sorry for her, angry with her too, for not having what it takes to hold on to him ... Well, yes and no ...' I fumbled for words. 'I mean, if she had, I'd never have met you ... and everything ...'

God, why was I being so inarticulate? I made an effort to focus. 'So the arrangement suited her,' I summed up, in a refrain of previously hazy recognition. Then, with more than a hint of cynicism, 'Pity she didn't explain.'

Flora rose and busied herself. I took out another cigarette, debated whether to light it, then stuffed it back in the packet again. 'In that case,' I demanded, more of myself than of Flora, 'why is she so angry with me? What is she blaming me *for*?'

I fiddled with my lighter, turning it over and over, backwards and forwards, balancing it on its end, catching it as it toppled. 'Unless of course,' the thought ballooned into my mind as I skimmed, in memory, over recent weekends and homed in on the image of Mother describing their wedding, those Easter roses, 'they *had* to get married.'

I rechecked my mental count to my birthday in a few weeks' time. That had to be it. I saw it all:

Mother seducing Father with her cordon bleu cookery; the inevitability of what must have followed; Father doing the honourable thing . . .

Flora cut short my speculation. 'No,' she said, 'I'm sure that wasn't so.'

'How do you know?'

'Your father may eventually have realised she wasn't the person he'd thought she was, but he wasn't pressured into it.'

It hadn't been a loveless marriage from the start, then. On balance I was more relieved than disappointed at that explanation falling by the wayside. I didn't, it occurred to me, really relish the idea of being an unwanted child.

'In that case,' I said, 'what went wrong? What is it *I'm* supposed to have done?'

Flora was drawing water into the washing-up bowl. 'Here,' I said, rousing myself, 'let me do that.'

I immersed my hands in the suds, the warmth of the water seeping up through my arms. With a damp finger, I flicked back a strand of hair which then flopped forward, spangled, over my forehead again. I blew upwards at it, and the froth erupted into tiny floating bubbles – and one big one, rainbow sided. 'Ooh, look,' I said. 'I haven't made those since I was a child.'

It was Father who'd brought home the small cylinder of soapy liquid one hot summer lunchtime. He'd taken me into the garden and shown me how to catch a film across the wire circle, then blow . . . just hard enough.

The image was as clear as if I were there, with him, now. We were standing in the middle of the lawn, he still in his office suit, the sun glinting on the parade of translucent spheres wafting gently upwards, the colours – reds, blues and violets – dancing within them; the magic of it delighting us both.

But then Mother, wiping her hands on a towel, had stepped out through the French windows and remarked crossly to Father: 'You spoil that child – forever playing with her.'

I looked up, now, from what I was doing. A fly was crawling across the window. I swatted at it with the dishcloth.

'My God, I hated her,' I said.

I was aware of Flora, somewhere behind me in the room, pausing. Then she appeared beside me with a teatowel. She picked out a plate from the drying rack.

'She accused me,' I said bitterly, 'of never having loved her.' I scooped up a knife and scrubbed at it. 'Maybe she was right.'

Flora's silence, as we continued our task together, was reassuringly companionable. I rescued the last teaspoon, upended the bowl and watched the water flood into the sink and down the drain.

We lit the promised fire, both of us down on our hands and knees, Flora demonstrating how to wind old newspaper into firelighters and build a pyramid of sticks before balancing logs strategically

above them: 'The air's got to get to it if it's to catch.'
It soon did, and we settled in chairs either side of
the flames.

Flora picked up a book, flipped it open and
transferred the postcard marking her place to the
back. She smiled comfortably at me before turning
her attention to the page.

I was left alone with my thoughts. Eventually I
said, 'Was it awful of me to say that about my
mother?'

Flora looked up.

'It was just that I was remembering one occasion.' I recounted it. 'Do you think . . . well, it was
almost as though she resented me; was jealous of
me.' I recanted hurriedly. 'It's crazy, of course.
Mothers aren't jealous of their children.'

'Whyever not? Particularly of their daughters.'

I stared at her, then giggled. 'You're not serious?'

Flora shrugged.

'Explain,' I demanded. But I wasn't sure I
needed her to.

'If she'd produced the son she told me he
wanted . . .' I mused. If I'd been that son . . .
Thoughts spilled over each other.

'Hang on,' I said. 'I don't see any sign of Aunt
Leah being jealous of Elspeth.'

'So?'

So why my mother of me, and not my aunt of
her daughter? I recalled Elspeth's comment: *her*
mother had had the sense to marry someone who –
how had she put it? – sublimated his sex urges in

the greenhouse. I smiled, shaking my head – Elspeth didn't mince words. But, remembering my conversation with Leah, I wasn't sure she was right; and even if she were, that wasn't all there was to marriage. For all that my aunt and uncle played out the hen-pecker and the hen-pecked, I had the sense that this was an act put on for other people's benefit – a cover in some way for some deep comfortableness with each other which they weren't about to share with the rest of the world. Even Elspeth, it occurred to me now, hadn't been able to challenge that. Maybe that was why she'd got out, kept away.

'I suppose,' I said, following my train of thought, 'mothers and daughters *are* in competition in some way.' Ruefully I recalled those times when I'd attempted to nudge my way between my parents when Father had been sitting close to Mother. And, on occasions when I'd run to open the door in the evenings, hadn't I experienced a sort of triumph when he'd swept me up in his arms, leaving Mother hovering in the background?

'But surely,' I said, the images clear in my mind, 'it's more a case of daughter vying with mother for father's attention than the other way round?'

Flora placed her book, face down, across the arm of the chair. 'Maybe she was afraid he cared more for you than for her?'

'That's nonsense. He loved us in different ways. Didn't he?'

'I suppose she might not have seen it quite like that.'

I considered this, echoes of the weekend just gone reverberating in my mind. 'You mean she wanted the fathering too?'

Come to think of it, given the picture I'd been piecing together, that made sense. 'Great,' I said. 'Caught up in sibling rivalry with my own mother.' A thought struck me. 'Presumably she didn't imagine that father had designs on me – ' I searched for words – 'in any other way?'

Flora smiled. 'Far more likely you simply reminded her, once you started growing up a bit, that she was getting older.'

I pondered. 'And she didn't like it. Still – ' I gestured a protest – 'I could hardly help that.'

The logs were well alight, glowing red now. I stared into them, at the wafering created as they burned. 'You know,' I said, 'being realistic, I can, I suppose, imagine other reasons too why she might have been jealous – or at least envious – of me. My education, my career. She wasn't exactly very academic herself, never totally at ease, for example, with Dad's parents; pretended to despise their . . . intellectual interests, I suppose you'd call them.' I thought about it; remembered Gran valiantly making conversation with her about cake recipes or the season's fashion colours – Mum *Vogue* smart, Gran in an old cardy over the print dress she resurrected each summer.

'And at home she always opted out when Dad helped me with homework. Sometimes one subject led to another . . . exploring ideas, that sort of thing. It didn't happen often though.' I leaned forward and picked up the poker, idling it in my hands. 'I think I was embarrassed to let her see . . . even admit to myself perhaps . . . I'm talking about my teens now . . . that I was enjoying just chatting with him.' I prodded among the flames. 'At the time I was only aware of this awful feeling of disloyalty. Now I'm not so sure. Maybe there was more to it than that.' I took a vicious lunge at a log, splitting it. Sparks flew up.

'Mind you.' I sat back, allowing my shoulders to relax. 'I don't know where all this is getting us. Even if Mother *was* jealous . . . envious of me, that had nothing to do with Dad turning to you. Which we've already decided she was happy about.' I shook my head. 'I can't see there's any connection between the two.'

Maybe, it was to occur to me later, I wasn't at that stage, ready to do so.

I cooked supper for Andrew that evening. He sat on a stool watching me, his elbows resting on the table, his chin in his hands.

Feeling disconcertingly self-conscious, almost as though I were acting out a part, I said, 'This is all terribly domesticated. But then,' I added, 'you're used to it of course.'

'If Ginny were doing it, she'd either have me

326

helping or bundle me out. No ceremony between brother and sister.'

'Something else for me to envy you for,' I said, sprinkling salt on the broccoli. 'Having a brother and sister. Half my problems probably arise from being an only child.' I told him some of what Flora and I had talked about. 'Too much on one pair of shoulders.'

'I take it,' said Andrew, choosing not to lead me any deeper into it all, 'you'll want a dozen when the time comes.'

'Or none.'

Unperturbed, Andrew got up and crossed the room. Reaching round me, he placed his hands over my stomach. 'You'd look great, pregnant,' he said.

'Do you mind? Long time before I start thinking about things like that.' I wriggled free. 'Now get off.' I pushed him away and, picking up a wooden spatula, waved it at him.

He dropped back a few paces and raised his arms in mock surrender. 'Now that,' he said, laughing, 'is what I recognise as being really domesticated. Never,' he retreated to the safety of the far side of the table, 'argue with a woman in her kitchen.'

I chased him. 'For that,' I said, thrusting the spatula at him, 'you can take over at the stove.'

CHAPTER 22

I came to the conclusion – lying awake beside Andrew that night – that there was nothing to be gained by chewing over the past any further.

It all seemed clear enough now. Father – as Andrew had forcefully reminded me men did – wanted a woman, both in bed and out of it, not a dependent child. Why he'd put up with Mother playing at being a wife for as long as he had was a mystery; maybe the timing of his eventual decision not to had little to do with anything other than opportunity. There was nothing to suggest he'd been actively looking; maybe he didn't even realise what he was missing until he came face to face with the alternative – Flora.

Hardly the bimbo Mother assumed. Maybe my budding adolescence did more than remind her the years were piling on; perhaps in Father's fondness for me she saw a predilection for a younger woman. How wrong she was! It wasn't something long-legged and nubile he craved, but warmth and companionship: someone who shared, or at least valued, his interests; who was sensitive to his needs and feelings.

Strange that I should be so sure – never having seen him and Flora together – that that was how they had been with each other. But, then again, not so strange – I'd got to know Flora now, and, yes, in some almost real, and enhanced, sense, him too.

I turned my head sideways. Andrew was sleeping peacefully. I could do worse, in my own relationships, I thought, than take a leaf out of Flora's book.

I stared back up at the ceiling again. And what about Mum? It was a bit startling to have to take on board the idea that she'd been – still was? – jealous of me. Did she really think I'd never loved her, cared about her? Whatever I'd said earlier today, I surely hadn't meant it? Not in general terms. It had just been hurt and anger; the heat of the moment; over-reaction. But – I pulled the covers closer under my chin and turned on my side – I supposed I had loved Father *more*. No doubt she'd been jealous of that – of us both. I felt my eyes closing. Well; that had certainly changed once Flora came on the scene. After that, surely Mother couldn't have been in any doubt it was she I cared about, supported . . .

I roused myself to prepare breakfast for Andrew next morning.

'Very cosy,' he commented. 'There's usually bedlam here at this time of the day – Ginny chasing around looking for lost socks; Tom and Justin arguing over whatever gadget they've found in the cornflakes packet . . .'

He downed the last forkful of bacon and egg. 'Makes me think—' He broke off as he glanced at his watch. 'Must go. Got an indomitable old dear coming in at nine – and she's always on the dot.'

I was round at Flora's by ten.

'I could do with going into town,' she said, as we debated how to spend our time.

It was market day. The place bristled with people and stalls, those selling genuine local produce vastly outnumbered by peripatetic vendors of the cheap and cheerful.

I glanced at Flora as we meandered through the crowds, allowing out attention to be caught now and then by some item of bric-a-brac or a second-hand gardening tool.

She returned my look quizzically.

'I'm waiting for you to say something about the good old days,' I said.

'When this would have been a real country market?' She shrugged philosophically. 'No point harking back. Things change.'

True, I thought.

Sidestepping a pile of litter at the edge of the pavement, I persuaded her into the local coffee shop. We sat over frothing hot chocolate and a slice each of home-made shortbread.

'This is deliciously self-indulgent,' I said. 'The prospect of going back to work next week—'

'I thought you thoroughly enjoyed your job?'

'Yes, of course.' I did. No question about it. 'It's a rather smug feeling though – ' elbows on the table, I smiled complacently – 'sitting here while everyone else is grinding away... But no, you're right. I'd miss it if it weren't there to go back to.'

I looked across at her. 'Have you *never* worked – apart from the bit of nursing you mentioned?'

Flora tipped her head on one side. 'You find that strange?'

'Well, even Mother,' I said, 'until she was married—'

'I suppose you could call looking after my aunt a job.'

I considered. 'That was a bit hard on you, wasn't it?'

'Not really. Her mind was as active as ever up to the very last. And she had so many fascinating friends – of all generations – with whom I was expected to keep up intellectually. I imagine it was just as stimulating a period in my life as your job makes yours now.'

I gave a moue of acknowledgement. 'I see.'

Flora laughed suddenly. '*And* she insisted I do all the things she'd loved to, but no longer could.'

'What! Disappear off on a Grand Tour?'

'Not quite. Mostly art exhibitions, theatre; occasionally – ' her expression became almost dreamy as she stared towards the window – 'dances – the old-fashioned formal kind with long evening gloves...' She turned back. 'And she *adored* the motor car. Broke her heart when she eventually let

331

the old Bentley go.' Amusement spread across her face as she recalled, 'You weren't so far off the mark when you guessed there was a would-be racing driver lurking inside me. Rallying. That became my big love. And Auntie encouraged it. We'd move her chair over to the window so she could sit and wave us off.'

'Us?'

Flora raised a tolerant eyebrow. 'Various people. Part of a crowd. We all promised ourselves that one day we'd do the Monte Carlo.' She picked up her cup, stared into it, and gave a regretful shrug. 'Once Auntie became bed-ridden . . . and then, when she died . . . well, it was the end of an era.'

'So what happened then?'

'Maybe I should have stayed in Bristol. But I had an urge to get out into the country.' She gave a small smile. 'To sit back and watch the flowers grow.'

'And that's what you've been doing ever since?'

She nodded, looking thoughtful. 'Perhaps I should have done more with my life. But then,' she straightened up, 'I've been quite content; lucky really. Haven't had to worry about the pennies – Auntie left everything to me and Donald. Thank goodness. It's meant I've been able to ensure that everything that could be done for him has been. Not – ' the robustness in her voice contrasted with an almost imperceptible slump in her shoulders – 'that that was much.'

I indicated my sympathy.

'In fact,' she said, 'it's this week I'm due to go

and see him. I should have mentioned it. Pity it's clashed with your visit – but I don't really want to put it off. Difficult to gauge how much concept he has of time passing, whether he'll be expecting me; but just in case—'

'Of course you must go. I can easily occupy myself.' I expected to feel disappointment; but the familiar sense of being let down failed to materialise.

'Phew. Give me a drink. 'Andrew flopped down at the kitchen table when he appeared that evening. 'It's been a heavy day.'

I passed the Scotch.

He took a long slurp, heaved a relaxing sigh, then fished in the inner pocket of his jacket to produce several folded sheets of A4. 'Slipped into the estate agents' at lunchtime,' he said, straightening out the papers and laying them out in front of him. 'I've been thinking – ' he lifted his glass again, took another sip and swallowed – 'maybe it's time I considered moving into a place of my own.'

I stared at him. 'But I thought—'

'Ginny? The boys? Well, yes; I don't know. Thing is . . . these last few days . . . it's brought it home that there are advantages – ' he peered expressively across at me from under raised eyebrows – 'in not having my style quite so cramped.'

Automatically I let him take my hand. 'Yes, but . . . maybe you shouldn't do anything too drastic. Not in a hurry. I mean . . .'

It was his turn to look puzzled. 'Why? Don't you like the idea?'

Like it? Of course I liked it. The fact of it. It was the implications behind it I wasn't too sure about.

'There's a cottage here – ' he was riffling through the papers – 'about halfway between here and Chadham . . .' He found what he was looking for. 'I know the place. Been empty for quite a while; probably needs quite a bit of work doing on it, but still . . .' He looked to me for approval. 'Now don't throw a dampener.'

'But what *about* the boys? You said yourself . . .'

Andrew reached forward and brushed the hair back from my face. 'Relax,' he said. 'This is my problem. I've let things slide far too long. Yes, of course; I'll have to talk to them about it, as well as to Ginny. But they're pretty sensible. Having to cope with Jonty's death has made them grow up faster – made them more realistic about the world.

'And after all, I'll still be around. No, I don't think that's the major problem. The big one – the one I've been sweeping under the carpet – is Ginny and her pride. Imagine I may have a hell of a job persuading her to accept gracefully that I don't want to lay any immediate claim to my share of the house.

'So,' he pushed over the sheet of details for me to read, 'why don't you come with me to look at this place? See if it's got possibilities.'

We did so the following day. Wednesday. Halfway

through my week's leave already.

Andrew juggled his appointments to allow himself an extended midday break. We took Flora along with us. I had an idea he valued her opinion at least as much as mine – though whether about the property specifically or about the principle of the idea, I wasn't sure. In a way, I guessed, he saw her presence as some form of implicit approval of it.

Lucke Cottage wasn't the sort of place one fell in love with at first sight – an old and undistinguished brick building set back from the road amid knee-high grass and untended bushes. Patches of bare wood leered from behind peeling paint on the doors and window frames, and bird droppings encrusted walls on either side of drainpipes.

Inside was better. If one mentally jettisoned the limp curtains hanging forlornly at rain-stained windows and ignored the occasional pile of abandoned rubbish, one could imagine the rooms redecorated and warmly furnished.

'I see what you mean about it needing some work,' I said. I wandered upstairs, made a face at the antiquarian plumbing in the bathroom, and peered into the bedrooms. In the second, larger one, I crossed creaking boards to the window. It faced the rear. I flapped a cobweb away. Then, 'Come and look,' I called as I heard Andrew's and Flora's steps on the stairs. 'A sundial.'

We inspected it at close quarters later: a tall stone plinth supporting a copper dial and arm, now olive-green with neglect. I trampled the undergrowth surrounding it, pointed to rose bushes struggling for air nearby.

Andrew turned his attention back to the cottage, surveying it as a whole. 'What do you think?' He looked from me to Flora and back again.

I gave a shrug of tentative encouragement.

Flora turned the question round. 'What do *you* think?'

I stared at the sundial. It had to be Andrew's decision.

'Worth considering,' he said.

I ran my fingers over the etched hieroglyphics as we turned to leave.

'Come and have supper with us tonight,' suggested Andrew to Flora as he dropped us back at Wood Edge.

As the Volvo disappeared along the lane and she and I retired into the house, I commented wryly, 'I expect he's planning to press you. About the cottage.'

'Probably.'

I picked up Columbus, napping on the chesterfield, and settled him, still curled, on my lap as I sank down.

'What *do* you think about it?'

'It looks solid enough. With a bit of effort—'

'Paint, elbow grease, and a scythe?'

'Precisely.'

I stroked the curve of ginger fur asleep on my knee. I could imagine Andrew, sleeves rolled up and in an ancient pair of jeans, balanced on a step-ladder with a pot of emulsion; or hacking back the weeds to reveal what, with a bit of luck, was a lawn beneath.

And what would I be doing? Somehow that picture was less clear. Polishing the sundial, I thought. Yes, that could be my contribution.

'I'm just wondering – ' I glanced up – 'whether he should be rushing into this.'

Flora, now seated and kicking off her shoes, nodded. 'I thought possibly you had reservations.'

'There's Ginny and the boys for a start. How are they going to react?' I recalled my conversation with Andrew yesterday evening. It was all very well him claiming it was his problem. 'What if they blame me?'

'They might be grateful.'

I blinked. 'Grateful?'

'Who's to say? Until Andrew's talked to Ginny, he won't know how she feels.'

I wondered. I supposed it wasn't impossible. Could she too have anticipated that Andrew's living at the Dower House would only be temporary? Come to think of it – financial implications apart – it wouldn't be easy for her to ask him to move out even if she wanted to. Could they both have got caught in a situation which neither of them felt able to break for fear of upsetting the other?

'But the boys,' I said. 'They'll miss him.'

I'll be around, Andrew had said. So had my

337

father, I thought – been around, that is. But then not, of course, in the way Andrew meant. He'd be the same as always with Tom and Justin when he saw them – and they with him. Was that just because he was their uncle not their father? Because they wouldn't have the same reason to feel let down; that their mother had been let down? Or was there something more to it than that?

I pictured Ginny when Andrew dropped in – on his way back from work perhaps. 'Hi,' she'd say. I conjured colour into her greeting: 'The boys want to ask you about . . . The boys want to show you . . . Be a gem and kick a football around with them while I . . .'

'Maybe it'll be all right,' I concluded.

Later, we went for a walk, the sky that pre-dusk opalescent grey. For some reason, I never ceased to tire of the stroll up the lane beyond the house. Columbus, disturbed by my moving, chose to accompany us. He strutted ahead, his tail held high like an antenna.

I stopped when we reached the stream and looked down at the water. Its summer languidness had melted into a steady current of movement, the weed at the edges streaming gently in the flow.

'It's not just Ginny and the boys . . . how they'll take it . . . that bothers me,' I said, reverting to our earlier conversation.

Flora had paused beside me. I was conscious of her eyes, if not her head, turning towards me.

'I'm not sure what Andrew's expecting.' I picked

a leaf from an overhead branch and dropped it into the water. It floated off. 'I love coming down here at weekends. Often. But not all the time. I've got a life in London too.'

'You're afraid Andrew might be hoping you'd give that up?'

'Entirely, you mean? Move in with him?' I wasn't sure whether my mind had leapt quite that far. 'I couldn't do that. Wouldn't want to.' I considered. 'Well, I might. If we both lived in London. But I'm not sure; it's a bit soon.'

We'd started walking on. 'Don't you think Andrew's probably sensitive to that?'

I supposed he might be. Come to think of it, on past experience he more than likely was. 'But why has he *suddenly* decided?'

'Perhaps you've just been the catalyst. Wanting the freedom to be on his own with you may simply be spurring him into doing something he's had in mind for quite a while.'

Which was more or less what he'd said to me himself.

'I'm not saying he may not be anticipating that perhaps in time . . . if you both decided . . .'

A weight seemed suddenly to have lifted. I halted and looked at Flora as she too stopped and turned. 'You must think me a self-centred idiot,' I said.

'No,' said Flora. 'I don't think that. But possibly you haven't been giving Andrew the credit for plain common sense. At a thoroughly pragmatic level, he's intelligent enough not to try bulldozing people into situations they're not happy with.'

'So it's all got very little to do with me?' Contrarily I now felt disappointment.

'To be thoroughly brutal,' said Flora,' if you and he should find you're not right for each other, he'd still have established the space to lead his own life, to develop some other relationship. What you *can* congratulate yourself on – ' she smiled now – 'is having woken him up to the realisation that some relationships are worth pursuing.'

I felt my own face lift. 'Maybe,' I said, 'he's done the same for me.'

Flora moved to my side and, for the first time ever, put an arm round me. She squeezed gently. 'That's my girl,' she said.

Shit, I scolded myself; why were my eyes filling up?

On the way back, I said, 'Andrew's never mentioned previous girlfriends.'

'Are you reading something into that?'

'Not necessarily.'

'No need that I'm aware of. He's had his share. Enough I guess – ' that smile again – 'for him to have discovered what he's looking for, what he values.'

I acknowledged the compliment.

'And what about you? Do you know yet what you want?'

'I think I'm still checking it out.'

Flora gave an understanding nod. 'Fair enough.'

She dealt succinctly, over supper, with Andrew's prodding for an opinion on Ginny's likely reaction. 'You'll just have to ask her.'

Andrew seemed satisfied. Maybe all he was looking for was some sort of encouragement to broach the matter. He succeeded in drawing Flora more on the subject of Lucke Cottage itself. We all agreed it could reward a measure of care and attention.

I couldn't resist mentioning the sundial. 'The first thing I'd want to do is clean it up.' Then, at ease after my conversation with Flora, I heard myself volunteering to make curtains. 'And I'm a dab hand with a paintbrush,' I claimed, conveniently ignoring my lack of experience – one could always learn.

'I'll talk to Ginny when she gets back tomorrow,' confirmed Andrew, helping himself to cream.

'Ah.' Flora looked from one to the other of us. 'You'll need the key then,' she said to me, smoothing the situation – with her reference to practicalities – that Ginny and the boys' imminent return threw up.

'Of course. You're going to be away.' I'd not so much forgotten as failed to connect the timings. It gave me pause. I'd be alone in the house with only Columbus for company – not a prospect I relished. On the other hand, nothing to stop Andrew sneaking in . . . No! Not behind Flora's back; I wouldn't feel right about it; and neither, I was pretty sure, would he. Moreover I was glad, in some perverse way, that for all her tolerance she'd not only never suggested he stay at Wood Edge but wasn't doing so now. There was nothing for it, I'd just have to take a deep breath and brave the country ghoulies. Unless . . .

Flora was spooning apple crumble. I turned to her.

'Why,' I said, wondering why I hadn't thought of it before, 'don't I come with you; drive you over? Would you mind? I think I'd like to meet Don.'

CHAPTER 23

Andrew glanced at me but made no comment.

Flora finished her mouthful. Then: 'If you like,' she said.

I wondered next day, as we skirted south of London, whether I'd been foolish to make my suggestion so impulsively. I was far from certain what I was letting myself in for.

I supposed I'd anticipated Flora would brief me – give me some idea of what to expect. But she'd hardly said a word since we set off, other than to respond to my comments on the scenery or the traffic.

And something was stopping me asking. Maybe I didn't want to admit my doubts, my apprehension. In what way was Don brain-damaged? What was the effect? And was he physically scarred – disfigured even – as well? If so, how would I react? Could I cope without shaming myself or embarrassing and even hurting Flora – and Don himself?

Well, Dad had done it. 'Supported her,' Andrew had said. So now it was my turn. Get a grip, girl.

Suddenly I felt more assured – as though Father was hovering at my ear, whispering, 'You'll manage.' Back to that pantomime again – only this time it was to be no on-stage performance: this was for real.

As though in tune with my thoughts, Flora broke her silence to volunteer, 'Your father often came with me, you know. When he could.'

'Then I'm glad I'm doing so.'

'So am I.'

She said no more, other than to issue directions, until we turned in at wrought-iron gates and followed the signs to the visitors' car park to one side of a large mock-Tudor building.

'Bring your coat,' she advised then.

'Oh?'

'It has to be pouring with rain or two feet of snow to keep Don inside. And even then he'll argue.'

We located him sitting on the ground beneath a cedar. Flora pointed him out, leaning against its trunk, picking randomly at the grass. When we were about ten yards away, she put out a hand to halt our approach.

'Hello, Don,' she said, just loudly enough for him to hear.

He turned his head, and I swallowed a gasp: he was quite one of the handsomest men I'd ever seen. In total contrast to Flora's, his eyes were startlingly blue, his classic features, under a still full head of, admittedly greying, hair, reminiscent of the heartthrob stars of old 1950s' films.

He rose cautiously – all six foot something of him, and broad with it.

'Hello, Don,' Flora repeated.

Inching back towards the tree, he put out a hand as though steadying himself against it.

'Wait there,' said Flora to me. Then she began walking forward slowly. 'It's me, Flora.'

I watched, mesmerised. Over to my left, a male nurse in high-collared, short white coat, was crossing the lawn. He glanced towards Don and Flora and slowed his pace. I looked back at Don. His eyes held all the fight-or-flight indecision of the hunted.

Flora had paused. 'It's only me. I've come to see you.' She put her hand in her coat pocket and pulled out a packet of sweets. The bag crackled as she opened it. Don flinched, cringing backwards.

'It's only the cellophane, nothing else. Here, would you like one?'

The nurse's careful stroll had brought him within a few feet of me. 'Not one of Donald's better days,' he remarked. 'Very edgy. Still, if anyone can calm him, his sister can.'

She'd taken a sweet out of the bag now and was holding it out to him. Hesitantly Don let go of the tree and began moving towards her, darting glances from left to right as he did so.

'It's OK, old chap – ' the nurse's tolerantly matter-of-fact commentary was for my ears, not Don's – 'you're not in the jungle now.'

I nodded. Understood.

Flora stood motionless as Don approached her.

Then he snatched the sweet – and simultaneously beamed. He popped it in his mouth and bent his cheek for a kiss.

'Phew, that's all right then.' The nurse turned and went on his way.

Flora was chatting to Don, brushing grass from his jacket, scolding him for sitting on damp ground. Then she called me over.

'Don,' she said, 'I've brought someone to meet you. Hugh's daughter. You remember Hugh?'

Don turned piercing eyes towards me – piercing in colour only; his expression was bland. 'No,' he said emphatically, in a voice that had the depth of a man's but the intonation of a child's.

'Yes, you do. This is Charissa.'

'Hello, Don.' I held out my hand.

He ignored it.

'Never mind,' said Flora.

She despatched me to fetch our picnic lunch from the car while she persuaded Don to a bench below the house. We sat there, huddled in coats, sharing out the sandwiches and warming ourselves with coffee from the flask. A member of staff occasionally emerged on to the terrace above and glanced in our direction. Everyone else appeared to have had the sense to retreat inside.

I was packing away the remnants when Don startled me by reaching out and slapping a hand on my knee. 'You're very pretty,' he said, as though having come to that conclusion after considerable thought.

'Thank you,' I said.

'But not as pretty as Amy.'

I looked across at Flora.'

'Who's Amy?' she asked.

'Hugh's daughter.'

'No, this,' she nodded towards me, 'is Hugh's daughter. Her name is Charissa. Is Amy one of the nurses?'

'Yes,' said Don. He directed a devastating smile at me and patted my knee again. 'Very pretty.'

We booked into the small hotel on the edge of town where Flora regularly stayed. We were close enough to London, it had occurred to me, to suggest we go up to the flat and stay there overnight, but something told me Flora needed the routine of the familiar.

For that matter, it wouldn't have been too late by the time we departed – following afternoon tea, brought out to us in already failing light on the terrace – to drive back to Cotterly. But Flora always made a two-day trip of it.

I asked about plans for the next day when she eventually came downstairs and joined me in front of the modest log fire.

'Friday's the morning when I can catch the psychiatrist as well as the GP,' she said. 'I like to make a point of having a word with them both.' She shrugged. 'Not that there's usually much for them to report – a bad episode here, a better one there. He swings so.'

'At least it ensures they know you're around; that Don's not forgotten.'

She glanced up. 'I suppose that *is* part of it. But it's also something to do with that dreadful feeling of helplessness – it's all I *can* do.' She turned on me, almost aggressively. 'Don't think I haven't wondered whether I could have had him at home.'

Something made me keep quiet.

She subsided. 'It was a pipe-dream, of course. Totally impractical. I was only a girl – younger than you are – when it happened.'

The reminder shook me. Supposing I, now, were faced with something like that.

'And there was Auntie to look after as well.' Flora was staring into the fire, her face taut. Was she remembering Bristol; wondering . . .

I hesitated. 'Your parents,' I said. 'I mean, you've never said much about them. Were they—?'

'Gone,' she replied tersely. She sat up and turned, concentrating her gaze over my shoulder towards the dining-room door. She checked her watch. 'Must be about time they started serving dinner.'

Over the soup I apologised. 'I'm sorry, I shouldn't have asked . . .'

She looked up, the stiffness eased from her expression.

'No, *I'm* sorry. Just touched a raw spot, that's all. I guess that particular scar's still tender; and visits here . . .' She gave a quiet rueful smile.

'Doesn't seem as though, even now, I've managed to forgive my parents totally, does it?' She looked reflective. 'Still haven't got rid of all the anger, I suppose.' She tipped her plate, scooping up the last spoonful of cream of mushroom. 'Virtually abandoning us as children was bad enough; but –' her voice almost imperceptibly rose – 'when they refused to face up to what had happened to Don . . .'

We waited while the soup plates were removed and roast lamb placed in front of us.

'They were like children, you understand,' Flora resumed. She shrugged. 'The war gave them a wonderful excuse to play hero and heroine. I guess they just became addicted to Never-Never-Land. Peter Pans, both of them.'

'Are they still alive?'

'I've no idea.'

I stared at her. She was cutting into her meat.

'You know you talked to me about my lost years with my father,' I said. 'Were you speaking from personal experience – your parents . . . and Don too, of course?'

Flora put down her knife and fork and dropped her hands to her lap. She sat there silently for a moment before replying. 'I suppose I was.'

I'd have liked to reach out and touch her. Instead: 'Oh, Flora,' I said.

She straightened her shoulders then and continued eating. 'Just one of those things,' she said firmly.

As we said goodnight on the landing, I gave her a hug.

'Will you be coming with me tomorrow morning?' she asked.

'What do you think? Would you like me to?'

'There are some quite interesting little shops in town.'

'Then I'll go and browse round there.' I hoped it was the right response.

Flora seemed more relaxed on the journey home, but preferring to enquire about my morning rather than reveal anything of her own. We arrived back at Wood Edge just after six.

As I pulled on the handbrake, I turned to her. 'Thanks for letting me come.'

She squeezed my hand. 'I'm glad you did. Now –' she opened the car door and swung herself round to alight – 'off you go and see Andrew. Find out if he's sorted things out with Ginny.'

It was she who, a few minutes later, opened the door to me. 'Hi. Come in.'

'I'm sorry,' I said. 'I've interrupted you.' I'd heard the sound of the piano as I switched off the car engine. I'd paused for a moment in the driveway, savouring the lightness of a single instrument merging with the muted music of everyday sounds. The playing had stopped abruptly as I rang the bell. 'Isn't Andrew . . . ?' I nodded towards the Volvo beside which I'd parked.

'He and Philip have taken the boys off to help

put the finishing touches to the bonfire. For tomorrow night,' she added in response to my look of incomprehension.

'Oh, Guy Fawkes.' Long time since I'd even thought about it. 'And Philip too!' I commented as Ginny closed the door behind me.

She laughed. 'Always likes to involve himself in village events. There's a bit of the would-be-squire in our Philip. Surprised you haven't noticed.'

I supposed I had, come to think of it.

'You could wander along and see what they're up to if you like.'

I made a face. 'I'd much rather flop down if you don't mind. It's been a long day. But – ' nodding guiltily in the general direction of the abandoned piano – 'don't let me stop you—'

'Nonsense.' Ginny headed for the kitchen. 'Nice to have a bit of female company for a change. Tea, coffee, or something stronger?'

I opted for tea. 'I'm parched.'

'You've been with Flora to see Donald?' said Ginny as she plugged in the kettle.

I nodded.

'You're privileged.'

'Am I?' I hadn't thought of it like that. Or had I? In a way, yes. Flora had certainly let me see a side of her – of her life – she'd previously kept firmly wrapped.

'So,' said Ginny, declining to probe further and now perching herself on a stool, 'what do you think of this cottage Andrew's considering moving into?'

'What do *I* think?' I'd have liked to add it had nothing to do with me. Instead I opted for neutrality. 'It seems OK.'

Ginny gave me a long look. She pushed a packet of biscuits in my direction. I shook my head. She retrieved them and helped herself. 'I think it's a great idea.'

'You do?'

She nibbled. 'I've been thinking about it all day. On and off. At first – last night – I felt a sort of panic. I mean . . . having Andrew living here with us . . . when we came back. . . . it smoothed the ground.' She grinned. 'Got the grass cut anyway. But – ' her expression became serious again – 'I guess that nice comfortable path has worn itself into a rut. For me anyway.'

She picked crumbs from her lap and made a neat pile of them on the table. 'We ended up having a really good talk about everything yesterday evening. Andrew's quite right – I've got to let Jonty go; start making a new life.'

'Is that what he said?'

Ginny looked up. 'Actually, no – I guess those are my words. But it's what he meant. And I can see it now. It's all been too cosily safe.

'I've been hanging on to Jonty, in whatever sense that is, because – this is what I've worked out, anyway – the possibility of getting involved with someone new is too damned scary.'

'I think I know that feeling,' I said.

'*Do* you?'

I considered. 'When you lose someone you love – in my case feel let down by them too – you're a bit cautious of risking being hurt like that again. Not,' I added hurriedly, 'that my experience is any way comparable with yours.'

'Who are you talking about?'

'My father. And a boyfriend. Not that I'm sure whether I really loved Mark – but I certainly felt he let me down.'

Ginny looked thoughtful. 'You know,' she said, 'in a crazy way I suppose I've always felt Jonty did just that. A sort of irrational feeling of "how dare he die and leave me to cope".' She prodded the biscuit crumbs into a heap, then smoothed them. She turned to me. 'And before you ask, no, I don't feel Andrew's abandoning me. Freeing me from leaning on him, more likely.'

I almost commented that that seemed to be becoming something of a habit for him, but changed my mind.

While I was debating instead whether to ask about the boys and their reaction, we heard the sound of what Ginny recognised as Philip's Land Rover pulling up outside.

'Oh, whoops!' She sprang to her feet. 'And I haven't even started preparing supper.'

There was a bustle at the front door. Tom and Justin came rushing through to the kitchen. 'Hi, Mum.' And on seeing me: 'Hi, Charissa.'

'Oh, my God.' Ginny's eyebrows shot up in

mock horror. 'You're filthy. What *have* you been doing?'

Andrew, closely followed by Philip, had appeared in the doorway. 'Having fun,' he said. 'You should see the size of the bonfire.' Then he looked across at me and winked a greeting. 'Hi.' Philip nodded.

'Baths. Now,' Ginny was instructing the boys.

'Yes but—'

'Now!'

Andrew made play of booting them in the direction of the stairs. 'And leave some hot water for me.' He and Philip moved forward into the room and started chatting. 'Three trailer-loads,' Andrew was saying, referring to old wood and dead branches cleared from the farm.

'Could do with a beer if you've got one,' suggested Philip, gruff as ever.

He leaned against a cupboard to the side of the rest of us, nursing his drink, saying little. I made my share of attempts at conversation with him but found it hard going.

'Stay and have supper,' Ginny invited.

'No thanks. Things to do.' He drained his glass. We heard him call up from the hall as he departed. 'Goodnight, boys.'

'Night.' There was a patter of feet on the stairs. A pause. 'Night. See you tomorrow.'

Justin, smelling of soap, appeared in pyjamas. 'Tom's just getting out,' he said.

'Right. My turn.' Andrew went off. Moments

later there was the sound of laughter and a scuffle on the landing.

'What was going on?' demanded Ginny, busy with a saucepan, when Tom strolled down.

He grinned. I was struck by how much more grown-up he suddenly seemed. Maybe it was the sleeked hair, wet from the shower; or that the long stripes of his pyjamas accentuated the inches he'd been almost imperceptibly putting on over the summer. 'I was measuring up,' he said, 'to decide where my stereo speakers would go in Andrew's room.'

'Goodness.' Ginny pulled a face. 'Anyone'd think you can't wait for him to move out.'

Again that teasing self-assurance. 'I can't, if it means I don't have to share a room any longer with this –' he made a playful lunge at Justin –'. . . this infant.'

Justin tossed his head. 'Can't wait to have our room to myself, either.'

I looked across at Ginny.

'So much for nepotal devotion,' she observed.

'What's nepotal mean?' It was Justin.

'Look it up,' said Ginny.

By the time Andrew came down, the boys were already seated at the table, gazing hungrily in the direction of the stove. Ginny related, with amusement, their conversation. She patted Andrew's shoulder. 'So you needn't worry you'll be missed.'

He pretended dismay.

Justin was the one concerned to reassure and be

reassured. 'But you'll see us often,' he said, 'won't you?'

'I'm going to need you to help me do the place up.'

Tom allowed himself interest. 'When can we see it? Can we have a look tomorrow?'

Andrew helped himself to another beer. 'Sunday, if you like.' He looked across at me. 'I was going to suggest we go and walk over the Quantocks again tomorrow. Good idea?'

'Great.'

He turned to Tom and Justin. 'Don't worry, Charissa and I will be back for the fireworks. Just you make sure – ' he prepared to dodge Ginny – 'that your mother's ready in good time.'

Flora, correctly assuming I would be included in supper at the Dower House, had already retired when I returned to Wood Edge. I crept upstairs with my bag and shook out the trousers and shirt I would need next day. I hung them over a chair, ready for an early start, before climbing into bed.

I lay there wondering how many more times I would stay in this room that had by now become so familiar. How long would it be before Andrew could move into Lucke Cottage – as it seemed he was now all set to do?

While Ginny had been chasing the boys up to clean their teeth – 'Come on, hurry up; it's late already' – I'd turned to him. 'I gather Ginny's accepted your plans happily enough?'

'To my relief.'

His version corroborated Ginny's. 'As for the boys –' he laughed – 'ever practical and pragmatic, my nephews. As you heard.'

There was a pounding overhead as someone scampered across the landing. Andrew stared up at the ceiling, grimacing in mock apprehension. 'Tom wanted to know,' the commotion seemed to prompt him to recount, 'whether you would be living there with me.'

'What did you say?' I strove for light-heartedness.

'I pointed out you could hardly commute to London from here.'

'And my work's important to me.'

Andrew abandoned his consideration of the plaster above and turned his gaze on me. He smiled. 'I know,' he said.

I reached across and slid my hand over his hair. 'Are you going to make an offer for the cottage, then?'

'First thing on Monday morning.'

'You don't hang about, do you?'

'Not once I've made up my mind.' He got up, sweeping plates together. 'I suppose we could clear these away before Ginny comes down.'

Later, walking me out across the darkened driveway to my car, he took the opportunity to ask about my trip to Sussex.

I leaned against the bonnet, explaining Don as best I could. 'It's such a lonely responsibility for her,' I said of Flora. 'At least while my father was alive she had someone to share it with. Her feelings about it anyway.'

Andrew nodded. 'Maybe,' he said, 'that was part of the reason your father sent you down here.'

'You mean, not just for my benefit?' The thought presented a new angle. Or rather, resurrected the one I'd discarded on coming face to face with Flora's forceful self-sufficiency.

'It's taken a long time for me to see it,' I remarked ruefully.

'Or for Flora to allow you to.'

I'd let his comment stand at the time but now, increasingly drowsy, I mulled it over. Andrew, I was at last beginning to appreciate, was considerably more astute than I'd realised.

I had prepared myself, as we drove westwards next day, for the disappointment of lost magic on this, my second, visit to the gently rolling Somerset hills. Instead, the beginnings of familiarity enhanced it. Seasonal differences were apparent, of course: a chill wind and light drizzle for a start; and colouring muted not only by the browning of trees and heather but by the angle of light now winter was approaching. But such changes seemed only to firm the ground; to emphasise some special quality that was more than permanence – though that was part of it.

I strode alongside Andrew, neither of us willing to intrude anything other than the occasional comment. Now and again, in tacit understanding, we stopped and looked around us. Once, paused at the top of a rise, I reached up and put my arms round his neck. Our kiss was light, its intimacy a function of our contentment.

If ever life were perfect, it was now.

Apart, that was, from the problem of Mother, and our mutual resentment. I saw no imminent prospect of resolving the situation; but then, who ever knows what tomorrow may bring?

CHAPTER 24

It was strange, I reflected later, that it should have been a death – my father's – that led to the estrangement between myself and Mother, and a death that was instrumental in bringing us together again.

The answerphone was winking when I arrived back in Fulham late that Sunday evening. My mother always ignored it – 'makes me nervous; it's not natural, speaking to a machine' – so I was taken aback, when it wound through to the final message, to hear her voice.

'Charissa.' Pause. Then in a rush: 'Ring me as soon as you come in, would you?' The pitch indicated more than unease with modern gadgetry.

I gave myself a couple of minutes before returning her call. 'What is it? What's happened?'

It was Nan.

'The warden called ... they found her in her chair ... she'd been taking an afternoon nap ... just slipped away, he said ...'

'Oh Mother, I'm so sorry.'

And within moments, as the news sank in, guilty too. It was ages since I'd last been to visit my grandmother. Usually I'd driven over with Mother every two or three months or so; taken Nan a box of sweets, tucked her shawl round her shoulders and listened with only half an ear to her ramblings while congratulating myself with the other half of my mind on a duty patiently performed. I winced. But even that had been better than forgetting her entirely as I had done this summer.

'It's such a shock,' Mother was saying. 'Such a shock.'

I calmed her as best I could. I checked the time. Realistically it made no sense to rush down now. 'I'll come over straight from work tomorrow,' I promised.

I did, and found Leah there; though on the point of departure.

'I think we've sorted out most things,' she said.

I went with her to the door.

'Your mother's taking it very hard,' she whispered.

I nodded. 'And what about you? Are you all right?'

'Maybe I'm more pragmatic. It was bound to happen sooner or later. And anyway, I've got Harold.'

After she'd gone, I shut the door and leaned against it. So true, what Leah had said. Dammit, why wasn't Father here to bear the brunt? Why did I always have to cope? And I wasn't just talking about now. I glared up at the ceiling, mentally piercing it to the ether above. 'Huh,' I said, directing my remarks there. 'Whatever happened to perfect parents?'

You'd have thought my grandmother had been one, the way Mother talked about her. I listened, and forbore to remind her of the many moans I'd heard over the years. But then, I supposed, one does prefer to remember only the good things. To hear Mother speak of Father these days you'd think he'd been a saint. Come to think of it – Mother's monologue allowed plenty of opportunity for my thoughts to wander – hadn't I been doing much the same thing where he was concerned? Was it hypocrisy or charity? Maybe just self-protection.

And which, or what combination of the three, was Mother displaying now in conveniently forgetting her fury with me? 'She doesn't want to lose you,' Leah had said. Any more, I conceded, than, whatever her faults, I wanted to lose her. Any more, it suddenly hit me, than *she* wanted to lose *her* mother. And she just had. I shifted closer on the sofa and put an arm round her. 'I'll make you some cocoa,' I said.

There's something oddly unreal about funerals, I assessed as, early the following week, I steadied my mother into the front pew and took my place beside her. On her far side, Harold had brought himself stiffly to attention while Leah and Elspeth fidgeted with bags and gloves, uncertain whether to put them down or hold on to them. Mother stared straight ahead.

That sense of time standing still while the rituals are performed seemed even more pronounced on this occasion than it had done at Father's funeral. Then the church had been packed and the black, grey and brown winter coats pressing behind me had somehow absorbed the vaulted echoes.

But there was only a handful of mourners for Nan. Mother had insisted on 'seeing her off' from home, and I'd spent the weekend with my sleeves rolled up in the kitchen helping prepare refreshments.

Who for, I wondered now, as the vicar strove to personalise the traditional phrases. Only one carload of the more mobile of her fellow residents had felt up to making the journey across London and out through the south-western suburbs. The numbers, such as they were, had been made up by various of Mother's acquaintances attending in a gesture of support.

It was a sad little ceremony, I thought as we trailed up to the crematorium and stood again in solemn, unnerving silence as the final farewells were intoned. Outside, afterwards, Mother and Leah were led off to choose a spot for the ashes to be scattered. Elspeth and I stood to one side as Harold led the perusal of cards on the laid-out wreaths.

'I hate these places,' said Elspeth.

'Can't say I'm too keen on them myself.'

I stared across the Garden of Remembrance to where our mothers were paused beneath a lilac tree. Mother was using her stick, still kept to hand for less steady moments, as a pointer.

'Come with me?' I whispered to Elspeth.

She raised an eyebrow in query, but followed me.

I skirted right and through a gap in the hedge, halting at one corner of a rectangular rose bed. 'Father,' I explained.

Elspeth's arm slid round me; she tipped her head briefly against my shoulder. I stared upwards. And suddenly I felt tall; reassuringly tall.

Back at the house, when all but family had departed, Elspeth and I excused ourselves to clear up in the kitchen.

'Glad that's over,' observed Elspeth, tearing off a length of cling-film to wrap left-overs.

I collected glasses on to the draining board and turned on the tap. 'How long are you staying down?'

'A couple more days, I expect. I have to admit,' she confessed in a tone of self-mockery, 'there's a lot to be said for checking out home comforts once in a while. I suppose my parents aren't such bad old sticks when it comes to the point.'

I let the acknowledgement pass. 'And how's Perry?'

We brought each other up to date on our love lives.

'So is your mother reconciled to Andrew yet?'

'Hardly. There's a mutual stand-off on the subject.' I sighed. 'The Flora connection just makes the whole situation impossible.'

Elspeth polished a glass thoughtfully. 'I suppose there isn't any more to it than that?'

'Like what?'

She shrugged. 'Like being afraid any man's going to take you away from her; turn you against her.'

I dunked a glass; watched the bubbles rise, one or two of them escaping and floating up over my wrists. I was in the garden again with Father, Mother standing in the doorway. And I was on the stairs with Mother glaring up at me. 'You never loved me,' I heard her say.

Elspeth's words continued to hang in the air – Mother's fears; fears which were in danger of proving self-fulfilling. Forced, as I'd seen it, into choosing between her and Andrew – and Flora, Cotterly, everything – I had chosen Father's world. This time. Last time she had been in control. Kept me away from my father – turned *me* against *him*. And, yes, I was afraid – had been afraid – she'd do something similar where Andrew was concerned. Not that, contrarily a good wedding wouldn't delight her. But then what? Whoever I were to marry. Would she and I be back in competition – but this time for *my* man?

'She really doesn't realise, does she,' I said, 'that you can love people in different ways, that there's room for all? It's as though if she hasn't got your undivided love, attention, loyalty, she's got nothing.

'And she can't see,' I carried on musing as Elspeth inspected a smudge and rubbed at it with the teatowel, 'that her demands are eventually so constraining that people burst away. My father; now me. Why – ' my voice rose with the frustration of incomprehension – 'is she like that?'

Elspeth lined up the glass she'd dried next to the others. 'Insecurity, I guess.'

'But why?'

'Upbringing? With all due respect to the recently departed . . . you have to admit Nan was something of an embittered old harridan.'

I frowned. 'Bit of an exaggeration, isn't it?'

'Well, a permanent whiner, anyway. Hardly an all-loving mother.'

I acknowledged it.

'And of course neither of them ever knew their father. Not to remember him, that is.'

The reminder jolted me. No wonder . . . Seeing me with Dad must have recalled for Mother what she'd missed. Not that that was my fault, but still . . .

'But Leah . . . your mother; she's not like that.'

'She might be; if she didn't have Dad.'

As if cued by the mention, Uncle Harold appeared. It was time, he apologised, they were leaving.

Mother and I stood by the porch as they climbed into the car. Elspeth held the door for Leah; smiled;

exchanged a cheerful comment with her father. The threesome departed.

'And I suppose you'll be wanting to be off soon?' said Mother, as we turned to go back inside. She looked, I thought, more weary than hard-done-by.

On the spur of the moment I reconsidered my plans. 'I could stay and go up first thing in the morning,' I suggested.

The lines around her eyes eased the merest fraction. 'That would be nice,' she said, as though – was I imagining it? – she had decided to stop, or perhaps was too tired to carry on, fighting me.

While she went up to have a bath – 'Good idea,' I'd agreed – I curled up in Father's Minty armchair, just as I used to as a teenager: shoes kicked off, feet tucked up under me. Above, I heard water running, then stop. Somewhere in the system, residual gurgles protested feebly. I'd been aware of them that night Mother was in hospital and I'd been here on my own. I was glad I'd decided to stay and keep her company this evening – now wasn't the moment to leave her with her loneliness.

I was, I realised, all she'd got left – apart from Leah. And I saw again, perhaps with Mother's eyes, that image of her sister, with her husband and daughter, driving away.

I stirred myself. By the time she came down, I had everything ready to whip up an omelette. She was grateful.

'How are you feeling?' I ventured after we'd eaten.

She gave a wan smile; shrugged.

'It's been a tough year, hasn't it?' I knew I was referring not only to my father's death, and now her mother's, but to my own behaviour.

'I'll survive.' She sounded resigned rather than belligerent.

She would too, of course. Hadn't she always? 'She's well able to look after herself,' Harold had said.

Yes, but at what cost? And how well in the over-all scheme of things? Strange that she hadn't fought harder against Flora.

Why had she settled, almost complacently, for the appearance only of marriage? Had there been some other compensation – over and above the one Elspeth had, some months ago, so bluntly identified, and which even Andrew had acknowledged?

I baulked at the direction in which my deductions were driving me. Surely – but even as the thought took shape I recognised it, inescapably, for the truth – she couldn't have welcomed the opportunity Flora afforded to sour my feelings for my father. Subtly, with her uncomplaining martyrdom. Better, had she decided, to lose him than – as her irrational jealousy must have persuaded her – to lose us both? To each other. And how much greater must her fear of being sidelined by the pair of us have become as I grew older? Hadn't the thought crossed my mind – I recalled the occasion: here, alone, rousing myself in my sprigged bedroom upstairs – that Mother maybe preferred him to find the companionship, the intellectual rapport I might have offered, with Flora than with me? That way at least, in her tattered perception, she retained the means to hold on to *me*, to exact *my* loyalty.

Maybe, in the years before he turned to Flora, she had been paving the way – by the withdrawal, to whatever extent that was, of bedroom intimacies – for his departure, emotionally, from the family scene. Or had that withdrawal been, in itself, a cry of protest at having to share his affection with me; a cry which Father had presumably failed to recognise or, if he had, had been either unable or unwilling to respond to? In which case, Elspeth's version of Mother's attitude to such closeness was over-simplified to the point of misconstruction.

Who was to say? And looking at Mother now – exhausted, defeated even – I doubted if even she, were she of a mind to explore her motivations, could unravel them. Moreover – I continued to study her, leaning back in her chair, eyes half-closed, her hands for once idle in her lap – whatever she'd done to me, I couldn't believe she'd consciously intended me any hurt. Any more than Father – or indeed Flora – had. Though they, at least, had been aware of it. Whether that was a plus or a minus on their account I was none too sure.

Mother was still motionless. What good would it do, I reflected, to confront her? In the name of survival, she too had lost out. Perhaps the most.

'Coffee?' I suggested quietly.

Mother opened her eyes. 'That would be lovely.'

The strip-lighting in the kitchen buzzed as I switched it on. Its fluorescent glare accentuated the gleam on the work surfaces and cupboard doors. Impossible not to compare the harsh reflections with the softness of wood and glow of lamps of Flora's kitchen; or even with Ginny's where the modern units were at least mellowed by the clutter of living. I found myself wondering how Andrew would design his at Lucke Cottage. Would he invite me to take a hand? Did I hope he would?

I reached for cups and coffee. Maybe, though I had dismissed the idea of confronting Mother with the past, it was time to face her with the future. Now; before she retreated behind those hostile barriers again. Flora had become an unassailable part of my life. If Mother could accept that – however unwillingly – she could accept Andrew. Only one way to find out if she was prepared to do so.

I carried the tray through, passed Mother the milk, added my own, and sat back against the firmness of the upholstery.

'Next weekend . . .' I said as she sipped.

'Your birthday.'

I nodded. 'Andrew's coming up to London on Friday evening.'

We'd arranged it over the phone. A crowd of us, at Clare's suggestion, were planning an evening out to celebrate: a drink, a meal, maybe go on somewhere afterwards. 'And we all pay for ourselves,' I'd explained firmly to Andrew. He'd laughed. 'Whatever you say, ma'am.'

'I was just wondering,' I said now to Mother. 'We'll be driving down to Cotterly on Saturday.' I decided not to mention that Flora had promised to make a cake, and Ginny to ice it. 'We – Andrew and I – could call in on the way.'

I lifted my chin and gave her a straight look. 'I'd like you to meet him,' I said.

Her mouth pursed into a tight line, her eyes focusing somewhere behind my head. 'I wouldn't want you to—'

'Mother . . .' I warned.

There was a pause while she steadied her cup in its saucer. Then: 'I'll rustle up some scones,' she said.

CHAPTER 25

If any apprehension about the meeting had tinged my overall comfortableness at a decision well made, it needn't have done.

Andrew greeted the proposal equably, and we drew up in front of the house, on the Saturday morning of my birthday, only a minute or two after the pre-arranged ten-thirty. Mother, dressed up for the occasion, opened the door before we reached it.

Over the promised scones, she exuded charm – so much so that I began to wonder whether Andrew was withstanding it. But as she turned to lift the coffee jug, he winked at me. Reassured, I hid my smile in my cup. Later, in amusement, I watched her dimple prettily as, on our departure, he kissed her proffered cheek.

We waved out of the car window as we reached the end of the Avenue. Once round the corner, Andrew allowed his face to crinkle. 'So much for the dragon I was expecting,' he said. 'You could have warned me I was to be introduced to a good old-fashioned flirt.'

I supposed she was. Hadn't I seen it in her

fluttering helplessness recently with Jack Webb? 'You seem to have handled her without too much difficulty,' I remarked.

He laughed, and I settled back, enjoying the novelty of being driven along this particular route.

'So where's that present she gave you?' Andrew interrupted the daydreaming into which I'd happily drifted. 'Let's have another look at it.'

I reached into my bag and took out the slim box. I eased off the lid and held up the gold necklace for Andrew to glance across at.

He gave a nod of approval.

'It matches that bracelet,' Mother had pointed out unnecessarily as I'd unwrapped it and recognised the etching on its links. The bracelet Father had chosen and Mother had considered, granted at the time, to be too sophisticated for me. Was there some acknowledgement which even she was unaware of in her selection today of its companion? The hug of thanks I'd given her had been for more than the delicate gift itself.

'And what,' I teased Andrew now, 'have *you* got for me?'

He turned back from checking over his shoulder as we joined the motorway. 'You could try the glove compartment for a start,' he said.

I clicked it open and pulled out a roughly wrapped parcel. I explored its feel – something soft, but with a hard circular object, a box perhaps, beneath.

'Go on, then. Open up.' The corners of his eyes and mouth twitched in amused anticipation.

I folded back the paper to reveal a yellow duster. 'What the . . . ?' From within it I unearthed a jar of polish.

'For the sundial,' he explained with a sideways grin.

I laughed. 'Does that mean . . . ?'

He confirmed it was just a matter of tying up the paperwork. I leaned back contentedly, closing my eyes. 'And what else,' I asked, 'might you have in store for me?'

I felt his hand against my cheek, lingering there for a moment. I put up my own and brushed it briefly against his. 'You'll just have to wait and see,' I heard him promise.

I smiled. 'By the way,' I said, the light shimmering through my eyelids, 'do you think the boys would like my father's old fishing rods?'

Later, as we crested the rise above Cotterly, I turned to Andrew. 'Pull in for a moment, will you?'

He drew on to the rough and looked at me enquiringly.

The track stretched to my left. 'I'd like to walk along to the meadow,' I said. 'No . . .' I put out a restraining hand as he made to turn off the engine. 'On my own. If you don't mind.'

I checked my watch. It was just gone one. 'Why don't you go ahead; round up the others? I'll meet you all in the pub in, say, half an hour.'

'If that's what you'd like.' He seemed neither surprised nor put out.

I nodded.

'I could wait for you. Or come back and pick you up.'

'No, I'll walk down.'

Fallen leaves crunched underfoot as I strolled, unhurriedly but with a certain briskness in my step, towards the gate at the far end. I leaned against it for a while marvelling, as though seeing it for the first time, at the familiar view of hedges, fields and woods. Or, rather, at the sense of space.

Less than a year since I first came here, convinced – that day in February – that my journey was a mistake. Smiling, I struggled with the spring latch on the gate and pushed it open sufficiently to allow me to squeeze through. I walked forward to the spot where Father had chosen, in his painting, to place me.

I flung my arms wide, stretching out towards horizons blurred against the mid-November sky. My mental reach encompassed the oak under which Andrew and I had sat that first time we'd come here together, the ponies grazing further down the slope, the rooftops of Cotterly – the chimneys of Wood Edge now identifiable among them – and the hills rising all around. In the stillness of a lull in the breeze, I could almost swear I discerned the sound of the stream bubbling through the dip below. I opened my mouth and breathed in the autumnal smell of nature resting after the activity of summer. I let the taste out gently. 'Thanks, Dad,' I said.

I stood for a moment or two longer, relishing the air smoothing across my face. Then I turned. Andrew, and Flora and Ginny too, were waiting for me.

If you enjoyed this book, you might also enjoy the following:

Puppies Are For Life by Linda Phillips

Now that their children have finally flown the nest, Susannah and Paul Harding are looking forward to a trouble-free middle age. But their nest isn't empty for long: daughter Katy comes home for comfort having lost her job, followed by her brother, licking the wounds of redundancy and a failed relationship – with a baby and a cat in tow. Finally Susannah's father and stepmother, seeking refuge from a disastrous attempt to settle in the Dordogne, set up camp in the garden. Paul is delighted to have his family home once more, but Susannah is horrified at the prospect of a return to domestic drudgery, and seeks solace with her sympathetic neighbour Harvey – who happens to have too much time on his hands . . .

The Company of Strangers by Eileen Campbell

It's the summer of 1959 and eleven-year-old Ellie Fairbairn is exiled to the Highland village of Inchbrae, to stay with a grandmother she hardly knows, after her mother's nervous breakdown. Her grandmother Dot is decidedly eccentric, partial to the odd dram of whisky and, worst of all, she's never been married. Once Ellie discovers this shameful secret, she's determined to find her missing grandfather.

Ellie is drawn into Inchbrae; its lifelong friendships, its half-buried secrets and its larger-than-life characters. When Johnny Starling comes to stay, it seems he holds the key to Dot's past and Ellie's future.

Eileen Campbell brilliantly evokes a young girl's awakening to the mysteries of adulthood in a heart-warming novel about the power of friendship, the pain of loss and the indomitable spirit of a Highland community.

If you would like to order a copy of *Puppies Are For Life* or *The Company of Strangers*, please turn the page for details.

If you would like to be put on a mailing list to receive regular updates on further new books from Fourth Estate, please send your name and address on a postcard to Meadowland, Press Office, Fourth Estate, 6 Salem Road, London W2 4BU.

To order a copy of *Puppies Are For Life* and/or *The Company of Strangers*, price £5.99 each, please complete the form below. Please allow 75p per book for post and packing in the UK. Overseas customers please allow £1.00 per book for post and packing.

Please send me . . . copy/copies (insert number required) of:
Puppies Are For Life by Linda Phillips.
The Company of Strangers by Eileen Campbell
(delete as appropriate)

Name ....

Address ....

....

....

Send this page with a cheque/eurocheque/postal order (sterling only), made payable to Book Service by Post, to:
   Fourth Estate Books,
   Book Service By Post,
   PO Box 29, Douglas
   I-O-M, IM99 1BQ

Alternatively you can pay by Access, Visa, or Mastercard: please complete the following details and return this page to the address above.

Card number ....

Expiry date ....

Signature ....

You can also order by phone, tel: 01624 675137; or by fax: 01624 670923

Please allow 28 days for delivery. Please tick box if you do not wish to receive any additional information. ❑

Prices and availability subject to change without notice.